# WHISPERS

# ROSIE GOODWIN

# WHISPERS

headline

First published in Great Britain in 2011
by HEADLINE PUBLISHING GROUP

1

Cataloguing in Publication Data is available from the British Library

ISBN 978 0 7553 5393 4

Typeset in Calisto MT by Palimpsest Book Production Ltd,
Falkirk, Stirlingshire

Printed and bound in Great Britain by Clays Ltd, St Ives plc

Headline's policy is to use papers that are natural, renewable and recyclable products and
made from wood grown in sustainable forests. The logging and manufacturing processes
are expected to conform to the environmental regulations of the country of origin.

HEADLINE PUBLISHING GROUP
An Hachette UK Company
338 Euston Road
London NW1 3BH

www.headline.co.uk
www.hachette.co.uk

This one is for Donna who asked for a ghost story – here it is.
Hope you enjoy it. Also for Steve who promotes my books at every
opportunity, thank you!
Love you both xx

As always, a big thank you to my lovely family for their patience and understanding during the writing of this book. Especially to my long-suffering husband for always making the time for me to write.

Also, sincerest thanks to the lovely staff at Headline for their unfailing support, not forgetting my copy editor and of course my readers.

We meet them at the doorway, on the stair,
Along the passage they come and go,
Impalpable impressions on the air,
A sense of something moving to and fro.

*Henry Wadsworth Longfellow, 1807–82*

# Prologue

As the estate agent fumbled with the keys, Jessica Beddows smiled at her husband. Simon was frowning and she could tell that he was less than impressed with what he had seen so far, but she was prepared to look around the house at least. Now that they had come this far it seemed silly not to, to her way of thinking. They had been house-hunting for months, but up until now Simon had picked fault with each one they had viewed. The two girls weren't looking too happy about it either as they stared around the overgrown courtyard, but Jess was determined to stay positive.

'Come on, you lot,' she urged, as the harassed estate agent finally located the right key and slipped it into the lock. 'It might be lovely inside.'

'I did warn you that Stonebridge House has been with another agent and that it has stood empty for some time,' the estate agent pointed out, already feeling a sale slipping away. 'Hence the ridiculously low asking price of less than half a million. You need to see the potential here and picture this wonderful property as it could be if it were returned to its former glory, rather than view it as it is now. When the recession has run its course, prices round here are going to rise, and the value of this place will go through the roof.'

He ushered them all into a large dim hallway.

'Here we are then,' he said jovially, spreading his hands as if he was about to escort them around Buckingham Palace. 'The place is quite *enormous*, as you can see. Would you like me to show you around, or would you rather have a mooch about by yourselves?'

'I think we'd like to explore on our own if you don't mind,' Jess told him quickly as she saw Simon wrinkle his nose in distaste. She had to admit the smell of damp was overpowering.

'No problem at all.' The man backed towards the door again. 'Take as long as you like. I shall be waiting for you in the car outside.'

The second he disappeared out of the door, eleven-year-old Josephine skipped ahead and promptly shot off into one of the numerous rooms

1

leading off the hallway. 'Jo, don't get going too far,' Jess warned, then turning back to her other daughter and Simon, she said brightly, 'Right. Let's get this show on the road then, shall we?'

Thirteen-year-old Melanie folded her arms and said, 'Do we *have* to?' She glanced up at the festoons of cobwebs that hung like lace from the ceilings. 'Ugh. It's like one of those haunted houses you see in horror films.'

'That's the problem with you, you watch far too much TV,' her mother scolded. 'Now come on, the pair of you.'

They moved forward, and after pushing a door open they found themselves in the biggest kitchen that Jess had ever seen. It was like stepping back in time. A deep stone sink stood beneath the window overlooking the courtyard, and a large Aga was set into an alcove on the wall facing them. Thick with dust and surrounded by six solidly built chairs, a long table took up the middle of the room. Mel grimaced as she looked at the plate that still stood there. Food had obviously been left on it but it had long since crumbled to dust.

'Ugh!' she shivered. 'How creepy is that? Someone left their meal there. Did someone die here or something? I bet you any money this place is haunted.'

'Don't be such a drama queen,' her mother told her. 'This kitchen could be wonderful if you'd just open your eyes to it.'

'Yes, it could – if you were willing to spend a small fortune on it,' Simon grunted. As a builder, he knew the real cost of renovations. 'This place would be like a bottomless money pit.'

Jess's tawny eyes stared coldly back at him. 'That's perfectly true, but we have the money to do it now, don't we?' She was obviously far more concerned about what her daughters thought of the place than her husband's opinion of it.

Simon seemed to deflate like a balloon as he looked away from her without arguing and Jess felt a little ripple of satisfaction. For the first time in the whole of their married life she had the upper hand. Her beloved gran had died and left her with substantial inheritance. Jess's parents had both been killed in a car crash when she was little more than a baby, and her gran had brought her up from that day on. Jess had never wanted for anything, least of all love, but even she had never realised how much money the old lady had had stashed away in the bank. She could still remember the look of shocked disbelief that had flashed across Simon's face when the solicitor had read out the will. Gran had never made a secret of the fact that she didn't like

2

Simon and felt that Jess could have done better for herself, but when Jess became pregnant at eighteen, her gran had begrudgingly given the pair her blessing to marry. And now here was Jessica with more money than she had ever dreamed of, and looking for her ideal home. She set off across the kitchen towards a door in the far wall.

'Look at this,' she shouted across her shoulder. 'It's a storage room and there are some steps here that must lead down to a cellar. How handy would that be, eh?' She clicked on the light switch at the side of the door and when nothing happened she sighed with disappointment. 'It looks like the electricity's off,' she murmured. 'And it's too dark to see anything. Never mind. Let's go and look at the rest of the place, eh?'

Simon and Melanie followed her resignedly down the hall. The wallpaper was hanging off the walls and the windows were so dirty that they could barely see anything through them. The next room they came to was an enormous dining room, and once again they found the furniture still in place although it was so shrouded with dust it was impossible to see what it was like.

'It's probably riddled with woodworm,' Simon said nastily, as Jess rubbed at the corner of a large sideboard with the sleeve of her cardigan.

'Actually, I think it's mahogany,' she replied, ignoring his tone. 'And I bet it would be quite beautiful if it was polished. It certainly goes with the style of the house.'

The next room they came to was a large sitting room boasting high sash-cord windows giving wonderful views across the garden.

'Just think, this place has got three whole acres,' Jess said dreamily as she ran her hand across the original wooden shutters. It was certainly a far cry from the tiny square of lawn they had at the back of the neat semi-detached house in Hinckley where they were living now.

Simon gazed grumpily out at the tangled mess. Their garden took him half an hour to mow, if that. This lot would need a whole team of gardeners to get it back into any sort of order.

It was then that they heard Jo's footsteps pounding up the stairs and Jess smiled. At least someone was enjoying themselves.

'Come on. Let's take a look at the upstairs. We can come down and see the rest of the rooms down here later,' she suggested.

They all trooped up a rather splendid staircase until they came to a galleried landing where they all went off in different directions to explore. There were seven bedrooms in total up there, all of a very reasonable size with high ceilings and elaborate cornices. As Jess stepped into each one her imagination began to run riot. Despite the outdated furniture and the need for total redecoration, she knew that they could be made beautiful. Halfway along one landing was a large bathroom, and Jess grinned when she stepped inside it. It was like walking into a museum! Faded linoleum covered the floor and above the toilet was a cistern from which dangled a tarnished brass chain. She was sure that the bath was quite large enough to swim in, but even so she found she could look beyond its present condition to what it could be like.

At the end of the landing she entered yet another bedroom and for the first time, she felt a little nervous. The sheets on the bed had been thrown back as if someone had just stepped out of it, and she glanced around half-expecting to see someone standing there. A huge mahogany wardrobe was leaning drunkenly on one wall, with one of the doors gaping open, and inside she found a row of clothes hanging on the rail. They had obviously belonged to a gentleman, from what she could see of them. When she heard footsteps behind her she grinned. 'Look at these,' she said, pointing. 'I wonder if they belonged to the old man who owned the house before it was shut up.'

She had expected Simon to answer her, but when all remained silent she turned and was surprised to find that she was alone. Thinking she must have imagined it, she moved on to the next room.

Half an hour later, the family congregated downstairs.

'So,' Simon said smugly, 'have you seen enough now? The whole place wants modernising from top to bottom.'

'You're quite right,' Jess agreed. 'And I think we are just the people to do it.'

'Oh Mum, you must be joking.' Melanie groaned as she stared around at the gloomy interior. 'The entire place is utterly *gross*.'

'It is now,' Jess admitted, 'but it won't be when *I've* finished with it. From the second I set foot through the front door I got the feeling . . . I don't know – it was as if I'd come home somehow.'

Just then, the estate agent poked his head around the door to ask brightly, 'So what do you think of it then? It's a snip for £450,000, isn't it? I reckon it could be worth a million-plus easily, if it were to be modernised.'

Ignoring the look of horror on her family's faces, Jess said, 'I shall be in touch to make you a cash offer. What's more, we'd like to move in as soon as possible.' Somehow she knew that this house had been waiting for her, and some time in the not too distant future, she would restore it to its former glory.

'Here, now, just hold on a minute,' Simon spluttered. 'Even if we did buy the place there's no way we could live in it in *this* state!'

'Why not?' Jess asked. 'Most of the rooms will be quite habitable once they've had a good clean and an airing, and we can take our time moving our things in. Our house hasn't sold yet. When it has, the money we get for it can go towards renovating and refurnishing this place.'

Simon glanced at the girls and sighed; he knew when he was beaten.

When they drove away, Jess glanced back at the house for a last look. The sun was shining on the grimy windows, and for no reason that she could explain, her eyes were drawn to one of the attics. Just for a moment, she could have sworn that there had been someone at the window, staring back at her. Probably just a trick of the light, she told herself, and then her mind went into overdrive as she began to plan all the things she wanted to do to Stonebridge House, once it was hers.

# Chapter One

'That's about the lot then, missus. Would you like to sign here, please?'

Jess took the paper and pen from the driver of the van and hurriedly scribbled her name. The removal firm she had hired had now shifted all the family's possessions into the new house and were scurrying about like ants, placing boxes in the rooms Simon was directing them to.

'Thank you very much indeed.' As she pressed a small bundle of notes into his hand as a bonus the man grinned from ear to ear and doffed his cap.

'That's very kind o' you, missus. I hope you'll be very happy here.' Secretly he thought the woman must have taken leave of her senses to move into such a run-down out of the way old place, but he wisely kept his opinion to himself and raced off to get his men together. They had another job to do before they went home that night and he wanted to get it over and done with.

'Right then, I reckon we've all earned a cuppa, don't you?' Jess said when the removal men had finally driven away. After a while she managed to light one of the gas rings on the outdated cooker and then she moved to the sink to fill the kettle. The tap squealed in protest and suddenly dark water squirted out of it.

'Oh, that's just great!' Melanie, who was sitting at the dusty table with her father and sister, sighed dramatically. 'Now as well as having to live in this dump we're going to get poisoned as well.'

'Don't be so silly,' Jess scolded. 'The water will run clear in a minute. The cleaners I hired to come in and give the place a bit of a onceover said they had the same problem, but the surveyor has given the thumbs-up on all the services. The taps just haven't been run in a long while, that's all. Now stop moaning, Mel, and get the sandwiches I packed out of that basket over there. Then when we've eaten and had a hot drink we'll set to and get your bedrooms sorted out. The old mattresses have already been carried outside and we'll have your beds made up in no time.'

Mel glumly did as she was told as Jess attacked the table with a damp cloth. The cleaners had got rid of the worst of the dirt and grime in the rooms they were going to be living in, but she supposed the dust would be settling for some time. Soon they were all tucking into ham sandwiches and packets of crisps. Simon seemed distracted, and so she said, 'Why don't you go and have a proper look at the outbuildings when you've eaten? You've already said they'd be perfect for you to run your business from, and your landlord has been trying to get you out of your yard so he can build a bungalow on it. Just think of the money you'll be saving, when you have all your stuff on your own premises.'

'But they're not *my* premises, are they?' His voice was heavy with sarcasm, and as both the girls looked towards him, an unspoken message seemed to flash between their mother and father.

Completely ignoring his tone, Jess bent to feed half of her sandwich to Alfie, their Golden Retriever, who wolfed it down hungrily. They had bought him that year for Jo as a birthday present, and now he was at the curious stage where he seemed to be all ears and legs. He certainly didn't resemble a Golden Retriever, that was for sure, although Jo adored him. Her feelings were returned and Alfie followed her about like a shadow.

'Come on, boy, let's go and play outside, shall we?' Jo chirped the minute she had swallowed her sandwich, then they both flew out of the door that led from the kitchen into the garden and bounded across the overgrown lawn.

Aw well, at least those two are happy about the move, Jess thought to herself as she put the used mugs into the sink. She could only hope that as they settled in, Simon and Mel would feel the same.

Once outside, Simon gave a deep sigh. He wasn't at all happy about the move, but had decided to hold his tongue and go along with it, although it went sorely against the grain. Up until now he had always organised everything for the family, right down to the last detail, and now he was shocked to learn that Jess was more than capable of managing on her own.

Abandoned at an early age by an alcoholic mother, Simon had then been shipped from one foster placement to another, with nowhere to call home. Despite her promises to come back for him, Simon had never seen his mother again and had grown up with a chip on his shoulder the size of a house-brick. He supposed that was why, when he left school, he had been determined to make something of himself and he had worked tirelessly ever since to build up his own business. He had met Jess when they were both very young, and when she told him that she was pregnant, he had decided to do right by his unborn child and marry her. Admittedly, he had found the prospect a little daunting at first, as he had never allowed himself to get close to anyone before. Even so, things hadn't turned out too badly and Jess had always been an obedient wife – until now, that was – but he had a horrible, insecure feeling that all that was about to change. Still, as Jess had quite rightly said, the outbuildings would make a brilliant base for his business, so feeling slightly more cheerful, he set about deciding where all his equipment and materials would go.

Once Simon had disappeared inside the barn Jess turned to Mel and said, 'How about you come and show me which room you'd like then, my love?'

Mel trailed ahead of her up the stairs with her shoulders stooped, but Jess was determined not to let anything spoil the day. She was well aware of the amount of work that needed doing to the house, but from the second she had set foot through the door, she could imagine it as it would look in the not too distant future, and hoped that soon her family would share the same vision.

Two hours later, the girls' rooms were tidy and their beds were neatly made up with fresh bedding. Jess left them to put some of their clothes away whilst she went into the room that she and Simon had decided to use. It was very spacious and overlooked the grounds at the back of the house. There was a huge bay window in there, and Jess grinned as she looked out and saw Jo and Alfie racing around the lake. This would be a lovely family house, once it was finished. She tried to imagine how this room would look with the wallpaper she had chosen and with new carpets and curtains. The girls had already chosen the paper for their bedrooms, and she hoped that once the improvements had been made, they would start to feel more at home.

For now, she would only be redecorating the rooms they would be living in because of the expense. Plumbers, painters and electricians were all booked to come in. She and Simon could do the rest of the redecoration at a later date. He simply had too many commitments to do the necessary major work on the house, and was very put out to be paying other firms to be doing it. However, Jess knew that he would be monitoring it all very closely.

Jess was standing in the window when she saw Simon suddenly appear at the back of the house. He stood pensively looking out at the overgrown lawns and her heart swelled. Their relationship had not been going well for some time now but she loved him so much, and wanted this to be a new start for them. Simon was now in his mid-thirties and still a very handsome man. Tall and dark-haired, he had always had an eye for the ladies, which had almost ended their marriage on more than one occasion. But Jess hoped that now things were easier financially, he might settle down a little. She had lost count of the times she had caught him out in sordid little affairs and knew that now, all that had to end for the sake of the children. Their constant bickering was beginning to affect Melanie, who had become very quiet and withdrawn lately. Of course, some of the girl's mood swings were no doubt due to her age. She was a teenager now, and Simon often referred to her tantrums as 'the battle of the hormones'. Melanie looked much like her mother, petite and fair-haired, whilst Jo took after her father in looks. She was taller, with his dark hair and blue eyes, which made a startling contrast.

Jess looked beyond Simon to where Jo was rampaging across the grass with Alfie in hot pursuit, and then yawning, she mentally tried to prioritise the list of jobs she still needed to do that day.

As darkness fell, Melanie began to glance nervously towards the windows. There had been streetlamps outside their home in Hinckley, but here there was nothing but inky blackness and she found it slightly unnerving, as if they had been shut off from the world.

'Everything all right, love?' Jess asked as she flipped some bacon she was cooking for supper in the frying pan.

'Yes. It's just strange not to be able to see any other houses,' Melanie told her quietly. 'I feel sort of . . . isolated.'

'You'll soon get used to it,' Jess said comfortingly as she manoeuvred the bacon onto a plate to keep warm before breaking an egg into the pan. 'And our nearest neighbour isn't that far away. There's a cottage just at the end of the drive.'

'I wonder who lives there?' Jo piped up as she waited for her food. 'It would be great if there was someone there the same age as me that I could play with.'

'I have no idea, but I've no doubt we'll find out soon enough,' Jess assured her, then turning her attention to Simon she asked, 'And when are you planning on moving all your supplies into the outbuildings?'

'I've already asked Bill and a couple of the lads if they'll help to move all the stuff here from the yard, though it's going to take a few days. I thought we could stack all the bricks in the Dutch barn,' he said.

'Well, there you are then. It's all going to work out just fine, isn't it?' she said.

Simon didn't reply but merely got up to fetch the tomato ketchup, and the meal passed in silence as the family ate hungrily.

Later that night, when the girls had gone to bed, Simon broached a subject that had been concerning him. 'Look, Jess, I know we have been able to afford to buy and do up this house with the sale of our home in Hinckley and with what your gran left you – but have you given any thought as to how we're going to live when that money is gone? I know I could earn enough to pay the mortgage on our old house, but this is a huge place and it's going to take some maintaining.'

Jess suddenly felt sad as she realised how precarious their relationship had become. This was something that they should have discussed before now, but Simon had left it until they were actually in the property before voicing his concerns.

'I have given it a lot of thought as it happens,' she replied. 'And I've decided that it's time I branched out and started a little business of my own to top the funds up.'

Simon looked incredulous. 'Oh yes, and what would that be then?'

'Once we've got everywhere ship-shape I'm going to open a little B and B. We have far more bedrooms than we need, so it makes sense to utilise the ones that are standing empty.'

He opened his mouth to protest but then clamped it shut again. This was yet another side of his wife that he had never seen before. For years she had been content just to stay at home and bring the girls up, but it seemed that now, she was ready to spread her wings.

'What do you think of the idea?' she asked eventually.

'I suppose it could be a viable proposition,' he answered cautiously. 'If you think you can manage the extra workload, that is?'

'You'd be surprised what I could manage if push came to shove,' she said tightly.

Hearing the hidden threat in her voice, he hurriedly dropped his eyes. His last affair had impacted badly on their relationship; to the point that he had thought for a time that their marriage wouldn't survive it. Jess had informed him in no uncertain terms that he was skating on very thin ice, and he knew that he would have to be on his very best behaviour for some time to come, if he wanted to keep his family together.

'If that's what you want to do, I won't stand in your way,' he told her.

'Good. Now how about we get ourselves off to bed? I don't know about you but I'm ready to drop and we have a lot to do tomorrow. The girls will be starting their new schools on Monday and I have to find what boxes their uniforms are packed in for a start-off.' Glancing apprehensively at the mountain of boxes stacked against one wall of the kitchen, Jess wondered if she would ever get straight again.

'Come on then.' Simon went to lock the back door before holding his hand out to her with a twinkle in his eye. 'Let's go and christen our new bedroom, eh?'

They had not slept together since his last misdemeanour, and for a moment he thought that she was going to refuse. But then she rose and took his hand as a slight blush pinked her cheeks. If they were going to stay together it was time to put the past behind them.

# Chapter Two

They were all sitting at breakfast the next morning when Mel said sulkily, 'Will you please knock next time you want to come into my room, Mum? I'm not a little baby who you have to check on any more, you know.'

Jess raised her eyes from her Weetabix. 'What do you mean? I didn't come into your room last night.'

'Well, someone did,' Mel stated emphatically.

'It wasn't me,' Jo told her, her mouth full of cornflakes.

'Perhaps you just thought you heard someone come in,' Jess suggested. 'These old houses tend to be noisy at night as they settle.'

Mel opened her mouth to protest but thought better of it.

'Can me and Alfie go out to play now?' Jo trilled as she pushed her empty cereal bowl away. 'We found a little bluebell wood on the other side of the lake yesterday and it's ever so pretty.'

'Yes, you can – but mind what you get up to,' Jess warned. 'Don't get going too near to the edge of that lake, please, young lady.'

'I ought to be getting off too,' Simon told her as he rose from the table. 'I've got a few of the lads together so we can start bringing some of the supplies over here today. The Dutch barn will be ideal for storing the sand and cement as well as the bricks. It seems quite dry in there.'

Apprehension flashed momentarily in his wife's eyes but then she masked it with a smile. Every time Simon went out she wondered if he was going to see another woman, but she knew she had to stop thinking like that, if they were going to make this work.

'All right. How long do you think you will be?'

'How long is a piece of string? You know how much stuff there is to shift. It will probably take most of the day just to load the lorry. And being Saturday, the lads won't want to work too late.'

She started to clear the table, saying, 'See you later then. Don't get working too hard now.'

Mel shot off upstairs at the first opportunity and in no time at all Jess found herself alone. Suddenly the enormity of what she had taken on hit her full force and she wondered if she had bitten off more than she could chew. But then she straightened her shoulders. She hadn't even found time to venture up into the attics yet, although she was longing to have a look around up there. But somehow she knew that this house had been waiting for her. She had been meant to live here, and every minute of work she put into it would be worth it in the end, she just knew it.

Later that morning, as Jess sat enjoying a well-earned tea-break, she pored over the kitchen brochures she had picked up a few weeks ago. There was one that both she and Simon liked, and although it was expensive she decided that she would ring the shop that very morning and book an appointment for them to come out and measure up. The units were solid oak and she knew that they would suit the room perfectly. It was then that she was interrupted by a tap on the back door and when she went to open it she found an attractive dark-haired woman who looked to be a little older than herself standing there with a teenager in tow.

'Hello there, I'm Laura Briggs,' the woman introduced herself. 'And this is my daughter, Bethany. We live in Blue Brick Cottage at the end of the drive. Anyway, I thought we should introduce ourselves. My husband Dennis is at work, but I'm sure you'll meet him soon. Oh, and I brought you these as a little house-warming present. They're home-made – I hope you'll like them.' As she spoke, she pressed a small wicker basket into Jess's hands. It contained a couple of bottles of wine with handwritten labels, along with an assortment of jars of jam.

'Why, how kind of you. Do come in,' Jess invited as she held the door wide. 'Have you got time for a cup of tea? I was just having one.'

'I never say no to a cuppa,' the woman grinned as she stepped inside.

'I'm Jess, by the way.' Jess urged her guests towards the table. 'My husband Simon is at work too. He's a builder and he has a small yard that he rents, but he's decided to store all the stuff here now so he's gone off to start shifting it. It seems silly not to, with all these outbuildings standing empty.'

Quickly carrying two more mugs to the table she lifted the teapot and glanced at Bethany. The girl was strikingly pretty. Tall and slim, she had eyes the colour of bluebells and a heart-shaped face. There were dimples in her cheeks and her skin was like fine porcelain, but she seemed to be very quiet. She hadn't uttered so much as a single word up to now.

'Bethany doesn't say much,' Laura informed her as if she could read what Jess was thinking. At that moment, Bethany spotted Jo and Alfie out of the window and she touched her mother, who smiled at her affectionately. 'She loves dogs. Would you mind very much if she went outside to meet him?'

'Of course not. That's Alfie, he's with my daughter, Jo. Go and introduce yourself.'

The young woman instantly rose and lumbered towards the back door, and in that instant, Jess realised that there was something not quite right about her.

'Bethany is a little . . . slow,' Laura told her hesitantly once the door had closed behind her. 'Unfortunately there were complications during her birth and she was left with slight brain damage. But even so she is our only child and we adore her,' she said defensively.

'I should think you do, she's absolutely beautiful,' Jess told her. It seemed so sad that anyone who looked so perfect should be disabled. 'And how old is she?'

'She's nineteen now.' Laura sighed. 'I'm afraid she'll never be able to live independently, and Dennis and I worry ourselves sick about what will become of her when anything happens to us.'

'Oh, my goodness. I'm sure that won't be for a very long time yet,' Jess assured her. She was warming to this woman by the minute and had the feeling that they could become friends. 'Does Bethany go to work?'

'Oh, no,' Laura said hastily, 'although she can cook and clean with the best of them. If you need any help getting this place back into shape I'm sure she'd love to help and it would give her something to do. She tends to get a little lonely sometimes with just her dad and myself for company. Dennis does run her to a youth club in town that caters for young people with special needs, but that's only once a week, and other than that she barely sets foot out of the door.'

'I might just take you up on that offer,' Jess said. 'To be honest I'm feeling a little overwhelmed with all I have to do today. This place must have stood empty for a long time.'

'Oh, it has – nearly two years by now, I should think.' Laura sipped at her tea and glanced around nervously before going on. 'Mr Fenton, the old man that lived here, left it to distant family in Texas when he passed away. The story goes that Mr Fenton was married once, a very long time ago, in the 1960s, but his wife left him when their son was quite small, and she was never heard of again. Then, shortly after she left, their son drowned in the river. After that, Mr Fenton became a bit of a recluse. The couple from Texas came over to check the place out a few months back, but they didn't stay long, and before we knew it, the place was on the market.' She leaned forward and admitted, 'As a matter of fact, I've never set foot in here before. But apparently the house has been in the Fenton family since it was built.'

'Really? Do you know anything about the history of the place?'

'Jake Fenton, who owned a mill in Attleborough, had it built in the early 1800s. It was originally called Stonebridge Farm, named after the stone bridge that crosses the river about a quarter of a mile away towards Caldecote. Jake was a bit of a wild one, if you can believe the old stories – you know, a ladies' man and a gambler. His genes must have passed down through the generations 'cos it's said that this has never really been a happy house.' Seeing the look of dismay that flitted across Jess's face she added quickly, 'Of course, I'm sure all that will change now that a nice new young family have moved in. It's just what the place needed – although I have to say I think you're very brave, taking all this work on. The place is in a bit of a state, isn't it?'

'I'd say that was putting it mildly,' Jess said wryly as she looked round at the outdated cupboards. No wonder the couple had taken fright and gone back to the USA, allowing the house to go out of the family after all this time.

'Oh, I'm sure you will manage to put it to rights.' Laura looked out and saw Bethany and Jo in the garden playing with Alfie. 'Is Jo your only child?' she asked.

'No, we have two girls. Her sister, Melanie, is thirteen. She's upstairs listening to her iPod, I should imagine.'

'Well, I suppose I should be going and let you get on, now that I've introduced myself,' Laura said as she rose from the table. 'It was lovely to meet you. If there's anything I can help with, do give me a shout. I'll just call Bethany now, shall I?'

'Oh no, you needn't do that,' Jess assured her. 'She and Jo seem to be getting along just fine. Let them be if they're enjoying themselves and I'll send Bethany home later when she's ready to come.'

'Are you quite sure?' Laura said hesitantly.

'Yes, I'm quite sure. And don't get worrying about her. I'll keep my eye on her, I promise.' She saw her neighbour to the door where they shook hands warmly as Jess said, 'Thanks for coming and also for the lovely gifts. You're very clever, making all these yourself. I think I might sample the wine tonight when I've done all my jobs for the day.'

'Looking round here, I think you'll be ready for a drink by then,' Laura chuckled, and striding off over the courtyard she headed for the cottage at the end of the drive leading to Stonebridge House.

Jess closed the door behind her with a smile on her face. At least the nearest neighbour seemed nice, which was one blessing at least. Humming softly to herself, she went off to tackle the upstairs.

In the bedroom that had been used by the old man, she shuddered as she looked at the unmade bed. In no time at all she had stripped the bedding from it and placed it in a pile ready for Simon to take to the tip in his lorry. Next she began to take Mr Fenton's clothes from the wardrobe, wrinkling her nose at the musty smell. After adding them to the pile, she tore one of the curtains down – sending a thick cloud of dust spiralling around the room. The other one quickly followed it and, coughing and spluttering, she struggled with the sash-cord window until she managed to open it.

Already the room was beginning to look much brighter and now as she turned, her eyes were drawn to a couple of charcoal sketches hanging on the wall opposite the bed. Their frames were riddled with woodworm, but the sketches themselves were excellent. The first was of a stone bridge that spanned what appeared to be a fast-moving river, and Jess guessed that this was the bridge that had given the house its name. The second was of a young man. He was tall and dark-haired, dressed as she imagined the Lord of the Manor might have been in times gone by; he was standing on the bridge that was featured in the first sketch, gazing off into the distance. Jess held her head to the side and placed her finger thoughtfully on her lip as she studied the sketches. They could actually look quite nice if they were reframed; she thought to herself, and put it on her fast-growing list of things to do before turning and bundling the bedding, clothes and curtains up to throw downstairs.

Simon returned mid-afternoon with the first lorryload of tools and building materials, and he and two of his workmen began to store them in the large barn. Jess made them all a tray of tea and some corned-beef sandwiches before hurrying back into the house to get on with her own chores. Bethany had stayed to have lunch with them but shortly before tea-time, Laura appeared in the courtyard just as Simon was leaving the barn.

'Oh hello, I'm Laura your neighbour,' she introduced herself. At that moment Jo and Bethany rounded the corner and as Bethany went to join her mother, Laura told Simon, 'This is Bethany. She's been keeping your daughter company but I've just come to fetch her home.'

Jess stepped out of the kitchen just in time to see Simon shaking their neighbour's hand, and her heart sank as she saw him smile charmingly at Laura and hang onto her hand for a fraction longer than was necessary. He never could resist a pretty face.

'Ah, so you've met then,' she said, forcing a smile as she hurried across to them.

'Yes, we have, and I've come to take Bethany out of your way,' Laura told her with an apologetic grin. 'I was just saying to your husband that you must be tired of her by now.'

'Not at all,' Jess said truthfully. 'In actual fact, she's been a really good help, keeping Jo entertained. You are welcome to come any time you like, Bethany.'

The young woman smiled shyly as she sidled up to her mother and Simon frowned. Jess shot him a warning look, and when Laura and Bethany were safely out of earshot she explained, 'Bethany suffered brain damage at birth and she's a little slow.'

'How sad, and such a lovely young girl as well.' Simon shook his head. 'It makes you realise how lucky we are to have our two healthy girls, doesn't it? Even if Mel *is* going through the terrible teens moods.'

Jess nodded in agreement before returning to the kitchen where she was tackling the unenviable job of scrubbing the Aga, which was literally caked with grease. This was another job that the cleaners hadn't touched. Jess knew that she could have afforded a new one, but Agas should last for ever, and the older models were lovely to look at.

Later that evening, she and Simon manhandled the old stained mattress from the late owner's room down the stairs and onto the back of his lorry.

'That's the best place for it,' Simon muttered.

'I absolutely agree,' Jess replied. 'But some of the bedframes, ward-robes and chests of drawers are solid mahogany; all they need is a bit of TLC.'

Simon nodded. His wife had always preferred modern furniture but it looked as if all that was about to change. As she had already explained to him, she intended to restore Stonebridge House to the way it had once been.

'Once I've got us basically straight I shall start having a look around the antique shops and auctions for suitable pieces,' she told him.

As far as Simon was aware, Jess had never so much as set foot in an antique shop or an auction room in her whole life, but then whilst she was so busy with the house, it would give him a little more freedom – so it wasn't all bad. Already it was more than clear that their whole way of life was in the process of dramatic change.

# Chapter Three

'It's really beginning to take shape now, isn't it?' As Jess stood back to admire their newly decorated bedroom, Simon nodded. The decorators had finished the girls' rooms and theirs too, and to Jess the place was beginning to feel like home. It was now mid-July and the family had been living at Stonebridge House for over three months. During that time the whole place had been rewired and a new central heating system had been installed. Downstairs, the kitchen fitters were sawing and hammering away as they put up the new units, and outside a team of gardeners were tackling the overgrown jungle. She herself had had to slow down a little as the girls were now on their summer holidays from school and she was having to entertain them, but Jess was quietly pleased with the progress so far.

'I daren't even begin to think what all this must be costing,' Simon said ruefully, as he examined the new dado rails. The original ones had been ripped off at some point in time, but Jess had insisted that new ones should be fitted. The decorators had also repaired the elaborate plasterwork on the ceilings and the original cornices, and now they were all freshly painted. A huge crystal chandelier dangled from an ornate rose in the centre of the room giving it an air of grandeur, and the walls were covered in a flock paper in soft shades of gold and cream.

'Well, none of it has come cheap,' Jess replied, 'but I have managed to save some money by making the curtains myself. I got the material for a snip in the Bull Ring when I went to Birmingham last week and I've only got the swags and tails to finish and then they're ready to go up. All we need now is the new carpet to go down and the carpet fitters are coming in to do that tomorrow.'

'And what do we do for furniture in here?' Simon asked.

'Oh, I've saved money there as well,' she hastened to assure him. 'I've cleaned up a whole suite for in here. It's solid mahogany and it's going to look beautiful.'

'Then I suppose I should be grateful for small blessings,' he quipped.

She punched him playfully on the arm.

'Oh, stop moaning, will you? It will all be worth it when it's done, you'll see. I'm going to have a good root around in the other bedrooms later this afternoon when the girls have gone swimming. You'd be surprised what little gems I'm finding.'

'Rather you than me.' Simon strode towards the door, saying, 'I'd better get off back to work, else Bill and the lads will think I've got lost. See you later.'

Once he was gone and Jess had heard the Land Rover roar off down the drive she fancied a cuppa, but there were kitchen fitters everywhere, and when she entered, one of them winked at her cheekily. Deciding that it was time for a bit of fresh air she beat a hasty retreat through the back door, with Alfie close on her heels.

She welcomed the feel of the sun on her face and meandered on, avoiding the gardeners who were mowing the extensive lawn to the left of the property. Eventually she came to the lake, where she sank down onto the grass. From here she had a wonderful view of the front of the house. She wondered when it had been renamed Stonebridge House, seeing as Laura had told her it had once been a farm. It must have been a very impressive farmhouse, she decided, and supposed that one of the Fentons must have renamed it to make it sound a little grander. By modern-day standards it was huge, and as she sat gazing at it, she fell in love with it all over again. It was built from local stone, which had mellowed to a warm golden colour over the years. Its tall chimneys loomed above the slate roof; and the high windows stood in regimental rows on either side of the front door. The latter was reached through a magnificent porch held up on two sides by marble pillars, and a profusion of ivy and wisteria grew in wild abundance all over it. Simon had said they ought to have it removed, but Jess had flatly refused to allow it, saying that it lent an air of olde-world charm to the property. Windows were also set into the roof of the attic. Laura had told her that this was where the servants used to live, but as yet she had still had no time to go up there and explore, although she had every intention of doing so, as soon as the opportunity arose.

A rabbit suddenly appeared from a burrow not far away from where Jess was sitting and, barking wildly, Alfie went in hot pursuit of it, his tail wagging as if it had developed a life of its own. There's one who is happy about the move, at least, she thought to herself with amusement. In their old house they had taken it in turns each day to take him for a walk to the local park, but here she could just open the door and let him run where he wished on their three acres of ground. Jo seemed quite happy with the move too and had settled remarkably well into her new school in Weddington before breaking up for the summer holidays. Already she and Bethany, their neighbour's daughter, had become good friends and Beth was now a regular visitor to the house. Sadly, Mel was missing her friends and her old school dreadfully. Even so, Jess was confident that she would eventually adapt, and in the meantime she was spending as much time as she could with her.

It was funny, when Jess came to think of it. Their new home was situated between Caldecote and Weddington along an unadopted road which the local people had named 'The Four Shillings'. It was just a few miles away from their old home in Hinckley and yet it felt like a world away. Staring into the lake, she suddenly thought of the request that Jo had made the night before. She had asked her dad if she could have a rowing boat, and as she was a good swimmer, he had agreed to get one for her. Jo was a real tomboy, always into some sort of mischief, and Jess had no doubt that once she had her boat there would be a few mishaps. Not that she minded. As long as her children were happy, she was happy.

Now she gazed contentedly back at the house, remembering how, from the second she had seen it advertised in the local paper, she had hounded Simon to go with her to view it – and once she had set foot through the door she had known that she had come home. Now, if only she and Simon could return to being as happy as they had once been, and Mel could settle, everything would be just perfect.

A movement in one of the attic windows caught her eye: someone was standing there staring out across the lawns, although from here she couldn't distinguish whether it was a man or a woman. Simon was at work and both the girls were out, so who could it be? Perhaps one of the workmen had wandered up there to have a nosy? Deciding there was only one way to find out, Jess rose and brushed the grass from her jeans before setting off back to the house.

When she entered the kitchen she had to stand for a second to allow her eyes to adjust to the light, but she soon saw that all four of the kitchen fitters were present and correct, busily at work. The key to the attic was still on the board in the hall, and that in itself Jess found strange. If the key was still there, how had anyone managed to get up there?

The door leading up to the attics was situated at the end of a long landing and she inched it open cautiously. The new light illuminated a plain wooden staircase. There was no wallpaper on the walls here, just bare plaster, which looked as if it hadn't been white-washed for years. The stairs were very steep, and at the top of them she inserted the key into the door there. It grated noisily as she struggled to turn it, then she pushed hard against the solid door and it slowly creaked open. Within seconds she had located another light switch and found herself confronting a long passage from which a number of rooms led off. The floorboards were thick with dust, apart from several sets of footprints that had no doubt been made by the surveyor when he'd come to check the property, and the electricians.

She stood for a while trying to get her bearings. The person she had glimpsed from the lawn had been standing in the first window at the back of the house, so she reasoned it must have been in one of the rooms to her right. She headed towards the first one and threw open the door. Instantly she was met by an overpowering scent of roses. It was a welcome change from the smell of damp and mildew that she had become accustomed to, although she had no idea where the scent could be coming from. This must once have been one of the original servants' rooms, and Jess blinked with amazement to find that it was still furnished exactly as it must have been, back nearly 200 years ago when it was occupied. A small window was set into a sloping roof, and against one wall was a wooden bed. An old-fashioned marble washstand with a plain china jug and bowl stood next to the bed, and against the other wall was a dark wooden wardrobe with no adornments of any kind, and a stout chest of drawers. Jess tentatively opened the wardrobe door and was shocked to find a number of clothes still inside it. Sadly, the moths had done their worst on most of them but she could still distinguish two long brown skirts of a thick calico-like material, and two plain white blouses with long sleeves and high necks. Excitedly, Jess next crossed to the chest of drawers and in the top drawer she found a number of enormous aprons made of starched white linen, yellowed with age. The second drawer held an assortment of plain underwear, but in the bottom one she found a straw bonnet and as she drew it out she smiled. This had obviously been someone's Sunday best hat long ago, and she tried to imagine the person who might have worn it. It was made of straw with a wide brim and had been trimmed with faded ribbons. Two longer ribbons that had obviously tied beneath the chin dangled down and she fingered them gently. Whoever these things had once belonged to must have been dead for a very long time now, and it struck her how strange life was. People died, but life went on as before. It was a sobering thought.

Something in the very bottom of the drawer then caught her eye, and laying the bonnet on the hard wooden bed, she drew out a small sampler that someone had clearly been working on, still stretched on a round wooden frame. The needle that was inserted into it contained scarlet thread. There were a number of flowers embroidered around the edges, and in the middle someone had neatly sewn a name. MARTHA. Jess sighed. If the size of the waistbands on the skirts she had discovered were anything to go by, the person who had slept in this room had only been a young girl, and she wondered why she would have left all her possessions behind. What was more puzzling still was the identity of the person she could swear she had seen standing at the window. It was obvious that no one apart from the electricians and surveyor had set foot in this room for many years, so it must have been just a trick of the light.

After placing everything back exactly as she had found it, she turned to leave the room and it was then that she spotted the charcoal sketch hanging on the wall. It was of a young girl picking wild flowers in a field, and in the background was a stone bridge spanning a river. It was a very simple sketch but Jess loved it and decided that it should be reframed to hang with the others she had found in the late owner's bedroom. Right now she was keen to explore what lay behind the other doors, so she left the sketch where it was for the time being.

The next room she entered was almost exactly the same as the first, but the wardrobe and chest of drawers were empty. The third room had obviously been used as some sort of schoolroom at one time and was much bigger than the servants' rooms, with a larger window set into the sloping roof. Three small wooden desks were placed in front of a large blackboard, which was now white with dust, but again, other than that the room was empty. It was quite cold up here despite the heat of the sun outside, and Jess rubbed her bare arms, wishing that she had put a sweatshirt on.

In the last room were a table and two chairs, and in the far corner, an old-fashioned swinging crib. The carving on it was beautiful. This room had obviously been used as a nursery, and Jess tried to imagine the baby or babies that must once have slept in there.

Finally she came to the end of the landing and another door that led into an enormous room. There was no light in here apart from the little that managed to filter through the filthy windows. Even so,

Jess could see the shapes of discarded furniture covered in dust sheets, and large wooden trunks placed here and there. *I'll come back again when I have more time*, she promised herself as a little ripple of excitement ran through her. It was like discovering an Aladdin's cave and she could hardly wait to explore it. But not on her own though, she decided. It was actually quite creepy in there and she'd wait until Simon could come with her. Thoughts of him made the corners of her mouth twitch into a smile. Things had been slightly better between them since they had moved into the house. He certainly hadn't been going out half as much as he used to. Truthfully she had kept him so busy that he never had the time, but even so she took that as a good sign. Despite the many times he had hurt her she still couldn't contemplate her life without him.

She had just stepped out onto the main landing again when a voice floated up the stairs to her.

'*Mum!* Are you up there?'

She realised that it must be the girls home from the swimming baths and shouted back, 'I'll be with you in a minute!' She felt guilty, as she'd completely forgotten the time. She had offered to drive them to the swimming baths and pick them up too, but as there was a bus stop less than half a mile away Mel had insisted that they go by bus. Jess had agreed and now she raced off downstairs to get them something to eat, aware that swimming made them ravenous, the person she had thought she saw in the window forgotten for now.

# Chapter Four

That evening, as Simon and Jess sat in the kitchen, she told him about the room she had discovered in the attic. 'Everything that the girl owned is still there as if she had just popped out for a while and never come back. Don't you find that strange?'

Simon sighed. 'I suppose you'll be telling me next the house has a resident ghost. Most places this age are supposed to have one, aren't they?'

'Don't be so mean,' she pouted. 'It's the age of the house that drew me to it. Don't you find it fascinating to think of all the people that must have lived here before us?'

'Not really,' Simon answered truthfully as he sipped at his cocoa. 'I just tend to look at the amount of work that still needs to be done.'

'Well, I'm very sorry but *I* think it's all going to be worth it!' Jess snapped. 'Laura was quite envious when she called in for a cuppa earlier on. She only has a small kitchen in Blue Brick Cottage.'

Simon privately thought Laura and Den's cottage had more than ample space for a family to live in but wisely refrained from saying so. Since moving into Stonebridge House, Jess seemed to have become obsessed with the place and wouldn't hear a wrong word said against it. They had got to know the couple and their daughter quite well during the time they had lived there, and both of them agreed that Laura and Den were lovely people, although Jess secretly wished that Simon wouldn't be quite so attentive to Laura. Until recently, Simon had always been a little nervous around people with disabilities but Jess was pleased to note that he seemed to have taken a real shine to young Beth. Once a week now he would deliver her to the door of the youth club she attended as he had to pass it on his way to his weekly game of darts at the Town Talk, a pub on Abbey Green, and then he would pick her up and deliver her back to her parents' door on his way home. Den was more than grateful as sometimes he had to rush home from his work on the railways to take her himself. Beth now spent almost as much time at their house with Jo as she did at

26

home, and Jess found it touching to see them play together. To hear them, no one would have believed that there was an age gap between them and it made her sad sometimes, for Beth was a stunning young woman with the brain of a child.

'I was thinking,' Simon said. 'Once we get around to clearing out the big attic room, it might make a great office. I could work up there without being disturbed when I've got my accounts to do.'

Jess was delighted by this sign of enthusiasm, but then becoming serious, she changed the subject, saying, 'I'm a bit worried about our Mel. She doesn't seem to be settling in at all, does she? And she's started to have awful nightmares. Funnily enough, I've noticed that they usually occur after I've been to see Karen on a Wednesday evening. Do you think she's afraid of being here on her own?'

Jess and Karen had been friends for years, and Jess still visited her each Wednesday evening, which was another thing that had shocked Simon. Although Jess had learned to drive some years ago, she had rarely done so until her gran died, but now she had bought herself a little Ford KA and was off all over the place. Karen had been given a royal tour of the house shortly after they had moved in and had declared bluntly that Jess must be off her trolley to buy such a mausoleum. But it seemed that even her closest friend's opinion could not swerve Jess from wanting to live there.

'No, I don't think it's anything to do with you going out,' Simon told her. 'When you go off to Karen's she's not on her own, is she? I'm always here, and Jo is too if she doesn't come with you.'

'Hm, I suppose you're right, but I wonder what it is then?'

'It's her age.' Simon seemed to put everything down to age. 'Now, how about we lock up and go and get some shut-eye. I'm dead on my feet and I've got to be up early in the morning. This extension me and the lads are building has turned out to be a lot bigger job than we'd thought.'

Jess secretly thought that Simon was working too hard, but at least he barely went out of an evening now apart from to his weekly darts match, so that was something to be thankful for at least.

After locking all the doors and turning off the lights they climbed the stairs together and Simon went off to the bathroom and Jess to their bedroom. She undressed quickly and was in the process of pulling her nightshirt over her head when she heard Simon enter the room and felt him come to stand behind her.

'Crikey, that was quick,' she laughed and turned. There was no one there. Frowning now, she stepped out onto the landing, thinking perhaps that Jo was playing a trick on her, but there was no one in sight. She moved back into the bedroom wondering where the smell of roses was coming from, but then realised that it must be wafting in through the open bedroom window. The gardeners had planted some rose bushes the week before.

It was then that Simon did enter, and seeing the look on her face he asked, 'Is everything all right?'

'Oh yes, I just thought . . .' Jess's voice trailed away as she knew what he would say if she told him that she had heard imaginary footsteps. 'Oh, it was nothing really,' she said lamely. 'Now shall we hit the sack?'

Within minutes they were tucked in and Simon's gentle snores were echoing around the room as Jess lay thinking of the room in the attic and the clothes that were hanging in the wardrobe there, and wondering who they might have belonged to . . . but it had been a long day and soon she was fast asleep too.

A bloodcurdling scream had them both springing awake in the middle of the night and they almost collided as they fell out of bed and headed for the door.

'It sounded as if it came from Mel's room,' Jess gasped as they raced along the landing. When they reached her door they flung it open to find the girl sitting up in bed with the duvet clutched to her chin and her eyes starting from her head.

'There was someone in my room, standing at the end of the bed!' she sobbed.

Jess hurried across to her daughter and took her in her arms. 'Shush,' she soothed, rocking her to and fro. 'There wasn't anybody in here. You were just having a bad dream.'

'No, I wasn't. They were standing at the end of the bed,' Mel hiccuped as Jo arrived in the doorway, knuckling the sleep from her eyes. Alfie was with her and suddenly his hackles rose and he began to bark furiously.

'Oh, that's all I need. A paranoid teenager *and* a mad dog,' Simon groaned as he grabbed Alfie's collar and began to haul him back towards Jo's room. 'Can't you keep this bloody mongrel under control?'

'He's *not* a mongrel and Alfie *never* barks for no reason,' Jo protested indignantly as she sped along after him.

'Well, just the same keep him in here and keep him quiet, will you? Some of us need to get our sleep.'

Jo glared at him as he shoved Alfie into her room before firmly closing the door on them. Alfie was shaking like a leaf and Jo hugged him protectively. She had never known him to do anything like this before, although thankfully he did seem to be calming down a little now. She wondered what it could have been that had upset him.

Simon meanwhile hurried back to Mel's room where Jess was still cuddling her and asked, 'Do you need me?'

'No, we don't – go *away!*' Mel hissed before Jess had a chance to answer him.

'*Melanie!* That's no way to talk to your father.' Jess was shocked, although now she came to think of it, Mel had been keeping well out of his way lately whenever she could. It was probably due to the fact that Simon tended to be a little heavy-handed with her and still tried to keep her as his baby. Whenever she asked if she could go out with her friends to the pictures or to a disco he would always insist on taking her and bringing her home.

'I'm old enough to go on my own now,' Mel would insist but Simon was having none of it and the rows between the two of them were becoming more frequent.

Simon seemed about to say something but then thinking better of it he turned and left the room as Mel clung to her mother.

'I don't like this room, Mum. Can I move to another one?'

'But we've only just had it all decorated for you,' Jess pointed out as she stroked her daughter's damp hair from her brow. 'Why don't we give it a little longer, eh? Everything is strange for you at the minute but I guarantee you'll love living here once we've got it how we want it.'

Mel didn't look too sure about that but remained silent until Jess rose to leave, tucking the duvet around her warmly and bending to kiss her cheek. 'Now you try and get some sleep and I'll leave the door open and the bedside lamp on for you, shall I?'

She headed back to her own room where she found that Simon had already dropped off again. She slid in beside him with a frown on her face. This was the second time that Mel had insisted that someone had been in her room. And then there had been the other two strange experiences that she herself had had when she had thought someone was standing behind her. Deciding that there wasn't much point in worrying about it for now she snuggled up to Simon's broad back and fell asleep from sheer exhaustion.

\*　　\*　　\*

29

When Laura and Beth called in the following morning, Jess took them into the newly decorated lounge out of the way of the kitchen fitters, who were still busily working.

'Well, I have to say you've certainly made a difference in here,' Laura said admiringly as she took in the fancy drapes and the thick Axminster carpet.

Beth wandered out onto the sunlit lawn with Alfie close behind her, and now that they were alone, Jess began to tell her neighbour about Mel's nightmare and the strange experiences she herself had had since moving into the house.

'Simon reckons we might have a ghost,' Jess chuckled. 'You don't think we could have, do you? I mean . . . there are no such things as ghosts, are there?' She had never been one to believe in ghosts and ghouls and things that went bump in the night, but the recent experiences had unnerved her.

'Actually . . .' Laura suddenly looked extremely uncomfortable, 'I believe there are spirits. You see, I have this gift – or at least, that is how my mother refers to it, although I sometimes think it's more of a curse. She has it too, and I became aware of it when I was very young.'

'What sort of a gift?' Jess asked curiously.

'I see things, sense things – that's the only way I can explain it – and I have no wish to frighten you but I've sensed a presence in this house from the moment you invited me in.'

'Oh, what nonsense!' Jess retorted brashly. 'You're just letting your imagination run away with you because of what I've just told you. This is a very old property. There are bound to be noises at night – pipes clanking and floorboards settling and so on. And as for what Mel thought she saw . . . well, she had her curtains open and the moon was out, so she probably just saw a shadow in her room when the moon hid behind the clouds.'

'Yes, yes, I'm sure you're right,' Laura agreed a little too quickly for Jess's liking. Then she put the mug of tea that Jess had made her down on the tray and stood up.

'Thanks for the tea and the chat,' she said, fidgeting with the buttons on her blouse, 'but I really ought to be off now. Things to do, you know – and I bet you have a lot to do too. I'll just call Beth, shall I?'

'No, leave her here – she can play with Jo and Alfie,' Jess told her.

Laura had gone quite pale. Without another word, she strode towards the door where she stopped abruptly as if there was something she wanted to say. Her mouth worked soundlessly for a second but then she seemed to think better of it and clamped it shut.

'Be seeing you,' she said. 'Send Beth home if she starts to get on your nerves, won't you?'

And with that she was gone, and as she crossed the courtyard Jess heard one of the workmen in the kitchen wolf-whistle at her appreciatively through the open window. She watched Laura's hasty retreat with bemusement. It was almost as if she couldn't get away quickly enough, but Jess couldn't for the life of her think what she had said to upset her. Sighing, she placed the empty mugs on the tray and headed back to the kitchen to see what progress the men were making.

# Chapter Five

'You're late tonight,' Jess commented as Simon walked in and threw his car keys onto the coffee-table. He had been to the Town Talk on Abbey Green for his weekly game of darts and she was curled up on the settee reading a magazine.

'Blame Beth,' he said as he sank wearily into a chair opposite. 'They had some disco or something on at the youth club when I went to collect her, so I had to wait for it to finish.'

'That was kind of you,' she said, noticing how tired he looked. Neither of them had had a proper day off work since moving into the house and she wondered if perhaps they shouldn't plan a short holiday. It would do them all good, the way she saw it. She suggested it now but Simon shook his head.

'No chance,' he said regretfully. 'Me and the lads have got work booked right through until the end of November and I can't turn it down.'

'No, of course you can't.' Jess tried not to sound disappointed. Simon had a lot of faults but he had always worked hard.

'Then perhaps you should slow down a bit on your days off?' she suggested. 'You look totally whacked.'

'Oh yes, there's fat chance of that happening, isn't there? If I paid workmen to do every single thing around here that needs doing, it would cost us a fortune. But then as you so quite rightly keep pointing out, it can't go on for ever, can it? I mean, hopefully we will get this place straight one day and then we can both take a breather.'

'Mm.' Feeling more than a little guilty, Jess headed for the kitchen to make him a last drink before they went to bed.

The girls were back at school now, and noticing one of Mel's exercise books left discarded on the central workstation, Jess flipped through the pages. She was becoming more and more concerned about Mel, who seemed to be sinking into a deep depression. She had lost weight too and only this morning at breakfast Jess had noticed dark circles under her eyes, although Mel hadn't complained of having any

32

more nightmares lately. Once or twice Jess had tried to ask her what was wrong, but after having her head almost snapped off, she had given up.

Just today she had received a phone call from Mel's teacher who had told her that Mel was slipping behind with her schoolwork. Jess hadn't known what to say. Mel had always been so bright in her lessons until recently. She made two mugs of cocoa and after carrying them back to the lounge she told Simon about the call from school.

'I suppose you're going to start worrying about that too now,' he grumbled. 'When is it going to sink in that Mel is a teenager? Christ, at her age everyone had a job to even *get* me to school.'

Jess eyed him coldly. Every time she tried to talk to him seriously about Mel he simply blamed it on her age or changed the subject.

But then he surprised her when he suggested, 'How about we plan a party for her birthday? You know – let her have some of her friends from her new school come here for a sleepover or something?'

Mel chewed on her lip as she considered. Mel would be fourteen soon and it sounded like a good idea, although she wasn't at all sure that Mel had even made any friends at her new school as yet. She had certainly never mentioned them if she had.

'It sounds like a plan,' she admitted. 'But I haven't heard her speak about anyone special, not even a boy.'

'We don't want boys here. She's too young for that sort of thing,' Simon said protectively. 'I think we should limit the invites to girls only.'

'Oh Simon, you're the one who's always telling me she's a teenager. It's normal for a girl her age to start taking an interest in lads. You can't wrap her in cotton wool and lock her away for ever, you know?'

He glared. 'Well, I can, for as long as she'll let me,' he muttered. 'There'll be plenty of time for that sort of thing when she's older.'

Feeling a row brewing, Jess stood up and said shortly, 'I'm going to bed. Goodnight.' And with that she left him to it.

Once upstairs in their room she crossed to the open window and stared out musingly over the lake which was sparkling in the moonlight. Rabbits were gambolling across the lawn and they could have been miles from anywhere rather than on the outskirts of a busy town. Jess supposed that was one of the things she loved about this place. It was like a little retreat from the world. The painters were now busily working on the outside of the house and it was beginning to look smart. She estimated that in approximately another year they should have it all as she wanted it and then she would see about starting her B and B business. In a happier frame of mind again she rolled into bed and within minutes she was sound asleep.

Saturday morning, Jess woke to the sound of birdsong and stretched lazily. For the first time in weeks Simon was not going to work today and as there were no workmen there at the weekend she was looking forward to a lazy day with her family. Or part of the family at least. Jo had been invited to a birthday party at the house of one of her new friends in Shanklin Drive in Weddington, and then once the party was over she was going to stay for the night. Jess had asked Mel if she would like to invite one of her friends to stay over, but the girl had silently shaken her head and disappeared off to her bedroom again.

As she lay listening to Simon's breathing, Jess tried to think of something they could do that might encourage Mel outside. And then it occurred to her. Laura had offered to take them all to see the stone bridge that their home had been named after. It was about half a mile away apparently, and Jess quite fancied a casual stroll across the fields. No doubt Laura would be happy to show them the way as Den would be working. He often spent the weekends repairing train tracks, which left Laura at a loose end.

Slipping out of the bed, Jess shrugged her arms into her dressing-gown and headed for the kitchen. She would make Simon his breakfast and take it to him in bed. That should put him in a good mood if nothing else did.

Alfie was lying in his basket when she entered the kitchen and Jess was surprised. He had always slept with Jo on her bed until recently, but for some reason he seemed reluctant to go upstairs now. Jess bent to stroke his silky golden coat then put the kettle on and began to rummage in the fridge.

Half an hour later, Simon rubbed his full stomach as he sat propped up in bed on pillows. 'I could get used to this treatment,' he grinned. 'What did I do to deserve this?'

'You work so hard – too hard really.' Jess was standing at the open window watching a heron that was hovering by the lake for a sight of some unsuspecting fish. 'I was thinking we ought to give ourselves a day off. How about we go for a nice walk? It's a lovely day and we have the whole afternoon to ourselves after I've dropped Jo off at her friend's house. Laura offered some time ago to show us the stone bridge but I've never got round to going and seeing it yet. What do you think?'

'It sounds lovely but I thought you wanted me to make a start on stripping the old wallpaper off the dining room.'

'Oh, sod the dining room!' Jess exclaimed uncharacteristically. 'I reckon we deserve a break. We've been going flat out ever since we moved in and we both need a rest.'

'In that case I'm all for it.'

Jess wondered briefly if it was the thought of spending time with Laura that appealed to him more than the walk. She had seen the way he looked at their neighbour. Not that she could blame him. Laura was a very attractive woman, and Jess knew she had let herself go a bit since moving into the house. She couldn't remember the last time she had been to the hairdressers or worn a skirt, and she promised herself she would make more of an effort in future.

They all had a lazy morning at home and then Jess drove Jo to her friend in Weddington. Back home, she found Laura and Beth already there, sitting on the bench in the courtyard with Alfie skittering about their feet.

She greeted them as she got out of the car before asking Simon, 'Where's Mel? Isn't she coming with us?'

'I'm afraid not. As usual she's closeted herself in her room.' He sighed. 'She's getting to be a right little madam, I don't mind telling you. If this is what living with a teenager is like I reckon I'll freeze Jo before she gets there and defrost her when she's twenty-one.'

Jess smiled at his joke but inside she felt uneasy. Mel was far too reclusive for a girl her age. She should be taking an interest in clothes and make-up and boys by now, and going out to discos instead of staying locked away in her room all the time. Still, there was no point in spoiling the afternoon, so after tossing her car keys through the open kitchen door onto the table she asked, 'Are we all ready then?'

It was nice to see Laura. She'd been avoiding the place lately, and Jess had missed her. Now they all strolled towards the sloping lawn at the bottom of the garden before walking along beside the River Anker, which slowly meandered into the distance ahead of them. Beth was as close to Simon as she could get, staring up at him like an adoring puppy, and again Jess was saddened. Beth really was a stunningly pretty young woman. It was only when she spoke or if you looked into her vacant eyes that it was apparent there was something not quite right about her. It somehow put the problems they were having with Mel into perspective. At least Mel was healthy and bright and once she came out of her mood swings she would be able to enjoy a full life, while poor Beth would always be dependent on someone to care for her.

'L . . . look. B . . . buttercups,' Beth now told Simon as she pointed to some.

'That's right. Clever girl,' Simon said approvingly, and Jess smiled at him, proud of the patience he showed to the girl. Laura looked pleased too as she grinned at her lovely daughter.

They had gone some way when Laura suddenly pointed. 'There's the stone bridge ahead – look. Or should I say what's left of it.'

Jess quickened her pace until she came to the remains of the bridge. The top of it had gone, tumbled into the river many years ago, but it was clear to see how it might once have looked. It had been built in three rough stone arches, the footings of which still stood above the waterline.

'It must have been a very pretty bridge at one time,' Jess said musingly.

'It probably was in the summer when the waterline was low, but from what I've researched, it was pretty treacherous in the winter,' Laura told her. 'This whole area is prone to flooding, and more than a few people were swept to their death from that bridge.' She flinched and took an involuntary step back, as if someone had trodden on her grave.

'Are you all right?' Jess noted how pale her friend had gone.

'I, err . . . yes, I'm fine. Now how about we go for a wander over the Weddington fields? It's too hot to stand about.' Without waiting for an answer, Laura strode off, as Simon and Jess exchanged a puzzled glance. But then they set off after her, and for the rest of the afternoon they thought no more about it.

It was shortly before tea-time when they arrived back in the court-yard of Stonebridge House pleasantly tired from their outing.

'Christ, it would have been easier to go to work,' Simon complained as he sank onto the bench. 'I reckon you lot have nearly walked my legs off. We must have covered *miles*.'

'Oh, stop moaning. Exercise is good for you,' Jess giggled. 'Now sit there while I go and get us all a nice cool drink.'

'Not for me thanks,' Laura said a little too quickly. 'I'm going to have to shoot off to get Den's meal ready. He should be in from work soon, but thanks for a pleasant afternoon.' With that she snatched Beth's hand and dragged her towards the drive.

Jess stepped into the kitchen just in time to see someone pass the door that led into the hallway.

'Is that you, Mel?' she called out, but a quick inspection of the hall showed no one in sight and the only sound was that of the loud music wafting down the stairs from Mel's bedroom. Sighing, she headed for the fridge to get the lemonade out, thinking that she must have imagined it.

# Chapter Six

It was three weeks later before Jess ventured into the attics again. She was going into Nuneaton that afternoon and had decided to take the three sketches she had found with her. There was an art shop in Abbey Street where she could get them reframed, and then she intended to hang them in their bedroom.

Once again she climbed the bare wooden staircase to the small room where she had found the other sketch and stood there in the doorway as her eyes adjusted to the gloomy light. The smell of roses still hung heavy on the air, which she found quite strange as the window was shut tight. She lifted the sketch from the wall, keen to get out of there for no reason that she could explain, and she didn't look round again until she was out on the landing with the door firmly closed behind her. She was shocked to discover that her heart was pounding fifteen to the dozen. *I reckon I've been listening to Laura too much*, she thought to herself.

It was then that her curiosity got the better of her. She hadn't been back into the big attic room and now that she was up here it seemed silly not to take a peek. Propping the picture up against the wall, she quickly headed for the big room, opened the door and put the light on. She was shocked at the size of the place and the amount of stuff that was stored up there. She hadn't realised on her first inspection just how much there was. Cobwebs hung in great festoons from the ceiling and she thought she heard something scuttle across the floorboards. Shuddering, Jess made a mental note to get Simon to put some mouse traps up there. The whole place could be infested with rodents for all she knew, and she'd had a fear of mice ever since she was a child.

Jess didn't know where to look first. To one side of her was a large dressmaking mannequin, obviously very old, with straw sticking out of it. Crossing to the nearest chest, she cautiously raised the lid to find herself staring down at a collection of china-faced dolls. They looked very old and she wondered if they might be worth anything.

The next chest she opened revealed bed linen, yellowed with age. Soon her trip into town was forgotten as she continued with her exploration. She found an old rocking horse with a beautiful if somewhat dusty mane beneath one of the sheets, and exclaimed aloud with delight. That would look beautiful in the bay window in the drawing room if I were to clean it up, she thought, and determined to get Simon to carry it downstairs for her. It was far too beautiful to be hidden away up here.

Beneath another dust-sheet she unearthed a set of six matching ladder-back chairs. One of them was wobbling dangerously and the seats were in dire need of re-upholstering, but even so Jess fell in love with them and vowed to restore them to their former glory. She knew that they would look superb in the dining room. She just hoped now that she might be lucky enough to come across the table they belonged to.

Another half an hour and a lot of rummaging later, she came to a smaller wooden chest with metal straps around it set beneath the eaves. She had to drop onto her knees to drag it towards her, causing a storm of dust to make her cough, but at last she managed it. The lid was stiff, and despite her best efforts she was beginning to think that she would have to wait until she could get Simon to force it open for her, but then the heavy brass hinges suddenly squealed in protest and slowly but surely the lid creaked open.

This time she found herself staring down at a number of crudely bound leather books. They certainly didn't appear to be of any value but all the same, Jess was consumed with curiosity as she lifted one out and blew the dust from its cover.

Opening it to the first page she read, *This Journal belongs to Martha Reid*. The handwriting was neat and now Jess became excited. The sampler she had found in the servant's room where the clothes still hung had been embroidered with the name *Martha*, and she wondered if this was the same girl's journal. Curious to find out, she tucked it under her arm and headed for the door where she hastily snapped off the light and hurried downstairs, the shopping trip ignored for now.

Jess made herself a large pot of tea and after plonking it on a tray with some custard creams, she headed for the drawing room where she curled up on the sofa and opened the journal to the first page.

The first entry was dated 20 June 1837. And as Jess read on through the painstakingly written pages, splotched with blots and sprays of faded ink, she was transported back in time . . .

Today I, Martha Reid, am seventeen years old. This book is a birthday present from my Granny Reid and from now I shall try to find a little time each day to write my journal in it, with my best grammer and handwriting. I know that I am fortunate to be able to write, as most of the staff that work here are only able to make their mark with a cross. But Granny had been taught how to read by the vicar before she married my grandad, in return for cleaning and baking for him, and she has taught me and my sister Grace our letters and how to do sums for as long as I can remember. My birthday has been slightly marred as word has reached us that today our King, King William VI, has died at Windsor at the age of 71 years. Princess Victoria, who is only one year older than me, will now become Queen of Great Britain and Ireland. It is strange to think that a girl of about my age should have so much responsibility placed upon her shoulders. My life is hard, and yet I am blessed, for I have Grace and my Granny Reid to look out for me. Until three years ago we had our own little cottage in Mancetter, which was tied to the pit our father worked in. Our mother died in childbirth some years ago, and sadly I only have vague memories of her, and then when Da was killed in a pitfall we had to leave our home. Thankfully, we were then taken on by Master Fenton and we came to live here. I know that we are fortunate that Master Fenton allows us to live in Stonebridge House but I do sometimes wish that he was a kinder master. Our granny is now very old, at least sixty years, so I believe, and I think sometimes that the kitchen work is becoming too much for her. Granny and I and Grace have rooms in the attic. They are freezing cold in the winter and unbearably hot in the summer. In the autumn when Grace marries her Bertie they will live in the accommodation above the stable, and the room that I now share with my sister will become all mine. Grace is the chambermaid and the scullerymaid, I am the kitchenmaid and Granny is the cook. Bertie is the groom, and I think that he and Grace love each other very much. I am quite envious of them sometimes and wonder if I shall ever meet a boy I will fall in love with. Granny tells me to be thankful for what I've got, but I cannot help but dream.

Besides us, another family called the Tolleys live in a cottage in the grounds. Phoebe and Hal Tolley have four boys and they also all work for the Master. Hal and the boys do all the jobs about the place as well as tending to the gardens, and Phoebe does the laundry work.

Today the tinker called by and Grace bought me a red velvet ribbon which I shall wear in my hair when I go to the fair on Saturday. It is presently in the Pingles Fields in Coton. I am going with Grace and Bertie, but Granny has warned me not to spend all my hard-earned pennies on fripperies. It is all right for her, she is an old woman, but I like to look nice on my afternoons off. I went to the fair last year and greatly enjoyed it. The only thing I didn't like was the great brown bear who was shackled to the ground with chains about his ankles. His eyes were sad, and I felt sorry for him. People were poking him with sticks to make him roar and I thought they were cruel.

I shall have to close now to go about my duties. Master Fenton has visitors arriving later today and I must help to prepare their rooms. Granny says they will no doubt be gambling in the study until the early hours of the morning as usual and so she will probably have to stay up too, to serve them drinks and food. She worries about the Master since the Mistress left him earlier in the year. She says it's a wonder his flour mill in Attleborough hasn't gone under because he is hardly ever there to run it properly now, but Bertie said the Master had a good manager in charge there. Bertie doesn't feel sorry for the Master, in fact he said it served him right that the Mistress had gone because of the way he treated her, and that it was a good thing they were childless. Maybe that's why the Master plays the fool: he might have wanted an heir. I miss the Mistress. She was kind. Sometimes she would give Grace and me her cast-off gowns, and Granny would alter them to fit us. Rumour has it that the Mistress has returned to live with her parents at their country estate in Shropshire and that she will never return. I hope they are wrong. The house is not the same without her.

As Jess gently closed the book on Martha's first entry a shudder rippled through her despite the heat that wafted in through the open French doors. She knew she should share the journal with Simon, but she felt

41

strangely reluctant to do so. It was as if she had discovered something very precious and for now she wanted to keep it to herself. After carrying the book up to her bedroom she went about her chores, but her heart wasn't in them now. She just wanted it to be bedtime so that she could read some more of the young maid's past. It was incredible to think that Martha had once known every room in this house just as she herself now did, and Jess was intrigued to read on and discover more about the girl's life.

Beth arrived on the kitchen doorstep later in the afternoon and Jess beckoned her inside where she was preparing a large bowl of salad to accompany the cooked ham they were going to have for their evening meal. Beth looked eagerly around the kitchen, the smile on her face as bright as an electric light bulb as she asked expectantly, 'S . . . Simon?'

'Sorry, sweetheart. Simon is still at work, and he's likely to be late back this evening. He has a very big job on and he's trying to get as much done as he can whilst the weather is still on his side.' Seeing the girl's crestfallen expression, she suggested, 'Why don't you take Alfie for a little walk around the lawn? He gets very lonely while Jo is at school and he loves to see you.'

Slightly more cheerful again, Beth instantly rose, and seconds later she flew out of the door with Alfie following close behind, his tail wagging joyfully.

The rest of the day passed uneventfully. Jess postponed her trip into town, intending to go the next day, and Simon arrived home late as she had expected, tired and more than a little frazzled. 'I reckon I'll have a soak in the bath and turn in, if you don't mind,' he said after he'd eaten his meal. 'I've got another early start tomorrow and I'm all in.'

Jess was secretly relieved, and once he was fast asleep in bed she slipped in at the side of him and took Martha's book from the drawer. Within no time at all everything else faded away as she was drawn back into the early summer of 1837 . . .

*June 24*
Despite all my good intentions, this is the first day I have had time to write anything in my book since Granny Reid gave it to me on my birthday. The Master's friends arrived later that day as expected and stayed for three whole days, during which time

we were all run off our feet seeing to their needs. Granny is none too pleased at all with the way they have conducted themselves . . .

'I don't know.' Granny Reid pushed a strand of greying hair from her forehead as she placed a damp huckaback cloth over the dough and left it to rise. 'This place is gettin' to be little better than a bawdy-house, wi' all the Master's goin's-on.' She clapped her hands, sending a cloud of flour into the hot kitchen. 'Thank the Lord the poor Mistress left when she did. I wonder the poor lamb stuck 'im for as long as she did.'

Grace and Martha exchanged an amused glance as the older woman shuffled away to the oven to check the goose that was cooking in it. They knew what their granny was like when she got a bee in her bonnet about the Master.

'An' has the wine arrived yet? I ordered it two days ago.'

'Not yet,' Grace answered.

'Huh! Happen it won't neither.' Granny Reid tutted. 'If he don't settle some of his bills soon, we're goin' to have to go further afield for supplies. Hammond's in town nearly shut the door in poor Bertie's face when he took the last order in, an' they told him there'll be no more till the accounts is settled.'

Bertie, who was sitting at the kitchen table eating his lunch, nodded in confirmation.

'They did that, an' so did Lumley's,' he said. 'The Master's bills are as long as yer arm, but when I told him what they'd said, you'd have thought it were *me* as had run the bills up.' He bit into a thick slice of bread and cheese. 'An' I'm tellin' you now,' he mumbled, 'the wine in the cellar is almost gone. Lord knows what he'll do when his guests turn up tonight if it don't arrive. No doubt that'll be *my* fault, an' all.'

'How can it be your fault?' Grace said protectively. 'An' what guests are these? You mean to say there are yet *more* comin'?'

Bertie nodded. Lowering his voice and leaning towards them, he said, 'Aye, there are ladies from the brothel in town comin' to entertain 'em, from what I overheard the Master tellin' his cronies.'

'God above!' Granny Reid quickly crossed herself as she wiped her hands on her apron. 'Didn't I tell you this place were becomin' a den o' vice? That lot in there ain't stopped drinkin' an' gamblin' since they arrived, an' now this. Huh! It's a fair disgrace, so it is. Martha – I want you to keep as far away from 'em as yer can. I don't want the likes o' them mixin' wi' my girls. Do you hear me?' She shook a large wooden spoon at Martha as the girl nodded mutely then turning back to Bertie she demanded, 'An' are these women goin' to be stayin' over? If they are, we'll have to get some more bedrooms ready.'

'I can only assume so,' Bertie muttered.

Granny Reid stared off through the window towards the lake. 'It'll be his mill in Attleborough goin' under next,' she said worriedly. 'An' if he loses that, what will become of us? He may only pay us a meagre wage, but at least we have a roof over us heads an' food in our bellies.'

'Now Granny, don't get thinkin' the worst,' Grace soothed as she placed her arm about the woman's slight shoulders. 'I'm sure it won't come to that. The Master has a good manager at the mill, doesn't he, Bertie?'

'Aye, he does,' Bertie agreed. 'The problem is, if the Master doesn't order in the stuff to keep the mill workin', then even the best manager in the world can't keep the place runnin' on fresh air.'

'Well, happen this ain't the time to be frettin' about it,' Granny now stated matter-of-factly. She ran her kitchen with military precision and even now when she was sorely vexed at the goings-on around her she had no intentions of letting her standards slip. 'Martha, you go and start to set the table in the dinin' room, an' you, Grace, help me to get these vegetables dished up. Happen all we can do is cross each bridge as we come to it.'

Lifting her long brown calico skirt, Martha scuttled away to do as she was told.

At seven o'clock that evening, a carriage pulled up outside and four women emerged, eyeing the house with interest.

'Just look at the state of 'em,' Granny Reid said scathingly, as she spied on them from the hall window. 'If their dresses were cut any lower, their titties would fall out of 'em, so they would. An' would yer just *look* at their painted faces.'

'Shush an' come away to the kitchen,' Martha urged as she took the woman's elbow. 'The Master will skin us alive if he catches us gawpin'.'

Once back in the sanctuary of the kitchen they found Grace busily working on a length of fine blue satin that the Mistress had left behind. She had found it in the loft and the Master had told her she might have it, so now she spent every spare minute, which were few and far between, transforming it into her wedding dress for when she married Bertie.

'Isn't it beautiful?' she sighed. They had just finished washing up all the dinner pots and now had a little spare time before they had to start the supper for the Master and his guests, and Grace didn't intend to waste a second of it.

'It is that,' Martha said. She adored her older sister for her kind and gentle ways, and would gladly have laid down her life for her, if need be.

Glancing up, she found Granny staring at her. 'You look worn out,' the old lady commented as she finished polishing one of the huge copper pans before hanging it with the others above the enormous range. 'Why don't you away and get an early night, love? Me an' Grace can see to the supper. The vegetables are all ready, an' I only have to slice the cold meats. Everythin' should run smooth now that the wine order 'as arrived. Happen his lordship will be in a better frame o' mind now.'

Martha hesitated but Granny stood firm. 'Go on now an' do as yer told. The further away from them hussies that have just arrived you are, the happier I'll be. I doubt as they'll even touch the meal anyway, they're all too busy gamblin' an whorin' to worry about food.' She shook her head in disgust as Martha bent to kiss Grace before scuttling away to her room. It had been a long day and in truth she was glad of a chance of an early night.

'Goodnight, love,' Bertie said as she passed him at the door to the hallway.

'Goodnight.' Martha hurried through the long hallway and once she had reached the first landing was just in time to see one of the Master's guests disappearing off into a bedroom with one of the gaudily dressed women who had just arrived. She stifled a grin as she thought of what her granny's reaction would have been. Up in the attic, she opened the small window and breathed in the muggy night air. The room was baking hot and she could see dark clouds building. It looked like they might be in for a thunderstorm, but Martha thought that would be no bad thing. At least it might clear the air and cool things down a little. It had been unbearably hot working in the kitchen today. They had all been hard at work since first light, and only now did she realise just how tired she was.

Shrugging out of her skirt, she then unfastened the row of tiny buttons down the front of her blouse and folded it neatly over the back of the small chair. She then hastily washed in the cold water in the bowl on the washstand and pulled her nightshirt on before releasing her hair from its long plait and falling into bed. She could faintly hear the sounds of laughter and shouting coming from the floor below, but she was so tired that in no time at all she was fast asleep.

The Master's guests stayed for three days and as the last carriage pulled away, Granny heaved a sigh of relief. 'Thank God that unholy lot 'ave gone,' she muttered. 'Though Lord knows 'ow much the Master must 'ave gambled away, an' lookin' at the state o' the house, it'll take us another three days at least to put it to rights. Why, they were worse than animals.'

'Aw well, that's what we're paid for,' Grace pointed out in her usual gentle way. 'An' at least now Bertie can start sortin' through the stuff in the attics again to see if there's anythin' else he can salvage for our rooms.'

The Master had given the young people permission to help themselves to any old pieces of furniture they found in the attics, which Bertie was only too happy to do.

'Yes, and we've got the fair at the Pingles Fields to look forward to on Saturday an' all,' Martha piped up with a grin, her lovely blue eyes sparkling.

Grace laughed. 'Well, I just hope they haven't still got that great bear chained up this time,' she commented teasingly. 'You didn't stop crying all the way home after you saw him last year.'

Martha tossed her head indignantly. 'So what if I did? It was cruel,' she retorted.

'That's enough chit chat, me gels,' Granny commented drily. 'Off you go an' get them mucky beds stripped. It's a good dryin' day today wi' this bit o' wind if you get a shufty on.'

'I've already got the coppers heatin' up,' Grace replied as she followed Martha, and soon the sisters were busily stripping the soiled linen from the beds, the fair forgotten for now as they worked side by side to get the house back to rights.

The day of the fair dawned bright and sunny, and Martha worked with a will to do her chores so that she could get ready.

'Eeh, yer look a rare treat,' Granny Reid remarked when she entered the kitchen all ready to go out later that afternoon. Martha's hair was free of its plait today and she had tied it back with the pretty red velvet ribbon. She was wearing her Sunday best dress, which Granny had fashioned from an old one that the Mistress had passed on to Grace. There seemed to be a glow about her, and the old lady eyed her suspiciously.

'Just goin' to the fair you're lookin' so pleased about, is it?' she enquired.

Martha had the good grace to blush as Grace quickly grabbed her hand.

'Come along, else it'll be time to come back afore we even get there,' she urged and so the two sisters set off.

They were going down the drive when Grace scolded, 'I hope you haven't arranged to meet young Jimmy Weeks at the fair, Martha?'

Martha had met Jimmy, who worked on the neighbouring Leathermill Farm, the week before at the market and he had walked her home and kindly carried her basket for her.

'I haven't, as it so happens,' Martha snapped. 'But what if I had? I'm not a child any more, Grace, and I like Jimmy. He's kind an' he's handsome.'

'That's as maybe, but you're a little young to be walking out with anyone just yet.'

Martha opened her mouth to protest but stopped when she saw the Master galloping towards them on his coal-black stallion.

They stepped to the side of the drive, but when he drew abreast of them, Master Fenton reined his horse in and looked at Martha approvingly.

'My, my, don't we look pretty today? Off to the fair, are we?' He leaned down from his saddle and tilted Martha's chin up to him.

She blushed at the compliment, thinking how nice it was of him, but Bertie's face turned a dull brick-red colour, and when he made to step forward, Grace clung on to his hand as she yanked Martha from his grasp with her other.

'Yes, sir, we are – an' so if you don't mind we'll be on our way else it will hardly be worth goin'.'

Without another word the young woman dragged Bertie and Martha along as the Master followed Martha with his eyes before slapping his whip sharply against Prince's flank and galloping away at breakneck speed, his tail-coats flapping wildly behind him.

'Poor bloody 'orse,' Bertie muttered as he clenched his fists. 'No doubt the beast will be all of a lather again by the time he gets him back to the stables.'

'Well, that's not for you to worry about tonight,' Grace told him sternly and then turning her attention to Martha she said forcefully, 'Don't you *ever* get yerself in a position where you're alone wi' him. Do yer hear me?'

'But he only said I looked pretty,' Martha objected.

'That's as maybe. But keep yer distance all the same.'

Totally confused, Martha nodded and they made the rest of their journey in silence.

Once at the fair, Martha was happy to find that the bear wasn't there, although she worried about what might have become of him. There was a snake charmer and a bearded lady, however, but Martha was too busy keeping an eye open for a sight of Jimmy Weeks to take much notice. They wandered about the side-shows, but somehow since the encounter with the Master the joy had gone from the day and the trio made their way home in a subdued mood.

Martha was feeling slightly angry at Grace because of the way she had talked to her, and although she had never kept a secret from her sister before, she decided that if she should see Jimmy again, she wouldn't tell her about it. She was tired of them all still treating her like a little girl. And what had all that been about, when the Master had told her she looked pretty? Grace and Bertie had looked fit to burst with anger. It was all very confusing.

Once back at the house, Martha kissed Granny Reid a hasty good-night and went upstairs to the attic. She had no wish to be in their company any more that evening.

Once in bed, she wrote the happenings of the day in her journal until her candle began to burn low.

As she came to the end of the page, Jess snapped back to the present with a jolt. The girl's writing had been so vivid she almost felt as if she had gone back in time and had actually been there. She sighed as she lay trying to imagine what Martha might have looked like. Already the picture that was emerging of Mr Fenton was not a good one. He had obviously been a waster and a scoundrel, and Jess wondered what had eventually become of him. No doubt she would find out later in the journal.

Yawning now, she replaced the book in the drawer and turned off the bedside light before slipping into a deep sleep. It was the early hours of the morning when someone shaking her arm brought her blinking awake to find Jo standing at the side of the bed, sobbing uncontrollably.

'Mum, there was someone in my room – a lady. She was standing at the side of my bed looking down on me. Can I come into bed with you and Dad?'

'Oh, darling.' Jess instantly hotched closer to Simon as Jo slid in beside her. 'You've just had a bad dream. Either that or it was the moon playing tricks as it shone through your window.'

'That's what you said to Mel when it happened to her,' Jo shot back accusingly. 'But I'm telling you she *was* there. I woke up and she was standing there – I *swear* it.'

Jess wrapped the child in her arms, alarmed to find that she was shaking.

'We'll talk about it in the morning. You just get back to sleep now,' she urged.

An uneasy feeling began to form in the pit of her stomach. What if Laura had been right and there really *was* a spirit here walking the corridors of Stonebridge? Both Mel and Jo had seen it now, and what about all the times she had thought she had heard someone close behind her, only to turn and find that she was alone?

*Pull yourself together girl*, she scolded herself, *or you'll be jumping at your own shadow next. There are no such things as ghosts*! And on that positive thought she eventually dropped off into a restless doze.

# Chapter Seven

Next morning, Jo was unwilling to go to school. 'I've got a headache and my belly aches,' she complained as she pushed her cereal round the bowl.

Jess paused in the act of buttering some toast as she eyed her youngest. She did look pale, admittedly, but her school attendance record was excellent, so Jess supposed that missing just one day wouldn't hurt.

'All right then, finish your breakfast and go and hop back into bed. You'll probably feel better later on if you have a good rest.'

Jo shook her head. 'I'm not going back into my room,' she stated. '*She* might still be there.'

Mel's ears were pricked up now, and not wanting to blow the situation up out of all proportion, Jess told Jo, 'Then go and get back into my bed and I'll come up and see how you are when I've got your dad off to work and I've run Mel to school.'

'I don't feel very well either,' Mel put in, keen to jump on the bandwagon, but Jess wasn't having any of it.

'You were quite all right until you knew that Jo was having a day off. So go and get your schoolbag, please, miss.'

Mel slouched away from the table, casting an evil glare at Jo as she went, but thankfully she didn't argue and minutes later she was sitting in the car at the side of her mother with her arms tightly crossed and a rebellious expression on her face. When Jess pulled up near the school gates, Mel got out of the car and stamped away without so much as a by your leave.

Jess sighed heavily. She was still running the girls to school each morning although they were now walking home alone in the afternoons while it was light, which had freed her considerably. Today however, she wondered if she had done the right thing in making Mel go. Oh well, there was nothing she could do about it now. It hadn't been the best start to the day, that was a fact.

By the time she got home, the decorators were unloading their van.

They were going to start work on the dining room today and Jess was looking forward to seeing it done.

She made them a tray of tea and carried it through to them before taking the stairs two at a time to check on Jo, whom she found fast asleep in the middle of her bed. Satisfied that the girl was resting, she softly closed the door and slipped away.

Jo came back downstairs shortly before lunchtime looking a little more like her old cheerful self.

'Feeling better are you, sweetie?' her mother asked, through a mouthful of pins. She was busily re-upholstering the chairs she had found in the attic.

'Yes, thanks.'

'Good, then why don't you go and get dressed and I'll make you something to eat. You can take Alfie for a walk then.'

Jo hesitated for just a fraction of a second. She was obviously still unsure about going back into her old room, but Jess sensed that if she didn't make her do it now she might never want to go in there again.

'Come on, chop-chop,' she ordered with a smile, and Jo reluctantly turned and left the room.

When she came back ten minutes later dressed in jeans and an old T-shirt, Jess pointed to a plateful of tuna sandwiches and a Kit-Kat on the table. Jo wolfed the whole lot down in seconds before calling Alfie and heading for the door as Jess heaved a silent sigh of relief.

After lunch, Jess put the sketches in the car, and she and Jo visited the art shop in Abbey Street where they chose three nice frames that Jess felt would fit in perfectly with the décor in her bedroom. The man who owned the shop assured her that he would have them done for her by the end of the following week, and she and Jo then went to do some food shopping at the supermarket. Laura and Beth were sitting on the bench in the courtyard waiting for them when they arrived back.

'Why didn't you go in and make yourself a cuppa?' Jess asked. 'The door's unlocked as the decorators are in.'

Laura shook her head. 'It's too nice to be indoors so we thought we'd wait for you here.'

Jess secretly thought that it was probably more due to the fact that Laura was reluctant to go into the house, but refrained from saying so. There was only so much drama she could stand in one day, and she felt she'd already had enough with Jo's episode.

Beth and Jo instantly shot off to play by the lake as Jess took a seat at the side of Laura.

'Has Jo not been to school today then?' Laura asked. She had noticed that the girl wasn't wearing her uniform.

'No, she hasn't. She had a nightmare last night and ended up in our bed with me and Simon. Then when she got up this morning she said she wasn't feeling well, so I thought I'd give her the benefit of the doubt, though she'll certainly be going in tomorrow.'

'What sort of a nightmare was it?' Laura probed.

'The poor lass thought she saw someone standing at the side of her bed looking down on her. It scared her.'

Laura didn't say anything. She could sense that Jess was as taut as a spring and didn't want to upset her. They were still sitting there chatting when Simon pulled into the courtyard in his lorry, and Jess started guiltily.

'Good grief. It's *never* that time already? I wasn't expecting him for at least another couple of hours.'

Simon hopped lithely down from the cab and strolled over to them with a charming smile on his face.

'Don't look so worried,' he told Jess. 'I had to finish early. The extra bricks we ordered didn't arrive, so there didn't seem to be much point sitting there twiddling our thumbs.' Then turning to Laura he told her, 'You're looking very nice today, Laura. Is that a new blouse you're wearing?'

Laura blushed becomingly as Jess silently seethed. Simon was such a flirt, and quite open with it too. She wondered how he would feel if she were to be as openly admiring to one of his friends.

'I'd better go in and start dinner,' she said shortly. 'Would you like to come in for a drink before you go, Laura?'

'No, thanks all the same but I ought to get back to start Den's dinner too. Bye for now.'

Jess nodded and went inside with Simon following close on her heels. Once they were in the privacy of the kitchen she slammed over to the sink and filled the kettle.

'So what's wrong with your health and temper then, eh, miss?' Dropping onto a chair, Simon stretched his long legs in front of him.

'Not a thing.' Jess would not give him the satisfaction of letting him see that he had upset her.

'If you say so,' he muttered, obviously not believing her. 'So where are Mel and Jo then?'

'Mel just got back from school. She's in her room as usual and Jo is playing outside with Beth,' she said tersely.

'No changes there then,' he commented. 'And are you off to see Karen tonight?'

'Yes, I am. Why, is there a problem?'

'Not at all. There's some snooker on the telly this evening so I shall be quite happy left to my own devices with that and a few cans of lager.'

Jess began to unwind, feeling slightly foolish now for the way she had acted. She really would have to curb her jealousy where Simon was concerned. She'd got to the stage where she imagined he was about to run off with every attractive woman he laid eyes on. At that moment, Beth and Jo burst into the kitchen and as usual, at the sight of Simon, Beth's pretty face lit up.

'Hello, love,' he said as she shot across to him. 'Been a good girl for your mum today, have you?'

She nodded eagerly as he put the flat of his hand gently in the small of her back and pushed her towards the door. 'You'd best get yourself off home now then. Jo will be having her dinner soon and your mum will think you've got lost.'

Jess instantly forgave him everything as she saw how tender he was with the girl. Beth obviously adored him, which Jess found very touching. The girl had so little in her life and his kindness obviously meant a lot to her.

As Jess was leaving their bedroom after getting changed to go and see Karen that evening, she saw Simon leaving Mel's room and heard Mel crying loudly.

'What's wrong now?' she asked.

Simon scowled. 'We've just had words. She wanted to come and see Karen with you, but after the school reports we've been getting I've told her she's got to stay here and get some studying done. And don't look at me like that – you're always saying I leave everything about the girls' schooling down to you. I'm only trying to help.'

Jess felt as if she was caught between the devil and the deep blue sea. Mel ventured out so rarely nowadays, apart from to go to school, that Jess thought it might have done her good to get out for a while. But on the other hand she knew that what Simon was saying was perfectly true. She *did* complain that he left too much responsibility for their schoolwork on her shoulders. And if she undermined his authority now it would only cause another row.

'I suppose you are right,' she said uncertainly, trying to ignore the sound of Mel's sobs. 'Jo and I will shoot off then. We shouldn't be too late, but don't wait up for us if you fancy an early night.'

He nodded as she padded along the landing, and soon she and Jo were in the car and heading down the drive, although strangely she didn't really feel like going now.

# Chapter Eight

The next morning, as soon as she was alone, Jess took Martha's journal from the drawer. There were a million and one jobs that needed doing, but she was feeling restless and wasn't in the mood.

I'll just allow myself ten minutes, she promised herself, but the second she opened the book to the next entry, 13 July 1837, she was oblivious to anything else as she went back in time once more.

'Granny, the tinker is here with his cart,' Martha shouted as she looked out of the kitchen window.

'Huh, so he is, an' no doubt yer wages will be burnin' a hole in yer pocket,' the old woman commented as she looked up from the pastry she was rolling.

Throwing her a cheeky grin, Martha raced away to her room and came back with a collection of small coins in her hand. Before her granny could stay her, she skipped outside and approached the man's car.

'Good mornin', me darlin', an' how might you be this fine day?' The old tinker doffed his cap as Martha's eyes swept over his wares.

'I'm very well thank you, Mr Dawson. An' what have you on offer today?'

'Well, there be some fine ribbons here. They'd look a rare treat in your bonny hair. Or there's a linctus will cure everythin' from a head-ache to a fever. Or perhaps you'd like to try the scent? Made from fresh roses petal, it is, an' guaranteed to 'ave the lads droppin' at yet feet.'

He pulled the stopper from a small glass bottle as he spoke and held it out to Martha with a flourish, and she almost swooned with delight and blushed as she thought of Jimmy.

'Oh, that's just beautiful,' she sighed. 'But is it *very* expensive? If I could afford it I would wear it to Grace's wedding and keep it for very special occasions.'

'To you, me dear, two o' them shiny coppers yer 'ave in yer fair 'and an' you'll be gettin' a bargain.'

'I think you're right,' Martha agreed, readily handing the coins over.

It was then that a commotion in one of the outbuildings caught their attention, and Martha saw Grace emerge at a run, almost tripping over her skirts in her haste. She was crying, but as Martha made to go towards her, the Master also emerged. He was red in the face and swayed dangerously on his feet as he tried to pick the straw from his breeches, cursing beneath his breath. It was then that he caught sight of the tinker and with a silly grin he swaggered towards him.

'Morning, my man. Come to tempt my girls with your wares, have you?' He seemed in a fine humour now but Martha was nervous and edged away. She saw Grace disappear into the dairy and would have followed her but the Master caught her arm and looked her up and down.

'She's growing into a little beauty, wouldn't you agree, Mr Dawson?'

The old tinker swiped his cap off and ran a hand over his balding head, clearly ill at ease. 'She is that, sir. Won't be long now afore some young fella-me-lad snaps her up, eh?'

'Not too soon, I hope.'

Martha squirmed as the Master's eyes seemed to bore into her very soul. Just then, Bertie rounded the corner, and seeing the Master's hand on Martha's arm, he began to stride towards them.

'Er . . . happen it's time I was on me way now. Good day to you, sir, miss!' And with that the tinker grabbed the handles of his cart and trundled it across the cobbled courtyard as if Old Nick himself were snapping at his heels. The Master meantime released Martha and with a scathing glance at Bertie disappeared off into the house.

'So what's going on here then?' Bertie demanded.

Martha clutched her precious rose water, saying, 'I ain't sure, Bertie, but our Grace is in a rare dither. I just saw her come out o' one o' the outbuildin's cryin', an' seconds later the Master followed her. He were swayin' about.'

'Where did she go?' Bertie demanded as his hands clenched into fists.

'Into the dairy,' Martha informed him in a small voice, and without another word he turned on his heel and headed in that direction as Martha scuttled away to the kitchen.

Granny Reid raised an eyebrow as Martha raced in and without wasting a second the girl launched into an explanation of what had happened.

'Damn him to hell an' back!' the old woman exclaimed as she leaned heavily on the edge of the scrubbed oak table. 'No doubt he's drunk again.'

'But it ain't even eleven o'clock in the mornin' yet,' Martha said incredulously.

'The time o' day don't matter to him,' her granny ground out. 'I've seen 'im drinkin' brandy wi' his breakfast. It'll be his downfall, you just mark my words. But for now give Bertie an' Grace a bit o' time to themselves, eh?'

Bemused, Martha nodded before going about her chores.

It was later that evening when Grace had served the Master his evening meal that Martha overheard her talking to Bertie in the courtyard. Their voices were raised.

'He is our employer and I must do as he orders,' Grace told him.

'Not *everything* he orders.' Bertie was clearly very distressed. 'I swear to you, Grace, much more o' this an' I'll kill the bastard, so help me.'

'Martha, come away from there this instant!'

Granny Reid's voice made Martha jump, and she flushed as she realised that the old woman had caught her eavesdropping.

'Really, I don't know what gets into you,' the old woman scolded. 'First of all yer go fritterin' yer hard-earned money away on rubbish from the tinker, an' then you go listenin' in to yer sister's private conversations.'

'I'm fed up with you all still treating me like a child, and perhaps I'm just trying to find out what's going on around here,' Martha dared to answer back. 'You've always served the Master his meals till lately, Granny, so why all of a sudden is he insistin' that Grace serves him? And why does Bertie get so upset when she does?'

'The lessen yer know, the lessen you'll 'ave to worry about. Now get that dinin' room cleared an' let's be havin' no more o' yer lip, eh?'

Snatching up a tray, Martha slammed into the dining room and began to load the dirty pots onto it. Something was going on here but it was clear that no one was going to tell her what it was. Once the table was cleared she placed the tray on the polished mahogany sideboard that ran the length of one wall while she whisked the snow-white damask cloth off the table. Then, with the cloth under her arm ready for the laundry, and balancing the heavy tray in her hands, she headed back to the kitchen.

She was trying to open the green baize door that led into the kitchen when she heard voices from within, and once more she became still as she listened intently.

'I swear, as God is me witness, I'll do fer 'im if I have to,' she heard Bertie say, and his voice was full of anguish.

'That's enough o' that sort o' talk,' she heard Granny reply. 'He's our Master, lad, and there's nowt we can do about it. His word is law an' we have no choice but to obey him. We either do as we're told or it's the poor house fer all of us, an' yer wouldn't be wantin' that fer Grace, now would yer?'

Deciding that she had heard enough, Martha pushed the door open with her hip and was just in time to see Bertie slam his fist onto the table, setting the milk jug dancing. He was crying, but when Martha appeared he stood up abruptly and left without another word.

'Where's Grace?' Martha asked, as she placed the tray on the table.

'She's gone up to her room – she ain't feelin' so good.'

Granny's lips were set in a hard line, and knowing that it would be pointless to ask any more questions, Martha carried the pots to the deep stone sink and began the unenviable task of washing them up.

That night, as Martha lay in bed, she heard her sister crying in the next bed, but feeling powerless to help her she turned her face into the pillow and tried to lose herself in sleep. They had all been so happy living there until the Mistress had left, but now things were going from bad to worse.

The next morning, as Martha helped her grandmother to prepare the breakfast, she peeped at her from the corner of her eye before venturing, 'I heard Grace cry herself to sleep last night.'

'There you go again, pokin' yer nose in where it ain't wanted,' the woman said crossly. 'I've a good mind to box yer ears, me gel. There's bad things goin' on here. Things as don't concern yer – an' if we're not careful we'll all be out on our arses, so just let things lie, eh?'

Mid-morning, Martha was working in the dairy churning butter when she heard Grace and Bertie walking past, 'Please, love, let's just up an' go,' she heard Bertie implore her.

'Granny is too old fer a life on the open road or the poorhouse. We must endure it,' she heard Grace reply, but then the couple moved out of earshot and Martha could only groan with frustration.

It was lunchtime when Martha next entered the kitchen to find Bertie and Grace chatting to Granny.

'His lordship come in 'ere this mornin' an' told me to prepare a lunch fer Farmer Codd from Leathermill Farm tomorrow,' Gran informed Martha. 'We're thinkin' he's happen plannin' on sellin' off some more of his land.'

'It'll be a dark day fer all of us including the Tolleys if he does,' Bertie muttered. The Tolley family lived in a cottage in the grounds.

'Not so long ago the land amounted to more than ten acres but I doubt he owns five now, an' there ain't goin' to be enough work fer 'im to keep us all on if any more goes.'

Mention of Leathermill instantly made Martha think of Jimmy and she felt colour burn into her cheeks. She had been working towards asking Granny if she could walk out with him as he had asked her to on the last market-day, but now didn't seem to be the right time. In fact, nothing felt right at present and yet Grace and Bertie were due to be wed in just three weeks' time at the charming little church, St Theobald and St Chad's in Caldecote. Surely this should be a happy time? It was all very worrying.

Jess paused and put down the journal as the first rumbles of thunder could be heard in the distance. The sky had gone ominously dark and she pulled her cardigan more tightly about her. Martha had mentioned the scented rosewater she had bought off the travelling tinker. Could this be the smell that had lingered in her room in the attic? She dismissed the idea almost immediately, and yet . . . A flash of lightning suddenly illuminated the room and Jess started in shock before leaping from the bed and rushing to the window. A strong wind had blown up from nowhere and the curtains were billowing into the room as the first heavy drops of rain began to fall. After a struggle she managed to close the window and looked back at the book on the bed. It was then that she sensed someone standing close behind her again and she whirled about to find that she was alone.

I'm not sure if it's doing me any good reading this journal, she thought to herself. And then she grinned. If she wasn't careful she would start to believe all the same gobbledegook as Laura. Spirits indeed! There was no such thing. Annoyed with herself, she set off purposefully down the stairs, intent on getting some work done.

'What's this then?' Simon asked that night as he lifted the journal from the duvet.

Jess groaned silently. She had meant to put it away. 'Oh, it's just an old journal I found up in the attic,' she said dismissively, shoving it into the drawer of the bedside table.

'Really? Whose was it?'

'Just some servant girl who used to work here, from what I can make of it.' Jess was keen to change the subject. She turned to Simon with a seductive smile as he slipped into bed. 'But never mind about that for now. Do you fancy a cuddle?'

Simon yawned. 'Can't say as I do, to be honest, love. I'm dead beat. Perhaps tomorrow, eh? Goodnight.'

Slightly miffed, Jess climbed in beside him. It was usually she who pleaded a headache or some such ailment but lately the tables were turning and she wondered briefly if he was having another fling. Almost immediately, she felt guilty. He was working hard from early in the morning until late at night most days. No wonder that he wasn't in the mood for romance. He probably just didn't have the energy for it.

They were getting dressed the next morning when Simon told her casually, 'I'm giving Laura a lift into town this morning on my way to work – did I mention it?'

'No, you didn't.' She kept her voice light. 'Why is that then?'

'She told me she needed to get Beth some new clothes. She asked me if I'd take her as I pulled into the drive last night.'

'I can't think why she doesn't take Social Services up on their offer of some respite,' Jess said. 'It must be hard caring for a young person like Beth twenty-four-seven.'

'That's easy for you to say, but I wonder if you'd want it if it was one of our girls in Beth's shoes.'

Jess could hear a note of reproach in his voice and instantly wished that she hadn't said anything. She supposed he was right. If Mel or Jo had been born like Beth she would have been just as protective of them. And yet, if Laura would only allow Beth to mix with other people more, surely it would be good for the girl instead of being kept tied to her mother's apron strings all the time? Beth seemed to come alive when she was with Jo or Simon, but Jess didn't say that now. At the end of the day she was aware that it was really none of her business.

'So what have you got planned for today then?' Simon asked as he pulled his shoes on.

'I thought I'd hang the new curtains in the dining room now that the decorators have finished in there and then I'm going into town to pick those pictures up that I've had reframed. They should be ready today.'

They went downstairs together and soon after Jess ran Mel and Jo to school and Simon shot off to work. Once she was home again, Jess wandered into the dining room and looked around with satisfaction.

The paper she had chosen for the walls in there was perfect for the room and the chairs that she had recovered looked as good as new. Simon had made a marvellous job of repairing the one that had been wobbly. Now all she had to do was scour the antique shops again until she found a table that would go with them. She briefly wondered what had happened to the original one, but then was soon absorbed in hanging the new curtains.

Outside, the rain poured down relentlessly just as it had since the thunderstorm the day before. The sky was black and overcast, and Jess wondered briefly if they had seen the last of the summer. At this rate, she would soon be trying the new central heating system out. It was decidedly chilly now.

Once the curtains were hung to her satisfaction she had a solitary lunch then popped upstairs to get changed before going into town. As she accelerated down the drive shortly afterwards, she glanced in the car mirror. The house looked dark and brooding without the sun shining down on it – nothing at all like the happy family home she was trying so hard to create. She scolded herself, *Don't be so daft, woman. Everywhere looks dull in this weather.*

Her spirits lifted slightly when she picked up the sketches. The frames she had chosen suited them to perfection and she could hardly wait to get home and hang them in her bedroom. On the way back she popped into the supermarket and loaded a trolley with food, and soon she was turning into the drive again, only to slam on her brakes when she saw Laura standing in the middle of it gazing at the house.

'You daft thing,' she scolded as she jumped out of the car. 'I could have run you down then.'

'What . . . ?' Laura seemed distracted for a second but then she smiled apologetically. 'Oh, I'm so sorry, Jess. I was miles away.'

'I could see that, but what are you doing?'

Laura glanced towards Beth, who was absorbed in dragging the piles of gravel on the drive into neat little piles with the toe of her trainers.

'Actually, I think it's time you and I had a little talk.' Laura kept her voice low.

Jess frowned. 'What about?'

Ignoring the question, Laura asked, 'How about tomorrow morning about elevenish? Den is off work with this awful flu bug that's flying about, so Beth could stay with him for an hour while I came up to you.'

Jess was momentarily lost for words. She normally had to almost

61

crowbar Laura into the house, and now here she was asking to visit of her own free will. 'Of course you can call in,' she told her eventually. 'You don't need to make an appointment. I've always told you you're welcome to pop in at any time. To be honest, now that the main part of the house is taking shape, I'd be glad of the company. But now get yourself home. You look like a pair of drowned rats. You'll catch your deaths, standing out in this weather.'

Laura grinned ruefully before taking Beth's hand. 'I'll see you in the morning then, shall I?'

Jess nodded and watched them move away before swiping the rain out of her eyes and clambering back into the car. She roared off up the drive and once she had parked up in the courtyard she made a run for the kitchen door with the sketches tucked securely under her arm.

After hastily throwing off her wet coat she put the kettle on to boil and laid the sketches out on the kitchen table to admire them. The one of the young girl picking wild flowers particularly held her attention and she studied it intently. The girl looked to be about sixteen or seventeen years old and had shoulder-length brown hair. She was slim, but as she was bending down it was impossible to see her face for the curtain of hair that draped across it, and Jess wondered if she had been pretty. She also suddenly wondered if this might be Martha, the young girl whose journal she was reading. At the thought a little shiver rippled through her but she had no time to dwell on it because at that moment someone shouted her name and she started. The voice had come from upstairs but she was certain that she was the only person in the house. Curious, she hurried into the hallway where she stood at the foot of the stairs gazing up them. It had sounded like a young girl's voice but both the girls were at school.

'Is anyone there?' she called uncertainly, but only silence answered her. Slowly she began to climb the stairs and once on the landing she looked left and right. The rain was lashing against the windows and she began to relax a little. That was probably what she had heard. There was certainly no one there.

As she prepared the vegetables for the evening meal, Jess wondered what it was that Laura wanted to see her about the next morning.

# Chapter Nine

If anything the weather got even worse during the night and Simon was not in the best of moods at breakfast the next morning. 'All this rain is going to put us right behind on the job we're doing,' he complained.

'Well, I'm afraid you can't order the weather.' Jess poured more tea into his mug and grinned, trying to stay cheerful. Jo looked slightly flushed today and Jess wondered if she was coming down with something, although the girl had insisted she was well enough for school. Mel was in her usual sulk, looking as if the end of the world was just around the corner and now Jess had Simon moaning too. Another great start to the day!

After seeing Simon off she ran the girls to school, watching Mel pick her way across the playground. Her daughter's hair was scraped back into a severe ponytail with two long bits dangling down around her face. She had obviously attacked it with the straighteners again this morning, but as Jess was discovering, curly hair nowadays was considered a curse by teenage girls. She could only begin to imagine what damage the heat was inflicting to Mel's crowning glory, but had long ago stopped trying to point it out because whenever she did, Mel just stared at her as if she was some sort of raving looney. The girl's school tie was knotted at the third button of her shirt, which was undone at the neck as were all the other girl's making their way into school, and the waistband of her skirt had been rolled over so that it sat just above her knees. It was as if they were trying to look like clones of each other but Jess was wise enough to know by now that she had to bow to fashion. Oh, to be young again, she thought as she restarted the car and drove away. Once back at the house she decided to have a few minutes to herself and read a little more of Martha's journal. In no time at all she was propped up against her headboard with the book open to the next page and soon everything else faded away as she became lost in the girl's story.

Today Grace and Bertie were married in St Theobald and St Chad's Church in Caldecote. I had expected it to be a happy day, a day for rejoicing, but for some reason it turned out to be almost like any other day . . .

The day of the wedding finally dawned and as Martha woke, a feeling of excitement coursed through her. She had her Sunday best green dress laid out across the chair and as she looked towards it she smiled. Once they had seen to the Master's breakfast they would be free to get ready, and she could hardly wait to see Grace in the gown she had fashioned from the length of blue silk. After pouring some water from the jug into the bowl she washed hastily and pulled on her drab work clothes. There was no point in wearing her best dress until the chores were done. The night before, she had washed her hair in water and vinegar, and after rubbing it with an old towel she had sat at the bedroom window and brushed it until it shone in the breeze that was wafting in.

Once she had secured it with a ribbon she skipped downstairs in a happy frame of mind just in time to see Bertie coming out of the Master's study, his mouth set in a grim line.

'So, the big day is finally here then?' Martha smiled tentatively as Bertie appeared to look straight through her.

'Aye, I suppose it is,' he muttered eventually then he turned and walked away as Martha chewed on her lip. The Master had obviously said something to upset him, although she had no idea what it might be. Surely Bertie should have been in a happier frame of mind on his wedding day? Shrugging, she moved on to the kitchen where she knew Grace and Granny would already be working.

On entering the room she saw Granny flipping bacon and kidneys in a large cast-iron pan on the range and Grace laying the Master's tray. Lately, if he didn't have guests, the Master preferred to take his breakfast in his room, which Martha had noticed Grace didn't seem at all happy about. But then it was a special day, so surely even Grace wouldn't mind waiting on him today?

'I just saw Bertie coming out of the Master's study, so he's obviously up and about. He'll probably have the tray in his study this morning,' she chirped cheerfully. 'And I have to say Bertie didn't look none too pleased, so I don't know what the Master's said to upset him.'

'Hold your tongue, girl, else I'll box yer ears fer yer,' Granny snapped.

Martha sighed. What was wrong with everyone today? It seemed that they'd all got out of the wrong side of the bed.

After fetching the large milk jug from the pantry she helped the two women prepare the rest of the meal in silence before slipping through the back door. Once outside she headed for the meadow where she quickly picked a bunch of wild flowers then carried them back to the kitchen and held them out to her granny.

'I thought these might be nice for Grace to carry as her bouquet,' she said quietly.

The old woman's faded grey eyes softened as she looked at her young granddaughter. It wasn't her fault, after all, that there was trouble on, and happen she'd been a bit hard on her.

'They're lovely.' She forced a smile. 'An' I reckon I've got a length o' blue ribbon up in me room to tie 'em with. They'll look a treat wi' Grace's dress.'

Slightly happier, Martha asked, 'And where is Grace?'

'Gone up to her room to get ready. She might be glad of a bit of help.'

Martha frowned. 'But shouldn't we be preparing the bridal meal for when we get back before we get dressed?'

'There'll be no bridal meal,' Granny said shortly. 'The Master's informed us that he has guests comin' again tonight, so soon as the service is over we'll have to come back an' prepare fer them.'

'Oh!' Martha could not stop the note of disappointment that crept into her voice. She had at least expected a small celebration with the Tolleys to mark the day. Hal Tolley was to accompany them to the church to act as best man to Bertie, but it appeared that it was not going to happen. Some wedding day this was turning out to be, she thought to herself.

'Why don't you go an' get ready an' all,' Granny now suggested, taking the flowers from Martha's hands. 'I can finish up in here an' I'm sure Grace will be grateful of a hand wi' her hair.'

Feeling somewhat deflated, Martha slipped out into the courtyard and headed for the stable block. She would check that everything was right in the rooms above it for Grace to return to as a bride before going to help her sister get dressed.

Bertie was there already, washed and dressed in his Sunday best suit when Martha tapped on the door and entered. He looked very nervous and very handsome as Martha grinned at him.

'By, you look posh,' she laughed. 'Happen our Grace will fall in love with yer all over again when she sees yer lookin' like that.'

Bertie's hand rose self-consciously to pat his hair, which at the moment was flattened to his head with Maccassar oil.

Martha then took a quick look around the rooms and sighed with satisfaction. They had all been working tirelessly to transfer the old furniture from the attics that the Master had told them they might have, and now the small rooms looked quite homely. There was a table with two sturdy wooden chairs at either side of it in the living area and an ancient couch that Granny had re-upholstered for them from a length of cloth they had found in one of the numerous trunks in the attic. Granny had also made them some pretty curtains to hang at the window. One corner of the room was partitioned off by a faded velvet curtain, another reject from the attic, and behind it was a sink and a small stove that would serve as their kitchen quarters. Bertie had hung a shelf there too which was full of mismatched plates and mugs, but Martha saw that everything was sparkling.

The last room to check was the bedroom. She knew how untidy Bertie could be and wanted everything to be just right for when he brought Grace back there as his wife. But she need not have worried. A quick glance assured her that Bertie had put everything away in the old wardrobe and the chest of drawers that stood to one side of the large brass bed. The same pretty flowered cotton curtains that hung in the living room graced the bedroom window, and Granny's wedding present to the young couple, a beautifully sewn patchwork quilt made from scraps of material all the colours of the rainbow, was spread across the bed. It felt strange to think that Grace would be sleeping here with Bertie from now on rather than in the servants' quarters with her, but Martha hoped that the couple would be happy. And once they had put Grace's bed into the storage room, she would have much more space, which would be nice.

'Well, everything seems to be in order here so I'll go and give Grace a hand in getting ready now,' she told Bertie brightly.

He nodded as he tugged at his tie and Martha giggled. 'At least *try* and look happy,' she teased. 'You look more like a chap that's about to go to the gallows than one that's about to be wed.'

'I'm happy enough. But now be gone wi' yer an' help Grace, eh? We've less than an hour to get to church an' I can't see the parson bein' none too happy if we keep him waitin'.'

Lifting her skirts, Martha carefully descended the stairs before skipping across the cobblestones and back into the kitchen. There was no sign of Granny, and Martha guessed that she had probably gone to get ready too.

On entering Grace's room she became still as she saw her sister lifting the blue satin gown over her head. It seemed to accentuate the colour of her eyes and Martha thought she looked truly beautiful. Almost like gentry.

'Ah, just in time. Could you help me with these buttons?'

'Of course I will.' Martha crossed to do as she was bid and within seconds was saying playfully, 'I think you must have put a bit of weight on since you finished this dress. I can scarce get the buttons to do up about your waist.'

To her amazement, Grace rounded on her, her lovely blue eyes flashing. 'I hope you won't get saying anything so thoughtless as that in front of Bertie!' she hissed.

'O' course I won't, an' I had no wish to cause offence,' Martha stammered.

Grace's hand flew to her brow and she sighed. 'Sorry, love. I didn't mean to snap yer head off. Happen I'm just a bit nervous.'

She dropped onto the chair and taking up the brush, Martha began to brush her hair. 'It's all right. I've heard it's quite normal fer folks to be nervous on their weddin' day.' In no time at all she had fastened Grace's long fine hair into a bun at the nape of her neck and now her sister lifted the second-hand bonnet she had bought from a stall in the market and put it on. It looked totally transformed now that Grace had covered it in tiny satin rosebuds and when she tied it beneath her chin, Martha sighed dreamily.

'Oh, our Grace. Yer look truly beautiful,' she breathed in a choky voice. Then side-by-side the sisters made their way down to the kitchen.

Hal Tolley was there, dressed in his best outfit as they all were, along with Granny and Bertie, and they all looked at Grace admiringly.

Granny was looking smart in a light grey gown she had bought from the pawn shop and altered, and over it she was wearing the Paisley shawl that Grace and Martha had bought for her the previous Christmas.

Bertie's eyes misted over as he viewed his bride-to-be. Taking her hands in his, he looked deeply into her eyes.

'Right then, we're not goin' to let *nothin'* spoil today,' he told Grace.

''Cos I know what a lucky fellow I am. Now – if everyone's ready, I reckon we should be off.'

The sun was riding high in a cloudless blue sky as they set off for the tiny church in Caldecote, and Martha found herself skipping happily ahead. The rest of the party still seemed somewhat subdued, however, although she had no idea why. The church was less than a mile as the crow flew, but Granny was puffing before they were halfway there. 'Happen me head still thinks I'm nor but a lass, but me old legs are tellin' me otherwise,' she huffed.

They had gone about halfway when they heard the sound of a horse and trap and glancing over their shoulders they saw Jimmy Weeks on his way to market. He winked at Martha cheekily, before turning his attention to Grace and Bertie. 'Good luck to you two,' he said, then shaking the reins he moved the horse on.

'Cheeky young whippersnapper,' snorted Granny, then wagging her finger at Martha she said warningly, 'I hope you're not up to no good wi' that young 'un, me gel.'

'Of course I'm not,' Martha replied indignantly, and lifting her skirts she stalked ahead.

The villagers in Caldecote called out their good wishes and greetings as the party passed, and soon Grace, clutching her posy nervously, and Bertie, were standing before the parson.

The service seemed to be over in the blink of an eye and in no time at all they were all outside again.

'It doesn't seem right that there's going to be no wedding meal,' Martha sighed as they made their way back to Stonebridge House.

'Happen we should just think 'usselves lucky that the Master allowed us time off fer the service,' Granny retorted and they made the remainder of the journey in silence, although Martha was happy to see that Bertie and Grace walked hand-in-hand and seemed to be happy.

They were nearing the house when Granny groaned and pointed ahead to where two carriages stood outside the front entrance. 'Would you just look at that! Seems some of his lordship's guests 'ave arrived already. That means I'll 'ave to get a spurt on gettin' the meal ready, else he'll be grumblin'.'

'Well, I'll nip back home an' get yer them two rabbits I snared last night,' Hal Tolley said. 'Happen they'll make up into a nice couple o' pies.'

'It's perhaps as well,' Granny said, a frown on her brow. 'The pantry's near empty an' most places are refusin' to send supplies now; lessen the Master settles his bills.'

They slipped into the house and Grace and Martha hurried to their rooms to change back into their work clothes. Martha was bitterly disappointed. 'I don't want it to be like this, just like any other day when I marry Jimmy,' she muttered to herself as she fastened an apron about her waist. She then ran back downstairs and in no time at all was too busy to think of anything.

'Would you just hark at that carry-on,' Granny said in disgust, cocking her head towards the door that led into the hall. 'Sounds like half of 'em are drunk already, so God only knows what they'll be like come evenin'! Just you stay away from the lot of 'em, our Grace. They're heathens, so they are.' She then went back to rolling the pastry for the pies with a vengeance as Martha continued to skin the rabbits Hal had supplied them with.

It was mid-afternoon when Granny asked, 'Would yer go an' collect me some eggs from the barn fer the egg custard, pet?'

'Of course I will.' Martha obligingly collected the wicker basket and lifting her skirts she set off across the courtyard. It was dark in the barn after leaving the bright sunshine outside and Martha stood for a moment letting her eyes adjust before going in search of the eggs. She knew all the hens' favourite laying places and in no time at all the bottom of the basket was covered with them. She was happily scouting about when a noise from the hay bales in the far corner caught her ear. That corner of the barn was in deep shadow and she was peering towards it when a naked woman suddenly shrieked with laughter and raced towards her, closely followed by a naked man.

Martha was so shocked that she dropped the basket and the eggs rolled all over the ground as her hand flew to her mouth.

'Ha-ha! Come to join in the frolics, have you, me pretty?' As the man lurched towards her laughing loudly, Martha lifted her skirts in a most unladylike manner and fled as if her life depended on it.

She almost fell into the kitchen door and Granny looked up sharply. 'Why, whatever's wrong wi' you?' she barked. 'An' where are me eggs?'

'I . . . I dropped them,' Martha gasped as she pressed her hand into the stitch in her side. 'There was a man . . . an' a woman . . . an' they were naked an' racin' round the barn. I'm sorry, Granny.'

Granny's face darkened. 'No lass, don't *you* be sorry. Yer did right to come away. I don't know – such sordid goin's-on! Whatever would the Mistress 'ave said to such shenanigans? Heathens they are, the whole lot of 'em. You stay here wi' me now an' damn the eggs. An' if the Master asks why he ain't got no egg custard I'll give 'im what for, you just watch me.'

It was late that evening before Grace and Bertie were finally able to return to their rooms for their wedding night, and Grace seemed shy and flustered as they said their goodnights.

'See yer both in the mornin',' Granny said as if it was just any night, and the young couple slipped out into the balmy evening with eyes only for each other.

'I reckon you should go an' get yer head down now an' all,' Granny told Martha. 'It's been a long day. Goodnight, love.'

Martha didn't need telling twice. She planted a kiss on her granny's cheek and headed for the door, every limb aching.

She was almost at the foot of the stairs when the drawing-room door banged open and the man she had seen in the barn earlier in the day staggered out.

'Ah, can't keep away from me, me pretty, can you?' he laughed, and lunging forward he caught Martha's arm in a strong grip.

She had just opened her mouth to scream when the Master appeared in the doorway. One of the women from the town was hanging around his neck and he told the man, 'Unhand her, James. *I* have first rights wi' that little maid an' when the time comes I want her pure.'

The man good-naturedly did as he was told and lurched drunkenly away as Martha fled up the stairs, not stopping to breathe until she had slammed her bedroom door and bolted it securely behind her. The room looked so big now that Bertie had dragged Grace's bed into the large attic, and Martha suddenly felt very lonely. It had certainly been a funny old day, one way or another. And what could the Master have meant about wanting to keep her pure? Tiredly, she began to undress as she tried to put the event from her mind.

Jess slammed the book shut and stared towards the window. What a sad wedding day Grace and Bertie had had. It just went to show how times had changed and how hard life must have been for working-class people in Martha's time. She was sorely tempted to read on but decided against it. Laura would be here soon and Jess was curious to hear what she had to say. Reluctantly putting the journal away in her drawer, she made her way back down to the kitchen.

Laura arrived punctually at eleven o'clock looking slightly ill-at-ease.

Jess had a percolator full of coffee bubbling away on the range and she carried it to the table along with a plateful of ginger nut biscuits. She knew Laura was rather partial to them.

'So?' she smiled, hoping to lighten the atmosphere a bit. 'How is Den today?'

'Oh, you know.' Laura raised her eyebrows. 'He's a man, isn't he? Need I say more? If he gets a cold it's flu. If he gets flu it's pneumonia.'

'I know what you mean, Simon is exactly the same.' Jess chuckled as she poured out their coffee.

Laura sipped at her drink, eyeing Jess pensively over the rim of her mug before asking, 'So how are you settling in?'

'Very well really. The house is shaping up nicely at last. I reckon I'll have it how I want it for this time next year.'

'Well, I have to say this looks stunning.' Laura glanced around at the gleaming kitchen. 'In fact, I think you have a flair for interior design.'

'I wouldn't go that far.' Jess blushed at the compliment. 'But now what was it you wanted to see me about?'

Laura gulped. 'I don't quite know where to start,' she said.

Jess smiled encouragingly. 'Then why don't you start at the very beginning?'

'I er . . . Well, the thing is, I know you don't believe in spiritual things, but I have to ask you: have you ever had anything strange happen since you've lived here? For instance, have you ever had the sense that you weren't alone when everyone else was out?'

Jess decided to answer truthfully. 'Yes, I have. On a few occasions I've thought that someone had come into a room behind me and when I've turned around there's been no one there. Another time I thought I heard someone call me from upstairs, but when I went up to check, all the rooms were empty. Oh, and there's Alfie too . . .' She glanced towards the dog, who was curled up in his basket. 'He always used to sleep in Jo's room when we lived in our other house, but since coming to live here he refuses to go upstairs.'

'And what about nightmares?'

Jess frowned. 'I haven't had any personally, but Mel has, and so has Jo. She said that someone was standing at the side of her bed watching her one night. In fact, she was so upset she came and got in with me and her dad.'

'I see.' Laura tapped the table thoughtfully. 'Anything else?'

71

Jess thought hard before nodding. 'Come to think of it, there's the smell. Well, not a smell exactly, it's more a scent of roses. The first time I noticed it was when I was up in the old servants' quarters in the attic. You really should come up and see it, Laura. It's like stepping back in time up there. One room still has old clothes hanging in the wardrobe and I discovered that they once belonged to a young girl who lived here.'

'How?' Laura was leaning forward in her seat, all ears now.

'I found her journal in the attic. It's quite fascinating, although I haven't read much of it up to now. The girl's name was Martha Reid. She and her family were servants here and they referred to the man who owned the place at the time as Master Fenton. He was a cruel bugger, if what I've read up to now is anything to go by, and the poor sods lived in fear of him turning them out and ending up in the workhouse. The first entry in the journal goes right back to 1837.'

Laura had gone quite pale. 'I knew it,' she said softly, more to herself than Jess. 'There *is* a restless spirit here.'

'Oh, come on! Don't let your imagination get running away with you. This is a very old house, Laura. I'm sure a lot of what we've experienced has been down to it settling at night. You know – floorboards creaking, et cetera.'

Laura shook her head. 'It's nothing to do with settling. I'm telling you there *is* a spirit here, and it's here for a reason.'

Jess sighed. 'And what makes you think that?'

'I don't *think* it, I *know* it. You see, I've seen her.'

A shiver ran up Jess's spine despite the fact that she was trying desperately hard to be logical. 'Oh yes, and what does she look like?'

'She is slim and dressed in an old brown skirt covered by a large white apron and a white blouse with very full sleeves. She has long dark hair and is quite pretty. About eighteen years old or so, I should imagine.'

'Come with me,' Jess said, and without giving Laura a chance to refuse she quickly left the kitchen and headed for the stairs. Laura followed reluctantly and once on the landing, Jess led her towards her bedroom where the sketches she had had reframed were now hanging on the wall.

She pointed towards them and as Laura followed her finger she gasped. 'That's her,' she croaked. 'I swear it is.'

Jess was seriously spooked now.

'Come on,' Laura said with a new determination. 'Show me the room where this girl slept.'

Jess led her to the narrow staircase that went up to the attics and as she pushed open the door to Martha's room, the overwhelming scent of roses greeted them.

'See!' she exclaimed triumphantly. 'Didn't I tell you there was the scent of roses in here? Can you smell it too?'

'Yes, I can,' Laura said, as she gazed around.

'But what do you think it all means?' Jess was fiddling nervously with the buttons on her cardigan. 'Not that I'm saying I believe she *is* actually still here,' she added hastily.

'I really don't know,' Laura admitted. 'But I know she *is* still here and that she's very unhappy, which is why she hasn't passed on to the other side. She wanted you to come, but I don't know why yet. Didn't you once tell me that you felt as if you belonged here, the first time you set foot in the place?'

'Now just hold on a minute,' Jess said quickly, not wanting to believe what Laura was telling her. 'That was just because I fell in love with the character of the house.'

Laura shook her head. 'I don't think it was. I think you were meant to come here.'

Jess groaned. 'So what are you suggesting I do then? Stick a For Sale board up.'

'Of course not,' Laura retaliated. 'Eventually it will become clear why Martha wants you here.'

Jess shuddered as she headed back towards the door. 'I don't know about you but I could do with another cup of coffee,' she said, eager to get away from the cloying smell and back into the warmth of the kitchen. 'It's damn cold in here, isn't it? Or is that just me imagining it?'

'No, it is cold,' Laura agreed as she followed her out onto the landing.

The two women hurried back downstairs where Jess quickly changed the subject to other things, mainly Mel's worsening moods.

'I'm getting seriously concerned about her,' she confided to her neighbour. 'She snaps her dad's head off every time he so much as looks at her, and she spends hours locked away in her room when she isn't at school. It can't be healthy for her, can it?'

'I can't really be a judge of that, with Beth being the way she is. I never got to have the teenage mood swings,' Laura said regretfully. 'In her head Beth is still a little girl and she always will be.'

Jess instantly felt ashamed. Poor Laura. Perhaps it was time to stop feeling so sorry for herself and start to count her blessings. After all, she could still clearly remember what a bad time she herself had put her gran through when she was Mel's age. In fact, looking back now she wondered how the dear soul had put up with her.

Reaching across the table she squeezed Laura's hand comfortingly. Laura squeezed hers back but then glancing at the clock she stood up. 'I should be going. Den really isn't well and Beth will be driving him to distraction by now.'

Jess saw her to the door where she asked, 'Will you pop in again soon?'

Laura nodded. 'If you want me to.' And then she was gone and as Jess closed the door behind her she stood there chewing on her lip. Laura was such a level-headed person that it was hard to imagine that she really believed in spirits and all that malarkey. But then, everyone was entitled to their own opinion and Jess set about her chores and tried not to think any more about it.

When she got in the car to pick the girls up from school later that afternoon she was not in the happiest frame of mind. They normally walked home alone now, but the rain that had poured down for two solid days had slowed to a drizzle and everywhere looked dark and miserable, so she had arranged to give them a lift.

She sat outside of Jo's school first and soon the girl flew out of the gates with a wide smile on her face like a little ray of sunshine.

'Had a good day, have you, love?' Jess asked as she clambered into the car all arms and legs.

'Yes,' Jo told her happily as she fastened her seat belt. 'I got a star in English and Matilda asked me if I can go to her house for tea on Saturday. May I, Mum?'

'I don't see why not, so long as her mum doesn't mind.' Jess smiled indulgently as she started the car and steered it out into the road. At least she could always rely on Jo to be cheerful. Well, for most of the time anyway. She drove the short way to Mel's school next to find the first of the pupils already emerging. She parked the car, keeping her eye on the gate but after fifteen minutes Mel still hadn't appeared and the flow of youngsters had steadied to a trickle now.

'That's strange,' she commented. 'I wonder if she'd already left when we got here.'

'I shouldn't think so,' Jo replied in her usual forthright way. 'If she'd come out we would have passed her up the road.'

Jess waited a further five minutes then opened the car door. 'You wait there,' she told Jo. 'I'll just pop into the school and see if I can find her. Perhaps she's got a detention she forgot to tell me about.'

She hurried across the now almost deserted playground and once inside headed for the reception desk.

'I wonder if you could tell me if Melanie Beddows has left yet?' she said to the woman behind the desk. 'She's in Mrs Congrave's class.'

'I'll just go and find out for you,' the young woman told her pleasantly before hurrying away through the swing doors.

A couple of minutes later she reappeared with Mrs Congrave at her side.

'Ah, Mrs Beddows.' The teacher smiled at her. 'I was actually going to ring you before I left school today. There seems to be some sort of a mix-up. Miss Holden here says you're looking for Melanie but she hasn't been in school today. I assumed that she was off sick.'

'But she *must* have been here,' Jess told her indignantly. 'I dropped her off myself at the school gates this morning, so . . .' As a thought suddenly occurred to her, her voice trailed away and she flushed with embarrassment. Mel must have waited until she had pulled away and then done a bunk for the day.

'Perhaps she felt unwell and decided to go home,' she said lamely, knowing full well that Mel hadn't put in an appearance back at the house. 'I'm so sorry, Mrs Congrave. Leave it with me and I'll get to the bottom of it.'

The teacher smiled at her sadly, guessing exactly what had happened. She had certainly seen it enough times before.

'Of course,' she said kindly, not wishing to cause Jess yet more embarrassment. 'And then perhaps you could call into school to see me one day next week? I'm quite concerned about Melanie as it happens. She doesn't seem to be settling in here at all well.'

'I'll do that.' Jess turned hastily, wishing that the ground would just open up and swallow her. One thing was for sure, Mel would feel the length of her tongue when she did catch up with her. She scuttled away like a scalded cat and once outside she climbed into the car and slammed the door resoundingly. Jo had been humming merrily along to Britney Spears on the car radio but she fell silent after one glance at her mother's face. That look usually meant trouble.

'Where's Mel?' she asked tentatively.

'Ah, now *that* seems to be the leading question at the moment,' Jess ground out as she jammed the car into gear and roared away from the kerb. 'I should think by now she's either slunk into her room at home or she's holed up at a friend's house somewhere.'

Jo frowned. 'But Mel doesn't have any friends.' One more glance at her mother's set face made her clamp her mouth shut and she kept it that way for the rest of the drive home, glad that she wasn't in Mel's shoes right now.

# Chapter Ten

'Mel, where are you?' Jess roared as she stormed into the kitchen a short time later and flung her bag onto the table.

Jo wisely kept her head down as she hurried over to Alfie's basket to fuss him. It was not often that her mum lost her temper but on the rare occasions when she did, Jo had learned to keep well out of her way until she calmed down.

Jess thundered up the stairs then marched along the landing and flung Mel's bedroom door open ready to blow her top, but the words died on her lips when she was confronted with an empty room. It was just as Mel had left it that morning. The duvet was kicked to the end of the bed and various items of clothing and CDs were scattered across the floor. Sighing heavily, Jess closed the door again before going back downstairs. No doubt Mel would turn up soon and the little madam would have some explaining to do when she did decide to put in an appearance.

The second she set foot back in the kitchen, Jo scooted out of the door with Alfie and Jess felt a pang of guilt. I must calm down, it isn't Jo's fault, she told herself and then set about preparing the dinner. Jo came back in half an hour later to the smell of bubbling cabbage and pork chops cooking under the grill. She immediately began to set the table to help her mum, who was obviously still very upset.

Some time later they ate their meal, then Jess covered Mel and Simon's portions with kitchen foil. They could be microwaved later when they came in.

As the hand of the clock crept towards six o'clock, Jess's anger was replaced by a niggling feeling of fear. Mel hadn't even bothered to phone to tell her where she was, and now for the first time Jess began to wonder if she was safe.

By the time Simon arrived home shortly before seven she was chewing her nails and smoking like a chimney, which instantly told him that something was wrong. Jess had given up months ago.

'What's up?' he asked.

'It's Mel. I dropped her off at school today but she never went in according to her teacher and she still isn't home.'

He could feel the tension in the air but shrugged. 'She's probably bunked off with one of her mates.'

Jess shook her head. 'You know she's hardly made any friends since we moved here and she hasn't even phoned. I can't reach her on her mobile either. It just keeps going to the answer machine. I've hardly been able to pry her out of the house just lately, so why would she suddenly do this?' As she was speaking she was putting his meal into the microwave.

'Didn't you ever bunk off when you were her age?' Simon asked, washing his hands before sitting at the table.

'Well, yes I did, but I wasn't the same temperament as Mel,' she told him, grinding her cigarette out in an ashtray. 'It's just so out of character for her to do something like this. Should I call the police?'

'No!' Simon said hastily. 'They'd laugh you under the table if you did. They must spend half their time looking for kids Mel's age who pull this stunt. Just wait a while longer. She'll be back when she gets hungry. She isn't stupid and she knows where her bread's buttered.'

As the microwave began to beep, Jess carried his meal to him and switched on the news on the small portable television set they kept in the kitchen. She supposed that Simon was right, but she still couldn't help worrying.

As soon as Simon had finished eating he shot away upstairs to get changed for his darts match.

'Surely you're not still going out tonight with Mel missing,' Jess said accusingly when he reappeared some short time later all showered and changed. His hair was still damp and he looked so handsome that she could understand why women were attracted to him like a magnet.

'Of course I am. You know I always drop Beth off at the youth club and I wouldn't want to let her down. The poor kid goes out little enough as it is. And anyway, by the time I get home Mel will be back with her tail between her legs. I bet she won't think of doing this again when I've finished with her.'

Jess sulkily stacked the dirty pots in the dishwasher until she heard the door close behind him. Jo was in the small lounge watching *Emmerdale Farm*, so Mel left her to it as she began to wander despondently from room to room. It suddenly struck her how few of the rooms they actually used. The drawing room looked very grand now with its expensive wallpaper and its grand swags and tails, but they'd soon discovered it was far too large for them unless they had company, and so they chose to sit in the small cosy room that adjoined the kitchen for the majority of the time. Perhaps this house is too big for us, she thought for the first time, but then she pushed the thought away. Once the rest of the house was finished she would start her B and B business and then perhaps all the rooms would be used as they should be.

Feeling at a loose end, Jess headed for her bedroom where she settled down to read the next extract from Martha's journal. At least it would give her something to keep her occupied until Mel decided to put in an appearance.

*1 September*

The Master has gone away to visit friends for a whole week so today we all went for a stroll in the meadow and Bertie did a sketch of me while I was picking some wild flowers. Bertie can draw beautifully and Granny often says he could have been an artist, had he been born into the gentry.

'I'm tellin' yer, things are goin' from bad to worse since the Master sold them fields off to Farmer Codd.'

Hal Tollcy was taking a tea break in the kitchen with Granny Reid, and as he spoke, his expression was grim. 'He called into the cottage to see us yesterday an' told us that now he only 'as two acres left, it's doubtful whether or not there'll be enough work left fer me to do.'

'But what'll 'appen if he turns you an' yer brood out o' the cottage?' Granny Reid asked worriedly.

Hal shrugged. 'I ain't even dared to think on it yet,' he said gruffly. 'It seems the work'ouse would be the safest option, but I'd rather live in a hovel an' take any job I could, afore I'd resort to me family goin' there, especially now we've discovered Phoebe is expectin' again.'

'Eeh, it makes yer wonder where it's all goin' to end,' Granny muttered as she lifted her heavy mug of steaming tea. 'Word has it that the mill is in trouble an' all.'

''T'wouldn't surprise me,' Hal rejoined. 'Money slips through that one's hands like water, an' it'll be all of us that suffer if he don't pull his reins in soon. But anyway, I'd best get on while I still 'ave a job, eh? Happen I'll be out o' one soon enough an' I don't wanna give his lordship an excuse to set me on the road. Thanks fer the tea, lass, it were right welcome.'

Granny Reid watched Hal walk from the cottage, his shoulders stooped with worry. 'Poor bugger,' she sighed, as much to herself as to Martha, who was rolling pastry at the table.

'Try not to worry too much,' the girl told her with all the optimism of youth. 'Perhaps things ain't as bad as we all fear?'

'Huh!' Granny shook her head before disappearing off into the large walk-in pantry to try and find something to serve for dinner as Martha and Grace exchanged worried glances. It seemed that things were indeed going from bad to worse, and they both silently wondered where it might end.

Later that afternoon, as Martha was going to feed the last remaining pig in the sty, a sound caught her ear. It was coming from the side of the Dutch Barn so, lifting her skirts, she tiptoed towards it. When she turned the corner she was confronted by Grace, who was leaning over being violently sick into the midden.

'Grace, whatever's wrong?' she asked as she rushed to her sister's side but Grace held her hand up as if to ward her off.

'It's nothin',' she gasped. 'You just get about yer chores an' don't fret, eh.' With that she straightened up and hurried away.

Martha quickly fed the pig and fled back to the kitchen to inform Granny, 'I just caught our Grace bein' really sick behind the Dutch Barn.'

Granny rounded on her, waggling a carving knife at her. She seemed about to scold the girl, but then her shoulders sagged and she said, 'I reckon it's quite normal fer women in the family way to be sick. I may as well tell yer now as let yer hear it from someone else.'

'In the family way . . . Yer mean our Grace is havin' a baby?' Martha couldn't disguise the shock and delight in her voice although Granny certainly didn't look any too happy about it.

'Aye she is, but I don't want yer goin' round broadcastin' it, an' don't get talkin' to Bertie about it neither.'

Martha looked confused. Grace and Bertie obviously loved each and they were married, so why shouldn't they have a baby and be happy about it? It was a natural progression, after all.

'I wonder if Phoebe's baby will come before Grace's,' Martha said musingly as she tied a large hessian apron about her slender waist.

'I've told you, ain't I?' Granny said sharply. 'Least said about it fer now the better, so button yer lip, me girl.'

Martha sighed as she crossed to the sink to attack the pile of washing-up there. She felt peeved at the way her granny had spoken to her but she couldn't stay miserable for long. The previous evening, just before retiring to bed, she had slipped out to meet Jimmy, and they had wandered along by the River Anker hand-in-hand. It had rained ceaselessly for the last two weeks and the stone bridge was underwater, while the river had burst its banks – but nothing could have spoiled the time she spent with him. She knew that Granny would not have approved of her sneaking off to meet him, but how else was she to see him? It was clear that Granny wasn't going to give her permission to walk out with him and Martha could not envisage not spending time with him now. He had kissed her when they parted and she had felt as if a million butterflies were fluttering about inside her stomach. On top of that the Master would be going away tomorrow to visit friends in Northamptonshire for a whole week and she could hardly wait to see the back of him. Whenever he wasn't there it was as if a great black cloud had lifted from over the house and Martha knew that the rest of her family were looking forward to him going too. Humming softly to herself, she got on with her chores.

The following afternoon when the Master had departed, they all went for a walk in the meadow. The rain had finally stopped and the sun was riding high in a cloudless blue sky. Grace and Granny sat on the grass, enjoying the feel of the sun on their faces whilst Bertie sketched Martha picking wild flowers for the kitchen windowsill.

When the sketch was done, Martha was amazed at how good it was. 'I reckon you should have a go at sellin' some of your pictures in the market place,' she told him.

'Do you really think folks hereabouts would have money to waste on sketches in these hard times?' Bertie pointed out sensibly, and Martha supposed he was right. With jobs so hard to come by, folks thought they were lucky if they could put food in their bellies. But oh, it did seem such an awful waste of his talent.

Jess reluctantly closed the journal. She would have liked to read on, but her thoughts were back on Mel's whereabouts. Glancing at the clock she saw that it was approaching nine o'clock and she got off the bed, pausing only to glance at the sketches on her bedroom wall. The girl picking wild flowers must be the sketch that Martha had written of in her journal – the one that Bertie had done. There was no doubt that he had been very talented.

As she walked along the landing she heard someone in the shower and guessed that this would be Jo. Perhaps when she got downstairs

Mel would be home and she could stop worrying. On this hopeful thought she hurried down the stairs.

The kitchen was deserted apart from Alfie and again a stab of fear rippled through her. It was almost dark outside now and feeling the need to do something useful she raced back to Mel's bedroom and began to rifle through the untidy drawers until she found her daughter's address book.

Back downstairs she dialled the number of Mel's mobile phone, chewing on her lip when she reached the answerphone again. 'This is Mum, would you *please* phone home and let me know where you are when you get this message?' she said, close to tears.

She then began to systematically work through the numbers in the book until eventually there was no one else she could think of to ring. It seemed that no one had seen her all day and now Jess was convinced that something was badly wrong. She checked that Jo was safely tucked up in bed, and after explaining that she was just popping to Laura's to see if Mel was there she let herself out into the dark courtyard and hurried down the drive.

When she reached Blue Brick Cottage she pounded on the back door and Laura opened it with a worried expression on her face. 'What is it? Has something happened to Beth?'

'No, Beth is fine,' Jess assured her. 'I should think Simon will be picking her up from the youth club any time now. It's Mel I'm concerned about. May I come in?'

'Of course you can.' Laura took her elbow and steered her into the small kitchen. 'Now what's wrong?' she questioned.

Jess wearily rubbed her brow where a headache was starting to throb. 'It's Mel. She hasn't come home.'

The kitchen here was probably a quarter of the size of the one at Stonebridge House, but what it lacked in size it made up for in olde-worlde charm, Jess thought dazedly. Oak beams crisscrossed the ceiling and a cheery fire was blazing in an inglenook fireplace, the flames bouncing off a selection of highly polished pans that were suspended from the thick beam above it. The floor was covered in red quarry tiles which lent a warm feel to the room, and against one wall was a huge old dresser laden with Laura's prized china collection.

'She didn't go to school today either, so where do you think she could be?' Jess asked despondently.

Not wishing to alarm her neighbour more than she already was,

Laura tactfully said, 'She's probably just gone round to a mate's house and lost track of time.'

Jess fiddled with the buttons on her coat. 'No, she hasn't. I've phoned every single number in her address book and no one has seen her. I know she's been moody lately but this isn't like her, Laura. In fact I've *never* known her to do this before. Do you think I should call the police?'

'Why don't you give her another hour or so?' Laura said gently. 'It's still quite early really, and I'm sure she's fine wherever she is.' As she swept a pile of paperwork aside to place a cup of tea in front of Jess she saw the latter glance at it curiously and she smiled self-consciously as she explained. 'I'm tracing my family tree. It's a hobby of mine and quite fascinating when you get into it. Den tends to go to bed quite early so he can be up with the lark in the morning, so I need something to keep me occupied. I'm also tracing the Fentons' family tree too.'

'Really?' Jess would have been very interested under other circumstances, but for now it was hard to think of anything except her missing daughter.

'Look, I know you must be worried sick,' Laura said kindly as she rubbed Jess's shoulder. 'But I'll bet you any money she'll turn up safe and sound within the next couple of hours and you'll wonder what you were worrying about. That's teenagers, I'm afraid. Even my Beth is worrying me at present, as Simon has probably told you. A boy who goes to the same youth club as her has taken a real shine to her and she hasn't been there the last couple of times your Simon has gone to pick her up. He's had to go looking for her, bless him.'

'Yes, he did mention something about it,' Jess said as she sipped at her tea and now Laura went on, 'The trouble is, my Beth is quite stunning to look at. Very often no one realises that there is anything different about her until she speaks. But she's so naïve and vulnerable. I worry that someone could take advantage of her. Between you and me, I asked Den if perhaps we shouldn't stop her going but he says it wouldn't be fair to deprive her of her only night out. I sometimes wish that I could just lock her away or wrap her up in cotton wool and keep her safe, but we can't do that with our kids, can we?'

'No, I don't suppose we can.' Jess suddenly felt very foolish. Laura was right. Mel would probably be home by the time she got back to the house full of excuses and now she just wanted to be there.

'Look, forgive me but I think I'd better get home.' Scraping her chair across the quarry tiles she rose, leaving her tea virtually untouched. 'Thanks for the advice, Laura. I'm probably just worrying for nothing. Goodnight.'

'Goodnight, love. Let me know how things are in the morning, won't you?'

Jess nodded as Laura let her out into the biting wind and then pulling up her collar she set off up the long winding drive to her home, jumping as the trees bent towards her in the wind. They looked as if they were involved in some sort of macabre dance and by the time she reached the courtyard her heart was thudding painfully in her chest.

'Mel!' she cried the second she set foot in the kitchen, but only silence greeted her and she settled down miserably to wait. It seemed that was all she could do for now.

# Chapter Eleven

It was now almost eleven o'clock and Jess was beside herself with worry as she paced up and down the kitchen like a caged animal. Simon should have been home long ago, but once again he was late and there was still no sign of Mel. Coming to a decision, Jess strode into the hall and lifted the phone. She had waited long enough and now every instinct she had was screaming that it was time to do something. She rang the police station and left a garbled missing person's report to a calm operator who assured her that someone would be with her as soon as possible. Jess thanked her before heading back into the kitchen where she lit another cigarette. The minutes on the clock ticked away ominously as anger and fear vied for first place inside her. Where the hell could Simon have got to? Why wasn't he here when she needed him?

His Land Rover finally drove into the courtyard at gone half past eleven and she flew to the door and threw it open.

Jess immediately let rip at him for going off when Mel was missing, but thankfully the exchange was prevented from developing into a full-scale row when a police car drew up beside them.

Seconds later, Jess ushered a young policewoman and a young constable with the worst case of acne she had ever seen into the room.

'I believe you've reported your daughter missing, Mrs Beddows,' he said, addressing Jess as he respectfully took off his hat.

'Yes, I have.' Jess promptly burst into tears. There was something very sinister about Mel not coming home now that the police were involved.

'Try not to get too distressed,' the young officer told her kindly. 'You'd be surprised how common this is. We seem to spend half our shifts looking for missing youngsters, and nine times out of ten they turn up safe and sound within twenty-four hours. But now how about I ask you a few questions?'

Jess sniffed loudly and nodded, so he went on. 'How old is your daughter and what is her name?'

Jess stumbled over the words while Simon looked on.

'And had you had an argument, or was anything worrying her?'

'She's been very moody since we moved here some months ago,' Jess admitted reluctantly. 'But we just put that down to teenage mood swings and the fact that she needed to adjust to living here.'

'Hm.'

All the while she was talking, the WPC was furiously scribbling away in a notebook.

'So now can you describe Melanie to me,' the young officer went on. 'Her height, hair colour, what she was wearing.'

Again, Jess did her best to answer him until at last he seemed satisfied.

'Right, now what we'll do is put a call out to all the cars in the area and we'll start to look for her. And you say that the last time you saw her was when you dropped her off at the gates of Highfram Lane School this morning?'

'Y . . . yes.' Jess blinked rapidly, trying her best not to look like some deranged parent. 'I take both the girls to school every morning.'

'And have you rung all her friends?'

'Every single number in her address book, but no one has seen her.' Jess could feel the panic rising in her again.

'Well, Mrs Beddows, I think we have all we need for now,' the young Constable said softly, handing her a small card. 'That's my number. If Melanie should come home, would one of you ring us straight away?'

Jess nodded numbly as he rose and put his hat back on.

He smiled at Jess and Simon. 'Try not to get worrying too much. I'm sure we shall find her. We'll start looking straight away and if we're successful we'll ring you immediately. Goodnight, all.'

Simon saw them out before saying, 'What are we supposed to do now then?'

'We wait,' Jess replied dully. 'And while we wait, we try to figure out why she might have run away.'

Hearing the accusation in his wife's voice, Simon bristled. 'And just what is that supposed to mean? Are you trying to insinuate that this is *my* fault?'

Jess looked him in the eye, her chin in the air. 'Well, I'd hardly say you've been fair to her just lately, would *you*?'

He opened his mouth to protest but before he got the chance, she rushed on: 'The poor kid can do no right for you any more. You're always nagging her over one thing and another.'

'That's not true,' he snarled, stabbing a finger at her. 'And if we're going to start apportioning blame, what about you – dragging her here to live in this godforsaken dump in the back of beyond away from all her friends.'

'This is *not* a godforsaken dump.' They were facing each other like two opponents in a boxing ring now as the argument escalated.

'Mel will settle here eventually. We just have to give her a little more—' Jess clamped her mouth shut when Jo suddenly appeared in the doorway, knuckling the sleep from her eyes.

'What's all the shouting about?' she asked fretfully, and Jess hurried over to give her a cuddle.

'We weren't shouting, sweetheart,' she lied. 'Or at least we didn't mean to. It's just that we're worried about Mel and our nerves are a bit on edge.'

Jo stared up at her before asking quietly, 'Will Mel come home?'

'Of course she will.' Jess sounded far more confident than she was feeling. 'Now why don't you get yourself back off to bed?'

Jo shook her head. 'I don't want to. That lady is in there watching me again.'

Jess felt as if someone had doused her in ice-cold water but she managed to raise a smile as she said, 'I'm sure there isn't anyone in there, but I'll tell you what, you can sleep in our bed tonight. How would that be?' She took Jo upstairs, and ten minutes later she reappeared after settling her daughter back down.

'Is she all right?' Simon asked.

Jess nodded tiredly as she peered out of the window over the dark gardens.

'Do you want me to go for a drive round and see if I can spot her?' Simon volunteered when the silence was becoming unbearable.

'What would be the point?' Jess sighed. 'The police are already doing that. The best thing we can do is stay put here in case they find her.'

Simon shrugged and dropped into the armchair at the side of the Aga. Then steepling his fingers, he stared off into space.

It was almost three o'clock when car headlights suddenly sliced through the darkness in the courtyard, and Jess sprang out of her seat so quickly she almost overturned it. The commotion woke Simon, and then Jess was racing towards the door as a police car switched its headlights off. The same young Constable who had called earlier stepped out of the driving seat while the young policewoman got out of the back closely followed by someone else.

Jess peered into the darkness then suddenly she shrieked and flew towards the car so quickly that her feet barely touched the ground.

'Mel? Oh, thank God! Where have you been? Are you all right? We've been worried half to death.'

'Oh Mum, get off me,' Mel said churlishly as Jess tried to hug her, and pushing past her mother she began to stamp towards the open door.

The Constable smiled at Jess as she stared at him bewildered. 'We found her wandering around the streets in Hinckley, not too far away from where you used to live,' he explained.

'And did she tell you why she ran away?'

He shook his head. 'I'm afraid not. In fact, she's barely said a word all the way home. But at least all's well that ends well. She's home now so I'll leave the rest to you, shall I?'

'Oh yes – and thank you,' Jess gabbled. Suddenly everything was right with the world again and she could willingly have kissed him. 'I'm so sorry you've been troubled, but I do appreciate what you've done.'

'Think nothing of it. It's all in a night's work.' He doffed his hat then after climbing back into the car with his colleague beside him, he restarted the engine and drove away.

Back in the kitchen, Mel was standing with her arms folded protectively across her chest as she waited for the onslaught that she was sure was to come. She looked totally worn out and all Jess wanted to do was hug her, but Mel's body language was telling her loud and clear that this wasn't what the girl wanted right now.

'So, are you going to answer some of the questions that I asked you outside now?' she said calmly.

Mel kept her head down avoiding eye-contact as Jess looked towards Simon for some help.

He merely shrugged, so now she tried again. 'Look Mel, there must be something that's upsetting you. Can't you tell us what it is? I'm sure there's nothing that can't be sorted, but if you won't tell us, we can't help you.'

'You *never* help me,' Mel burst out. 'All you care about is this damn house and Jo!' Her head was up now and Jess recoiled from the hatred she saw in her daughter's eyes. It was if she was confronting a stranger and she instinctively moved forward, but Mel side-stepped her, slapping her mother's outstretched hands away, her eyes flashing.

'Do you know what? I *hate* you!' Mel cried. And then stabbing a finger towards her father she continued, 'And I hate *him* even more. I wish that I was *dead*!' And with that she stormed out of the room and pounded up the stairs.

# Chapter Twelve

'So is Mel OK then?' Jo asked the next morning as she loaded her books into her bag.

'Yes, love, she's fine,' Jess replied absently.

'Then why isn't she going to school?'

'Because it was very late when she got home and she's worn out.' Jess refrained from telling her that Mel had only come home because the police had brought her back, figuring that the least said about the incident the sooner it could be forgotten and put behind them.

'So where had she been then?' Jo was like a dog with a bone and Jess feared that she wouldn't be fobbed off so easily. Deciding that a little white lie was called for, she told her, 'Oh, she'd just been round to some friend's house and they'd lost track of time.'

'Mel doesn't have any friends any more,' Jo stated, clearly not believing her.

'Look, why don't you just finish getting ready for school, miss. You're going to be late at this rate and I'm not in the mood for all these questions.'

'Oh, sorry I'm sure,' Jo growled. 'Bite my head off, why don't you!'

'Sorry, love. I didn't mean to . . . I'm just tired. Now let's get off, eh?'

Jo sulkily slammed her bag shut and followed her mother out to the car as Jess sighed. Why don't older kids come with manuals telling you how to handle them? she wondered as they got into the car.

After dropping Jo off at school she was thoughtful as she drove home. The things that Mel had said to her the night before when the police returned her home were whirling around in her head and she began to wonder if perhaps she hadn't neglected her elder daughter since moving into the house. The renovation had kept her very busy and she realised with a little start that it was quite some time since they had done something together as a family. She knew that it would be pointless trying to plan a holiday. She had already suggested that, and Simon had told her he was far too busy. But perhaps she could organise a shopping trip and treat Mel to some new clothes? All teenage girls took a pride in their appearance and it might just be the thing they needed to get them back on track again. In fact, she decided, she would suggest it as soon as she got home; there was no time like the present. They could go today if Mel was agreeable and she might mellow a little away from the house and confide to her what was troubling her.

She found Laura standing at the end of the drive with Beth at her side staring off into space. As she pulled up beside them Laura instantly asked, 'Is Mel home?'

Jess nodded. 'Yes, the police found her early this morning wandering about in Hinckley and brought her back.'

Laura breathed a sigh of relief. 'And is she OK?'

'She seems to be but she won't tell me why she did it.' Jess pursed her lips. 'I'm going to go and make her some breakfast and see if she'll open up while we're on our own.'

'In that case I won't keep you,' Laura told her understandingly as she took Beth's hand firmly in her own. 'Good luck, love.'

'I've got a horrible feeling I'm going to need it if the mood she was in when she came home is anything to go by.' Jess smiled wryly. 'Bye for now.'

Laura stood and watched the car disappear up the drive with a worried frown on her face. Something bad was about to happen, she could feel it, although as yet she had no idea what it was. The feeling had been there since the day the Beddows had moved into Stonebridge House and it was slowly getting worse.

Sighing, she turned Beth about and guided her back to Blue Brick Cottage.

As soon as Jess got home she stroked Alfie then hurriedly set about making a breakfast tray for Mel. She soft-boiled two eggs and cut up some bread and butter into soldiers; Mel had loved this when she was a little girl and Jess hoped that it would put her in a better mood. She added a glass of freshly squeezed orange juice before carefully carrying the whole lot upstairs.

'Morning, sweetie,' she chirped brightly as she entered Mel's room, balancing the tray on one hand. The curtains were still tightly drawn and Mel was just a bump beneath the duvet. 'Come on, wakey-wakey. It's a brand new day so let's make the most of it, eh?' After placing the tray on the bedside table she swished the curtains aside and Mel groaned as she surfaced from beneath the duvet, blinking in the harsh morning light.

Jess was shocked to see how ill and pale she looked. Her hair was all over the place and her eyes seemed to have sunk into her head. Forcing herself to sound cheerful she said, 'I was thinking we might go and do a bit of retail therapy today. It's been ages since we had a bit of quality time together and you've been complaining for weeks that you need some new jeans. What do you think?'

Ignoring the question, Mel screwed up her nose as she looked at the tray. 'What the hell is that, Mum? *Soldiers!* I'm fourteen next month, in case you'd forgotten. I'm not a little girl any more, you know.'

'Then perhaps it's time you stopped acting like one!' The second the words had left Jess's lips she could have bitten her tongue off but the harm was done now and Mel glowered at her.

'Sorry, love. I didn't mean that.' Jess ran her hand distractedly through her hair as she sank down on the side of the mattress. 'I suppose I'm still just a bit wound up after last night. I was sick with worry when you didn't come home. I had visions of you lying dead in a ditch somewhere and I don't know what I'd do if anything happened to you.'

The words were said so genuinely that Mel's face relaxed a little as she pulled herself up onto her pillows.

Now Jess cautiously took her hand as she asked, 'Why did you run away, Mel?'

The girl was instantly on her guard again as she snatched her hand away, and desperate to get to the bottom of what was troubling her now, Jess went on, 'Is it something you can tell me about?'

Mel wagged her head miserably as tears sprang to her eyes and Jess felt as if her heart was breaking. But she knew her daughter well enough to know that now was not the time to push her, so she forced a smile. 'Well, what about that shopping trip then? We could go to Coventry and hit all your favourite shops. Monsoon, Next, River Island. What do you think?'

'I . . . I don't really feel up to it,' Mel muttered, keeping her eyes averted from her mother's.

'Rubbish! It's just what we both need.' Jess wasn't going to give up without a fight. 'You were right about one thing – I *have* been too busy on this house and I feel as if I've neglected you. So please come . . . if it's only for me.'

Sensing victory when Mel didn't immediately refuse, Jess added,

'We could go and have a bit of lunch too and take a look in that cut-price jeweller's you like so much.'

Still no refusal, so Jess decided to quit while she was ahead and rushed for the door. 'Right, eat your breakfast and get a quick shower and we'll go in about an hour.' Flashing a smile in Mel's direction, she scurried away to get ready.

Mel finally appeared in the kitchen some time later with a closed look on her face, but at least she was clean and tidy.

'I'm looking forward to this,' Jess trilled falsely, snatching up the car keys. 'Come on, let's go while the going's good. We've got loads of time before Jo gets home from school.'

Mel reluctantly pulled a sweatshirt over her T-shirt and slid her feet into the trainers at the side of the door before following her mother out to the KA.

On the way into Coventry Jess tried to engage her daughter in conversation but they had barely passed the Bedworth bypass when it became apparent that she might as well bang her head up a brick wall. Mel was staring off out of the window, completely ignoring her, so eventually she gave up and concentrated on her driving. When they arrived in Coventry, Jess put a parking ticket on the car and they headed for the city centre. They visited all Mel's favourite shops and Jess treated her to new jeans, two new tops and a pair of new trainers, but even these treats didn't manage to put a smile on the girl's face and Jess's patience began to wear thin.

'How about we go in here for a bit of lunch?' she suggested, peering through the huge plate-glass window of a very posh-looking Chinese restaurant. Mel loved Chinese food and would normally have jumped at the chance.

'Actually, I'm not that hungry,' Mel mumbled, shifting her shopping bags from one hand to the other and looking completely disinterested.

'Well, that's tough luck because *I* am.' Jess pushed the door open and glowered at Mel until she stepped past her. A small Chinese waiter instantly ushered them into a window seat and Jess lifted the menu. 'Hmm, now what shall we have? Is there anything you particularly fancy, or do you want me to order for you?'

Slouching in her seat with her arms firmly crossed, Mel shrugged but with an effort Jess kept the smile on her face fixed firmly in place. 'Right, I think we'll have some chicken chow-mein, some beansprouts and some egg fried rice, please. Oh, and we'll have a bottle of sparkling water too.'

The waiter wrote furiously in his book then bowing slightly he scuttled away in the direction of the kitchen as Jess looked at Mel solemnly.

'So, are you ready to talk to me yet?' she asked softly.

'What about?'

'Oh, come on, Mel. About why you ran away for a start! Do you have *any* idea at all how worried your father and I were? Something must have made you do it. Can't you tell me about it? I want to help you.'

'Nobody can help me,' Mel whispered bleakly as her eyes welled with tears.

Jess felt as if someone had slapped her in the face. Whatever the problem was, it was clearly much more serious than she had thought. She would have probed further but just then the waiter reappeared with their drinks and began to lay out their cutlery. They barely touched their meal. Jess was glad when it was over and hastily paid the bill and ushered Mel outside.

'Is there anything else you need?' she asked, wondering why she had thought that this was such a good idea in the first place. It had hardly turned out to be a roaring success.

Mel shook her head and they headed back to the car in silence. Jess sensed that Mel wasn't ready to confide in her yet, so wisely held her tongue all the way home. The instant they arrived back, Mel flung the bags containing her new clothes onto a chair and shot off to her room, leaving Jess to stare helplessly after her. There was still well over an hour until it was time to fetch Jo from school and she didn't feel like starting any household chores, so she too went upstairs, hoping that reading a little more of Martha's journal would help take her mind off her own troubles.

*10 September*

Something terrible happened today. I had been working in the dairy as Phoebe is ill. She lost her baby last week and Granny says it is through worrying what will become of them if the Master gets rid of them. They will have nowhere to go and Hal fears that he will not be able to get work . . .

'That's all the vegetables chopped, Granny.' Martha stood and rubbed her back as Granny Reid looked up from the pastry she was rolling. 'What would you like me to do now? Shall I pop along to the cottage and see how Phoebe is?'

'No, not yet, lass. Go into the dairy an' see to what needs doin' there then you can take one o' these hare pies over to Phoebe later on. Bless 'er. She won't be in no fit state fer cookin, havin' just lost the baby.' She shook her head sadly. 'Truth be told, the Tolleys could ill afford another mouth to feed but it's a terrible thing to lose a child all the same. I blame that one in there.' She cocked her head towards the green baize door.

Martha chewed on her lip as she nodded in agreement.

'I've no doubt him indoors will moan about hare pie fer his dinner an' all,' Granny went on. 'But he's lucky to have that, if he did but know it. Our supplies are dwindlin' by the day.' Looking out onto the yard, she advised Martha: 'You just mind as yer don't go yer length out there. The whole place is like a mudslide what wi' all the rain we've had, an' it don't show no sign o' ceasin' yet neither.'

Martha nodded as she lifted her shawl from a hook on the back of the door, then lifting it over her head she set off through the driving rain. It was as she was passing the barn with her head bent that a piercing scream brought her to a shuddering halt. She looked towards the great wooden doors just as another scream sounded, and sped across the cobbles, avoiding the puddles as best she could.

Once in the barn she paused for a second as her eyes adjusted to the dim light and then the sight that met her eyes made her hand spring to her mouth. The Master had young Joey Tolley bent across a hay bale with his shirt lifted and his trousers round his ankles, and he was whipping him cruelly, the sound of the leather whip slicing through the air. Without stopping to think, Martha ran forward and caught the Master's arm just in time to stop the next blow landing on the small boy's bare buttocks.

'Eeh, Master, whatever are yer doin'?' she sobbed breathlessly. 'You'll kill the poor lad. For God's sake stop now!'

'Get off, you interfering little bitch,' the master ground out, throwing her off his arm. Martha fell heavily and then before she knew what was happening he had turned the whip on her and it was she that was screaming now as Joey slid into a heap on the ground.

Seconds later, the barn door flew open yet again, and seeing what was happening Bertie launched himself at the Master as Martha lay in a whimpering heap. Bertie snatched the whip from the Master's hand and flung it into a far corner and then the two men were grappling with each other as obscenities spewed from Bertie's mouth.

'You cruel, perverted bastard,' he spat. It was then that Granny and

95

Grace appeared, and taking in the situation at a glance, they sprang forward and somehow managed to drag the two men apart. It took both Granny and Grace all their time to hold Bertie back and as the Master rose to his feet, wiping a smear of blood from his lip, he sneered.

'I won't be the only bastard about here soon, will I?' he taunted. 'Not when Grace drops that load she's carryin'. *My* bastard will be poddlin' about here then too, won't it?'

Bertie was like a man possessed and it was all Grace and Granny could do to hold him now as the Master laughed in his face. He then brushed himself down and strode away without another word.

'I'll kill that swine if it's the last thing I do,' Bertie vowed to Grace as she took him in her arms. 'And let's hope as yer lose that bastard growin' inside you an' all!'

With tears pouring down her ashen cheeks, Grace looked soundlessly back at him.

'Never mind yer threats fer now,' Granny barked as Martha looked on in confusion. 'Little Joey looks to be in a bad way.'

The child was unconscious. The Master had whipped the skin from his back and his shirt was in tatters.

'Grace, stop yer blubbin' an' get out to the pump,' Granny told her. 'Fetch me a bucket o' water. We'll need to clean the poor lad up a bit afore we send him back to Phoebe. An' God alone knows what Hal will do when he sees what that cruel bugger has done to his lad.'

Minutes later, Granny gently sponged the worst of the lad's injuries as blood ran freely down his back. She was still in the process of doing this when he started to rouse round and Granny asked him gently, 'What did yer do to upset the Master so?'

'I . . . I stole an apple from them stacked in the barrels at the back o' the barn,' Joey whimpered. 'I'm sorry, Granny Reid, but I were hungry.'

Granny's breath came out on a hiss. 'An' he did this all fer an apple?' she said disbelievingly. 'I'm beginnin' to think that life on the road might not be so bad, after all. It would be better than havin' to pander to that wicked sod!' she sat back on her heels as she wrung the bloody cloth out in the bucket then, gently drawing the shirt down over the open wounds, she wrapped him in her woollen shawl and told Bertie, 'You'd best carry him back to the cottage, lad. Tell Phoebe she'll need to keep the wounds clean in case of infection an' say I'll be over as soon as I can.'

With that she patted Joey on the head and struggling painfully to her knees she set off back to the kitchen as Bertie lifted Joey as if he weighed no more than a feather and strode out into the rain.

Meanwhile, Martha rose and brushed the hay from her brown serge skirt as she looked towards Grace who was leaning heavily against the wall.

'What did Bertie mean when he said he hoped you'd lose the baby, Grace?' she asked in a small voice. 'Isn't he looking forward to it being born?'

Grace suddenly let out a sob and with her hand across her mouth she skittered away, her drab work skirts billowing around her, leaving Martha to shake her head in bewilderment.

Slowly now she made her way to the dairy, and while she churned, she tried to take her mind off what had happened. Once the butter was made, she placed it on the cool shelf and hurried back to the kitchen.

Striding inside, she threw off her wet shawl and demanded, 'What's going on, Granny? I'm not a child any more and I want to know. What did the Master mean when he said that there would be another bastard about the place when Grace has her baby?'

Martha had never stood up to her Granny before and half expected to get her ear skelped, but instead the old woman kept her eyes downcast. And then suddenly the meaning of the Master's words hit Martha like a blow between the eyes: Grace was carrying the Master's child! But her sister was married to Bertie and they loved each other . . . didn't they? How could Grace have done such a thing?

'The penny's dropped, 'as it?' Granny asked wearily. 'Now don't you get layin' no blame at your sister's door. The poor lamb had no choice in the matter. The Master believes that it's his right to take the virginity of any servant girl in his employ afore she weds, and poor Grace went to him like a Christian to the lions.'

Martha felt vomit rise in her throat. Would the Master consider that he could have first right with her too if he discovered that she was walking out with Jimmy? It didn't bear thinking about, and Martha was suddenly glad that she had kept their relationship a secret. On many occasions she had been aware of the Master coupling with women who had come from the town, but she had never dreamed that he could have done such a thing to her own sister. Poor Grace . . . and poor Bertie too. No wonder he hated the Master so much. What man wouldn't in that situation?

'Between you an' me, on his afternoon off Bertie's been scourin' the town an' the neighbourin' farms fer work wi' livin' accommodation included, but up to now he's had no luck,' Granny confided.

Suddenly, Martha understood why Bertie had seemed so sad on the day of their wedding and why he had been so snappy lately. She could only imagine how awful it must be for him to know that another man's child was growing inside the woman he loved. It was then that another terrible thought occurred to her. It was no secret that the Master had never forgiven the Mistress for not giving him a son and heir. Would he want to claim the child for his own when it was born, if it was a boy?

She was just about to ask Granny what she thought when the kitchen door was suddenly swung so wide that it struck the wall and danced on its hinges.

Hal Tolley stood there, rain dripping off his hair and his face contorted with rage.

'Where is he?' he ground out, his fists clenching and unclenching as Bertie followed him in. 'I'm goin' to kill him fer what he's done to my lad, so 'elp me God. An' all fer a stinkin' apple!'

'Calm down, Hal. I know exactly how yer feel, man, but think what yer doin'. You an' yer family'll be out on yer arses an' on the road if yer raise yer hand to 'im.'

'The lad's developin' a fever.' Hal's shoulders sagged. 'What'll it do to Phoebe if we lose Joey so soon after losin' the baby? The poor little sod'll be scarred fer life even if he does survive.'

'Just bide yer time,' Bertie urged. 'We'll have our day wi' that lousy swine, you just see if we don't. But fer now we 'ave to be patient.'

He took Hal's elbow and led him away as Martha chewed on her knuckles. Whatever was going to become of them all? The only place where she could be really safe was in her little room in the attic. There was a stout lock on the door and from now on she intended to use it. But would the lock be strong enough to keep the Master out if he decided that it was her turn to be taken down? Martha could only pray now that Bertie would find them somewhere else to go – and as soon as possible.

Jess shuddered as she closed the book. Poor Martha must have been terrified of her unscrupulous Master. And poor Grace, to be used like that and to be forced to carry his child . . .

Her sombre thoughts were interrupted by the sound of someone crying. Thinking that it must be Mel, she hurried towards the girl's bedroom door, but the only sound she could hear from within was the Black-Eyed Peas. Glancing towards the door at the end of the corridor, she slowly went and opened it, then began to climb the stairs with her heart in her mouth. Once outside Martha's room she stood completely still as the sound of someone sobbing broken-heartedly floated around her. Every hair on her body was standing to attention, but she gripped the door handle and threw the door open before she could change her mind and run back the way she had come, which every instinct she had was telling her to do.

The noise stopped abruptly and she found herself staring into an empty room. And yet someone *had* been crying in there. She would have staked her life on it.

Cautiously she stepped inside, her eyes focused on the narrow wooden bed. It was bitterly cold in here, and she wondered how Martha had stood it. But then she knew that back in the early 1800s there had been no central heating, so she would probably have been used to it.

'Oh Martha, I'm so sorry for what you had to go through,' she whispered to the empty room and then moving through the scent of roses, she gently closed the door and went back downstairs.

# Chapter Thirteen

Later that day, it suddenly hit Jess how little Simon had said to Mel about running away when the police had returned her home the evening before. Whilst they had been waiting for news he had been full of what he was planning to do to her when she got back. And yet when she did, he had actually said nothing at all. It was almost Mel's birthday. Perhaps she could organise something special for that? Something that would bring her daughter out of the depression into which she seemed to have sunk.

'What do you think? Any suggestions?' she asked Jo who was sitting at the kitchen table doing her homework.

'How about a weekend away somewhere?' the younger girl said.

Jess grinned. 'Do you know, that might be a good idea. Anywhere in particular?'

Jo tapped her top lip thoughtfully with her forefinger. Then: 'How about Paris?'

'Paris!' Jess was so shocked that she almost choked. Their holiday venues up to now had stretched to Yarmouth, Skegness and Blackpool, and even then the trips had been few and far between because the summer was the busiest time for Simon.

Seeing her mother's reaction, Jo chuckled. 'I'm not suggesting going to the moon, Mum.'

'I know – but Paris! Why, I've never even been on a plane.'

'Then it's time you did,' Jo said matter-of-factly. 'I reckon it would cheer Mel up no end and I'd love to see the Eiffel Tower. Kirsty at school went with her mum and dad a few weeks ago and she said it was wicked.'

'Right . . . well, I'll have a think about it,' Jess said doubtfully, 'but don't go mentioning it to your sister just yet until I've had time to run the idea by your dad, eh?'

'All right.' Jo settled back in her seat to read the magazine she had just taken from her schoolbag as Jess mulled the idea of the impromptu break over in her mind.

*   *   *

Simon was late home again that evening. Jess was getting used to it by now and although she knew that he was busy, she still found it annoying. When they had first moved in he had made a conscious effort to arrive home at a reasonable hour, so they could all have some quality family time together, but all his good intentions seemed to be flying out of the window again now.

Determined not to start an argument she put his meal in the microwave and said casually, 'Jo thought it might be a good idea if we had a weekend away for Mel's birthday.'

He snorted with derision as he pulled his workboots off. 'Huh! Fat chance of that happening with the amount of work I've got on. And anyway, should we really reward bad behaviour? She did run away, in case you'd forgotten.'

'Firstly, if she ran away there has to be a reason. I don't consider it was bad behaviour. Something is troubling her and if we're away from home she might be more willing to talk about it. Secondly, I am quite aware of how busy you are so if you don't want to come I shall take the girls myself. I think a change of scene would do them good. We've been so busy on the house I worry that we haven't spent enough time with them lately.'

Simon rolled his eyes. '*You* take them away?'

'Yes, *me*.' Jess's chin tilted indignantly. 'I'm perfectly capable of looking after our daughters for a few days.'

'Of course you are, and you have your own house too, don't you.'

Ignoring the spite in his voice she rushed on, 'There's no need to be like that, Simon. I'm just trying to make some sense of what's happening here. Mel isn't even fourteen yet but she looks like she's got the weight of the world on her shoulders.'

'And just where were you thinking of taking them? Blackpool, Skegness?'

'Er . . . actually Jo suggested Paris.'

Simon sputtered a mouthful of tea all over the table. '*Paris*, did you say? But you don't even have passports!'

'So, I can get them,' she retorted haughtily. 'I'm not completely useless, you know. We could fly from Birmingham and be there in a couple of hours or so.'

He shook his head, clearly unhappy about the whole idea. 'I think you should wait until we can all go away as a family. I don't believe in couples having separate holidays.'

'Then I'm sorry to hear it, but I think I should tell you I intend to take the girls whether you like it or not. Of course, it would be wonderful if you could somehow manage to come with us, but we're going, come hell or high water, so you'd better get used to the idea. I intend to get the passport applications from the post office first thing in the morning and fill them in. Shall I pick one up for you?'

Simon pushed away the meal she had just put in front of him. Jess was certainly spreading her wings now and he didn't like it one bit. She had always been so biddable before. 'No, you needn't bother,' he ground out, his mouth set in a grim line. 'Some of us have to work, in case you'd forgotten.' And with that he slammed out of the kitchen.

Biting down the urge to cry, Jess lifted his meal and scraped it into the bin. She'd had an idea that Simon wouldn't be too happy about their plan but she hadn't expected him to react quite so violently. Anyone would think she'd told him that she was going to leave him for good, the way he was going on.

She hastily followed him upstairs, but after a quick glance into their room she saw that he wasn't there so she moved further along the landing. Approaching Mel's bedroom, she heard the sound of muffled sobs and flinging the door open, she saw the girl curled on the bed as her father towered threateningly over her.

'What's going on here?' she demanded.

'I was just trying to find out why she pulled that stupid stunt and almost scared us to death last night,' Simon retaliated. 'Somebody's got to get to the bottom of it. You're just pussyfooting about and making things worse.'

Without waiting for her to answer he then pushed past her with a face like a thundercloud and disappeared off down the landing as Jess hurried over to Melanie. 'Are you all right, love?' she asked as she wiped the limp hair from her daughter's damp brow.

'Y . . . yes,' Mel sniffed.

Unsure of what to do or say, Jess backed towards the door. 'Well, I'm here if there's anything you want to talk to me about.' She closed the door softly behind her feeling more useless than she had ever felt in her life. Simon had just gone and made things worse now with his bull in a china shop attempts to find out what was troubling the girl. But then that was Simon all over. Tact had never been one of his strong points.

She followed him to their own room where she found him climbing into clean jeans and a sweatshirt.

'Where are you going?' she asked.

'Out!' he informed her shortly. 'And expect me when you see me.' And with that he marched past her and seconds later she heard him thudding down the stairs. Wearily, Jess sank onto the edge of the bed and after a moment or two she looked towards the sketch of the girl on the wall.

'Oh, Martha,' she whispered. 'Everything seems to be falling apart and I'm not sure what I can do about it.' She heard the Land Rover roar out of the courtyard. No doubt Simon would clear off now and get legless with his pals, or worse still, he might find solace in the arms of another woman. Either way there was nothing she could do about it – and she realised with a little shock that right at this minute she didn't much care.

Later that evening, when both the girls were fast asleep, Jess once again went up to Martha's room in the attic. The peace of the place calmed her as she sank down onto the side of the bed. She could understand why Martha had liked this room for all it was sparsely furnished and cold. She could imagine her lying here, writing in her journal by the light of a candle. And after all, the poor girl had had far more to put up with than she had. Jess had taken her anger and frustration out on an enormous pile of ironing and now she just wished that Simon would come home so that they could talk and hopefully put things right between them. Her gran had always told her that a married couple should never go to sleep on an argument, and it was a piece of excellent advice that Jess had always tried to live by.

'Goodnight,' she whispered as she left the room and went down the attic stairs to her own room, to undress, jump into bed and return to Martha's journal.

*3 October*
We were all in the kitchen having a cup of tea this afternoon before starting preparations for the Master's evening meal when Bertie entered with a face like thunder, not that this is a rarity nowadays . . .

'I were just talking to Farmer Codd while I were down in the lower field an' he reckons he's heard on the wind that the Master's mill is in serious financial trouble,' he told them.

'Aye, well happen it were only a matter o' time,' Granny muttered philosophically.

Grace stroked her swollen stomach fearfully. Her baby was due in January and she had been praying that they would still have a home when it was born. But now this latest news made them all wonder.

Granny suddenly began to cough, a deep wracking cough that had them all looking towards her. It had come on her some weeks ago and she couldn't seem to shift it, much to Martha's concern. She saw the old woman cough into a piece of muslin she took from her apron pocket and, hoping that none of them was still looking, she flung it hastily into the heart of the fire – but not before Martha had seen the smear of blood on it.

It was then that the door opened and Hal Tolley appeared, his shoulders stooped. He quickly took his cap off and nodded towards Granny respectfully before telling them, 'The Master just called into the cottage to see us an' he's given us notice to quit.'

'Aw, lad, no.' Granny sighed loudly. 'An' just when I were thinkin' things couldn't get no worse an' all. When do yer 'ave to be out?'

'End of the week,' Hal replied dismally. 'Though God knows where we'll go. One thing's fer sure, I'll take to the open road afore I'll let me family go into the workhouse.'

They were saved from replying when the sound of a horse and carriage reached them. Seconds later the great brass knocker on the front door reverberated through the house.

'Grace, change yer apron quick an' go an' see who it is,' Granny ordered.

Grace quickly took off her great bibbed work apron and slipped on the white linen one that she wore for waiting on table before she hurried off to do as she was told. Minutes later she was back with a face whiter than her apron. 'It's the bailiffs,' she told them in a low voice. 'They had an official paper from the magistrate and they said they've come to do an inventory of all the furniture an' silverware. I told 'em the Master weren't at home but they just barged right in. What shall I do?'

'Ain't nothin' yer can do,' Granny replied with a toss of her head. 'Eeh, who'd 'ave thought it would come to this, eh?'

Bertie rose from his seat after slamming his fist on the table so hard that the teapot danced across it, then commenced walking up and down the room like a bear with a sore head.

'It's just a matter o' time afore we're all chucked out on us ears an' all now,' he muttered to no one in particular.

Unable to listen to any more, Martha fled to the sanctuary of the barn where she perched on a hale bale, rocking herself to and fro. The thought of having nowhere to live and no job was daunting, but the atmosphere in the house was such that she wondered if it wouldn't in fact, be preferable. One thing was for sure, things certainly couldn't get any worse. The pantry was empty, as was the cellar, and the evening before, when Grace had served the Master with vegetable soup for his dinner he had flung it up the wall and roared at her, 'What sort of meal do you call *this* to lay before a working man?'

'The pantry is sadly depleted, sir, an' no one will let us have any more supplies till the bills are settled,' Grace had whispered fearfully.

'Get out! You're all bloody useless! Do you hear me? GET OUT!'

Poor Grace had arrived back in the kitchen in a right old tizzy and once again Granny had had to stop Bertie from going in and knocking the Master's block off.

But now it seemed that none of them would have to put up with the Master's tantrums for much longer . . .

*10 October*
We were all going about our business this morning in a melancholy frame of mind when a splendid horse and carriage drawn by four matching black stallions drew to a halt outside. The Master had told us to expect his nephew and his wife and we could only assume that this was them arriving . . .

'Hasten away an' let 'em in, our Grace,' Granny urged, suddenly all of a dither. Hal Tolley had called in at the Anker Inn the evening before to drown his sorrows and had heard talk that Leonard Fenton, the Master's nephew, had been called upon to help him out of his dire financial situation. They could only pray that the rumours were true.

The Master greeted Leonard and his wife personally in the hallway and then whilst Melody, Leonard's wife, went to her room to freshen up after her journey, the two men closeted themselves in the Master's study. The Master had made Martha prepare the best guest bedroom for them and when Martha showed Miss Melody to her room, the woman smiled at her kindly.

'Eeh, she's *so* beautiful,' Martha sighed dreamily once back in the kitchen. 'An' kind – an' yer should have seen the costume she were wearin' . . . I reckon it was made o' velvet an' she had on a lovely little hat to match, all trimmed wi' feathers.'

'Aye, well, it appears that young Master Leonard stands to inherit this place when owt 'appens to the Master, seein' as the Mistress never had no children, so it's in his interests to help 'im out o' the mire.'

'We'll see,' Bertie replied grumpily, then rising from his seat on the wooden settle at the side of the fire, he wrapped a warm scarf about his neck and donned his heavy work coat before going about his chores.

The family had their first glimpse of Miss Melody later that morning when she swept into the kitchen like a breath of fresh air.

'Ah,' she smiled, holding out her hand and addressing Granny. 'You must be Mrs Reid. Do forgive me for intruding in your kitchen but I so wanted to meet you all.' Granny bobbed a curtsy as Melody turned to Grace. 'And you must be Grace.' Her eyes dropped to Grace's protruding stomach. 'And when is the baby due? You must be so excited.'

'In January, ma'am,' Grace said awkwardly.

'Oh, please call me Miss Melody.' Lastly the young woman turned to Martha and winked at her. 'And you and I have already met, haven't we, when you showed me to my room this morning.'

Martha was suddenly tonguetied as she looked into the eyes the colour of bluebells and nodded numbly.

'Right, now that we have all been introduced, shall we get down to business?' Melody turned back to Granny. 'I believe from what I've been told that your supplies are running quite low, so if you could write me a list of all the things that you need, my groom will ride into town and get them ordered for you straight away.'

'Thank you, Miss Melody.'

'Excellent! Secondly, I wanted to congratulate you all on the way you keep the house running. It's a credit to you. As my husband and I will be dividing our time between here and our country seat in Herefordshire for the foreseeable future, I thought it might be pleasant to carry out a little refurbishment here. I shall be going into Coventry tomorrow for samples of curtain material and wallpapers. I thought it might be good to do the drawing room and the dining room first. But there . . . Leonard is always scolding me for chattering on. I am sure I must be keeping you all from your work, so I shall leave you in peace now. Do let me have your list as soon as it is completed, Mrs Reid, and be sure to write down *everything* you need. Good morning.'

With that she lifted her skirt and left the room in a swish of silk, leaving a waft of perfume in her wake.

'Well I'll be.' Granny scratched her head. 'I understand what yer mean now, our Martha. She does seem to be a lovely young woman. Perhaps this is the start o' better times?'

'I don't reckon the Master thinks so,' Martha said with a wry smile. 'I saw him go off to the mill a while back with young Master Leonard and he had a face on him like a slapped arse. Happen it's goin' against the grain fer his young nephew to bale him out o' trouble.'

'Happen it is,' Granny replied with a stern glare. 'But that don't give you licence to go usin' bad language so watch yer lip, me gel. An' it don't make things no better fer the Tolleys either, bless their hearts. Phoebe's been packin' all day, though God alone knows where they're goin' to go.'

Martha nodded in agreement. She had seen Phoebe and Hal loading their meagre possessions onto a handcart and it had almost broken her heart.

'What time will they be leaving?' she asked.

'No doubt when the Master gets back from the mill and pays Hal his dues,' Granny commented and they then both went about their business.

It was mid-afternoon when Miss Melody's groom knocked at the kitchen door.

'Just to inform you, ma'am, that I have placed all your orders and they will be delivered shortly,' he said, addressing Granny Reid.

Her eyes gleamed as she nodded her thanks. 'He must have settled the bills up,' she said to Martha once he had tipped his cap respectfully and left. 'It'll be nice to 'ave some decent food to cook wi' again after havin' to make do.'

Sure enough, within the hour, the deliveries began to arrive: meat from the butcher's, wine for the cellar, and all manner of foodstuff that had Granny smiling as she put it all neatly away in the enormous walk-in pantry. The Master and young Master Leonard had arrived back home by then and were closeted in the study when Hal tapped on the kitchen door and entered.

Granny Reid was suddenly stuck for words. What could she possibly say that would make things any better for their poor friend?

Nodding towards the green baize door she informed him, 'He's in the study, lad. Go on through an' I'll mek yer a nice cup o' tea fer when you come back.' She swung the kettle into the heart of the fire to boil as Hal made his way to the study with his head bent.

Minutes later he was back, but instead of being upset he had a broad smile on his face.

'God bless that young Master Leonard,' he grinned. 'Me an' the family are goin' to be allowed to stay on, after all.'

'Eeh – never!' Granny's jaw dropped so low that it almost rested on her chest.

'It's true,' he nodded. 'The Master was about to pay me off when his nephew asked why me an' the family had to leave. The Master explained that now he's sold off yet more o' the land, there ain't enough to keep me in work here, so then young Master Leonard suggested that I could work in the mill. The Master didn't seem none too pleased wi' the idea, I don't mind tellin' yer. But I reckon he's afraid of upsettin' the young 'un so he had no choice but to agree. Eeh, I can 'ardly believe me luck!'

'Why, that's wonderful, Hal,' Granny beamed as she poured boiling water into the large teapot. 'Now get off an' tell Phoebe the good news an' then come back fer a sup o' tea, eh? Happen things are lookin' up around here, after all.'

Martha chopped the vegetables for the evening meal with a light heart. At least that was one crisis that had been averted. Long may it last.

# Chapter Fourteen

The sound of the bedroom door opening brought Jess springing awake and she realised with a little start that she had fallen asleep reading Martha's journal.

'Simon, what time is it?' she asked as she hastily shoved the book into the bedside drawer.

'It's about one o'clock,' he muttered sulkily as he undressed and tossed his clothes into an untidy heap on the bedside chair. He then climbed into bed beside her and the smell of the alcohol on his breath made her recoil from him.

'I hope you didn't drive home,' she said accusingly then instantly wished she hadn't. There had been enough bad feeling for one night and she wanted them to make their peace before she fell asleep again.

'Now I know who the term "the nagging wife" was invented for,' he said drily as he snapped the bedside light off. He then turned his back on her as she blinked into the darkness.

'Where have you been?'

'Can we save the twenty questions until the morning?' he snarled. 'Or is a working man not even allowed to get a decent night's sleep now?'

'Sorry.' I certainly handled that well, Jess thought to herself and then, as the sound of his snores echoed around the room, she too tried to lose herself in sleep.

Simon had already left for work the next morning when the shrill ringing of the alarm clock brought Jess from a disturbed sleep. She hated to upset Simon, promising herself that she would make it up to him that evening, but even so she went straight from dropping the girls off to the post office where she got the passport applications before heading back to the house. She was still determined to take the girls to Paris in the next school break and if Simon didn't like it, he would just have to lump it.

Karen called in just before lunch-time, and as she and Jess sat drinking coffee she asked, 'So what's up with you then? You look like a wet weekend.'

That was one of the things Jess had always loved about her friend; she always said what she thought, offend or please. Karen was totally opposite to Jess in every way, which Jess supposed was part of her charm. It was a known fact that opposites attract. Karen was well built, with lovely long thick fair hair which had a tendency to curl. She was forever complaining about it and trying to straighten it whilst Jess kept telling her that she herself would have died for it. Karen was a jolly sort of person who let nothing worry her, and sometimes Jess cringed when she saw the state of her house. Karen would never be a slave to housework as she herself was, and yet for all that she lived very happily with her husband who was a fireman, and their three sons.

'Oh, I don't know,' Jess sighed. 'It just feels like everything is going wrong again, that's all.'

'I'm not surprised, living here in the back of beyond.' Karen glanced about apprehensively. 'I don't mind telling you, this place gives me the creeps.'

'It's hardly the back of beyond,' Jess objected. 'Caldecote is only a stone's throw away.'

'It may well be, but you still feel shut off when you start up that bloody drive. But come on, spill the beans . . . is Simon up to his old tricks again?'

Jess felt herself flushing. She always got the feeling that Karen could read her like a book, so she shrugged. 'I'm not sure to be honest, although he is starting to stay out again. But it's Mel too. She ran away the other night and the police brought her back in the early hours of the next morning. She won't tell me why she went and she just seems so down all the time. It can't be natural for a girl her age. She should be out and about enjoying herself, instead of spending half her life locked away in her room. She and Simon seem to be at each other's throats for the majority of the time. He barely gives her an inch of space and it gets you down after a while.'

'Well, I can understand why it would do,' Karen agreed. 'Although I'm shocked to hear it. Simon has his faults, God knows, but he's always been good to the girls. Perhaps he's just being over-protective because he's afraid of her growing up and moving away from him? I mean, let's face it, you and the girls are the first bit of stability he's had in his life, aren't you? He didn't have much of a start, what with being shunted from place to place like a parcel when he was a kid.'

'I suppose there could be something in that, but he can't keep her locked away for ever, can he?'

'Look . . .' Karen said hesitantly. 'I reckon we've known each other long enough for me to say this without you being offended. I reckon Simon is feeling somewhat put out at the minute. Ever since you got married he's been the breadwinner, and now suddenly you have money of your own and you're not reliant on him any more. Not financially, at least. I mean, look at this place for a start.' She spread her hands to add emphasis to what she was saying. 'You could never have afforded somewhere like this if your gran hadn't left you all that dosh. And you have your own car now too, so you don't have to rely on him to get you out and about. You've come out of your shell, kiddo – not that I think it's a bad thing,' she added hastily, 'but Simon's had his nose put out of joint good and proper. That could explain why he's being so hard on Mel. He can't control you any more, so he's taking his frustration out on her.'

'Hmm, I suppose you could be right,' Jess admitted musingly. It did make a lot of sense.

'Are you quite sure that's all that's bothering you?' Karen went on. 'You're jumping at your own shadow lately.'

Jess chewed on her lip for a moment, and then it all came tumbling out. 'Actually, there is something else, and before I even tell you, I know you're going to think I've gone off my rocker. The thing is . . .' She looked slightly embarrassed before rushing on, 'Soon after I moved here, my neighbour, Laura, from Blue Brick Cottage at the end of the drive, told me that she could sense a presence here.'

When Karen raised an eyebrow she hurried on, 'Laura is sort of spiritual. You know – she senses things. Now the first time she told me about this presence I scoffed at her, but lately . . . Well, I sometimes get the feeling that I'm not alone when there's no one else but me in the house.'

'Now you really are letting your imagination run away with you,' Karen scoffed, as predicted. 'You're not telling me that there's a resident ghost here, are you?'

'Call it what you will – a ghost, an angel, a presence – but yes, I *do* hear things.'

'Such as what?'

'Well, sometimes I hear someone crying. Other times I've sensed

111

someone standing behind me and I've smelled roses, even when there are no roses in the house. Other times I've thought I heard someone whispering. And that's not all. I think I might know who it is. I found this old journal, you see; it was up in the attic, and it was written by a young maid who used to live here, long ago. Laura told me that she's here for a reason and that reason has something to do with me. And don't look at me like that. Jo and Mel have seen things too. Jo insists that sometimes she sees the shape of a young woman in a long dress standing at the side of her bed.'

'I reckon it's all in the mind,' Karen said stoically. 'If the girls know that you're nervous, they will be – and then they'll start to imagine things too.'

'But I haven't said anything to them,' Jess objected hotly. 'In fact, I haven't even admitted to Laura that I think there might be something in what she said. I've never believed in things like this, but now I'm beginning to wonder. You just said yourself that this place gives you the creeps.'

'That's only because it's isolated, but if it's bothering you, why don't you do something about it? Get the place exorcised or whatever it is they do to haunted places.'

Jess suddenly giggled nervously. 'Oh, you're probably right. It's just me imagining things, like you say. Now how about I refill your mug, eh?' And with that she deliberately changed the course of the conversation and spoke of other things until Karen eventually left after a light lunch some time later.

She then shot off upstairs. She still had a little time before the girls came home from school, and the book was like a magnet to her now.

*2 November*
Miss Melody, as she insists we should call her, has made such changes to the place and suddenly there is laughter here again . . .

'Who would have thought it, eh?' Granny said to her granddaughters as she peeped into the newly decorated drawing room, a look of awe on her face. The walls had been covered in fine red flock paper, and elegant swags and tails hung at the windows. The floor was covered in silk-fringed rugs.

'Me heart is in me throat every mornin' when I clear the ashes out o' the fireplace,' Grace confided in a whisper. 'I'm scared to death o' droppin' 'em on the new rugs. It's the same in the dinin' room an' all.'

The dining room had been painted in various shades of green and was just as elegant as the drawing room. But then, considering the amount of workmen who had been swarming all over the place since Miss Melody's arrival, it was hardly surprising.

'I'd best get back to the kitchen an' start the breakfast,' Granny commented after a final peep at the room, but then a bout of coughing brought her bending almost double. Eventually she straightened and pressed her clenched fist into her chest as she waggled the other hand at the two girls.

'Now don't go lookin' at me like that,' she gasped. ''Tis only a bit of a cough, an' once the weather picks up it'll go. Now go on the both of yer and get away to yer chores.'

The two young women scuttled away as Granny stood watching them, a smile twitching at the corners of her lips. They were good girls, there was no doubt about it, and she thought herself a fortunate woman indeed. She had looked after them since their mother had died in a cholera epidemic when the girls were little more than nippers, and when her son had been killed in a pitfall, and she didn't regret a single day of it. In a happier frame of mind she pottered off back to the kitchen. Miss Melody was welcome to all her finery; Granny Reid was never happier than when she was ensconced in her kitchen which she considered to be very much her domain.

'What about the latest bit o' news then?' Granny gossiped to Phoebe as they sat in the kitchen later that day enjoying a well-earned sit-down. 'Miss Melody's informed us that she's expectin' a child too – an' not long after our Grace's is due. I have to admit we're all made up about it, an' her an' Master Leonard seem tickled pink wi' the idea o' becomin' parents. Maybe this will mean she'll be stayin' fer a good while longer. She told us at lunch that her lady's maid is comin' to join 'er from Herefordshire. Her name is Miss Prim an' we can only hope that she don't live up to it else I can see a few sparks flyin' atween us. But then I'm prepared to give the woman a chance. There's a seamstress callin' this afternoon to measure Miss Melody fer some new gowns to see her through till the nipper arrives. Eeh, yer should see the gowns she gave to our Grace an' Martha. They're beautiful, although as Grace pointed out, it's 'ighly unlikely they'll ever go anywhere grand enough to wear 'em. But she's a kind-hearted soul.

The other bit o' news is she's throwin' a dinner party come the weekend. It'll be the first this place 'as seen since the Mistress left an' I don't think the Master is none too pleased about it. But then he wouldn't dare to say so, he's too scared o' Master Leonard withdrawin' his financial support from what we can make of it.'

'I think yer could be right there,' Phoebe agreed musingly. 'Hal reckons Master Leonard has the mill runnin' like a well-oiled spring again – no thanks to the old 'un.' Granny chuckled. 'Do you know summat? I ain't seen the Master drunk once since his nephew arrived. An' long may it continue that's what I say.'

'Hear, hear,' Phoebe agreed, helping herself to a piece of Gran's gingerbread. 'An' I agree wi' what you said about the young Mistress bein' kind an' all. Did yer know she'd sent the doctor in to take a look at our Joey's back? God knows how she found out about it, but the ointment he prescribed is workin' a treat.'

Granny would never forget the terrible sight of the lad's injuries. 'I doubt very much the Master will even be here on the night o' the party,' she confided. 'He keeps out o' the young 'uns' way as much as he can – an' that suits us all just fine, devil that he is.'

It was then that the sound of a pony and trap entering the courtyard interrupted their conversation and minutes later a small, smartly dressed woman tapped at the kitchen door. 'Hello, I'm Miss Prim,' she introduced herself with a kindly smile and Granny Reid hurried forward and took her valise from her.

'Ah, we've been expectin' yer. Would yer like a sup o' tea before yer go up to the Mistress?'

'That would be lovely, thank you.' The woman took a hatpin from her hat and laid it neatly on the edge of the large pine dresser before joining the two women at the table.

'Been ladies' maid to Miss Melody fer long, 'ave yer?' Granny enquired pleasantly as she strained tea into a clean cup.

'Well, between you and me I was Miss Melody's nanny when she was a child,' Miss Prim confided. 'And then when she grew too old to need a nanny I took on the role of ladies' maid.'

'Ah, so yer've never been married then?'

Miss Prim threw her hands up in horror. 'Oh dear me, no!' she exclaimed. 'That would have meant me leaving my dear sweet child.'

Phoebe and Granny exchanged an amused glance. Miss Prim had referred to Miss Melody as if she was her own flesh and blood and they all knew in that instant that they were going to get along famously.

Later on that same day, another snippet of gossip filtered into the kitchen when Hal returned from the mill.

'I've heard tell that Master Leonard has bought a ribbon-weavin' factory in the town,' he told his captive audience.

'Then let's hope it's true,' Granny answered. 'The more ties he has here the longer he'll stay an' that would suit us all just fine.'

The speculation on whether the rumour he had heard was true was stopped from going any further when Bertie too strode in with a broad smile on his face as he hurried over to his wife.

'You'll never guess what's happened, pet,' he said animatedly.

'I dare say we won't if you don't tell us,' Grace agreed wryly.

'Well, the thing is, whilst I was at work today young Master Leonard waylaid me an' asked me how you an' me were copin' in the rooms above the stables. I told him we were right cosy, but he said that seein' as we're to have a baby he wants to build us a little cottage in the grounds! Think on it, Grace – our own four walls – an' he's aimin' to have it started as soon as possible. The Master didn't look none too pleased wi' the idea at all, but seein' as it's Master Leonard's money as will pay fer it, he didn't dare open his mouth.'

'Our own little cottage?' Grace looked astounded. 'Why, I can scarcely believe it. That man has a heart o' pure gold.' Tears stood in her eyes.

Martha glanced at the clock. It was her afternoon off, and she'd spent it at home. Despite all the good news, she was keen to get out of the house for a while.

'I'll be off now then, Granny,' she said, as she lifted her shawl and inched towards the back door.

Granny frowned. 'Eeh, yer never goin' out in this, lass? It's been rainin' cats an' dogs fer days. Everywhere is like a quagmire.'

'That's as maybe, but I feel the need fer a bit o' fresh air, an' it ain't rainin' now.' When she saw the look of concern on the old woman's face, she then promised, 'I shan't go far, an' I'll be back in time to help yer wi' the evenin' meal.'

Granny shrugged. 'Have it yer own way, lass, but mind yer wrap up warm.' She then turned her attention to the exciting news that Hal and Bertie had just told her as Martha slipped away.

She immediately headed down the long lawn to where the River

Anker ran. The river had broken its banks after the prolonged rain and the bottom of the garden was flooded but Martha set off sure-footedly towards the stone bridge, glad of the fog that was swirling in from the river. The currents were treacherous at present and only the week before, a man had drowned in it when his boat capsized. But it wasn't of this that Martha was thinking now, but of Jimmy, whom she now met each week on her afternoon off. Sure enough she saw him waiting for her with his hands thrust deep into his coat pockets as he stared into the swirling water. Her heart began to beat a tattoo in her chest. Eeh, he was a handsome lad, and she was sure now that she loved him. Perhaps soon she might be able to have a word with Miss Melody and ask if she would give her permission for her to walk out with him? The Master would never dare say anything to oppose it if Miss Melody had given her blessing, and then they needn't keep their meetings a secret any more. She hurried on with a spring in her step.

The day before the party, the seamstress that Miss Melody had employed to make her new gowns called at the house. She had taken both Grace's and Martha's measurements on her last visit and now as well as a beautiful new gown for the young Mistress, she was deliv-ering their new uniforms.

Granny looked on with amusement as Martha sashayed up and down the kitchen in hers. The new outfit consisted of a grey serge dress over which went a long white bibbed pinafore trimmed with lace, and she had also made them both a new mobcap of broderie anglaise.

'Eeh, I feel that posh I reckon I could attend the party in this,' Martha laughed.

'Don't you go forgettin' yer place, girl,' Granny warned but the words were said with affection. 'An' I suggest yer take it off before yer muck it up. I don't reckon the Mistress will be too pleased if you ruin it before the party.' They were all in high good spirits as they had been paid for the first time in months – a fact they had all taken advantage of when the talley man had called the day before. Martha had bought a fine woollen shawl for Granny and a pair of gloves for Grace as well as a scarf for Bertie, and she had now hidden them away until Christmas came. The mood in the house had lightened further when Master Leonard had informed them that he and Miss Melody would now be staying until after their baby was born. He was concerned that the long journey back to Herefordshire might be too much for her, and so now they were all envisaging a happy Christmas. Granny had been busily crocheting little hats and a shawl ready for her great-grandchild's arrival every spare second she had, and Martha had sewn some tiny nightgowns from a piece of flannel she had bought off the market, which she was very pleased with. It had already been agreed that the care of the baby would be shared between the three women once he or she arrived, so that Grace could go about her duties, and they were all looking forward to it as the time drew closer.

And now the house was alive with activity as they all prepared for the party. Master Leonard had ordered caterers to come in and help Granny with the food, and there would also be maids he had hired especially for the occasion. For the first time in a very long while they were all content and prayed that the happy atmosphere might continue.

Jess closed the book with an enormous lump in her throat. Now when she shut her eyes she could imagine the house as it had once been, and she found herself caring for Martha and her family. It was almost as if she was coming to know the girl through the journal she had left behind. But that in itself was a concern. Why would Martha have left her clothes and her journal upstairs? Did Martha marry her Jimmy? Was Grace's baby delivered safely? Did Granny Reid recover from her dreadful cough? Did the kindly Mistress restore peace to Stonebridge House?

Jess hoped that the journal would eventually supply her with the answers. Sometimes she was tempted to read the end of it to find out what had become of Martha – but that, she told herself, would be like reading the end of a good book and would spoil it. And so she forced herself to be patient and tried instead to concentrate on the trip to Paris that she was organising for herself and the girls.

# Chapter Fifteen

During the half-term holiday in October, shortly after Mel's fourteenth birthday, Simon drove them all to Birmingham International Airport early in the morning to get on the flight to Paris.

Jess was nervous, Jo was excited and Mel was, as usual, very quiet and unresponsive despite Jess's best efforts to involve her in the planning of the trip.

'She'll perk up once we get on the plane,' Jess whispered to Simon.

'Hmm!' His tone said without words that he wasn't convinced but she chose to ignore it. This was supposed to be a little holiday and she didn't want it to get off to a bad start.

'We are going to see the Eiffel Tower, aren't we?' Jo asked for at least the tenth time. 'We've been reading about it at school and it will be so *cool* to be able to tell the teacher that I've actually been there. I already know all about it. It was built in 1889 to commemorate the centenary of the French Revolution, and King Edward VII opened it.'

'Yes, well, why don't you wait until we get there and then you can give us the rest of the history lesson,' Jess said indulgently. At least Jo was looking forward to it, while Mel looked more like she was going to her doom than on holiday.

'And is there anywhere special you'd like to go, Mel?' she now asked hopefully.

When the girl shrugged Jess didn't push it. It really didn't matter as Jo was chatting away enough for all of them. Jess was feeling very mixed at present. Half of her was excited at the prospect of the break ahead; the other half was feeling apprehensive. She and Simon had never holidayed apart before, and she had never flown either, but then she knew deep down that he could have come if he had really wanted to. The men who worked for him were very trustworthy and reliable, and she was sure they would have covered for them had he asked them to. But then, he was conscientious when it came to work, so she didn't hold it against him. And they were only going for five days, after all. They'd be back before she'd had time to miss him.

Gazing from the car window she admired the Warwickshire countryside as it flashed by. The leaves were fluttering to the ground in shades of russet and gold, and she knew that winter would soon be upon them. She hoped that the central-heating system they'd had installed would prove to be adequate. Stonebridge House was a great barn of a place and Jess hardly dared imagine what the heating bills were going to be. But then she had known that when she bought the house, so she supposed there was no point in worrying about it now.

Simon drew up outside the terminal and quickly unloaded their cases from the Land Rover before pecking Jo on the cheek and turning to Mel. Completely ignoring him, Mel strode away towards the doors leading inside without giving him so much as a backward glance, and he turned back to Jess with a resigned look on his face.

'So, are you sure you've got everything? Passports, tickets, Euros?'

She nodded, too afraid to speak in case she started to cry. She suddenly felt as if she was saying goodbye to him for ever instead of for five days.

'Right – you'd better get inside then and get your luggage checked in.'

They were facing each other like strangers and it was tearing her apart. Once again, a gulf had developed between them.

'Take care of yourself, won't you?' she said. 'There's plenty of food in the fridge and the freezer so there's no need for you to go hungry.'

He chuckled. 'I hardly think I'm going to waste away before you get home. Now go on, get off and enjoy yourselves.' He leaned towards her and kissed her on the lips, and then she hastily grabbed the handle of the case and turned away. 'Bye, love. I'll be here to pick you up on Friday.'

Nodding numbly she quickly followed the girls into the airport wondering if this had really been such a good idea after all.

Mid-afternoon, the coach that arrived at the airport to take them to their hotel in central Paris pulled up outside the Hôtel du Chat d'Or and Jo bounced with excitement as she peered out of the window.

'Cor, look how posh it is! There's a doorman in a uniform and everything. I think I'm going to like it here.'

Jess ushered the girls off the coach and waited whilst the driver unloaded their cases. A porter appeared as if by magic, placed their luggage on a special trolley, and wheeled it inside. The foyer was very luxurious, with chocolate-brown leather settees placed here and there, and a huge crystal chandelier dangling from the centre of the ceiling, shooting prisms of multi-coloured lights all about the room. As their feet sank into a thick pile carpet in a lovely shade of blue, Jo's eyes were like saucers as she clung to her mother's hand.

'It's like something you see on the telly, isn't it?' she whispered in awe as Jess approached the desk.

Once they had checked in and had been given their key, Jess led them to a glass elevator and in no time at all they were up on the fifteenth floor.

'We're in room number 512,' she told the girls as they walked along the corridor peering at the numbers on the doors.

Eventually they found it and once inside were shocked to find a young woman unpacking their cases and hanging their clothes away in the wardrobe for them. Jess had decided to push the boat out and had paid for a suite of rooms. After all, it wasn't often that they got to go away. She certainly wasn't disappointed and began to feel like she'd walked into some sort of Hollywood movie set. There was a lounge boasting a panoramic view of Notre Dame and the Louvre, a room with a king-sized bed in it and another room with two single beds, as well as two en-suite bathrooms.

Once the young woman had finished their unpacking Jess gave her a generous tip and ordered afternoon tea to be sent up to their rooms before joining the girls at the window, pleased to see that even Mel looked slightly more interested now.

'Wow! This is *ace*,' Jo stated dramatically. 'Just wait till I get back to school and tell the other girls about this. They'll be *green* with envy.'

Chuckling, Jess slid her arms about the two girls' shoulders. 'Well, I figured if we were going to do it, we might as well do it in style.'

Jo slipped away, keen to explore their room with its stylish en-suite bathroom. 'Blimey, I reckon everything in here is made of solid marble, and the taps are gold,' she shouted out to them, and curious despite the fact that she had promised herself she wasn't going to enjoy it, Mel sped off to have a look while Jess went to her own room.

A little pang of regret sliced through her as she gazed at the huge bed and pictured herself and Simon curled up in it. *When the girls are a little older, I'll bring him here,* she promised herself. *And we'll finally have the honeymoon we never got around to.*

Minutes later, a maid arrived with their tea laid out on a trolley and the girls tucked in as if they hadn't eaten for a week. Everything was beautifully presented and Jess grinned as she watched Jo tucking into the finely sliced cucumber sandwiches and the assortment of fresh cream cakes displayed on a fine bone china three-tier cake-stand. She poured them tea from a solid silver teapot and they all drank from cups so fine that she could see through them. Even Mel ate heartily for a change, which was a relief for Jess as the girl seemed to have lost quite a bit of weight lately. She herself picked at the food like a bird. She hadn't been too keen on flying and felt quite nauseous, although she didn't mention it to her daughters because she didn't want to spoil it for them.

'Now,' she said, wiping her mouth on a starched white napkin when they had all eaten their fill. 'What would you like to do this afternoon?'

'Can we just have a mooch around and get our bearings?' Jo asked instantly. 'Then we can start sightseeing properly tomorrow.'

'I think that's an excellent idea,' Jess agreed, although truthfully she would have rather stayed in the hotel to rest. 'Are you up for that, Mel?'

Mel shrugged, so taking that as a yes they all put on comfortable trainers and fetched their cameras from their room.

In no time at all they were strolling through the fashionable area called Le Marais, entranced with all they saw, and thankfully Jess began to feel slightly better. The streets around the magnificent Hôtel de Ville were full of animated cafés where tourists and Parisians alike sat outside at small tables sipping wine and coffee. They crossed the River Seine and slowly Jess felt herself begin to unwind as they gazed in awe at the sheer beauty of this city.

They arrived back at the hotel at gone six o'clock, by which time the light was fast fading.

'I think we'll treat ourselves to a meal in the hotel dining room this evening,' Jess decided as they crossed the foyer and headed for the lift. 'So we'd better go and get changed into something a little dressier than our jeans. I've a feeling it's going to be quite smart.'

'I bet it will be really expensive too,' Mel ventured.

'So what?' Jess smiled at her. 'We're worth it! We're only here for five days so let's make the best of it, eh?'

Only too happy to oblige, Jo hastily shot off to the bathroom when they got back to their rooms and emerged in record time wearing one of the new outfits her mum had bought her especially for the trip.

'You look lovely!' Jess stared at her admiringly as Jo happily preened in her new skirt and top. Mel followed her out only minutes later and again Jess was complimentary as she saw how grown-up Mel looked. She was wearing black bootleg trousers and a rather pretty blouse that Jess had treated her to from Monsoon. It was red and quite glittery, and Jess suspected that it would rarely see daylight again except for special occasions once they got home. But even so it had put a smile back on her daughter's face, so as far as she was concerned it was worth every penny.

She herself changed into a simple black dress that just grazed her knees, and high-heel shoes, and the girls tittered when she came out of her room fastening a string of pearls that Simon had bought her for their last anniversary about her neck. She had swept her fair hair into a neat knot high on the back of her head and she looked elegant and sophisticated.

'Oh Mum, it's funny to see you in a skirt instead of old jeans all covered in paint,' Jo teased.

Jess smiled ruefully. It had been so long since she'd had cause to get dressed up that she'd almost forgotten how good it could make her feel. She suddenly wished that Simon were there to see her and quickly blinked to hold back the tears before saying, 'Well, come on then, girls. I don't know about you two but all that walking has made me hungry enough to eat a horse.'

In high good spirits they all made their way to the dining room where a waiter in a smart black tailcoat bowed to them before showing them to a table.

'I wonder if we'll see any film stars in here,' Jo hissed as her mother and Mel stared at the menus with concern. They were written entirely in French and none of them could read a word of it.

'Oh dear,' Jess muttered, much to the amusement of a very handsome young gentleman sitting on his own on the table next to them.

Leaning towards them, he whispered discreetly, 'Pardon me, madame, but if you are having problems ordering, may I suggest that you stick to le plat du jour? This is the daily fixed menu, and today it consists of Salade des Pyrenées for your hors d'oeuvres, which is a combination of bacon, Roquefort cheese and walnuts on a bed of fresh crisp salad, followed by canard à l'orange – duck with orange sauce and with fresh vegetables. You may then choose your dessert from the trolley. I can thoroughly recommend the plat du jour as I have just had it myself.'

Jess blushed as she smiled at him gratefully. 'Thank you, that all sounds delicious. What do you say, girls?'

'Sounds good to me,' they chorused, and so Jess summoned the waiter and quickly placed their food order along with a request for a glass of red wine. She had never been a wine connoisseur and hoped that whatever the wine was, it would be palatable.

Jo meanwhile was fascinated by the young man on the next table and told him, 'We're here on holiday.'

'How wonderful, and are you enjoying it?'

'Oh yes, but we haven't gone to many places yet because we only got here today.'

'I see.'

His voice had a heavy French accent although he spoke impeccable English so next, much to Jess's embarrassment, Jo asked him, 'Do you live here?'

He smiled affably. 'No, but I used to when I was small with my family. My mother was English but my papa was French. Now I live in England.'

'Really?' Jo wiggled on her seat. 'Whereabouts?'

'Jo *really*,' Jess scolded. 'Stop asking questions. You are spoiling the gentleman's meal.' He had, in fact, just finished his dessert and was drinking a cup of coffee.

'It is quite all right,' he assured her, then turning his attention back to Jo he told her, 'I live in Birmingham, in the Midlands. I am a teacher at a school there. Do you know it?'

'Oh yes, we live not that far from there in a town called Nuneaton.' Jo was grinning like a Cheshire cat now. 'We go there sometimes on the train 'cos Mum likes to shop in the Bullring shopping centre. But why did you move there when you could have lived in a cool place like this?'

Jess was beginning to wish that the ground would just open up and swallow her, but knew of old that once Jo was on a roll there was no stopping her.

'Sadly, my papa died when I was ten and then my mother and I moved back to England. She too then passed away when I was in my teens and so I then lived with an aunt in a village called Wolvey and went to university. When I qualified I went on to become a French teacher, so you see, I have the best of both worlds. I too am here on a little holiday although things have changed greatly since I lived here as a child.'

He held his hand out. 'My name is Emile Lefavre. How do you do.'

Feeling very grown up, Jo shook his hand with a broad smile on her face. Jess meanwhile was thinking what a handsome man Emile was. His hair was so dark that it was almost black, with a natural wave in it that gave him a gypsy-like appearance, and he was tall and well-muscled. But it was his eyes that were his most striking feature: they were an incredible indigo blue and they seemed to twinkle when he spoke. He was very smartly dressed in a dark suit. The crease in the trousers was so sharp she felt she might have been able to cut her fingers on it. With his pale blue shirt he wore a darker blue tie that exactly matched the colour of his eyes. She tried to gauge how old he might be and decided that he was possibly two or three years younger than herself. And then she blushed for even thinking about it. She was a married woman, for goodness sake! Simon had been her first and only love, and here she was ogling another man on her first night in Paris.

Feeling suddenly that she ought to intervene, she told Jo a little sharply, 'That's quite enough now, Jo. I'm sure Mr Lefavre would like to enjoy his coffee in peace without you chewing his ear off.'

Thankfully, the waiter appeared then with their starters and Jo goodnaturedly turned her attention back to her meal as Jess smiled apologetically at their neighbour.

Much to Jess's relief, Jo was so hungry that she concentrated on the food for the next half an hour as one delicious course followed another. Jess allowed both the girls to have a little sip of wine and was delighted to see that even Mel seemed to be enjoying herself. They were just about to start on their main courses when Emile Lefavre stood up and bowed to them.

'Goodnight, ladies,' he said. 'I am about to go for a stroll now before I retire for the night. I hope we shall meet again, but if we don't, do enjoy your holiday.'

'Thank you,' they all chorused. By the time they had finished a delicious assortment of desserts, Jo was yawning.

'Right, young lady, I think it's bedtime for you,' Jess told her with an affectionate grin. 'You're worn out, what with the journey and all the excitement, even if you won't admit it. But I want us to be up bright and early tomorrow, so if we get a good night's sleep we'll be raring to go. I tell you what – there's a television in your room and I'll let you watch that for a while until you drop off.'

Jo reluctantly followed after her mother and sister as they headed for the lift, and in no time at all she was tucked up warm and cosy in bed.

'I'm not at all tired,' she whined, but by the time Jess had put her clothes away she was amused to see that Jo was already fast asleep. So much for her not being tired, she thought as she joined Mel in the sumptuously furnished lounge. The girl was flicking through the TV channels, but when Jess appeared she mumbled, 'Actually, I think I might get an early night too. I'm done in.'

Jess sighed. She'd been hoping that in different surroundings when they were alone together Mel might confide in her about what had been troubling her. But it was already apparent it wasn't going to happen tonight.

'All right, love. If that's what you want,' she told her tenderly, and watched as her oldest daughter slipped away to her room. And then she grinned wryly. Here she was in Gay Paree – with only the telly to keep her company!

# Chapter Sixteen

Once the girls had gone to bed, Jess paced the room feeling strangely unsettled. She knew that it would be useless going to bed just yet, as there was no way she was going to be able to rest, so after checking that the girls were both asleep she wrote them a hasty note telling them where she would be in case they woke up, then snatched up her bag and headed for the door to the suite. Once she was sure that the door was locked firmly behind her she then went downstairs to the bar for a nightcap feeling in a slightly reckless mood. Jess had never been much of a drinker, but then she told herself, *I might never get this opportunity again, so why not make the most of it?* The bar was much like the rest of the hotel, extravagant and plush with deep leather settees and glass-topped tables placed here and there, and soft music was playing. A few of the gentlemen drinking in there glanced at her appreciatively as she picked her way to the mirror-backed bar, but Jess kept her eyes straight ahead.

'A gin and tonic, please,' she told the young barman as she slid onto a high stool and fiddled in her bag for her purse.

'Please, allow me.'

Jess quickly looked to her right and then her face relaxed into a smile when she saw Emile Lefavre standing there.

'That's very kind of you, thank you.'

'You are most welcome, but where are your charming daughters?'

'They're tucked up in bed fast asleep,' she answered. She was actually quite pleased to have him there as she had felt rather self-conscious walking into the bar on her own.

Once the barman had poured her drink, Emile gestured to one of the leather settees. 'Shall we sit over there?' he asked pleasantly. 'I think it might be rather more comfortable than perched here on these high stools.'

When he lifted her drink she followed him willingly and soon they were seated staring out of the window onto Paris at night.

'I can see why they call it the City of Lights,' Jess said dreamily as she sipped at her drink. 'It's quite awesome, isn't it?'

'Absolutely,' Emile agreed. 'You must try to do the after-dinner Paris By Night Illuminations tour. It's quite breathtaking. I'm sure you and your daughters would enjoy it. Although I have to say I find it hard to believe you are old enough to have two daughters.'

Jess was beginning to relax now as the gin and tonic worked its magic, and she giggled. It had been a long time since anyone had paid her such a blatant compliment, and she found that she quite liked it.

'Ah, so it's true then,' she said. 'I heard that Frenchmen had the gift of the gab.'

Emile's blue eyes twinkled as he raised his glass to her. 'It is best not to believe everything you are told,' he said. 'I also find it difficult to believe that your husband would allow such a beautiful woman to come here on her own.'

'But I'm not on my own,' Jess pointed out defensively. 'I have the girls with me and Simon, that's my husband, couldn't come because of work commitments. He is a builder and so he has to work when he can. Building work tends to slacken off through the winter. We're actually here to celebrate Melanie's fourteenth birthday, which was in September.'

'She looks a delightful young woman,' he told her.

Jess nodded. 'She is, but . . .'

'But what?'

'Well, she hasn't been herself for a while and I was hoping that this break might perk her up a bit.'

'Ah.' He nodded understandingly. 'I see it many times, the teenage problems in my job as a teacher, especially with the girls. Teenagers can be very moody, can they not?'

'That's putting it mildly.' Jess could hardly believe that she was sitting here in a bar in the middle of Paris pouring her heart out to a man she had only just met, but Emile, as she was fast discovering, was remarkably easy to talk to.

'And have her moods affected her schoolwork?' he asked now.

Jess nodded sadly. 'Yes, I'm afraid they have. Mel is a very intelligent girl and up until recently her school reports were excellent, but now . . .'

When her voice trailed away he smiled at her sympathetically. 'Perhaps you should think of getting her some extra home tuition? I do quite a lot of private tuition myself. At the school during the day

127

I teach French, but I also teach maths and English evenings and weekends. It wouldn't be so far for me to come down the M6.'

Jess chewed on her lip uncertainly. She wasn't sure what Mel would think of that idea; or Simon for that matter.

'I'll think about it,' she promised as she drained her glass with every intention of returning to her room. But before she could stand Emile had snatched the glass up and was heading for the bar again, and she didn't wish to appear rude so she sat there studying him. He really was a remarkably good-looking man. Not quite as muscular as Simon but very attractive all the same. He had changed now from his smart suit into more casual attire, and she decided that it suited him. He wore beige trousers and a navy-blue polo-shirt with the top button undone exposing a tantalising glimpse of thick dark hairs on his chest.

Blushing again, she quickly diverted her gaze, wondering once more what the hell she was doing sitting there. She was a happily married woman and this time next week she would be back at home in the daily grind with all this nothing more than a memory. She found everything about Emile attractive, which was surprising as she could never remember feeling vaguely drawn to any man but Simon. But then she had never found herself in Paris without Simon before, sitting in a bar with romantic music playing in the background and an attentive man at her side. She tried to think of other things and suddenly remembered the journal safely tucked away back in the bedside drawer at home. She wished that she had brought it with her now. Perhaps then she would have stayed up in her room reading about Martha's life and not have been tempted down to the bar. But then, she reasoned, what harm was she doing? She was merely enjoying a conversation and a drink, or a few drinks, with a pleasant acquaintance. They were hardly having a passionate affair, which was more than could be said for Simon, who had clocked up more than a few over the years with different women who had caught his eye. For all she knew, he could be with another woman right at this very minute. What was the saying? While the cat's away the mice will play? The relaxed mood suddenly fled.

'Is something wrong, Jessica?' Emile asked as he returned to the table with the drinks in his hands.

Even the sound of his French accent made her tingle and she shook herself mentally. She was behaving more like a teenager than the one who was tucked up in bed upstairs.

'No, but I er . . . I think I ought to go up after this one,' she mumbled. 'You know – to check on the girls.' But later, when she glanced at the wall clock behind the bar, she was shocked to see that it was almost one o'clock in the morning. The time had flown by while they had discussed everything from art to politics. At home, she and Simon never seemed to have time to talk about anything other than the more mundane matters such as what job he was working on or the children. The realisation saddened her and she determined to try harder when she got back.

As her eyes fastened on Emile's hands she couldn't help but notice the difference between his and Simon's. Emile's fingers were long and tapering, almost like a pianist's fingers, and his hands were smooth and well cared for, whereas Simon's were always red and chaffed from the outdoor work he did.

'So where were you thinking of taking the girls tomorrow?' As his voice sliced into her thoughts, she came back to the present.

'I – I thought perhaps we might visit the Louvre,' she stammered. 'Jo wants to see the *Mona Lisa*.'

'That's an excellent choice.' He smiled at her approvingly over the rim of his glass as she hastily raised hers and took a final sip. She was feeling more than a little tipsy now and was anxious to return to her room.

'Well, thank you for a most enjoyable evening,' she said as she extended her hand and wobbled to her feet.

The corners of his lips twitched with amusement as he solemnly bowed and kissed her hand. 'The pleasure was all mine, I assure you,' he told her. 'Goodnight, Jessica. I am sure we shall meet again.'

She nodded as she carefully turned and began to pick her way amongst the tables to the door. The bar was almost empty now, with only the odd couple here and there still talking animatedly.

After crossing the foyer she entered the lift and in no time at all she was back in their suite of rooms. A quick peek into the girls' room assured her that they were still fast asleep and she sighed with relief as she pulled the pins out of her hair and let it tumble about her shoulders. She then kicked off her high heels and hurried over to the phone. Suddenly she needed to hear Simon's voice, and although it was very late she hoped that he wouldn't mind her disturbing him.

As she dialled her home number she strummed the table impatiently with her free hand as she waited for Simon to lift the phone. But after waiting for five whole minutes she slammed the receiver back into the cradle with a frown on her face. Why hadn't he answered? There was a phone right at the side of their bed! Then her face softened. She, better than anyone, knew that once Simon was asleep wild horses galloping over him couldn't waken him, so he had probably slept through it. She crossed to the window to admire the view once more then slowly took herself off to bed where she slept like a baby right through until eight o'clock the next morning.

'Mum, Mum, wake up!' Someone bouncing on the bed at the side of her brought her eyes blearily open and she squinted to see Jo grinning down at her. Her mouth felt like the bottom of a birdcage and she had a raging headache, but then as she thought back to how much she had drunk the night before, she had to admit it served her right.

'Morning, love.' The words came out as a groan and Jo stared at her in concern.

'Are you ill, Mum?'

'No, sweethcart. I just had a couple of drinks last night after you'd gone to bed and I'm paying for it now.'

Jo grinned. She hadn't seen her mum with a hangover before and found it mildly comical.

'So what shall we do today?' she asked now. 'We need to get down to the dining room for a start-off or they'll be finished serving.'

'Where's Mel?' Jess croaked as she pulled the duvet back over her head.

'She's in the shower. I've already had one and I'm all dressed too.'

'All right then, I can take a hint. Buzz off and I'll get up.'

A hot shower, three glasses of bottled water and two Paracetamol tablets later, Jess felt almost human again and they were downstairs in the hotel dining room by nine.

Glancing about as a waiter ushered them to a table, Jess wondered if Emile would be there and was relieved when she couldn't see him. She felt strangely embarrassed about the way she had knocked the drinks back in his company the night before and was sure he must think she always behaved like that.

Jo tucked into her meal as if she hadn't eaten for a month and even though Mel didn't eat half as much, Jess was pleased to see that she made an effort at least. She herself stuck to fruit juice and a yogurt, and was relieved when they could leave the restaurant to return to their rooms.

'Now wrap up warmly,' she advised them. 'It's cool out there.'

The girls did as they were told then they all trooped down to the foyer armed once again with their cameras.

'I think we'll hop on the tour bus,' Jess told them as they stepped out into the chilly air. 'That way we can get on and off as we like. Where would you like to go first?'

'The Eiffel Tower,' Jo whooped excitedly.

'Right, according to the concierge I just asked, there's a stop just up here,' Jess said, peering at her street map. It was as they rounded the corner that she saw Emile standing at the stop and her heart sank.

'Good morning, ladies,' he greeted them jovially as he saw them approaching. 'It would appear that great minds think alike. You are taking the bus tour, yes?'

Jo nodded. 'Yes, and we're going to see the Eiffel Tower first.'

'How extraordinary, that is just what I was planning on doing. Would you mind very much if I tagged along with you? It is so much more fun seeing places if you have company.'

Jess's stomach turned over but she kept her smile fixed firmly in place as they all joined Emile at the bus stop.

In no time at all he and Jo were chattering away as if they had known each other for years, and even Mel was occasionally chipping in with the odd remark. Jess sighed resignedly as they all boarded the bus. She would much have preferred it to be just herself and the girls, but now that Emile had latched on to them she supposed she would just have to make the best of it.

# Chapter Seventeen

Despite Jess's apprehension the day flew by and everyone thoroughly enjoyed themselves. They spent the morning in the Eiffel Tower and even Mel got excited about the panoramic views from the top of it. Jo was like a fountain of knowledge and happily spouted all about its history, facts that she had learned at school. Jess wasn't particularly interested in discovering how many rivets it had taken to erect it, or even about the forty tons of paint it had taken to paint it, but even so she smiled indulgently, pleased to see Jo enjoying herself. Emile and the girls seemed to be getting along famously.

They all had lunch in a little café in one of the many tree-lined boulevards, by which time Jo was already planning what they should do that afternoon. Eventually they boarded the tour bus again and set off to visit the Concorde and Vendome Squares, where Jo snapped away furiously with her camera, determined to take as many photographs as she possibly could. The girls were both keen to see all the sights, and Jess didn't mind. It was so nice to see Mel smiling again that it was worth having sore feet.

By the time they arrived back at the hotel in the early evening, Jess was tired but Jo and Mel were still raring to go.

'What shall we do tonight?' Jo asked expectantly as Jess eased her trainers off. They had walked for miles and she had discovered that she wasn't as fit as she had thought she was. No doubt she would be as stiff as a board the next morning.

'Well, before we decide on that, I'm going to have a nice long soak in the bath and see if I can get through to your dad on the phone,' Jess replied.

At the mention of Simon, Mel frowned and so Jess hurried on, 'I hope he's eating properly and not working too hard.'

'Oh, he'll be fine,' Jo chirped airily as she gazed from the window. 'I'm going for a shower.' She skipped away, closely followed by Mel who dropped onto one of the beds in their room and flipped the TV on.

Now that she had a moment alone, Jess quickly lifted the phone and dialled home, but once again the call was directed to the answer machine.

'Damn,' Jess cursed softly as she then tried Simon's mobile number, but again she was put through to voicemail. 'Hello, Simon, it's me,' she said, deciding to leave a message. 'I was just ringing to check you are OK. We're all having a great time, the girls are loving it. We've been to the Eiffel Tower today. Could you ring me on my mobile? Bye for now.'

She placed the phone down and sighed heavily before heading off for the bath.

She came back into the lounge half an hour later rubbing her damp hair on one of the thick fluffy towels, which were all embroidered in one corner with a golden cat, and wearing the soft dressing-gown that the hotel had provided, finding the girls curled up on the settee watching the TV in there. She was feeling refreshed and was just about to ask the girls where they would like to eat, when Mel's mobile phone rang.

Mel took it out of the pocket of her jeans and flipped it open. 'Hello?' Her face set into grim lines as she listened to whoever was on the other end. 'Yes,' she muttered tersely in reply to whoever was speaking, and unable to contain her curiosity, Jess mouthed, 'Who is it?'

'It's Dad,' Mel replied flatly.

'Oh!' Jess was mildly surprised that Simon had chosen to ring Mel rather than her, but even so she reached for the phone eagerly. 'May I have a word with him?'

Mel grunted something inaudible in reply and passed her the phone without argument.

'Hello, love. How are you?' she asked.

'I'm fine,' Simon assured her. 'And it sounds like you lot are having a whale of a time if your message is anything to go by.'

'We are,' Jess assured him. 'But I wish you were here too. Is everything all right at home?'

'Of course it is. You're only gone for five days, you know,' Simon replied with a hint of amusement in his voice. 'Alfie is pining a bit, and I think Beth is missing you all too. She's been moping about here like a bitch that's lost its puppy. I don't think she understands the concept of time, so although I've told her you won't be gone for long she's still missing you all.'

'I miss her too . . . and you.' Jess was desperately aware of the girls

133

listening in and flushed with embarrassment as Jo giggled behind her hand.

'Right, well, I won't keep you. This call is costing a fortune,' Simon said, practical as ever. 'Be careful what you get up to and have a great time and I'll see you on Friday.' The phone went dead in her hand and Jess handed it back to Mel feeling vaguely irritated with herself. She had forgotten to ask him why he had rung Mel and not her. But then she supposed with how bad things were between the two of them he had probably just been trying to soften Mel up, which was no bad thing.

Jo was like a cat on hot bricks again now, keen to go out and enjoy herself.

'Is Emile coming out to dinner with us this evening?' she asked as Jess headed back to her room to get changed.

'No, why should he be? It was only a coincidence that we happened to bump into him today.'

'Aw, that's a shame then. I like Emile,' Jo told her. 'He seems to know all the best places to go and see.'

'He would do, wouldn't he, if he used to live here?' Jess pointed out. 'But I'm sure we shall manage perfectly well by ourselves.'

She glanced at Mel who had changed into baggy jeans and a T-shirt that looked at least two sizes too big for her. She had a lovely selection of new clothes that Jess had bought her for her birthday but always seemed to favour things that swamped her slight frame.

'So, do you want to eat in the restaurant here again or go out?' she asked the girls twenty minutes later when she had dried her hair and changed into trousers and a smart new red jumper.

'I think I'd like to eat here again,' Jo told her promptly.

Normally, Jess would have cringed as the hotel restaurant was quite expensive. But what the hell, she thought. We're only here for another three nights so we may as well spoil ourselves.

After dinner, which was just as delicious as it had been the evening before, they wrapped up warmly and went for a walk along the banks of the River Seine. The golden leaves that had fallen from the trees crunched beneath their feet as they passed couples holding hands and staring into each other's eyes. Jess could well understand why Paris had been nicknamed the City of Lovers. With the myriad lights sparkling off the water it was very romantic and she once more thought of Simon all alone at home. *If he is alone*, a little voice inside her head whispered, but she pushed the thought away.

\* \* \*

134

Tuesday passed in a blur. They visited the Louvre and saw Leonardo Da Vinci's masterpiece, the *Mona Lisa*, and the Ancient Greek sculpture of *Venus de Milo*. They also went to see the *Winged Victory*, which had been painstakingly put back together after being found in 118 pieces on a hillside on a small island called Samothrace in the Aegean Sea. They then went to view the transparent pyramid in the courtyard of the Louvre before wandering in the Tuileries Gardens. Jo was beside herself with excitement at finally seeing all the works of art that they had been talking about at school and took so many photographs that she made Jess feel dizzy.

They got back to the hotel slightly earlier that afternoon and as they were walking through the foyer they saw Emile studying a brochure on one of the smart leather settees that were dotted here and there.

'Emile,' Jo called as she hurried across to him. 'We've had the most wonderful day.' She immediately launched into an account of all they had done as Emile smiled at her. 'And what are you looking at there?' she finished breathlessly as Jess stared at her in exasperation.

He glanced at Jess with a hint of amusement in his eyes before telling her, 'I am looking at the Night Illumination Tour. I thought I might go on it this evening. Sadly, I have to return to England on Thursday, so like you I am trying to fit in as many sights as I can.'

'Wow! Can we go on it too, Mum? Please!' Jo breathed.

'I er . . . I'm sure Mr Lefavre wouldn't want us trailing along,' Jess said quietly, feeling desperately embarrassed.

'Nonsense. On the contrary – I would enjoy your company,' he told her. 'It is so much more fun to see places of interest if you have someone to share it with.'

Feeling that she had no alternative but to go along with the plans without looking unreasonable, Jess said politely, 'All right then. If you're quite sure you don't mind.'

And so it was decided. The evening actually turned out to be a great success and when they returned to the hotel they were all in fine high spirits.

'So what shall we do tomorrow?' Jo asked before they had even had a chance to reach the lift.

Emile grinned. 'I am going to visit the Cathedral of Notre Dame.'

'I've seen a film about that. Quasimodo, a poor hunchback, lived in the belltowers there. He fell in love with a beautiful girl called

135

Esmeralda but she didn't love him because he was so ugly,' Mel piped up unexpectedly.

Jess couldn't stop herself from smiling. Little by little, Mel was coming out of her shell again and was much more like her old self with every hour that passed. She had even laughed a few times today, which Jess took as a good sign.

'Oh, Mum, *please* can we go too?' Jo pleaded, wringing her hands dramatically.

'Of course we can, if Emile doesn't mind.'

'I would be delighted to have the enchanting company of three such beautiful ladies again,' he assured her, and then to Jess's mortification he caught her hand and kissed it softly. '*À demain* – until tomorrow,' he grinned before heading off for the bar.

Jo tittered. 'I reckon he fancies you, Mum.'

'Don't be so silly,' Jess said, going red. 'All Frenchmen do that. It's just like an Englishman shaking hands, that's all.'

'If you say so,' Jo shot back cheekily and then she launched herself into the lift out of the way of Jess's flailing hand.

The next morning, Jess found Notre Dame was just as beautiful as she'd expected, and realised that she was beginning to feel at home in Paris. Emile was his usual excellent company, and it was clear that the two girls had really taken to him.

'Whereabouts in Paris did you used to live with your parents?' Jess asked him curiously as they strolled along the rue de Rivoli.

She watched a flicker of sadness flare in his eyes as memories poured back.

'We lived in an apartment on the Left Bank on the Rue de Grenelle. Whenever I think of it now I remember the smell of coffee and fresh croissants, and my mother's perfume.' He smiled ruefully. 'My mother was a wonderful cook and was always experimenting with new recipes. She and my father were very much in love, to the point that sometimes I felt in the way, not that they deliberately set out to make me feel like that. In fairness they were very good parents and I never wanted for anything. But I often wonder if I was a mistake. You know – surplus to their requirements? They sent me away to boarding school when I was ten years old and most of my school holidays were spent in England with my aunt.'

Jess felt sorry for him as she then asked softly, 'And have you never been married?'

He shook his head. 'No. I have come close to it a couple of times.

Once when I was at university and once with a young teacher at the school where I work. But when it came down to getting committed, I backed out. I suppose I just haven't met the right person yet.' He grinned cheekily at her then. 'I think all the best ones are already spoken for.'

Jess blushed furiously. 'Well, you're still very young. There's plenty of time,' she told him like an old maiden aunt.

He laughed aloud, making Jo and Mel peer round to see what the joke was.

'You must have been very young when you got married,' he said, solemn now.

'I suppose I was really. It seems like a lifetime ago. I shall be thirty-three next birthday.' She said it as if that was some great milestone.

'Then you still have a long way to go before you get a telegram from your Queen,' he teased her. 'I shall be thirty myself this year.'

Jess was glad now that they had met Emile. He certainly seemed to have perked Mel up, and Jess had even heard her laugh on a number of occasions during the day. But then she supposed that being a teacher, Emile was used to talking to young people and knew how to put them at ease. If only Simon had the same talent. Then Stonebridge House might not feel like such a battlefield all the time.

Her thoughts were pulled back to the present when Emile next asked, 'And whereabouts did you say you lived?'

'Actually we recently moved into an old house and over the last few months I've been trying to restore it to its former glory. My grandmother died and left me a considerable sum of money, and looking back I suppose I bought the house on a whim,' Jess admitted. 'It was really strange when we went to view it because from the second I set foot through the door I felt as if I belonged there.' She smiled self-consciously. 'I have to admit I didn't realise the amount of work we were taking on. Simon wasn't too keen on the place from day one, so I think I bullied him into living there really. Mel wasn't happy about the move either. Not long after we moved in I came across an old journal that had been written by Martha Reid, a young maid who used to work there, and it's absolutely intriguing. The house has quite a dramatic history and every time I read an entry I feel as if I've gone back in time.' Jess felt that she was talking too much. 'That's partly why I fell in love with the place, because of its history. But there you are . . . we all make mistakes and I wouldn't want to leave it now until I've done what I set out to do.'

137

Emile looked interested. 'I love places with history attached to them. And you may find that by the time you've done all the renovations, everyone will love the place as much as you do.'

'I can always live in hope,' Jess muttered and then she lapsed into silence until they drew to a halt outside the hotel.

'And what were you planning to do this evening?' Emile asked as they all strolled into the foyer.

Jess grinned as she nodded towards Jo, who was yawning widely. 'If that's anything to go by I think we might order a meal to be brought to our rooms and have a quiet night. I have a feeling that this little lady is going to go out like a light.'

He nodded in agreement. 'I think you may be right, but should you get bored, come to the cocktail bar on the top floor and I will be happy to buy you a drink.'

'Thank you.' She smiled at him although she had no intentions of taking him up on his offer, then she ushered the girls towards the lift and they made their way upstairs.

Just as Jess had predicted, Jo ate her meal and promptly fell fast asleep curled up on the settee in the lounge. Mel helped her mother to get her tucked into bed then yawned herself.

'I think I might turn in myself if you don't mind, Mum,' she said.

Jess swallowed her disappointment. She had been hoping for a chance to have a heart-to-heart with Mel once Jo was asleep. But it didn't look like that was going to happen again now, and the holiday was going so well that she didn't want to spoil it.

'All right, love. Sweet dreams.' She smiled as she pecked Mel on the cheek and then turned the TV on and began to flick aimlessly through the channels as the evening stretched ahead of her.

# Chapter Eighteen

At ten o'clock, Jess finally gave in to temptation and got dressed. She put on a smart pair of black trousers and high heels, and topped the look off with a sparkly Lurex top she had bought on impulse. She doubted very much if it would ever see the light of day, or night for that matter, again, once she got home, but it felt just right for this particular evening. She carefully applied her make-up and brushed her hair till it shone, leaving it loose about her shoulders. And then after checking on the girls and leaving a note telling them where she was in case they woke up she picked up her bag and headed for the top floor. Emile would be gone by this time tomorrow night, so where was the harm in having one last drink with him?

She spotted him instantly sitting on a high stool by the window with a cocktail in his hand. 'We've Only Just Begun' by the Carpenters was softly playing in the background as she made her way over to him.

'Hello. I thought I'd take you up on your offer of a drink, after all,' she told him as she drew level.

His face lit up when he saw her. 'Jess! Why, how wonderful! Come and sit down and I'll go and get you one of their special cocktails.'

'Very well, but I insist on paying this time.' She handed him some euros.

As Emile hurried to the bar she slid onto the stool next to his feeling like a teenager on her first date. But that's quite absurd, she scolded herself. They were just two adult acquaintances about to share a drink together. What was so wrong with that? She would probably never see Emile again after tonight and that would be the end of it.

He came back to her with some weird and wonderful concoction in his hand and she grinned.

'I don't suppose this is non-alcoholic, is it?'

'I'm afraid not. It is called *Nuits de Paris* – Paris Nights – and it is truly delicious,' Emile assured her.

He was right and before she knew it Jess was sipping her second one.

'Have you thought any more about some private tuition for Mel?' he asked after a while.

She shook her head. 'No, I haven't to be honest. And anyway I would have to ask Simon how he felt about it before I agreed to anything.'

'Of course.' He fiddled in his wallet and handed her a card. 'If you do decide to go ahead, you can reach me on that number.'

After jamming it into her purse she smiled her thanks before gazing out of the window again. The view from up here was panoramic, and she could see for miles. In the distance the River Seine twinkled in the moonlight and she was suddenly glad that she had decided to come here. It was a sight that she knew she would never forget.

'So what are you planning on doing tomorrow?' he asked her now.

'The girls want to visit Versailles,' Jess said. 'They also wanted to go to the Moulin Rouge but I put my foot down on that one. Perhaps if we ever come again when they're both a little older.'

'I think you could be right,' he agreed. 'But it is sad that you did not get to go there. The Moulin Rouge has been the home of the French Cancan for over a century. It is quite a spectacular sight and not one to be missed. I don't suppose I could tempt you to come with me right now, could I?'

Jess was shocked. 'But what about the girls? I couldn't just leave them all alone. And wouldn't we be too late for the show?'

'I know the hotel has a babysitting service you could use and we would just about catch the last show if we were to hurry.' As he spoke he was glancing at the expensive Rolex on his wrist and Jess was sorely tempted. She had been told by numerous people that the show was amazing. And after all, she tried to convince herself, when would she ever get this chance again?

'All right then.' She couldn't believe she had agreed to it, but was excited all at the same time. 'But only if you allow me to buy my own ticket.' She had heard that it was very expensive, but what the hell! They drained their glasses and hurried down to the reception, where Jess arranged a sitter for the girls and in no time at all they were in a taxi and on their way, and delighted to find there were a couple of vacant seats.

As they sat sipping their complimentary glasses of champagne, a troupe of over a hundred dancers appeared onstage, dressed in exotic costumes adorned with rhinestones, feathers and numerous sequins. The show's sumptuous sets included moving staircases, swings and a garden setting, as well as a giant aquarium that provided a brilliant backdrop for the beautifully choreographed cabaret.

Jess was completely entranced, and when the show was over, she clapped until she felt her hands would drop off.

'Are you glad you went now?' Emile asked as their taxi crawled its way back through the traffic to the hotel.

'Oh *yes*!' Jess said. 'I can't remember when I've enjoyed myself so much. I suppose I've led a very sheltered life really. I got married very young and had Mel, and ever since then my life has revolved around my girls and my home.'

'They are a credit to you,' he told her sincerely. 'I'm quite envious of you in a way. It must be nice to have your own family.'

Hearing the sadness in his voice, she glanced at him from the corner of her eye.

'You are very pensive,' Emile remarked.

She forced a smile. 'Oh, I was just thinking, that's all. Life is a funny thing, isn't it?'

He nodded in agreement. 'It certainly is.'

When they arrived back at the hotel she thanked Emile for a wonderful evening and went immediately back to her suite, where she found the girls still sleeping like babies. She thanked the sitter, who was dozing in the chair, and gave her a tip and then on a sudden urge she rang home – but once again the call was unanswered so she got ready for bed and slept like a log until morning.

Emile was waiting for them all in the foyer the next morning. His plane wasn't flying out until later that evening, so she had guessed that he would choose to visit Versailles with them. Afterwards, everyone agreed that the trip was the highlight of their holiday. To Jess's delight, everything from the guided tour to the food was perfect, and Mel seemed more relaxed than ever. As they finally boarded the coach to go back to the hotel, Jo told Emile sadly, 'I wish you didn't have to go home tonight. Will we ever see you again?'

'I hope so, *ma petite*,' he answered. 'I have enjoyed being in your company so very much. It would have been a very lonely break for me, had we not all met.'

Jess could scarcely believe how quickly the time had passed. They would be flying home themselves tomorrow, and then it would be back to school and to work on the house.

'What time will you be leaving for the airport?' Jo asked.

Emile glanced at his watch. 'In about an hour, so I ought to go and get my packing done.'

The coach had stopped outside the hotel now and they all trooped into the foyer.

'May Mel and I come down to say goodbye to you before you leave?' Jo asked him.

He ruffled her hair affectionately. 'That would be very nice.' He then turned to Jess and held out his hand. 'I shall say my goodbyes to you now. It has been a pleasure to be in your company.'

Jess shook his hand warmly. 'Thank you, and it was nice to meet you too. Goodbye. Safe journey.'

As she and the girls made for the lift she realised that Emile had acted like a perfect gentleman for the whole of the time she had been in his company. He had never once tried to push their relationship beyond friendship and she was glad of that fact, because a little part of her knew deep down that had he done so, she just might have been tempted. He was an extremely attractive man, after all. But then she was a married woman and three whole years older than him anyway. Grinning to herself she led the girls to their rooms. It was time she started a little packing of her own. They would be heading for the airport straight after breakfast the next day and she didn't want to leave everything until the last minute.

An hour later both girls went down to the foyer to say goodbye to Emile and after a while Jo returned alone.

'Where's Mel?' Jess demanded, instantly flying into a panic. As lovely as Paris was, it was no place for a fourteen-year-old girl to be wandering about on her own.

'It's all right, Mum. She's just having a mooch around the hotel gift shop,' Jo told her.

Jess's heart slowed to a steadier rhythm. 'Oh, that's all right then – just so long as she doesn't get going off.'

Mel appeared fifteen minutes later clutching her purse and the small flight bag with her personals in that she'd bought on the plane.

'Get anything nice, did you?' Jess asked cheerfully.

Mel shrugged. 'Not really. Just bits and bobs. A few souvenirs.' She then ducked into her bedroom and seconds later Jess heard the shower click on. Judging by the sullen look on Mel's face the good mood was going to end with the holiday, which was a shame. She'd been so much more like her old self over the last couple of days. But then as Jess was fast discovering, that was teenagers for you and there wasn't much she could do about it. Sighing, she returned to packing her case.

The next morning after breakfast they all went back to their suite to do their last-minute packing.

'Mum, can I just pop down to the gift shop? I want to get something for Dad,' Jo said. She was not looking forward to going home and had made no secret of the fact. Jess was sure she would have stayed for at least another month if she'd had the chance.

'All right then,' she said. 'But only if Mel will go with you. I should be finished here by the time you get back, but don't be too long. I've booked us a taxi to the airport and I have to settle up the bill.'

Jo turned to Mel who had her head stuck in a magazine. 'Will you come with me then, Mel? *Please?*'

With a martyred look on her face, Mel slung the magazine down and slouched towards the door, and within seconds they were gone.

Now Jess quickly checked that everything was done. There were just their toiletries left in the bathrooms to pack now and that would take no more than a few minutes to do. First she packed her own before heading for the en-suite that the girls had shared.

She took the girls' flight bags in with her and after packing Jo's things she then lifted Mel's bag and her toothbrush and toothpaste from the sink. It was as she was putting them inside that something caught her eye, tucked well down beneath Mel's iPod. It was a large carrier bag, and quite heavy by the looks of it. She supposed it would contain the things that Mel had bought from the gift shop the night before, and curious now, she lifted it out and peeped inside. As she did so, the colour drained from her face. The bag was full of tiny plastic wallets full of white powder.

Jess had never had anything to do with drugs in her whole life. They were the one thing she abhorred, and she had always told the girls that if they ever dabbled in them she would wash her hands of them for ever. And now here was her daughter's flight bag stuffed full of the damn stuff. But where could she have got it from? Mel had barely been out of her sight for the whole of the time they had been there . . . apart from when she had gone to say goodbye to Emile in the foyer the night before. Shock coursed through her as she sat down heavily on the toilet lid. *Emile!* He must have targeted them. And she had fallen for his charm hook, line and sinker when all he had wanted was a young vulnerable girl to smuggle this dreadful stuff back into England for him. No wonder

143

he had been so flush with cash for a humble teacher. She remembered the Rolex.

Tears threatened to choke her as she stared down at the wallets in her hand. Emile must have reasoned that the customs wouldn't look twice at a young girl on holiday with her mother and sister. She began to shake. What would have happened if she hadn't accidentally discovered them and Mel *had* been stopped? Just the thought of it made vomit rise in her throat. How would they have explained it away? '*Oh, I'm so sorry; I didn't know they were there*!' And how could Mel have been so *stupid* as to agree to do this for him? But then he had been very charming, and Mel was a young impressionable girl. She wouldn't have realised how serious it was, what he was asking her to do.

Anger began to take the place of the shock. She didn't have a clue as to what sort of drugs they were, but she didn't need to be a member of the Drugs Squad to recognise them as such. And now what was she going to do with them? There was no way she was going to let Mel go through with trying to smuggle them out of France. Her first reaction was to ring for the hotel manager and show him what she had found, but she dismissed that idea almost instantly. If she did that, the manager would send for the police and the three of them would undoubtedly be detained and miss their flight back to England.

It was then that she heard the door to their suite of rooms open and she dropped the bag as if it had burned her as she raced into the lounge. If it was a maid she would have to get rid of her somehow until she had spoken to Mel.

Relief flowed through her veins like iced water when she saw Jo excitedly holding up a plastic model of the Eiffel Tower.

'Look what I got for Dad, Mum. Do you think he'll like it?' she bubbled.

'Er . . . yes, I'm sure he will. Mel, will you come in here, please?'

Mel looked vaguely uneasy as she stepped through the door her mother was holding open. And then once it was closed behind her, Jess rounded on her furiously, her eyes flashing fire. She caught her by the arm and dragged her into the bathroom before stabbing her finger at the bag.

'I think you've got some explaining to do, don't you, madam? Just what the *hell* is this – and where did you get it?'

The colour drained out of Mel's face like water out of a dam as she lowered her head and stared at the floor.

'Well?' Jess realised that she was screeching like a banshee but she couldn't seem to stop herself. What had begun as a wonderful break for them all had suddenly turned into a nightmare. Taking Mel by the shoulders, she shook her roughly. She had never so much as laid a finger on either of her girls before but she had to do something to make Mel understand the seriousness of the situation.

'It was Emile who gave you these and asked you to get them into England, wasn't it?' she choked as Mel's head rolled from side to side.

'No, it wasn't,' Mel cried as she shook herself free, and she then folded her arms and remained stubbornly silent.

'Oh, you must think I've fallen off a Christmas tree.' Jess tipped the wallets onto the floor, appalled to see how many of them there were. 'I'm not stupid, you know. Who else could have given you these? *Answer* me, Mel.'

Still Mel refused to speak and now Jess ran her hands through her hair, totally distraught. And it was then that an idea occurred to her and, quickly lifting the toilet lid, she began to flush the wallets away a few at a time. There was no other way she could think of to get rid of them, and she could hardly leave them in their rooms. If she did there was no doubt the police would be after them before they even got as far as the airport. She was torn between fury with Mel for being so stupid and for refusing to confide in her, and her anger at whoever had pushed her girl into doing this.

'What are you doing?' Mel whimpered as tears began to flow down her cheeks.

'What does it look like I'm doing,' Jess snapped back. 'You don't really think I'm going to allow you to try and take these through customs, do you? You're fourteen now – old enough to be criminally responsible for your actions. If they catch you with this lot, they'll lock you away!'

'Is everything all right in there?' Jo's worried voice wafted from the other side of the door and Jess tried to sound calm as she shouted, 'Yes, love. You go and watch TV for a while. Everything's fine.'

Jess systematically continued with what she was doing, flushing away four or five of the little plastic wallets at a time as Mel's wails grew louder. At last it was done and all that was left was the plastic carrier bag that had contained the drugs. There was no way that this would flush down the loo but Jess tucked it well down in the small rubbish bin in the corner of the room. There was nothing conspicuous about it, so hopefully the maids would simply throw it away with the rest of the rubbish when they came to clean the rooms.

145

She would have liked to interrogate Mel further but was painfully aware that the time was slipping away. They would have to leave now, or they would miss their flight and suddenly she just wanted to be home.

'Come on, get your things ready,' she told Mel shakily. 'But don't think this is the end of it, young lady; not by a long shot! It makes my blood run cold to think what might have happened to you, if I hadn't found those things.'

# Chapter Nineteen

It was a relief for Jess when they eventually boarded the plane and she could finally have time to think. Mel and Jo were sitting together in the seats in front of her as the flight attendant went through the safety precautions with the passengers. Jess didn't hear a word of it; she simply mechanically buckled her seat belt and stared out of the window at the runway as her mind raced ahead. What was she going to do? She couldn't just let this go. And what would Simon say when he found out? He would probably lock Mel in her room and throw away the key. Things had been bad enough between Mel and her father before the holiday, without this.

The phone number that Emile had given her was still tucked away in her bag, and now Jess cursed herself for a fool. No wonder he had wanted to keep in touch. He would want to collect his drugs. Jess's first instinct had been to ring him and tell him what a lowlife she thought he was, but that might have been asking for trouble. He wasn't going to be happy when he discovered that the drugs he had given to Mel had been flushed down the toilet. She couldn't even begin to imagine how much the drugs had been worth, and beneath her anger was a knot of fear about what the consequences of flushing them away might be, although hopefully there would be nothing he could do about it. He would be too afraid of Jess informing the police of what he had done. Or would he? There was no evidence now, so it would be her word against his. And if she told Simon, she would also have to explain why they had spent the majority of their time in Paris in the company of a handsome Frenchman, and she could only assume that he wouldn't be too happy about that.

All the way back her mind chopped from one idea to another, but by the time the plane was coming in to land she was no further towards knowing what to do for the best.

When they had gone through customs and were waiting to collect their cases she pulled Mel to one side and hissed, 'Not one word of what has happened to your father, do you understand? I'm not sure what we should do about it yet, so it's best to say nothing until I do. But don't think you've got away with this, Mel. This is far from over, I assure you. I just can't believe you could have been so stupid!'

Mel looked away from the anger and fear in her mother's eyes as their cases appeared on the conveyor belt. Jess yanked them off and after pushing one unceremoniously towards Mel she growled, 'Come along. Your dad will be waiting for us.'

Once outside in the bitterly cold wind they glanced this way and that but there was no sign of Simon. Normally Jess wouldn't have minded waiting for a few minutes, but today she wasn't in the best of humours.

'That man will be late for his own funeral,' she grumbled as she stamped her feet to keep warm. Sensing that her mum was not in the best of moods, Jo wisely said nothing.

Simon appeared twenty minutes later, and Jess saw that Beth was with him.

'Sorry I'm late, love,' he apologised. 'I got caught up on a job and while I was at home changing to come and collect you, young Beth here turned up and asked if she could come along too. Have you all had a good time?' He pecked Jess perfunctorily on the cheek as Jo immediately began to tell him about all the places they had seen as they followed him back to the car park.

Jess was actually glad of her chatter, it gave her time to compose herself and put her thoughts into some sort of order. The afternoon was darkening as they pulled into the long drive leading to Stonebridge House and Jess was glad to be home. One thing was for sure; it would be a very long time before she took Mel away again after the stupid stunt she had almost pulled. Had she not come across the drugs, Mel might be under interrogation by the Customs and Excise Department at this very moment. Jess came out in goosebumps and she felt nauseous again. As soon as they entered the kitchen Mel shot off upstairs whilst Jo disappeared into the garden with Alfie and Beth.

'So,' said Simon as he filled the kettle at the sink. 'After all that coffee they serve you over there I dare say you'll be dying for a decent cuppa now, won't you? How did it go?'

'It was very nice,' she answered quietly.

Simon raised his eyebrows. 'Just very *nice*, after all the money it cost? I expected you to come back full of it.'

'I probably will be later on,' she replied weakly. 'But I've got this

148

rotten headache at the moment. In fact, I think I'll cancel that tea for now if you don't mind and go and have a lie-down.'

Upstairs, Jess quickly undressed and slipped into her warm dressing-gown before crossing to the window. She could see Beth and Jo frolicking on the lawn with Alfie, and tears pricked at her eyes. Now that she had calmed down a little she realised that most of what had happened had been her fault. If she hadn't encouraged Emile's advances, he would never have been able to get to Mel, and she was sorry now that she had ever set eyes on him. He had seemed such a genuinely nice person, but then she knew that most conmen usually were. He had probably been sitting in that restaurant that evening just waiting for some unsuspecting female to appear with a youngster he could twist around his little finger, and like a fool she had fallen straight into his lap. She might as well have served Mel up to him on a plate.

Dropping onto the bed, she placed a hand across her eyes. She hadn't been lying when she'd told Simon she had a headache. It had probably been brought on by all the stress and suddenly she was so tired she could barely keep her eyes open. *I'll just rest for ten minutes*, she promised herself, *and then I'll start the unpacking*, and that was the last thing she remembered.

The sound of crying woke her some time later, and when her eyes snapped open she found herself in darkness. The wind was howling outside and rain was lashing against the window. Rising quickly, she put the lamp on before venturing out onto the landing where she paused to listen. The sound was coming from Mel's room. Before she could reach the door, it opened and Simon appeared, his face twisted with anger.

He stabbed a finger towards the door. 'I thought she might come back in a slightly better mood but I suppose that would have been asking too much. I just took her a cup of tea in and tried to be pleasant, and all I got for my trouble was a mouthful of abuse. I'm telling you, Jess, I've just about had it with that spoiled little bitch. She needs taking down a peg or two.'

Despite what had happened Jess found herself rushing to Mel's defence just as she always did.

'She's probably just tired after the flight,' she told him, her eyes flashing. 'Why don't you just lay off her for a while, Simon? I think you just make her moods worse. You don't seem to have any idea how to handle a teenager.'

'Oh, that's just *great* coming from you, that is.' Simon threw his hands in the air. 'Her mood swings are all *my* fault now, are they? Well, I'll leave her to you in future then. I'm off out.'

'Where are you going?'

'To the pub. Do I have to clock out?'

Jess watched him storm off down the stairs. Some homecoming this was turning out to be. She arrived downstairs just in time to hear the Land Rover accelerate out of the courtyard. Normally after a row with Simon she would be in floods of tears, but tonight she was so emotionally drained that she felt nothing.

It was as she was sitting there that someone tapped on the back door and Laura poked her head round it with a broad smile on her face.

'Hello, I thought I'd just pop in and see how the holiday went. I'm not disturbing you, am I? If you're tired I can come back in the morning.'

'Don't be so daft, of course you're not disturbing me,' Jess chided. 'Come on in. I was just about to have a coffee. I think I must have got the taste for it in Paris. Do you fancy one?'

'Yes, please.' Laura took her coat off, hung it over the back of a chair and sat down. 'Brr, it's enough to freeze you out there,' she said with a shudder as Jess put the kettle on. 'But come on – tell me all about your break.'

'There's not that much to tell really,' Jess replied cagily. 'We just did the usual things sightseers do.'

'Oh.' Laura looked mildly surprised. She had expected Jess to be full of it. She knew she certainly would have been if she'd just come back from Paris.

'And what about the girls? Did they enjoy it?'

'Yes, I think they did.' Jess kept her head lowered as she spooned instant coffee and sugar into two mugs. She was bursting to confide in someone about what had happened with Mel but was too afraid to, at least until she had decided what to do about it. She still hadn't worked out whether she should confide in Simon or not, and if she were to tell Laura and him only afterwards, that could make things even worse than they already were. And so she remained silent as she made the coffee and carried the mugs to the table.

'Something is wrong, isn't it?' Laura gazed at her seriously. 'Is it something to do with Simon? I just passed him haring off down the drive like a boy racer.'

When Jess didn't answer, she went on, 'I'm sorry. I'm sticking my nose in where it isn't wanted. Just ignore me.'

150

'No, it's all right.' Jess knew that Laura was only trying to help, but at this moment in time she was so confused she didn't know if anyone could. 'To tell the truth, Simon and I had a bit of a row over Mel, and as usual he's gone off to seek solace in the bottom of a pint glass.'

'Oh, what a shame and on your first night home too.' Laura looked at her sympathetically and Jess couldn't help but notice how her neighbour's eyes kept flitting nervously about the room. She was just about to comment on it when Laura suddenly burst out, 'I think something really bad is about to happen. I can *feel* it.'

Shocked, Jess stared at her. 'What do you mean, something bad?'

Laura clutched her mug with both hands.

'I don't know. Bad things have happened here in the past. Really bad things – and there's more to come. I'm sorry, Jess – I don't mean to upset you, but you need to know.'

If what she had read in Martha's journal was true, Jess knew that Laura was right. Bad things *had* happened here – in the past – but it was her home now, and there was no way she was ready to leave it just yet.

'I sense there's a young woman standing over there in the corner and she's not happy,' Laura told her as she gazed over Jess's shoulder. 'It could be the young girl from the sketch in your room.'

Not so long ago, Jess would have scoffed at her but now strangely she wondered if Laura might be right. This had been Martha's home long before it had been hers, so perhaps Laura really could sense her there even if she couldn't.

'Can't you ask her what's wrong?' Jess breathed quietly.

'She won't tell me.' Laura was as pale as putty now and shaking, slopping coffee over the rim of her mug onto the table. Suddenly she exclaimed, 'She's gone!'

'Perhaps I should start charging her rent,' Jess said, trying to lighten the atmosphere.

Laura gave a lopsided grin. 'Perhaps you should. But now where were we?' She was clearly badly shaken by whatever she had sensed, or thought she had sensed, and was desperate to get back to more everyday matters.

'You were telling me that Simon had gone off in a strop. Well, between you and me, I haven't had the best of times with Beth while you've been away.'

'Really? But she's such a sweet kid and as innocent as a lamb,' Jess said in surprise.

'That's the problem. She's so naïve – a young woman with the mind of a child. She would be so easy to take advantage of and I'm worried sick about her. I have to say though, that since your family moved here she's come out of her shell tremendously. She adores your Jo and Simon. In fact, we couldn't keep her away from here last week while you were gone. I think she missed you all and Simon was wonderful with her.'

'I know what you mean,' Jess sighed regretfully. 'I sometimes wish he could show as much patience to his own daughter. They just rub each other up the wrong way as soon as they look at each other. It's probably because they're so alike in temperament.'

The conversation then turned to the trip to Paris again and Jess told Laura about all the places they had visited until Laura rose and slid her arms back into her coat. 'I ought to be getting back now, else Den will be worrying about where I've got to. And I er . . . I'm sorry if I scared you earlier on.'

'You didn't scare me,' Jess admitted solemnly. 'To be honest, I'm beginning to wonder if there isn't something or someone here now, and the funny thing is, I've never believed in stuff like this before. But sometimes – I just get the feeling that I'm not alone, that someone is close by even when Simon and the girls are out.'

Laura squeezed Jess's arm wordlessly then slipped away.

Jess made herself another coffee and carried it up to bed. She felt so sorry for Laura as she recalled their conversation about Beth. Once more, it had put her situation into perspective. Of course, what Mel had done back in Paris was foolish and unforgivable, but she was young and bright and with time she would grow out of her moods and have a future in front of her, whereas Beth . . . Jess could well understand why her mother worried so much about her. There were unscrupulous men out there who would take advantage of her, given half a chance, and she knew that Laura would never stop worrying about her. She had formed the opinion long ago that Laura's husband Den left the parenting very much up to his wife. He was a nice man, but very quiet and unassuming. Now that she came to think about it, she doubted if she had met him more than half a dozen times in all the months she had lived there. It appeared that as long as he could go to work, come home and put his feet up, he was happy with his lot and she wondered if sometimes Laura didn't yearn for a little more out of life than just a special needs daughter and a pipe and slippers husband. Laura must have been really pretty when she was younger, and she was still a very attractive woman. And yet she barely left the house, and even when she did, she always had Beth in tow as if she was afraid to let her out of her sight. It was all very sad.

Hoping to take her mind off things she decided to read some more of Martha's journal. As she lifted it from the drawer she found herself smiling for the first time since she had discovered the drugs in Mel's bag that morning. She was shocked to find that the thought of Martha being here no longer frightened her. It was as if she had been blessed with her own guardian angel, if there were such things, and again she was keen to discover the next chapter in Martha's life.

*25 November*
Miss Melody sent for the doctor today. Granny has taken a turn for the worse and the Mistress has said she must stay in bed until she improves. Meantime Phoebe has taken over Granny's cooking and her chores in the kitchen . . .

'I'll take them up to her,' Polly offered as Martha loaded some broth and the potion the doctor had prescribed onto a tray for Granny. Polly was Miss Melody's maid and had joined the household shortly after Miss Prim. She was about the same age as Martha and the two girls were getting along famously. A small round girl with mousy brown hair, she was not the prettiest of creatures but her sunny personality more than made up for that. She was responsible for laundering all the young Mistress's gowns and keeping her rooms tidy, and like Miss Prim she was very fond of Miss Melody. She had certainly been a great help in looking after Granny who was not proving to be a good patient at all and complained endlessly about being confined to bed. Polly also had a knack of making Granny take her medicine whereas she would refuse it from the others.

'Here, take her one o' these up an' all,' Phoebe piped in. 'I know she's partial to a jam tart.' She loaded a tart fresh from the oven onto the tray as she spoke.

'Right you are, missus.' Lifting the tray, Polly disappeared through the green baize door.

'She's a nice girl, ain't she?' Phoebe commented. 'This place 'as certainly been a lot happier since the young Master an' Mistress arrived.'

Grace, who was sitting at the side of the fire on the wooden settle, working on a peg rug, nodded in agreement. Her ankles were badly swollen now that she was in the advanced stages of her pregnancy, but whenever she was forced to rest she spent every spare minute stitching curtains, cushions, rugs and bedclothes ready for her new home. 'It certainly has. And as for the young Mistress . . . it's thanks to her that Bertie an' me will have our very own home. It's comin' on a treat, though I don't get to see much o' me husband any more. He's too busy with the buildin' now, since they delivered the blue bricks. We've decided to call it Blue Brick Cottage once it's finished.'

'Do yer reckon it will be done fer when the baby comes?' Phoebe asked as she folded a pile of clean clothes.

'Oh no, I don't think there's any chance o' that, but I reckon we could be in fer next summer. Meantime we're managin' perfectly well where we are. How is your Joey now, by the way?'

'Eeh, that ointment the doctor prescribed fer his back 'as worked wonders,' Phoebe told her. 'It's cleared all the infections up, but the little soul will be scarred fer life, thanks to that cruel, wicked bugger.' She tossed her head in the direction of the main house and both Martha and Grace knew that she was referring to the Master.

Grace's face clouded. She still avoided Master Fenton whenever she could, and Bertie hated the man with a vengeance. Deliberately turning the conversation to happier things, she asked, 'How is Hal gettin' on at the mill?'

Phoebe's eyes twinkled. 'He loves it an' says everythin' is runnin' like clockwork again since the young Master took over. Seems his ribbon factory is doin' well an' all. He heard that the ribbons they're turnin' out now are so fine that some of 'em are bein' transported to Paris to trim the ladies' bonnets.'

Phoebe glanced towards Martha, who was busily sweeping the ashes from the hearth, and winking at Grace she commented, 'An' you seem chipper an' all, miss, since young Jimmy called to see the Mistress the other day.'

Martha blushed becomingly. 'She's given Jimmy an' me permission to walk out together,' she admitted. 'But he were so embarrassed. He were red as a beetroot. Miss Melody asked him if his intentions were honourable and he were so tonguetied all he could do was nod.' She chuckled at the memory. 'Then she told 'im that she expected 'im to behave wi' propriety. But when he'd left she called me back into the parlour an' told me that she thought Jimmy was a lovely, well-mannered young man an' gave me her permission to court him, so we won't 'ave to meet in secret any more fer fear of upsettin' the Master.'

154

Her face became solemn again now at mention of him. They all acknowledged that things had improved tenfold since the arrival of the young Master and Mistress, but *he* was still there, like a dark shadow in the background.

*3 December*
There is great excitement here in the lead up to Christmas. The decorators have been in yet again and the whole of the ground floor, along with all the bedrooms on the first floor, have been totally transformed. Huge wagonloads of brand new furniture have been delivered and everywhere looks wonderful . . .

'Oh, I shall never get these menus sorted out,' Melody sighed as she chewed on the end of the pencil. Leonard dropped a kiss on the top of her head as he passed the small desk where she was seated.

'I'm sure you will,' he assured her affectionately. 'I just hope that this party isn't going to prove to be too much for you. I don't want you overdoing it so close to your confinement. I wonder if we shouldn't perhaps have waited and had the party once the baby was born?'

'But I want it to go ahead,' she answered firmly. 'And I shall be quite all right. I'm so looking forward to Mama and Papa arriving, and I know all the staff are looking forward to meeting them too.'

Lord and Lady Longman, her parents, were due to arrive along with the other fifteen guests who had been invited on the day before Christmas Eve, and as Granny Reid reckoned that there had never been a Lord and Lady staying at Stonebridge before, the staff were all greatly excited at the prospect.

'Well, if you're quite sure that it isn't going to overtax you, then so be it,' Leonard agreed. He could never deny his wife anything and adored the very ground she walked on.

Now her face became mischievous as she giggled, 'Beside, I know Uncle is totally set against the idea of a party so I can't cancel it now.'

'Oh, you wicked woman,' he scolded. 'I sometimes think you take pleasure in tormenting him.'

'Well, you must admit, darling, he is very full of himself, not that he has cause to be, from what we have seen of it. If you hadn't stepped in when you did, I have no doubt he would have lost everything.'

Leonard nodded in silent agreement and lifting his copy of *The Times* he then became absorbed in the news whilst Melody battled with the Christmas Day menu. He had sent for yet more of their

155

servants from their Herefordshire home to help with the party, so Melody would only have to supervise. He actually found her attitude towards his uncle quite amusing at times. Master Fenton's lack of enthusiasm about the changes she was making to the house only made her tease him shamelessly, and for the majority of the time now he had taken to staying away from the place, only returning late at night to sleep. It was a fact that seemed to suit everyone very well.

Jess laid the book aside and stared about the room, and in her mind's eye she saw the house as it might have looked then. She could imagine the buzz of excitement as maids in their starched white aprons and mobcaps rushed here and there preparing for the guests, and the delicious smells that would have been issuing from the kitchen. For all she knew, this might be the very room that had been allocated to Lord and Lady Longman for the duration of their stay. Her eyes lingered on the wooden dado rails and the ornate plaster cornices that she'd had lovingly restored to their former glory. She was tempted to read on but her eyes were heavy now as the strain of the long day caught up with her. Normally she would not have been able to sleep soundly until she knew that Simon was home safe and sound. But tonight she was in no mood for his tantrums, so she turned off the light, snuggled beneath the duvet and in minutes was sleeping like a baby.

# Chapter Twenty

Simon had already left for work the next morning when Jess woke up. She knew he had been home because his work clothes were gone from the back of the chair and the clothes he had gone out in the night before were tossed in an untidy heap on the floor. The smell of bacon wafted up the stairs to her so after pulling her dressing-gown on she hurried down to the kitchen where she found Mel standing at the stove and Jo sitting at the table in her *High School Musical* pyjamas with her hair looking like a bird's nest.

'Mel is cooking me some breakfast, Mum,' Jo chirped brightly. 'Do you want her to do you some too?'

'I think I might manage a bacon sandwich.' It was a rare occasion when Mel bothered to cook anything and Jess wondered if she was trying to get back in her good books. Seating herself at the table she bent to tickle Alfie under the chin as she asked, 'Did either of you see your dad this morning before he left for work?'

'I didn't,' Jo told her as Mel flipped some rather overdone bacon onto her plate.

Mel didn't say anything but merely shook her head.

'Aw well, I dare say he's old and ugly enough to have gotten himself something to eat if he was hungry.'

Jo giggled as she tucked into her food and Jess poured herself a cup of tea from the pot on the table. It looked and tasted rather stewed but she didn't comment. If Mel was trying then she would too.

'Me and Alfie are going to call for Beth this morning and go for a walk along the river,' Jo told her later through a mouthful of toast and marmalade. Jess smiled indulgently as crumbs sprayed everywhere. Like most young people, Jo had very strange eating habits. Toast, marmalade and bacon were delicious but not eaten together as Jo was doing now. Still, she seemed to be enjoying it, so Jess wisely said nothing. She didn't bother to ask Mel what she had planned for the day, guessing that she wouldn't get an answer. In actual fact she had every intention of trying to talk to her today once Jo was safely out of the way. She just might be feeling a little more amenable now that she'd had a chance to think about what she'd almost done and what the consequences might have been.

Once Jo had cleared her plate she drained a large glass of milk then, wiping the back of her hand across her mouth, she set off towards the stairs door to get dressed as if she hadn't got a moment to live. And now at last she was alone with Mel, Jess seized the opportunity and asked quietly, 'And how are you feeling today?'

'I'm all right.' Mel fiddled with the handle of her mug.

'And are you prepared to tell me what's going on now?' Jess kept her voice deceptively light, praying that her daughter would confide in her.

When no answer was immediately forthcoming she pulled her handbag towards her and reached inside for her cigarettes. As her hand fumbled for them her fingers brushed against the card that Emile had given her in Paris and she withdrew them as if they had been scalded.

'Do you even begin to realise how serious it was, what you were going to do, Mel?'

Again only silence, so pushing her hair from her face Jess tried again. 'It was Emile who asked you to bring the drugs into the country for him, wasn't it? That's why you went off downstairs on your own the night before we left on the pretence of visiting the gift shop, wasn't it? So that he could hand them over.'

'NO!' Mel's head shot up and Jess saw colour burn into her cheeks.

'I'm not a fool, Mel. We scarcely spoke to anyone else but him the whole time we were there, so who else could it have been?'

'Look – just leave it can't you? You're always on at me! It's done now – and I'm sorry.' With that, the girl ran from the room as Jess lit up and puffed furiously on her cigarette. I handled that well, she thought wryly. But somehow she *would* get to the bottom of this mess. She was determined to, one way or another.

Jo appeared seconds later dressed for the outdoors with a big grin on her face, and Jess couldn't help but notice the difference between Jo and her sister. Nothing ever upset Jo for long whereas very little ever seemed to please Mel.

'Me and Alfie are going to call for Beth now,' she told her mother as Alfie sloped out of his basket to join her.

'That's fine, but be very careful. The river will be up with all the rain we've had and I don't want you falling in. You'd have no chance of getting out with that current,' Jess cautioned her. She felt as if she'd had quite enough dramas in her life over the last couple of days and didn't want to be faced with another one.

'We'll be careful,' Jo promised as she barged out of the back door with Alfie close behind her. Jess then flipped through a book of wall-paper samples to see if there was anything that caught her eye for the small lounge, but she discovered very quickly that she wasn't really concentrating, so she slammed the book shut and went upstairs to get dressed.

After a quick shower she decided to start sorting out the attic. When they had first moved in, Simon had expressed a wish to use the big room up there as his office, but he'd had neither the time nor the inclination recently to tackle it. *Well, it certainly ain't going to sort itself,* Jess told herself as she flipped on the overhead light in the gloomy room. *And perhaps if I make a start it will put me in his good books again.*

Hands on hips she gazed about at the masses of old packing cases and furniture, wondering where to start, and it was then that the overpowering smell of roses reached her. Instead of being afraid as she had been in the past, she smiled. Martha was close by, she could sense it. But why had she stayed here? Laura was insistent that Martha was worried about something to do with her.

'I know you're here,' she whispered to the empty room. 'And I wish I could talk to you.' She knew that Simon would think she had lost the plot if he could hear her, but she didn't care now. There was a mystery to solve and somehow she was going to solve it. She wandered about, peering at the old-fashioned sideboards and chairs. Some of them were lovely and she decided she would get Simon and his workmen to carry them downstairs so that she could take a closer look at them when he had the time. Some of them might be worth restoring; the rest could go to an antique shop or to the council tip. They were certainly too heavy for her to move on her own, so now she turned her attention to the chests. The last time she had started rooting around up here she had found Martha's journal and she wondered what she might find this time.

After a few minutes, however, Jess realised that she was still too worked up and worried about what had happened in Paris with Mel to fully concentrate on anything. She was still no nearer to knowing what to do about it. Walking towards the attic window she peered out across the rolling lawns just in time to see Jo haring towards the house with her hair flying out behind her and Alfie and Beth following.

Frowning, Jess hurried downstairs and arrived in the kitchen at the same time as Jo did. She saw at a glance that the child was breathless and excited about something, and waited while she clutched her side and got her breath back to tell her.

'There's some gypsy caravans on our land down by the river,' Jo gulped eventually, wildly gesticulating in that direction. 'An' Dad just got home and saw them and now he's down there rowing with them.'

'Oh no.' Jess groaned. She knew what Simon was like when he lost his temper. 'Just hold on while I get my coat and my wellies on and I'll come back there with you.'

In seconds they were all chasing across the lawn again and just as Jo had said, after a couple of minutes the caravans came into sight. She could see Simon wildly flailing his arms about in front of a large red-faced man who looked just as angry as Simon was. They were shouting at each other, and her heart sank. When Simon got into a temper, things could get out of hand, and this situation looked dangerously as if it might end with fists flying.

'Simon!'

He stopped shouting when he heard her cry out and turned towards her as she ran closer.

'Right,' she said breathlessly as she slithered to a halt on the muddy ground at the side of him. 'What's the problem here?'

'What do you mean – what's the *problem*?' He stared at her incredulously. 'This lot here are the problem.' He thumbed towards the small gathering of people. 'They've had the downright cheek to bring their caravans onto my land without asking!'

The man with whom Simon had been arguing stepped forward then and took his cap off respectfully as he addressed Jess. 'Look, missus, we ain't plannin' on stayin' here fer long. An' we'll be willin' to pay yer some rent if that's what yer wantin'. Me wife there . . .' he waved a hand towards a heavily pregnant woman who was watching with a frightened look in her eyes from the entrance of one of the vans, 'she's expectin' the child any day now an' I just wanted some peace an' quiet fer her till the birthin's over. I can't have her droppin' the kid while we're on the road. You'll not even know we're here if you'll give us yer permission to stay fer a while. We didn't realise that this bit o' land here belonged to anyone when we pulled on, but I promise yer we won't be no trouble.'

'Well, it bloody well *does* belong to me and—'

Jess squeezed Simon's arm and he fell silent although the look on his face was murderous. Truthfully she wasn't much happier about the gypsies being there than he was, but the pregnant woman looked so tired and worn out that she couldn't help but feel sorry for her.

'Perhaps if it's only until the baby is born they could stay, couldn't they?'

Simon glared at her for a moment before snapping sarcastically, 'Well, you're the boss, aren't you? It's *your* bloody house and grounds, so I suppose if that's what you want, that's how it will be!' With that he turned and stalked away as Jess looked back towards the gypsies apologetically.

'Excuse my husband,' she muttered. 'He's been working really hard lately and he's on a bit of a short fuse.'

'I appreciate this, missus,' the man told her, screwing his cap in his hands. 'You'll not know we're here, I promise yer, an' soon as the babby comes we'll be off.'

Jess nodded and quickly turned away as Beth and Jo hastily followed her.

'Dad isn't very pleased, is he?' Jo asked, as she ran to keep up with her mother. 'He hates gypsies.'

'I'm afraid he'll just have to live with it then, won't he?' Jess told her. 'They are only people at the end of the day and that poor woman looks as though she's at the end of her tether.'

Once back at the house, Jo and Beth hastily kicked their shoes off and shot up to Jo's bedroom. Jo could sense a row coming and wanted to put as much space between her parents and herself as she could.

'So what the bloody hell did you do *that* for?' Simon exploded the second the girls were out of sight. He was pacing up and down the kitchen like a caged animal and Jess knew she had upset him. Again! It seemed that they were always arguing over something or another these days.

'Look,' she said, trying to be reasonable. 'I know they shouldn't have just pulled onto our land like that, but that poor woman looked really ill. I wouldn't mind betting she'll have had that baby within a couple of days and then they'll be gone. And it's not as if they're hurting us, is it? I mean, they're far enough away from the house, we won't even know that they're there.'

'Huh! I wonder if you'll still be saying that when things start to go missing and getting vandalised,' he growled.

'Oh Simon, don't be so dramatic. Gypsies aren't all thieves and vandals, you know.'

'No? Well, we'll wait and see then, shall we? But don't come crying to me when it all goes pear-shaped.'

'Can't we just stop all this bickering now?' she pleaded. 'We've barely said two civil words to each other since I got back yesterday.'

'And whose fault is that, eh? You were hardly in a good mood when I came to pick you up from the airport, and then you'd barely set foot in the house before you shot off to bed with a headache. If that's the way holidays affect you, I suggest you think twice before going anywhere again.'

Jess bowed her head, knowing that what he had said was true. She longed to tell him about Mel and the drugs, but now more than ever she realised that it could only lead to more trouble. She had to put it behind her. Again she wished they had never met Emile. But it had taught her a valuable lesson and she knew that she would be a lot more cautious about who she got involved with in the future.

'How about I make us both a nice cuppa and we start again eh?' she said softly.

He sniffed but nodded as she hurried over to the kettle and then quickly started to ask him about his latest job. Simon might have his faults but he was a hard-working man and usually once he got on the subject of his work he could talk the hind leg off a donkey.

Later that afternoon, Simon was watching a football match on TV, Jo had gone home with Beth, and Mel was closeted in her room as usual, so feeling at a bit of a loose end, Jess headed back up to the big attic room and was soon engrossed in finding out what was in the chests. Most of it was rubbish – old sheets and pillowcases that the moths had made a meal of; broken kitchen utensils and old bottles. She piled everything she didn't want to keep by the door and methodically worked her way through the rest. The large wooden chests were still in surprisingly good condition and she decided she would keep them to store Christmas decorations in and all the other usual odds and ends.

And then she came upon yet another chest set slightly apart from the others, and when she lifted the lid she gasped with surprise. It was full of tiny baby clothes, all carefully wrapped in brown paper. She instantly thought of Grace's baby. There were tiny crocheted bonnets and hand-made nightgowns, as well as a number of little coats and bootees. But why had they never been worn? As she closed the lid of the chest she smiled, keen to read more of Martha's journal now and

162

find out what Grace had given birth to. The clothes in the chest could have been worn by either sex and gave her no clue.

Sitting back on her heels and swiping her dusty hands across her forehead, Jess's mind drifted, just as it always did when she thought of Martha. Somehow over the last weeks she had come to regard the girl as a friend, someone she could relate to – and if she really *was* still there as Laura insisted, then as far as Jess was concerned, she was welcome. After all, it had been Martha's home long before Jess had been born.

# Chapter Twenty-One

It was late on Sunday afternoon before Jess finally spoke to Mel properly again. Simon was out giving someone a quote on an extension, and Jo had gone to a friend's house for tea, so Jess decided to take full advantage of the fact that they could speak without fear of being overheard or interrupted.

Mel was lying on her stomach on the bed with her head buried in a magazine when Jess went in, and the girl instantly tensed. She had tried to keep out of her mother's way as much as she could since coming back from Paris, but the confrontation she had been dreading could no longer be avoided.

'It's all right, I haven't come in to read you the riot act,' Jess told her as she perched on the edge of the bed. 'But we really *do* need to talk, Mel. What you did, or almost did, is far too serious to be ignored. I think you understand that, don't you?'

Mel nodded as tears stung her eyes.

'Right, then let's talk about it and get it out of the way, shall we?' Jess straightened her back and folded her hands primly in her lap. 'I've done a lot of thinking about this and I've reached a decision. I have to admit my first reaction was to ring the police and pass Emile Lefavre's number onto them. But if I do that, Social Services and the police will become involved and I don't think you'd like that, would you?'

When Mel slowly shook her head Jess continued, 'I thought about telling your dad too. In fact, with something as serious as this I know I *should* tell him, but . . . Well, I'm hoping that you've learned your lesson and I don't need to tell you that your dad would hit the roof if he ever found out what you've done. Of course, if Emile turns up looking for the drugs I shall have no choice. Has he tried to contact you on your mobile? It's important you tell me the truth now.'

When Mel shook her head, Jess sighed with relief. 'Then if you can promise me faithfully that you'll never do anything as mad as this again, I think the best thing we can do is to try and put it behind us.'

Mel was crying now and Jess had to resist the urge to take her in her arms. But she didn't want her to get off too lightly.

She stood up now and walked towards the door before pausing to ask, 'Can you give me that promise, Mel?'

The girl nodded and Jess left the room, praying that she'd made the right decision. Should she have pushed Mel harder to confide in her? Worse still was the underlying guilt that she had exposed the girl to Emile Lefavre – but there was nothing she could do about that now. What was done was done, and she hoped that they'd be able to put it behind them.

The rain had stopped, so she decided to take Alfie for a walk to clear her head. Ten minutes later she stepped out into the darkening afternoon, well wrapped up in a waterproof coat and Wellington boots, with Alfie prancing along at the side of her. Once they reached the lake she struck off to the right and began to follow the river, her wellies squelching as she marched through the mud. Soon the gypsy caravans came into sight and she stopped, wondering if she should turn around and walk the other way. True to their word, the gypsies had kept themselves very much to themselves up to now, and she just prayed that they would continue to do so or she knew she would never hear the last of it from Simon. It was as she was hovering there that the door on one of the caravans opened and the pregnant woman she had met the day before stepped out. She hesitated for a moment when she saw Jess but then began to walk towards her, her arms wrapped protectively around her swollen belly.

'Thanks for lettin' us stay a while, missus,' she said solemnly as she came to a halt in front of Jess. Jess judged the woman to be about the same age as herself. She was tall, and no doubt would be slim when she was not pregnant. Her hair was long and a natural silver-blonde, tied back with an autumn-coloured headsquare, and she had on a man's jacket that strained across her stomach. A gaudy-coloured skirt flapped about her ankles.

'It's quite all right,' Jess told her with a smile. 'I hope everything goes well with the birth. And er . . . if you need fresh water there is an outside tap in the courtyard at the house. You are more than welcome to help yourself.'

The woman shook her head rapidly as she glanced across Jess's shoulder to the house in the distance. 'Thanks, but you'll not catch me up there. Bad things have happened there. It ain't a happy house. You'd do well to get yerself an' yer young 'uns away from there.'

Jess bristled with indignation. 'That house happens to be my home,' she told the woman imperiously. 'And I have no intention of leaving it.'

'Then on your own head be it,' the woman said sorrowfully, quickly making the sign of the cross on her chest. And then without warning she reached out and rested her hand on Jess's stomach. 'It's a little lad, God bless his soul,' she whispered, her voice heavy with sorrow.

Jess gasped and took a step back, while the woman scuttled back to the warmth of her home on wheels.

Flustered, Jess called Alfie and set off back towards the house, her mind racing. What had the woman meant by '*It's a little lad.*'

And then suddenly she stopped dead as something occurred to her. Now she came to think of it, she might have missed a period – or even two, if it came to that. She had been so busy working on the house that she hadn't even noticed. By the time she pushed her way through the kitchen door she was panting breathlessly. Leaving a trail of mud on the tiles in her wake she grabbed her handbag and took out her diary before furiously flicking back through the pages. She always marked the day her period had begun, but there was no tick against the last two months. She sat down heavily on the nearest chair as the colour drained out of her. *I can't be pregnant,* she tried to convince herself. *The girls are twelve and fourteen now. I'm too old to start again, and anyway Simon and I agreed that there would be no more babies after we had Jo.* And yet . . . there was no getting away from the fact that she had missed two periods, and then there was the sickness. She hadn't felt really well for weeks now but had put it down to a virus or something. One way or another, she needed to know the truth.

First thing on Monday morning, when she had dropped the girls off at their schools, Jess made for the nearest branch of Boots and bought a pregnancy tester kit. As soon as she got home she headed for the bathroom . . . twenty minutes later found her perching on the edge of her bed in complete shock. The test had proved positive. But how could the gypsy woman have *known*? And how was she going to tell Simon? She really couldn't envisage him being pleased about it. And she didn't even know if she wanted any more children herself. She was happy with Jo and Mel, for most of the time anyway. They were getting more independent now that they were older, but if she had another baby she would soon be back to sleepless nights, making bottles and changing nappies again. It was just too much to take in.

And what about the B and B business she had been hoping to set up? A new baby would certainly put the kibosh on that idea for quite some time – and yet . . . Her hand stroked her stomach wonderingly. A new baby might also mean the new start she had hoped for when they had moved into the house. She had no doubt that the girls would be tickled pink at the thought of having a new baby brother or sister.

As she slowly descended the stairs she heard a tap at the back door and moments later Laura walked into the kitchen with Beth. 'Are you OK?' she asked Jess. 'You look like you've seen a ghost.'

Jess thought that was rather a strange choice of words coming from Laura, and grinned ruefully as Beth stooped to fondle Alfie's ears. She knew that she really shouldn't say anything to anyone until she had spoken to Simon about it, but she was bursting to tell someone and Laura was there.

'I er . . . actually, I just found out that I'm pregnant,' she mumbled.

Laura gasped then seemed to leap across the room to her. 'Why, that's wonderful news . . . isn't it?'

'I'm not sure,' Jess admitted. 'And I don't know what Simon is going to say about it. We hadn't planned on having any more children.'

'Well, it's one of those things,' Laura said matter-of-factly. 'Sometimes the best-laid plans have a habit of backfiring on you. And what can he say? He obviously had a hand in it. You don't make babies on your own. I bet he'll be thrilled to bits when he gets used to the idea. I know I would be if it were me.' Laura gave her a hug and hustled her onto the nearest chair. 'You sit there,' she told her like a mother hen. 'You've had a bit of a shock and look like you could do with a hot drink. I'll make you one.'

'That's a slight understatement, to say the least,' Jess grinned. 'It's more like a bolt out of the blue. What are the girls going to say?'

'I reckon they'll be over the moon. But why don't you stop worrying about what everyone else is going to say? How do *you* feel about it? You're the one that's got to carry it and do all the hard work once it arrives.'

'I don't know how I feel, to be honest.' Jess fiddled with her wedding ring. 'It's all just so unexpected. I thought my baby days were well and truly behind me.'

Laura giggled as she spooned sugar into two mugs. 'Then it just goes to show you don't know everything, doesn't it? When did you start to suspect that you might be pregnant?'

Jess quickly told her about the encounter with the gypsy woman the day before, and Laura whistled though her teeth. 'Gypsies have been known to have the second sight for thousands of years, and that woman obviously saw something, didn't she?'

'She even told me that it was going to be a boy,' Jess answered, feeling strangely detached from everything. It was as if this was happening to someone else and not her.

'Let's hope she was right about that as well then. Just think how cool it would be to have a son after two daughters.'

'Will you do me a favour?' Jess suddenly asked.

'Of course, what is it?'

'Will you not say anything to anyone about this until I've had time to speak to Simon?'

'I wouldn't dream of it,' Laura promised. 'When are you going to tell him?'

'I doubt I'll get a chance until he gets home this evening, unless he pops back for anything.'

Laura plonked down on to the chair opposite and squeezed Jess's hand. 'Will you please stop looking as if the end of the world is nigh?' she asked. 'Just think how many people there are out there who can't have any children. They'd cut off their little fingers to be in your position.'

Jess suddenly felt guilty. Laura had once told her that one of her biggest regrets had been not being able to have any more babies after Beth. The news she had just told her must be cutting her like a knife, and yet she was putting a brave face on for her.

When she managed a wobbly smile, Laura patted her hand. 'That's better,' she said approvingly. 'Now why don't you give yourself time to get used to the idea, and then cook a nice romantic meal this evening just for two, and then tell Simon. I could feed the two girls if you like and give you both a bit of space.'

Jess's guilt intensified. She had always had a niggling suspicion that something might be going on between Laura and Simon, but if her reaction to this news was anything to go by, she had been sorely off the mark.

'I appreciate the offer but it isn't as simple as that,' she confided. 'Simon is rolling in at all hours at the moment, so a romantic meal for two might be quite hard to organise.'

'All right then. Tonight tell him that you have something important to talk to him about tomorrow and give him a time you'd like him to be home for.'

Jess grinned ruefully. Simon was his own master and not at all good at doing as he was told. If Jess were to order him home for a certain time he would probably stay out late just to make a point. But she didn't want to hurt her kindly neighbour's feelings, so she told her, 'Leave it with me. I'll figure something out.'

She then changed the subject and Laura told her how she was getting on with tracing her family tree. 'It's really quite fascinating when you get into it,' she told her. 'And the Fentons' family tree is too, seeing as I only live at the end of the drive. It's interesting to know who has lived here over the years and I've found quite a bit out. You might like to have a look at it when I've done as much as I can on it.'

'I would like to see it actually.' Jess thought of Martha's journal tucked away in her drawer upstairs but decided not to say any more about it for now to Laura. She had enough of her own worries to think about for now without telling Laura about how badly Martha and Grace had been treated. She had managed to get Mel off to school today but she was still seriously worried about the drugs incident. Up to now Emile Lefavre had made no effort to contact them, but Jess had no doubt that he would at some point soon and so she had confiscated Mel's mobile phone for the time being. If he tried to ring then it would be she who answered instead of Mel and she intended to put the fear of God into him.

Thankfully she had managed to avert what might have turned into a disaster for Mel, but how many more innocent girls was Emile preying on? He had been so charming and they had been so gullible. She was still feeling guilty about not telling Simon about it too. He was Mel's father, after all, and he had every right to know what had happened, but with the relationship between him and Mel being so fragile at present she hardly dared to think how he would react if he found out how stupid Mel had been. And now on top of everything else she had learned that she was going to have another baby! The old saying was certainly true: it never rained but it poured.

She suddenly wished with all her heart that her gran was still alive. She had been such a wise old woman, she would have known what to do for the best, but as it was, Jess was going to have to work things out for herself.

She was almost relieved when Laura left a short while later. It wasn't that she didn't enjoy her company but she seriously needed some quiet time to think.

Sliding her feet into her wellingtons again she donned a wet weather coat, then calling Alfie to heel she slipped out into the garden. Dark clouds were scudding across the sky and the trees were bending in the wind as the first sharp drops of rain splashed onto her face. She walked blindly on towards the lake, turning once to glance back at the house. And that's when she saw it – a small pale face solemnly watching her progress from the window in the attic bedroom.

# Chapter Twenty-Two

Jess's breath caught in her throat and she hastily swiped the rain from her eyes. When she looked back, whoever had been there was gone. Seriously unnerved, she forced herself to move on. Her Wellington boots squelched on the soggy grass as Alfie splashed through the puddles, his tail wagging furiously. It was strange, now she came to think of it – he always seemed to perk up once he got away from the house. She watched his antics, her mind not really on where she was going as she tried to put her thoughts into some sort of order. After a while she glanced up to see the gypsy folk all standing in a huddled little group about one particular caravan. Quickening her steps, she approached them and one of the women turned to look at her suspiciously. 'Amber's havin' the babby,' she told Jess solemnly.

'What . . . now? Right this minute?' Jess's eyes stretched wide.

'Aye, that's right.'

'But . . . but shouldn't she be in the hospital?' Jess stuttered nervously as her eyes licked over the caravan.

The woman shook her head, sending a shower of raindrops over Jess's face.

'Naw, Ma Biddy is in wi' her,' the woman informed her. 'She delivers all our souls into the world, God love 'em.'

'I see.' Jess chewed on her lip before asking, 'Do they have everything they need in there?'

The woman's face softened now as she nodded. 'Aye, they do. Now all we have to do is wait.' Even as she spoke, a scream rent the air and Alfie tucked his tail between his legs and slunk closer to Jess.

'Wouldn't you all be better to go into your caravans and wait?' Jess suggested tentatively. It was bitterly cold now and the little group looked as if they were soaked to the skin. 'Naw, not till the little 'un's put in an appearance,' the woman said stolidly. 'We'll all stand here in case we're needed.'

Jess was impressed. The travellers obviously had a strong loyalty to each other and she found that very touching. 'I'll leave you all to it then,' she said as she thrust her hands deeper into her pockets and turned to go. 'If you should find there's anything you need, don't hesitate to come to the house and ask.'

At that instant, a newborn baby's wail filled the air and Jess stopped in her tracks. Seconds later the caravan door banged open and an old woman appeared, clutching the infant in her two hands. 'It's a boy!' she boomed, holding the screaming infant aloft for them all to see. 'An' a right bonny lad he is, an' all!'

Jess felt as if she was watching some strange documentary on television as the group surged forward and started to cheer. The old woman was one of the oddest characters she had ever seen. She was dressed in a gaudy skirt that whipped about her legs in the wind, and her hair was covered in a purple headscarf tied at the back of her neck. Huge gold hoops dangled from her ears and there were so many wrinkles on her face that it was impossible for Jess to even begin to guess how old she might be. She desperately wanted to advise the old woman to get the child back into the warm but felt reluctant to intrude on this strange ceremony, so she simply stood there gaping as the people one by one kissed the child before stepping back.

And then at last the old woman disappeared, slamming the door unceremoniously behind her, and the people began to trudge back to their vans across the sludgy ground. The rain was coming down in torrents now and Jess's hair was plastered to her head. She felt moved by the birth that had just taken place and it made her think again about the child that she was carrying. She had wondered if she shouldn't just book herself into a clinic and have an abortion without saying anything to Simon, but now she had grave concerns about that idea. It was a child, after all, even if it hadn't been planned, and did she really have the right to take its life without telling her husband? It was as much his as hers at the end of the day, so she supposed he had a right to know about it. Not that she expected him to be too pleased about the idea. Simon had very much left the bringing up of the girls to her, and she guessed he would do the same with this one. He was very old-fashioned in some ways and believed that it was the woman's place to rear the family while the man went out to work.

Jess's head was whirling with all the things she had to contend with at present. One second she was thinking about Emile, and the way he had sweet-talked her, and then she was back in the bathroom in Paris again, staring down at the drugs he had intended Mel to smuggle back into the country. And now the unexpected news about the baby had

172

left her wondering if she was coming or going! She felt as if she had the weight of the world on her shoulders and was totally out of her depth. Things were almost as bad between her and Simon as they had been before they moved into the house, and she was wondering now if the move had been worth it. And yet . . . as she narrowed her eyes and peered through the sheeting rain, the house seemed to be beckoning to her just as it had the very first time she had set eyes on it.

That evening, she waited until the girls had finished eating and gone to their rooms to do their homework before hurrying into the dining room. It was as she spread a fine linen cloth across the highly polished mahogany table that she realised with a little start that this would be the first time that any of them had actually eaten in here. They usually ate at the large pine table in the kitchen, and up until now this had been nothing more than a show room, much like the other rooms that she had had decorated. Once the table was laid to her satisfaction with the finest silver cutlery and cut glass she stood back and smiled as the light from the overhead crystal chandelier cast a warm glow about the room. She had already placed a candelabra in the centre of the table but she would not light the candles until Simon put in an appearance, which would probably be much later if his recent track record was anything to go by. She then hurried back to the kitchen. She intended to cook all Simon's favourites tonight and get him in a good mood before she told him her news.

Just as she had expected he arrived home well after seven o'clock, soaked to the skin and not in the best of humours. Even so she greeted him with a smile and helped him to peel his sodden coat off as he eyed her suspiciously.

'What's all this in aid of then?' he questioned as he kicked his work boots off, spraying mud all across the tiles.

'I thought it was about time we treated ourselves, so why don't you nip up and get a quick shower? Your meal will be ready by the time you come down and we're going to eat in the dining room.'

He raised an eyebrow but went to do as he was told. When he came back downstairs with his hair still damp but looking clean and tidy she ushered him into the dining room where he stared at the table in amazement while she rushed away to fetch the first course.

'French onion soup!' he remarked as she ladled some into his dish from a fine china tureen. 'And home-made too, by the looks of it. Is it my birthday or our anniversary? Have I forgotten something?'

'Not at all,' she grinned. 'I just thought it would be nice to do things in style for a change. But don't get too used to it. I can't promise this sort of treatment every night.'

He watched her as she started her meal. She had made a real effort tonight and looked very pretty in the little black dress and high-heeled shoes that she'd worn in Paris. Once again, she'd piled her hair on top of her head in loose curls and it made her look elegant and sophisticated.

'The gypsy woman had her baby today,' she informed him as Simon helped himself to a bread roll. 'A little boy and he's gorgeous.'

'Good! Perhaps they'll clear off now then,' he retorted ungraciously. When he had finished his soup she brought in the main course, two large T-Bone steaks, a dish of salad and home-made French fries.

'That was delicious,' Simon told her when he'd eaten his fill. 'Now what's for pudding?'

'You'll see,' she said, as she gathered the dirty plates and whipped them away. 'Just wait there.' She was back in no time with a home-made apple pie and a large jug of thick creamy custard.

'Crikey, I reckon I might have died and gone to heaven,' Simon laughed as she ladled a large slice onto a clean dish for him.

She smiled demurely as she refilled his wine glass and helped herself to a small slice. He ate his in minutes but held his hand up in defeat when she offered second helpings.

'I couldn't eat another thing or I'll burst,' he told her. 'But now why don't you tell me what this is all about, eh?'

'Actually, there *is* something I need to talk to you about,' she admitted as she poured coffee for them both.

He groaned. 'Oh blimey, this sounds serious. I thought all this was too good to be true. Couldn't it wait until later? I promised the lads I'd meet them for a drink tonight up at the Anchor.'

Annoyance flashed in Jess's eyes. 'Couldn't you put it off just for once? You've been out almost every night since the girls and I got home from Paris.'

He peered at her over the rim of his cup. 'Out with it then if it's so important,' he said impatiently.

Jess nervously pleated the edge of the tablecloth. 'All right then . . . The thing is . . .' She gulped deep in her throat as she looked him in the eye. 'The thing is, I found out today that . . . that I'm pregnant.'

Simon coughed and spurted a mouthful of coffee all over the clean cloth as his eyes almost started from his head.

'You're *what*?'

Jess shrugged. 'I'm pregnant – and believe me, I was as shocked as you are.'

'I doubt that very much,' he ground out as he wiped his mouth on a napkin. 'How far on are you?'

'I haven't actually been to the doctor's yet but I should think a couple of months or so,' she said sheepishly, somehow feeling as if she had achieved this all by herself.

'But I thought after Jo we agreed that we wouldn't have any more kids,' he roared, as anger replaced the shock of what she had just told him.

'We did,' she agreed. 'And I didn't plan this, if that's what you're thinking. It's knocked me for six, I don't mind telling you.'

'Aw well, it should be easy to sort if you're only a couple of months,' he retorted unfeelingly.

As the meaning of his words sank in, she stared at him in horror. 'Are you saying you want me to get rid of it?'

'Of course I am,' he told her. 'We agreed two was enough.'

'But that was back then,' she objected. 'We barely had two pennies to rub together and we couldn't afford any more children, but we're better off now.'

'Jo is twelve years old and Mel is fourteen now. How do you think they'd feel if we suddenly told them they were going to have a brother or sister? They'd probably be embarrassed to death.'

'Why should they be?' Jess retorted hotly. 'We are *married*. It isn't as if we're doing anything wrong. Married people *do* have children.'

He shook his head. 'Well, I certainly don't want any more and if you want to go all through that baby palaver again, you must be mad. We'll be a complete laughing stock!'

'And since when have *you* ever been so concerned about what people will say?' she roared back, realising that this was fast turning into an argument.

'Since now!' he spat. 'So get rid of it, Jess, and do the sensible thing. We're too old to be starting again.'

'Too old?' she gasped incredulously. 'I'm only in my early thirties, Simon. Some career women don't even *start* having children until they're forty nowadays.'

He stood up so abruptly that he nearly overturned his chair. 'This subject is not up for discussion,' he said, ominously quietly. 'I've told you how I feel, so deal with it.'

As he made to stride past her she caught at his arm with tears in her eyes. 'Where are you going?'

'*Out*! And when I get back I don't want to talk about this any more.'

Sagging back into her seat she listened to the sound of the kitchen door slam, followed by the noise of his vehicle reversing erratically out of the courtyard again. And then she gave way to her tears. The worst part of it was the guilt she felt. After all, she had briefly considered having an abortion herself without even telling Simon about the pregnancy. But then she had seen the newborn gypsy baby and somehow she had known that she couldn't go through with taking an innocent life for no good reason. As she began to calm down a little she tried to look at the situation more logically. Simon was bound to be shocked. She herself had been, so perhaps he just needed some time to come to terms with the idea? But one thing was for sure. The test had been positive. There was a baby growing inside her whether they liked it or not. She thought of the children that had been born in this very house many years ago – Miss Melody and Grace's babies – and she wondered what had become of them. No doubt Martha's journal would give her the answers.

It was then that she became aware of a noise and she cocked her head to one side as she listened intently. It sounded like someone whispering. But then she decided it was probably just the wind she could hear and set about clearing the table she had laid so carefully, and with such high hopes, earlier in the evening.

# Chapter Twenty-Three

*23 December*

The young Master and Mistress's guests have all arrived for Christmas now and I have never known the house to be so full. It is bursting at the seams and there don't seem to be enough hours in the day to get everything done. Thankfully, many of Miss Melody's staff from her other home have arrived to help out . . .

The girls' first sight of Mrs Bloom, Miss Melody's cook from her home in Herefordshire, who had come to help Phoebe with the cooking, terrified them. Mrs Bloom was enormous. She had hands as large as hams and arms that would have put an all-in wrestler's to shame. She also had at least five chins and was very keen at barking out orders, but in a very short time they all discovered that her bark was far worse than her bite. On learning that Granny Reid was still ill in bed, Mrs Bloom instantly took it upon herself to make tasty snacks to tempt the old woman to eat at regular intervals throughout the day, even carrying them to Granny's room herself where she would cajole and bully her into eating. One evening, Grace also caught her filling a basket of Christmas goodies for Joey to take home to his family, and from then on none of them were quite so afraid of her.

Another new addition to the household was Miss Wigg, Miss Melody's housekeeper. A thin, stern-looking woman, she rarely smiled and would sweep about the house in a full-skirted bombazine dress with the keys to each room dangling from a chain about her waist, her salt-and-pepper-coloured hair twisted into two tight buns, one behind each ear.

'I think she might 'ave been a beauty once,' Grace commented as they all sat in the kitchen over lunch. 'An' the way she talks – she's obviously from a good family. I bet she were slighted in love and reduced to bein' a housekeeper.'

Mrs Bloom laughed, 'I'll say this fer yer, gel, yer've got a lively imagination. But I'm afraid I can't tell you nowt. Miss Wigg keeps 'erself very much to 'erself, though to her credit she does a good job. So long as the staff do as they're told, I reckon they won't have a problem wi' 'er. She's firm, but she's also fair, I think you'll find. But what did the doctor 'ave to say about yer granny today after his visit?' she asked Martha.

The girl's face fell. Miss Melody had the doctor calling on Granny weekly now, but she still seemed to be fading away before their very eyes.

'He was talkin' to Miss Melody about her when I went up to check if he'd done,' Martha said quietly. 'An' Miss Melody didn't look none too pleased wi' what she was hearin'. But when I asked how Gran was, she just flashed me that lovely smile an' said that she was sure Granny would start to pick up as the weather improved in the spring. As much as I want to believe her, I have me doubts. Granny suddenly looks so old and fragile and she's lost a frightening amount of weight. When me and Grace washed her yesterday, she weighed no more than a feather, did she, Grace?'

Grace sadly shook her head and Martha rushed on, 'I know Phoebe an' Mrs Bloom are sendin' her up good food regularly, but the trouble is I have me jobs to do, so I can't be wi' her constantly an' I don't think she's eating it.'

'Well, yer can only do what yer can do, love,' Mrs Bloom said philosophically as she slurped at her tea and they all lapsed into a thoughtful silence.

Half an hour later, after putting on her pretty mobcap and straightening her apron, Martha carried a tray towards the drawing room for Miss Melody, stopping to admire one of the three Christmas trees that had been delivered the day before in the entrance hall. Miss Melody and Master Leonard had spent the afternoon decorating it with fine glass baubles and tiny candles which the young Master had had sent from London. The other two trees now stood in the drawing room and the dining room, and as her contribution, Martha had spent the afternoon scouring the woods for holly, which was now strewn about the downstairs in ornate glass vases. Grace was no longer able to wait on the young Master and Mistress because she was so enormous that she waddled like a duck now. Miss Melody was not far behind her and Martha excitedly tried to imagine what it would be like to have two babies in the house.

The nursery that Miss Melody had had prepared for her baby was fit for a little prince or princess, and it had already been decided that the child would have a nanny who would travel between the two homes when it was old enough.

Dragging her thoughts back to the present, Martha hurried on, mindful that she still had an awful lot of chores to get through before she could finish for the day.

When she arrived back in the kitchen she found Grace telling Mrs Bloom excitedly about the progress on her cottage. 'We were hoping to be in fer the summer. But the roof's on now, so we might even manage it fer the spring.'

'That'd be a good time to move in,' the woman agreed as she basted the leg of lamb that was roasting in the oven. 'An' would any of yer happen to know if his lordship will be in fer dinner tonight?'

'I doubt it.' Grace chuckled wickedly. 'It's no secret that he's very put out about the party so he's still keepin' out o' the way fer most o' the time. Look at when he went off to London a couple of weeks since – he didn't come back fer a whole week. But he did come back eventually, more's the pity! Did yer know he raised his fist to young Polly last week?'

'No, we didn't. What happened?'

'Well, from what Bertie an' Hal have managed to glean from it, while the Master were in London he lost a deal o' money at the gamin' tables there an' he had to go cap in hand to Master Leonard to bail him out again. He an' the young Master were closeted in the study fer a very long while, and their voices could be heard all over the house. Anyway, the outcome of it was that the young Master informed him in no uncertain terms that this would be the very last time he would help him out financially, and the Master come out of the room wi' a face like a dark thundercloud on him. Young Polly just happened to be passin', returnin' one o' Miss Melody's gowns to her room, an' they almost collided. Poor lass, she were terrified. He raised his fist an' she were sure that he was goin' to strike her. But then he seemed to have second thoughts, an' roarin' at her to get out of his way, he stormed out o' the house instead. I reckon he realised that the young Master wouldn't tolerate any more cruelty to the servants and he's now so deeply in debt that he's afraid of upsetting him, which is one blessing at least.'

They all nodded in agreement before scuttling away to their chores.

That evening, a tap came on the green baize door and Miss Melody entered with a sweet smile on her face.

'I'm sorry to disturb you but my husband and I have just been talking, and as a reward for how hard you have all worked to entertain our guests, we thought it would be nice if we gave permission for you all to have a party in the barn. New Year's Eve might be a nice evening for it, if you're all agreeable? Our guests will have departed by then. And Martha – you must invite Jimmy, of course.'

Martha flushed prettily as she dipped her knee. 'That would be wonderful, Miss Melody. Thank you.'

'I shall provide all the food and drink,' Melody told them. 'So now I'll be off to leave you all to make your arrangements.' And with that she sailed from the room as Martha hugged herself with delight. Things were just getting better and better! If only Granny would improve, things would be almost perfect.

Jess closed the book and placed it safely away. It was mid-morning and she had become so engrossed in the journal that she had lost track of time. Simon had stayed out all night after their argument the night before and she had struggled to act normally earlier on in the morning when she took the girls to school.

'Is everything all right, Mum?' Jo had asked anxiously when Jess drew up outside her school gates.

'Everything's fine, love,' Jess had assured her as she leaned across her and threw the car door open. 'I've just got a bit of a headache, that's all. Now you get off and have a good day. Look, your friend is waiting for you over there.'

Jo had instantly perked up and shot off with a smile on her face. She was very intuitive where her mum was concerned and always seemed to be able to sense when Jess wasn't at her best. But then she'd seen so much over the years, Jess had thought ruefully as she headed back to the house.

She was tidying her hair in the mirror when a voice wafted up the stairs to her. '*Hellooo*! Is anybody there?'

Jess grinned. She had forgotten that Karen was coming round to see her. Her friend always managed to put a smile back on her face, and Jess wondered what she would have done without her over the last few years. Karen was her shoulder to cry on and her confidante, and she certainly had enough to confide in her today.

'Christ, you look awful,' Karen said bluntly as Jess entered the kitchen. 'What's the story?'

'You're just not going to believe it,' Jess muttered as she went to grab the coffee pot.

'So try me then.' Karen helped herself to a ginger nut biscuit from the plate on the work station and peered at her. 'Is it Simon again? Up to his old tricks, is he?'

Tears pricked at the back of Jess's eyes as she poured coffee into two mugs. 'In a way,' she admitted reluctantly. 'He didn't come home at all last night. But it's worse than that . . .' She gulped before blurting out, 'I told him I was pregnant, you see, and he didn't much like the idea.'

'*Christ Almighty!*' Karen almost choked on her biscuit as she gazed at Jess incredulously. 'Well, I have to admit it must have come as a shock to him. It certainly has to me. I had no idea you were planning on having any more kids.'

'I wasn't,' Jess said dismally. 'And now I don't know what to do about it. Simon's made it more than clear that he doesn't want it.'

'Huh! The last I heard, it took two to tango, so the least he could do is sit down and talk it through sensibly,' Karen stated indignantly. 'Burying his head in the sand isn't going to help, is it? He ain't a bloody ostrich.'

Jess grinned despite being so miserable. She could always rely on Karen to tell it like it was, which was one of the things she loved about her.

'But how do *you* feel about another baby?' Karen asked now.

Jess spread her hands in a helpless gesture. 'To be honest, I'm not sure. When I first found out I was horrified. Then I thought it might be a blessing in disguise. You know, that a new baby might bring Simon and me closer together again? And *then* I thought it might be best if I just got rid of it without telling him – and *now* I just don't know what I want!' Tears were spilling down her cheeks.

'You know, you haven't been right since you moved into this bloody great mausoleum,' Karen commented, looking around with distaste. 'I personally can't see what you ever saw in it. Do you think it's all getting a bit too much for you?'

'Everything is getting too much for me at the moment,' Jess admitted through sobs. 'There are Mel's mood swings, Simon staying out again till all hours, and now finding out about this baby is just the last straw.' She then went on to tell Karen all about meeting Emile Lefavre and what had happened in Paris as Karen listened attentively.

181

When Jess had finished the whole sorry tale she whistled through her teeth. 'Blimey, think what might have happened if you hadn't found the drugs,' she breathed. 'The lousy bastard – preying on a young girl like that. Has he been in touch with you or Mel since you got home?'

Jess shook her head. 'No, I haven't heard from him and I confiscated Mel's mobile, so I would have known if he had tried to ring her, but there have been no missed calls.'

Karen tapped the table thoughtfully with her fingertips. 'It doesn't make sense,' she said eventually. 'There must have been hundreds if not thousands of pounds' worth of drugs went down that loo. And he wouldn't have known that you'd found them and flushed them away, so why hasn't he got in touch? What does Simon think about it?'

'I haven't dared to tell him.' Jess flushed guiltily. 'Things are so bad between him and Mel at the moment that I thought this could only make them a million times worse. What's more, if Simon decided to involve the police they might bring Social Services in then and I think I'd die of shame. At the end of the day it's more my fault than Mel's. I shouldn't have let her go wandering off round the hotel on her own. The trouble is, I'm living on tenterhooks now. I keep checking Mel's room when she's gone to school in case she has any more drugs stashed away anywhere.'

'I can understand that,' Karen said sympathetically. 'And you really weren't joking when you said everything is a mess. You've sure had enough on your plate lately. But now back to the baby. You've got to make your mind up what you're going to do about it sooner rather than later if you're considering having an abortion. It's not like it used to be you know. They give you one tablet on the first day and another tablet the next and then that's it now. There's no operation involved any more.'

'I know,' Jess said brokenly. 'I suppose that a termination would be the easy solution. But I don't think I could bring myself to go through with it.'

'Well, this is something you're going to have to decide for yourself. It's your body, so you should do what feels right for you.'

'I know.' Jess stared out of the window as Karen squeezed her hand. She would have to think very carefully before reaching a decision either way.

'And is that the lot then?' Karen teased, trying to lighten the atmosphere.

'No . . . actually it isn't.' Seeing as they were having a heart-to-heart, Jess decided to tell her everything. When she had managed to compose herself a little, she told her friend, 'I think this house is haunted. What I mean is, I don't see ghosts floating about the place or anything like that, but I know there's a presence here. It's watching over me.'

'Oh, lordie! This just takes the biscuit, girl. You really *are* letting your imagination run away with you now,' Karen scoffed.

'I'm not, I swear it. And I can prove it.' Jumping up from the chair, Jess scuttled away upstairs to return minutes later clutching Martha's journal. She then hurried on to tell Karen how she had come across it and about the room in the attic as Karen flicked through the pages.

'And you think it's the girl who wrote this who is still hanging around here, do you?' Karen asked as she stole a nervous glance across her shoulder despite herself.

Jess couldn't help but smile. 'Yes, I do, as a matter of fact. It was Laura from Blue Brick Cottage who first told me that someone was still here. Of course I didn't believe her then, but now . . .' She knew that she must sound as if she had lost her marbles, but it was such a relief to talk to someone about it at last. 'Laura reckons that this person is here for a reason and it's something to do with me, although I have no idea what it is.'

'I see.' Karen peered at her friend closely. It seemed to her that Jess was fast approaching some sort of nervous breakdown, but she didn't want to say that for risk of offending her, so instead she said cautiously, 'But why would a spirit, or ghost or whatever you want to call it, know anything about you?'

'I don't know, but Laura can sense these things. She's sort of psychic.'

'Hmm.' Karen was a firm believer that there was a logical explanation for everything, and she certainly didn't believe in the afterlife. As far as she was concerned, when you were dead you were dead and that was the end of it, which was probably why she lived her life to the full, determined to enjoy each and every day.

'Do you know what I think?' she said, changing the subject abruptly. 'I think a bit of retail therapy is called for. Apart from that trip to Paris, which turned out to be quite stressful, one way and another, you've worked yourself almost to death since you moved in here. There's no time like the present, so go and get your glad rags on.'

'But the girls will be home from school,' Jess objected.

'That's hours away yet and I'm not going to take no for an answer, so go and get changed. I won't budge from here until you do,' Karen warned.

Knowing what Karen could be like when she had her stubborn head on, Jess slipped away to her bedroom where she quickly changed into a black trouser suit and a crisp white blouse. I look more like I'm going for a job interview, she thought as she brushed her hair. But at least I'm respectable now, so that will have to do.

An hour later they were browsing through the shops in Nuneaton. They had both decided it was a little late to venture any farther afield. In Next Jess bought a lovely little pair of denim dungarees and a matching T-shirt for the new baby that had been born within the grounds of Stonebridge House but her heart wasn't really in it and she just wanted to go home.

'Why are you buying that?' Karen enquired with a disapproving lift of her eyebrow. 'I thought Simon wanted the gypsies gone as soon as possible? I reckon they've got a bloody cheek parking there in the first place, if you were to ask me.'

'Well, they haven't been any trouble and it's not the baby's fault, is it?' Jess retorted.

Karen sighed. 'You're such a soft touch,' she said as she dragged Jess off to look at the Per Una section in Marks & Spencers.

Jess trailed around from shop to shop after Karen for another hour but then she put her foot down, saying, 'I really ought to be going else I'll be late getting back for the girls.' They had each gone in their own cars so at least she didn't have to give Karen a lift home.

'They're damn well old enough to look after themselves for an hour or two instead of having you run around after them like a blue-arsed fly all the time,' Karen replied but she didn't push it. She could see Jess was preoccupied. 'Oh go on – be off with you, you're like a cat on hot bricks. I'll be round at the same time next week, but if you need me before then you know where I am. And Jess . . . try not to worry too much about everything. It will all come out in the wash, you'll see, and don't go letting your imagination run away with you either.'

Jess managed a smile and after pecking Karen on the cheek she shot off to the car park to collect her car. At home, she quickly changed into her jeans and wellies again and set off for the gypsy van clutching the small gift she had bought for the baby.

She was surprised to see that the small encampment was a hive of activity and guessed that they were preparing to leave. The menfolk

184

were busily hooking up the caravans to the huge lorries they drove and the women were shepherding the children into the backs of them.

As she drew closer she saw Amber emerge from one of the vans. She had the baby tied in a shawl at her breast.

'We'll not be botherin' yer any longer, missus,' she said, 'but thanks fer lettin' us stay. You've been right civil.'

'You're very welcome and I'm very pleased everything went well at the birth,' Jess replied as she admired the baby. She could just see his face peeping out of the shawl and he really was a beautiful little child with a mop of thick dark hair and bright blue eyes.

'I er . . . I got this for him,' she said, feeling suddenly embarrassed as she passed the small gift to the woman. When the woman withdrew the dungarees and the little matching top her face creased into a smile. 'Why, they're lovely. Thanks, missus. It's right kindly of yer.'

'Come on then, Amber,' a male voice suddenly boomed. 'Let's be havin' yer then while we have the light.'

The woman glanced towards her husband before looking back at Jess and now her face was solemn as she gripped her hand. 'Take care o' yourself, missus. I see bad things ahead for yer.' Glancing towards the house, she shuddered. 'That place has seen a lot o' heartache, an' there's more to come.' She quickly made the sign of the cross on her chest, as she had done the first time, and then scurried away to clamber into the front of the van with her husband. And then one by one the caravans formed an orderly line and drove away as Jess looked silently on.

# Chapter Twenty-Four

Simon nodded curtly in Jess's direction when he came in from work that evening and she hurried away to fetch his meal from the oven. The girls were both in the small lounge and Jess was thankful for that, in case another row blew up, which judging by the look on Simon's face was more than likely.

She wanted to scream at him and ask him where he had been all night but instead she said quietly, 'The gypsies have moved on.'

'And so they bloody well should,' he growled. 'They had no right to come onto our land in the first place. Oops, *sorry* . . . I should have said *your* land, shouldn't I?'

'Just because I bought the place with Gran's money doesn't mean it isn't half yours,' Jess said quietly. 'We're married, for Christ's sake, so what's mine is yours and hopefully vice versa.'

Simon's lips curled back from his teeth and for the first time since she had known him, Jess felt like slapping him. He was behaving very childishly and she was almost at the end of her tether.

'Anyway . . .' Jess struggled to remain calm. 'How about we try and talk sensibly about more important issues? Like the baby, for instance. Have you had time to think about how you feel about it?'

She placed his meal in front of him and he grunted his thanks as he lifted his knife and fork and dug into the lamb chops on his plate. 'I haven't thought about much else,' he mumbled through a mouthful.

'And?' She looked at him, hoping that now he'd had time to come to terms with it, he might be feeling a little differently.

'And what? I haven't changed my mind about it. I reckon the last thing we need right now is another baby hanging around our necks.'

Jess took a deep breath. 'Then I'm sorry to hear that because I've decided that I want to keep it.'

His face darkened into a scowl. 'There's really no point in me saying any more on the subject then, is there?'

'Not really.' Jess stuck her chin in the air in a rare act of defiance.

'But you might like to tell me where you were all night. I was worried sick.'

'I dossed down on Mick's settee after we'd had a game of darts at the pub, if you must know,' he said sullenly, keeping his eyes fixed firmly on his plate.

Jess didn't believe him for an instant but she knew better than to question him. Simon could be as stubborn as a mule when he wanted to be. Slumping down on the chair opposite him, she suggested softly, 'Couldn't we start again? We seem to be going off track again lately.'

'Meaning?'

'Well . . .' she spread her hands helplessly. 'You're going out more and more again and—'

'Oh, we're back to *that*, are we? Can't a man even go and enjoy a quiet drink when he's been working all day?'

'Of course, but . . . well, it would be nice if you didn't go out every night.'

Slamming his knife and fork down, Simon stood up and towered over her threateningly. 'It always comes back to the same old thing, doesn't it? And just in case you've forgotten, I give Beth a lift to the youth club tonight. Do you want me to go and tell her I'm not allowed to take her?'

'Of course not,' Jess said hastily. 'I have no objections at all to you going out a couple of nights a week; I'm just saying I'd be happier if it wasn't *every* night.'

For a horrible moment she thought he was going to hit her as his face distorted with temper but then he slammed away upstairs without another word as she sat glumly looking at his half-eaten meal.

I made a good job of that again, she thought wryly, and lifting the remaining lamb chop she tossed it to Alfie before scraping the rest into the bin.

Simon left half an hour later without so much as another word to her, and Jess sat there, tears trickling down her cheeks. Everything was such a mess and this time she wasn't at all sure that she could put things right between them.

She was loading the dishwasher and feeling very sorry for herself when Laura appeared looking just as stressed and worried as she felt.

'Come and join the sad club,' Jess invited. 'You look as miserable as I feel. What's wrong?'

'It's Beth,' Laura said miserably. 'We've just had an awful row. She's been really off-colour for days now, so when Simon called to give her a lift to the youth club I told him I'd rather she didn't go tonight. Well, to say she kicked off big time would be putting it mildly! She was screaming and crying at me as if I was the Wicked Witch from the West. I can't understand it at all. Beth is usually as meek as a lamb, but lately she's changed. I'm sure it's something to do with that boy she's been going off with from the youth club.'

'*Beth?* Kicking off? I know you said she was playing up while I was away but I thought she would have settled back down by now,' Jess commented.

Laura shook her head as she took a pack of cigarettes from her bag and offered one to Jess before lighting one herself.

'So what happened next? Have you let her go?'

'No, I haven't.' Laura blew a plume of smoke into the air. 'Luckily her dad arrived home while all this was going on and he sent her up to her room. But she isn't happy about it at all.'

Because Beth was special needs, Jess had always assumed that she would be willing to do as she was told, but it seemed that even Beth could have her moments.

'What a pair we are, eh?' she grinned sadly.

'Too true,' Laura agreed. 'Anyway, I'm going to take her to the doctor's tomorrow. She might be behaving like this because she isn't feeling well. It's so unlike her to lose her temper like that. I don't know if it was because she didn't get to have a ride in the car with Simon or because she didn't get to see this boy.'

'It's probably a combination of both,' Jess said wisely. 'She worships Simon and I have to admit he's got the patience of Job with her. I just wish he'd show the same consideration to Mel.'

'Mm.' Laura stubbed her unfinished cigarette out in the ashtray before asking, 'And how did Simon take the news about the baby? Have you told him yet?'

'Oh, I told him all right,' Jess nodded. 'Last night, as a matter of fact, and we ended up having a flaming row. He walked out and didn't come back all night. He reckons he stayed at his mate's house but between you and me, Simon tends to have a roving eye and I just wonder if he doesn't have some girlfriend on the side. It wouldn't be the first time, believe me.'

Laura looked shocked. She had never heard Jess talk about her husband like this before.

'When we moved here, things were pretty bad between us,' Jess confided, 'and I hoped this would be a new start for us. But it certainly

188

doesn't seem to be working out that way. And now, what with finding out about the baby, everything seems a hundred times worse. To say that Simon isn't happy about the idea would be putting it mildly.'

'I'm sorry to hear that.' Laura was genuinely upset for her. She'd grown fond of Jess and didn't like to think of her being miserable. 'So what are you going to do about it?'

'I'm going to keep this baby,' Jess told her with determination. 'I did briefly think of having an abortion but I don't think I could go through with it, so that's that.'

'I don't blame you. Have you told the girls yet?'

'No.' Jess sighed wearily. 'I thought I'd hang on until I've been to the doctor's and had it definitely confirmed.'

The sound of a mobile phone going off suddenly echoed around the kitchen and after hastily fishing in her bag Jess saw that it was the one she had confiscated from Mel. She answered it, thinking that it would be one of Mel's friends.

'Hello?'

'Hello, Mel. How are you? Did you arrive home safely and have a good journey?'

As the sound of Emile Lefavre's voice reached her, Jess felt ice-cold rage pump through her veins.

'It isn't Mel, it's her mother,' she said tonelessly.

'Ah, Jess. Jo gave me her and Mel's numbers, but I didn't realise that I had not asked for yours until I had boarded my plane – and as I had not heard from you, I thought I would see if you were interested in going ahead with some home tuition for Mel. I was just about to ask her for your number.'

'I just *bet* you were,' Jess murmured.

'Jess . . . is everything all right? Have I upset you in some way?' Emile enquired.

'How *dare* you even have the nerve to ask?' Jess spat, her voice rising dangerously. 'I wouldn't let you near my daughter again if my very life depended upon it. And furthermore, if you *ever* try to get in touch with Mel again, I shall call the police and tell them what you tried to make her do.'

'I . . . I don't understand,' Emile said in that throaty voice that she had once found so attractive.

'Oh, but I think you do.' Jess was so furious now that she could barely speak. She ended the call, shaking, then flung the phone onto the table as Laura looked on, wide-eyed and uncomprehending.

'Can you *believe* the nerve of that bastard?' Jess stormed as she watched the phone as if it was going to bite her.

'Well, I doubt he'll dare ring again,' Laura soothed, wondering what all the fuss was about but not wanting to ask. 'But now you must calm down, love. Think of the baby.' Jess then promptly burst into a torrent of tears as Laura wrapped her arms around her and let her cry it all out.

Two weeks later, Jess sat the girls down at the kitchen table and looked at them nervously. She had been to the doctor's the week before and now knew that the baby was due early in May. She had been trying to find the right time to tell them ever since her appointment, and as Simon wasn't home from work yet, now seemed as good a time as any.

'So what is it that you want to tell us then, Mum?' Jo asked brightly as she tickled Alfie under the chin. 'Is it something to do with Christmas?' It was now mid-November and they were racing towards Christmas at an alarming rate. Jess hadn't even started the Christmas shopping yet whereas in previous years she had had all the presents bought and wrapped by now.

'No, love, it isn't.' Jess wished that Simon was there to tell them with her, but there was fat chance of that happening. He had only spoken to her when he had to over the last couple of weeks, and the atmosphere between them was strained, to say the very least. 'The thing is,' she went on, peering uncomfortably from one to the other of them, 'I've just found out that I'm going to have a baby . . . You're going to have a new brother or sister.'

There was a stunned silence for a moment before Jo whooped with delight and ran around the table to hug her.

'Why, that's *so* cool. When is it due?'

Ignoring the look of horror on Mel's face, Jess forced herself to smile. 'About the beginning of May next year,' she managed to choke out.

'Well, I think it's absolutely gross!' Mel shot at her mother, wrapping her arms across her chest even more tightly. 'Everyone at school is going to laugh at me when they find out. You're far too old to have another baby!'

'I know it must have come as a bit of a shock. To be honest, it was to me and your dad too,' Jess replied, keeping her voice calm. 'But when you get used to the idea you might actually find that it won't

190

be so bad, after all. This house is huge and there's more than enough room. And yes, I know that I must seem old to you, but early thirties isn't that old really.'

Mel bounced up out of her chair. As usual, she was dressed in her most shapeless clothes and her lovely hair was pulled back into a tight unbecoming ponytail on the back of her head.

'Well, don't expect *me* to be pleased about it,' she said loudly, and before Jess could say another word she stormed out and stamped away up the stairs.

Jo smiled at her mum sadly. 'Don't mind Mel,' she whispered. 'Nothing makes her smile any more. She's a right old misery guts.'

Jess smiled despite the ache inside her. She had never expected Simon to be happy about the baby, but she had hoped the girls might. It seemed that no one, even herself, really wanted this baby except Jo, who was grinning like a Cheshire cat again now.

'We shall have to start thinking of names,' she said, as she stared off into space with a dreamy expression on her face. 'How about Angelique if it's a little girl? That's a really romantic name, isn't it?'

'Er . . . don't you think it might be a bit too fussy?' Jess replied, not wanting to dampen the girl's enthusiasm.

'All right, how about Henrietta then or Magdalane?'

Jess gulped, very pleased that the choice of names for the infant would not be left solely up to Jo.

'We'll see nearer the time,' she said tactfully. 'Meanwhile you can help me start to choose the colours for the new nursery. I shall get the decorators in once we have Christmas out of the way. What do you fancy?'

Jo tapped her lip. 'How about we do it in lemon and white? Then it won't matter if it's a boy or a girl,' she suggested.

'Good choice,' Jess agreed. 'Now off to your room, miss, and get your homework done, there's a good girl.'

Jo skipped away, her head full of the news, as the smile slid from Jess's face. She couldn't pretend that she'd had a good reaction from Mel, but then in fairness she hadn't really expected one. And at least she had told them now, which was a weight off her mind.

She was all ready to go off and enjoy an evening with Karen when Simon came in from work. She pointed towards the oven as she picked up her car keys. He was late in again, and if she didn't get off soon there would be hardly any point in going.

'Your dinner's in the oven,' she told him. 'And I'm off to Karen's. See you later.'

He grunted an acknowledgement and sighing, Jess went on her way, more than ever aware of the gaping chasm that seemed to be developing between them.

# Chapter Twenty-Five

As Jess sat in Karen's small lounge later that evening she couldn't help but notice the difference between this room and her own sumptuous drawing room back at Stonebridge House. Karen's was tiny, with slightly worn leather settees on either side of the room and a carpet that looked as if it could do with a good shampooing. And yet Karen's room had a cosy, lived-in feel about it, whereas Jess had to admit that hers felt formal and uninviting.

'Penny for your thoughts,' Karen said suddenly. Her kids had been rampaging about the place until ten minutes ago when they had gone off to bed, and now Karen was curled up on one of the settees with her legs tucked up underneath her, a large glass of wine in her hand and a contented smile on her face.

'I was just thinking how peaceful it is,' Jess muttered.

Karen snorted with laughter. '*Peaceful?* You must be joking. The only time we get any peace is when the nippers go to bed. Mind you, I wouldn't want it any other way. They'll be grown up and flown the nest before we know it, so we may as well enjoy the mayhem while we can. How are things at your end? Have you told the girls about the baby yet?'

'As a matter of fact I told them just before I came here,' Jess told her.

'And?'

'It was just as I expected really. Jo was made up with the idea and Mel said it was gross and stormed off to her room.'

Karen chuckled. 'No surprises there then, but that's teenagers for you. Anyone over twenty is old to them and it's sort of strange to think of your mum and dad . . . you know. But I've no doubt she'll come round once she's got used to the idea. You might even find you have a built-in babysitter.'

'I don't think there's much chance of that', Jess said sadly. 'She hasn't even got time for Jo any more, let alone a wailing baby.'

'And how about Simon? Is he getting over the shock of discovering he's going to be a dad again yet?'

He's walking about like a bear with a sore head and we're barely speaking.'

'Aw well, things can only get better,' Karen said optimistically as she poured another glass of orange juice for Mel and then they went on to talk of other things, and as the night wore on Jess felt herself slowly beginning to unwind.

She was in a happier frame of mind as she drove home, even humming to herself by the time she parked the car in the courtyard. Simon was upstairs when she entered the house, so after quickly locking the doors and settling Alfie in his basket she headed for their bedroom. He wasn't there but she could hear him in the shower so she went along the landing to check on the girls before getting ready for bed. Jo was sound asleep and Jess smiled as she looked down at her. She looked like an angel with her hair fanned out across the pillow and her long eyelashes curled on her cheeks. Jess bent down and kissed her before switching off her lamp and moving on to Mel's room. She heard her crying even before she got to the door, and all the happy feelings she had had disappeared like mist in the morning.

Not bothering to knock she opened the door then stopped dead in her tracks. Mel was sitting in the middle of the bed hugging her pillow as she rocked back and forth. Her hair was wild and dishevelled and Jess was shocked to see how thin her arms were as they poked out from the sleeves of her nightshirt. She was sitting cross-legged and Jess noticed a large bruise just above her knee on one leg and another, even larger one, on one of her arms.

'Why, love, whatever's the matter?' she gasped. 'And how on earth did you get those bruises?' Hurrying over to her daughter she tried to put her arms around her, but Mel angrily pushed her away.

'Get out!' she shouted, waving her hand towards the door. 'And just leave me alone, can't you?'

'I'm going nowhere, madam, until you tell me where those came from,' Jess said firmly, pointing at the marks.

Mel's lips quivered and for a moment Jess thought that she was going to talk to her, but then the shuttered look came over her face again.

'I . . . I got them playing hockey at school,' she muttered, lowering her eyes from her mother's searching look.

'But they look quite nasty. Do you want me to put something on them for you?'

Mel shook her head as Jess looked helplessly on. 'Why were you crying?' she probed gently, her own heart full of pain for her beloved daughter.

'I was watching a sad film on the telly and it upset me.'

'Really?' Jess clearly didn't believe her, and Mel began to get agitated again.

'Does it really matter, Mum? Can't you just go now and let me get some sleep? I'm so tired.' Diving under the duvet she pulled it up over her head, and knowing that she was going to say no more, Jess stepped out onto the landing and softly closed the door.

Further along the landing, she paused to look out of the window. A full moon was riding in a black velvet sky, and the thick frost on the lawn looked as if it had been sprinkled with diamond dust. Out there, everything looked so peaceful – and yet inside the house, everything was in turmoil.

*I'll get Mel to the doctor's tomorrow,* Jess promised herself. *This depression has gone on for long enough now.* And it was then that she sensed someone standing, whispering behind her. She turned just in time to see a shadowy figure in a long skirt fade into the shadows, and suddenly the silence was deafening. Her heart leaped as she made her way to the bedroom, knowing that Martha was close by.

Simon was in bed with his back to her; it was becoming the norm now, but after quickly undressing Jess climbed in beside him and placed her arm around his broad shoulders.

'Everything all right, love?' she whispered into the darkness. A grunt was her only answer. After a while, when sleep refused to come, she clicked on the bedside light and took Martha's journal from the drawer. There was no chance of waking Simon. He slept like the dead so Jess decided to read a little until she was tired.

*26 December*

The house is bursting at the seams with all the guests but this afternoon when the meal had been served and all the washing-up had been done, I managed to sneak away and see Jimmy for a short time . . .

'Aw lass, I was wonderin' if you'd manage it,' Jimmy said delightedly as he saw Martha racing towards him across the frosty grass. Her cheeks were flushed, and with her eyes shining he thought he had never seen her look so pretty.

'I were wonderin' if I would an' all,' she answered breathlessly. 'It's absolute chaos back there an' I won't be able to stay fer long. We're all run off our feet.' She swiped a lock of hair back from her face as he took her hand and drew her into the shelter of the copse.

'I got you a little somethin' fer Christmas,' Jimmy said, fumbling in his coat pocket.

'An' I got you somethin' an' all,' Martha laughed as she withdrew a small, hastily wrapped parcel from beneath her cloak.

Jimmy beamed when he unwrapped a smart penknife with a mother-of-pearl handle.

'Aw, thanks, pet,' he murmured, turning it over in his hand and flicking the blade open. 'I can't begin to tell yer how handy this will be. But come on . . . open yours now.'

Blushing, Martha did as she was told and then gasped with delight when she revealed a small silver brooch in the shape of a leaf.

'Oh, Jimmy . . .' She was so thrilled she scarcely knew what to say. 'I ain't never owned a single piece of jewellery in the whole o' me life. It's beautiful an' I'll treasure it always.'

'Not half so much as I'll treasure you,' Jimmy stated as he drew her into his arms. 'We're goin' to be so happy together, I just know it.'

Martha sighed with contentment as she rested her head against his chest and thought of the life they would share together.

'Do yer reckon we'll have any little 'uns when we're wed?' she asked, and Jimmy threw his head back and laughed aloud, startling a rabbit that was hopping by.

'At least half a dozen, if I have my way,' he promised. 'An' I want all the little girls to look just like their mam.'

'Just so long as the lads all look like their dad,' Martha chuckled, and then everything else was forgotten as their lips joined and they made the most of the few precious, stolen moments.

Martha left him shortly afterwards and skipped back towards the house. Wasn't this just turning out to be the best Christmas ever?

Jess slid the journal back into her drawer and clicked the bedside lamp off in a slightly happier frame of mind, and soon her gentle snores joined Simon's.

Whilst Mel was pushing her breakfast around the plate the next day, Jess suggested that she might take the morning off to go to the doctor's, but Mel got so agitated that eventually Jess gave in and reluctantly let her go off to school.

'But you're so thin!' she had pointed out, only to be told that it was fashionable to be thin. It seemed there was no point in arguing with a teenager, although Jess promised herself that if Mel lost any more weight she would take her, even if she had to drag her there kicking and screaming. It was as she was putting a load of washing into the machine later that morning that she suddenly realised she hadn't seen anything of Laura for a while. It was unusual for her neighbour not to have popped in for a quick coffee, and as Jess recalled the last time she had spoken to her, she became concerned. She had been so wrapped up in her own worries that she hadn't given it a thought, but now she remembered that Laura had said Beth was unwell and she was going to take her to the doctor's. Jess hoped that they hadn't found anything seriously wrong with the girl, and after starting the machine she slipped her coat on and set off down the drive to find out. It was a bitterly cold day and a slight fog had fallen over the countryside.

When Laura opened the door to Blue Brick Cottage, Jess was shocked to see how ill she looked. There were dark circles beneath her eyes and she looked as though she had been crying. Beth was huddled in a chair at the side of the inglenook fireplace and didn't even glance up as Jess walked in.

'I just realised I hadn't seen you for a while so I thought I'd pop down and check everything is OK,' Jess told her. 'Are you all right, Laura? You look awfully pale.'

Laura walked over to the deep stone sink and crossed her arms. 'I'm OK, but Beth isn't,' she said bluntly.

'Why – what's wrong with her?' Jess looked towards the girl, feeling worried.

Laura leaned heavily on the edge of the wooden draining board. Her chin sank to her chest and Jess's heart began to race as she realised that something must be seriously wrong.

'Tell me what it is then,' she implored. 'Did you take her to the doctor's?'

Laura nodded. 'Oh, I took her all right and he told me . . .' She gulped deep in her throat before forcing herself to go on. 'He told me that she's pregnant.'

'She's *what*?' Jess sank onto the nearest chair as shock coursed through her. 'Are you quite sure?'

Laura nodded miserably. 'I'm sure all right. The doctor sent a test off to the hospital to double-check and it came back positive. She's nearly four months' gone.'

'So what are you going to do about it?' Jess asked tentatively as Laura threw three tea bags into three mugs.

'Our first instincts were to take her for an abortion,' Laura admitted. 'And if it was left to Den we'd still be doing that. But the doctor was worried about the impact that might have on her, with her being so far gone. He seems to think that she's able to cope with the birth and to be honest I can't bear the thought of getting rid of it, much as you couldn't when you found out about your baby.'

'But Beth could never look after a child,' Jess pointed out. 'She can't even look after herself. You've admitted that yourself.'

'I know she couldn't, but *I* could.'

'But what if.' Jess paused as she chose her words carefully. 'What if the baby has special needs too? It would be a tremendous amount of extra work for you.'

Laura nodded. 'I realise that, but it will still be our grandchild, and I always wanted another baby. Perhaps this has happened for a reason.'

Jess had her sensible head on, now that the first shock of what Laura had told her had worn off. 'Poor lass. Does she even understand that she's having a baby?'

'She doesn't seem to understand what's happening at all,' Laura said, wiping her eyes. 'She doesn't like being sick, of course, but the doctor assured us that she's well and healthy and that she will manage. If he'd thought otherwise I would have taken her for a termination even though it would have broken my heart.'

'And what about the baby's father? Does he know about it? Is it the boy from the youth club?'

Laura shook her head wearily. 'Den and I went to see the youth-club leader and he had no idea at all who it might be. It seems that for weeks, once your Simon has dropped her off, she's gone walk-about, and as some of the boys do the same thing, it could be any one of three of them. The problem is, all the young people who go there have special needs like Beth so there's no way of telling which one it is.'

'My God!' Jess was so appalled that for a moment she couldn't think of a single thing to say. Surely the staff at the youth club should have kept a better eye on the sexually mature young people? 'Is there anything that I can do to help?'

Laura shook her head. 'No, but thanks for asking. I suppose this is every mother's worst nightmare come true; even more so in Beth's case, and I just have to deal with it now. I blame myself, Jess. I've always known how vulnerable Beth is, and I shouldn't have let her out of my sight. But I just wanted her to have some sort of normality in her life.'

'Of course you did. Any mother would, so you mustn't blame yourself.' Jess felt tears sting at the back of her eyes.

'I dare say we'll get through it,' Laura replied, trying to be optimistic but failing dismally. 'I just dread the birth though. I don't know how Beth will deal with it, despite what the doctor said.'

'She will get lots of support,' Jess said encouragingly. Laura looked as if she was about to crack, and she too needed all the support she could get right now.

When Jess got home and saw Simon's Land Rover she perked up considerably. He'd probably come home because of the poor weather conditions and it would be nice for them to spend a little time together on their own.

He was sitting at the kitchen table reading the newspaper when she entered the house and he glanced up briefly as she took her coat off.

'Weather stopped play, has it?' Jess said trying to keep her voice light. He nodded but didn't reply, so now her voice became solemn as she went on, 'Laura just told me some dreadful news. I feel so sorry for her.'

'Why? What's happened?' She had his full attention now as she sat down opposite him.

'Well, it's not actually Laura – it's Beth. Laura has just discovered that she's pregnant.'

'She's *what*?' Simon stared at her in disbelief. 'But she can't be! She's just a kid.'

'Actually she isn't,' Jess reminded him. 'She's a young woman. Laura is so distressed, but then she would be, wouldn't she? And the worst of it is, they don't even know who the father is. It appears that when you've been dropping her off at the youth club each week, she's been clearing off so it could be any one of three boys who go there.'

Simon had gone deathly pale, but Jess wasn't surprised. She knew that her husband was very fond of Beth. In fact, he was like a mother hen when he was around her and very protective.

'So what are they going to do about it?' he asked eventually.

'Den wants her to have an abortion but Laura doesn't think she can go through with it, and they haven't much time left before it's too late for an abortion anyway.'

'But how will Beth cope with a baby?' he spluttered, much as Jess herself had done only minutes ago.

'She won't, will she?' Jess replied practically. 'It will be down to Laura and Den to bring it up, particularly if the baby is special needs like Beth. They're certainly going to have their hands full.'

'And how are they going to find out who the father is?'

'They didn't seem overly concerned about that. I mean, there wouldn't be much point in knowing, would there? All the boys who attend the youth club are special needs like Beth, so even if they knew who he was he'd probably be more of a hindrance than a help. It's all just so sad and such a mess.'

'You're not kidding.' Simon closed the newspaper and threw it across the table as he rose from his seat. 'I'm going for a bath,' he informed her shortly, and seconds later Jess found herself alone again – but then she was getting used to that by now.

# Chapter Twenty-Six

It was almost a week later when Jess next saw Laura again. She came up to the house one tea-time when Jess was baking. Simon had gone out, as was usual nowadays, and the girls were upstairs in their rooms.

'Hello,' Jess greeted her warmly. 'Come on in and take your coat off. The wind is enough to cut you in two out there.' And where is Beth, then?'

'Oh, she's tucked up in bed.' Laura plonked herself down at the table looking thoroughly miserable. 'She's still feeling very queasy and she doesn't understand why, although I've tried to explain to her. She's hated being sick ever since she was a little girl.'

'It isn't very nice,' Jess agreed. 'Thankfully I seem to have got over that stage now.' The waistbands on her jeans were becoming uncomfortably tight now and today she had felt a movement in her stomach for the first time. It wasn't what she could have classed as a kick, more of a flutter, but it had made the baby seem more real to her all the same.

'So how are you feeling about your new addition now?' Laura asked.

Jess smiled. 'I think I felt a little flutter today and it brought it home to me that there's really a baby there,' she answered. 'But as to how I feel about it . . . still mixed, I suppose. Sometimes I can't help but look forward to it and then other times I feel resentful. Probably because Mel and her dad have barely spoken to me since they found out. The way Mel goes on, you wouldn't think me and her dad were married. It's as if we've committed a cardinal sin. The only one who is really thrilled about it is Jo. She can't wait and she's thinking of names already, bless her.'

Dipping her finger in the cake mixture Jess was stirring and then licking it, Laura said, 'Well, at least you know what you're letting yourself in for. Poor Beth doesn't have a clue. She's not good at dealing with pain and I'm beginning to wonder now if an abortion wouldn't be the best thing, after all. The trouble is, I shall have to make a decision very soon. Time is fast running out.'

'It must be very hard for you.' Jess tried to imagine how she would feel if it was Mel in that position. She piled the mixture into cake tins, then after popping them in the oven, she said hesitantly, 'You know what you told me some time ago – about there being some sort of presence here? Well, I'm beginning to think you were right.'

'That's a bit of a turn-around, isn't it!' Laura exclaimed. 'You looked at me as if I was barmy when I told you. What brought about this change of heart?'

'Lots of things,' Jess finally admitted. 'I hear things – someone crying – and sometimes I get the feeling that someone is standing behind me. I've seen a face peering out from a window in the attics and then recently I caught a glimpse of a young woman on the landing. She was dressed in a long skirt. At other times I've heard whispering, as if someone is trying to talk to me, and lately things have started to go missing – and then they turn up in the most improbable places. I'm sure it has something to do with the journal that I told you about, that I found in the attic. I think if anyone really *is* here, it's Martha.'

'It's certainly a young woman,' Laura agreed solemnly. 'I've sensed her too. I think she *wanted* you to come here – and that's why you felt so drawn to the house.'

'But *why* is she still here?' Jess asked. 'I thought when people died they passed over to the other side, through some sort of light or something.'

'I really don't know,' Laura admitted. 'But I know she's here for a reason and it's definitely something to do with you.'

'The gypsy woman told me almost the same thing.' Jess stared towards the high ceiling. 'I haven't read much of the journal for a while now. I thought if I stopped reading it so much, the strange things wouldn't keep happening – but it hasn't made any difference.'

'They won't stop,' Laura assured her. 'Whoever is here won't leave now until they've done what they stayed to do, so you've just got to go with it. I don't think she actually wishes *you* any harm – but she's certainly got issues with someone here.'

'So why don't *you* just ask her what it is then?' Jess snapped. 'If you can see or sense these things, surely you can talk to her?' Then her shoulders sagged. 'I'm sorry, Laura, I didn't mean to take it out on you.'

Hoping to change the subject, Laura said, 'It was so nice of your Simon to call in to see Beth the other day. She was really pleased to see him. I think she misses him giving her a lift to the youth club.'

'Simon called in?' It was the first Jess had heard of it, and she was mildly surprised.

'Yes, he asked if Den and I wanted him to try and find out who was responsible for getting her into this mess but we told him we don't want to pursue that. There wouldn't be any point. It's our problem and we'll have to deal with it the best way we can. At least the youth club now keep all the youngsters under much stricter surveillance so it can't happen again.'

Once Laura had gone back to her own cottage Jess got on the computer and did some shopping, stocking up on food for the freezer, then she went on various sites hunting for wallpaper that might be suitable for the nursery. She knew that if she was going to keep this baby she ought to start getting prepared for it, and as she had nothing better to do, now was as good a time as any. There were two or three patterns that she quite liked but in the end she decided to wait until Jo was with her and let her have the final choice. It was the least she could do, seeing as Jo was the only one who was pleased about the baby.

She cooked a spaghetti Bolognese for tea, and then both the girls shot off back to their rooms to do their homework, leaving Jess to clear away the supper.

When the kitchen was tidy again she settled down to read the local newspaper at the table and was surprised to see headlights flash into the courtyard. She was even more shocked when Simon breezed in seconds later with a wide smile on his face. It was the first time he had been home early and in a good mood for ages, and she could hardly believe it.

'Hello, love.' He slid out of his coat before planting a sloppy kiss on her cheek. 'How are you feeling then?'

'I er . . . I'm fine,' Jess faltered, amazed at the change in him. Here he was, home on time, and falling over himself to be nice to her. 'You're early.'

'Yep, it's bitter out there, so I told the lads we were knocking off early so I could come home and spend a nice quiet night cuddled up by the fire with my missus.'

'You're not going out, then?' Jess asked, trying to sound as normal as possible.

'Not on your nelly. When I've eaten I'm going to go and have a nice hot bath and then I'm settling down in front of the telly. Now what's that I can smell? Is it spaghetti Bolognese?' When Jess nodded he rubbed his stomach in anticipation. 'Just what the doctor ordered. I'm so hungry I could eat a scabby horse.'

Still bemused, Jess hastily dished up his meal before scuttling away to put the kettle on.

He cleared his plate in no time and then as she put a steaming mug of tea in front of him he playfully slapped her bottom and told her, 'Delicious. Just like the woman that cooked it.'

'Is everything all right?' she asked tentatively and he laughed.

'Everything is fine. Why, shouldn't it be?'

'It's just that you seem to be in such a good mood. You haven't won the lottery, have you?'

'I wish. But a bloke can be in a good mood, can't he? I know I've been a bit of a grump lately, but now I've had time to get my head round it I reckon having another baby might not be such a bad idea, after all.'

'Really?' Jess gasped.

He gave her the lopsided grin that could always make her legs turn to jelly. 'Yes, really, and I'm sorry for the way I've behaved, love. I suppose it just came as a bit of a shock, that's all.'

'It was for me too,' she pointed out, still struggling to come to terms with the sudden change in him, welcome though it was.

'Right then.' He took a swig of his tea and stood up. 'I'm off for a nice soak in the bath. You go and have a look what's on the box, eh, and I'll be down in no time.'

He breezed through the door and it was then that the whispers started like white noise in her head. Convinced that someone was standing right behind her, Jess whirled about but there was no one there although the whispers were louder. Clamping her hands over her ears she screwed her eyes tight shut and slowly the whispers receded and she dared to open her eyes again. Badly shaken, she sat down heavily and for the first time she began to wonder if she was losing her mind. After all, she had been under a lot of stress just lately, what with Simon's mood swings and Mel's tantrums. Was this what it was like to have a breakdown? All manner of things began to skip through her head until Simon suddenly appeared again in his dressing-gown.

'What's up, sweetheart?' he asked with concern as he saw how pale she was.

'Oh . . . it's nothing. I just felt a bit dizzy.' She managed to raise a weak smile as she rose unsteadily from her seat.

Simon instantly grabbed her elbow and steered her into the small lounge where he sat her on the settee with a stool beneath her feet. 'You sit there while I go and get you a drink,' he told her as he shot off to the kitchen. He was back in seconds sloshing water all over the rim of a glass.

'Here, drink this,' he ordered, and she obediently took it from him and sipped it.

'Is that better?'

She nodded as he sat beside her and slid his arm across her shoulder. 'You've been overdoing things,' he muttered, 'and I blame myself. I should have been around to help out more.'

'I'm fine now,' she said as she rested her head on his shoulder. It had been such a long time since they had been like this that she didn't want anything to spoil it.

They sat in companionable silence until Jess dozed off, and when Simon gently woke her some time later, she started.

'It's all right,' he soothed. 'You've been out for the count but it's bedtime now. Go on, you go up. I'll lock up and I'll join you in a minute.'

'Thanks, love,' she murmured, feeling more contented than she had in a long time.

She was propped against the headboard waiting for him when he came into the bedroom ten minutes later and smiled at her suggestively. 'Move over and let your husband make love to you,' he said softly.

Only too happy to oblige Jess did as she was told, burning with desire as his warm hands found their way beneath her nightshirt. And suddenly she remembered why she had fallen in love with him as he kissed away all her concerns, and there was no one but the two of them in the whole world.

An hour later she lay with her head on his broad chest listening to his heartbeat. The rain was hammering against the windows but she was oblivious to everything but the man lying at her side.

'Are you all right?' he whispered into the darkness.

'Mm, *better* than all right.'

'Good.' He kissed the top of her head before saying hesitantly, 'Actually Jess, I need to ask you something.'

'So ask away then,' she purred as she played with the hairs on his chest.

'Well . . . um, the thing is . . . I need a favour.'

Leaning on her elbow she stared down at him, watching the shadows

205

play across his face and thinking how handsome he was as she waited for him to go on.

'I – look, I need to borrow some money. I hate to ask but I'm pretty desperate, to be honest.'

The smile disappeared to be replaced by a frown. She had never known Simon to be short before, particularly since she had come into her gran's inheritance. Until then he had always been the breadwinner, but since then she had never expected a single penny from him. She paid for all the housekeeping expenses and all the bills, apart from the various insurances, which Simon had always seen to, and had assumed that his business was doing well.

'The thing is,' he hurried on when she didn't immediately answer him, 'work is fine but I have some clients who haven't paid me for fairly large jobs yet, and until they do I'm a bit strapped. I've got suppliers waiting to be paid and I need wages for the men. It shouldn't be for long though. As soon as they do pay me I can give it you back.'

'How much do you need?' she asked.

'About ten thousand should do it.'

'Ten thousand *pounds*!' Jess couldn't keep the shock from sounding in her voice and she felt him tense.

'I wouldn't ask if I didn't have to,' he muttered resentfully, and she instantly felt guilty as she thought of all the years he had kept her and the children.

'Well, of course you can have it. I was just surprised when I heard how much you needed,' she explained hurriedly.

'Building materials don't come cheap,' he told her. 'And it is only a loan until the clients that owe me cough up.'

'Don't be so silly,' she scolded him. 'The money might be in a bank account in my name, but it belongs to both of us. We're married, aren't we? When do you need it?'

'I was wondering if you could perhaps write me a cheque?'

'Of course I will,' she assured him.

'Thanks,' he said shortly, and as he turned his back to her she realised how much it must have cost him to ask. As it was, she could afford that amount comfortably. She still had over a hundred thousand pounds of her gran's money left, although she knew that most of that would go when she finished the rest of the renovations. Everything was so expensive and she sometimes felt that she was throwing money into a bottomless pit; she just hoped that it would be all worth it. It would certainly be a comfortable inheritance for the girls one day, and that knowledge gave her a great deal of comfort. Hopefully they wouldn't have to struggle as she and Simon had done when they had first got married. Every penny had counted back then and they had often had to rob Peter to pay Paul. But all that was behind them now and they were comparatively well-off compared to most people.

Snuggling down beneath the duvet she closed her eyes and soon she was fast asleep.

The weather was appalling the following day and so Simon decided it would be useless to try and work in it.

Jess wrote him a cheque out and handed it to him with a bright smile.

'Thanks, love,' he said as he stuffed it in his pocket. 'I think I'll go into town and pay it into my account, then I'm going to go and chase up some of these clients that owe me. But I shouldn't be too long.'

Jess felt vaguely disappointed. She had hoped they might spend the day together, but it was nice to see Simon cheerful again so she nodded.

'Why don't you call in the butcher's in Chapel End while I'm gone and get us all a nice bit of steak for our dinner?' he suggested as he left the house a short time later.

'You're on, if that's what you fancy,' she said cheerfully, and when he strode away she found herself humming merrily. Simon certainly seemed to be happy again. If she could just get Mel out of her moods, things would be looking up at last.

# Chapter Twenty-Seven

'That's it then. No more school for two whole weeks now,' Jess smiled when she and the girls arrived home one day in late December.

'I can't believe it's Christmas in just one more week,' Jo said excitedly. 'I've asked Dad if I can have a pony. We have plenty of room to keep one, don't we?'

'But I thought you said a couple of weeks ago that you wanted a computer?' Jess queried. That was Jo all over; she changed her mind like the wind.

'Well, I suppose that would do if I can't have a pony,' Jo shot back with a grin.

'And what would you like, pet?' Jess asked her other daughter.

Mel shrugged. 'I'm not bothered. I don't want anything really.'

Jess sighed. Mel was getting no easier at all, although things between Jess herself and Simon had improved vastly over the last couple of weeks, which was one blessing.

'Dad's picking a Christmas tree up this evening on his way home from work,' Jess now informed them. 'You can help decorate it if you like.'

'I will,' Jo volunteered. 'And I can go out and collect some holly for you too if you like. I saw some in the woods the other day when I took Alfie for a walk.'

'That would be nice, love. We could put some along the mantelpiece, and I'll get some mistletoe too when I go into town tomorrow.'

Jess had been shopping for presents almost non-stop for the last two weeks but thankfully she was almost finished now, which just left all of the wrapping to do.

'Can I stay over at my friend's house tomorrow night after her birthday party?' Jo asked, and Jess nodded obligingly.

'I don't see why not, so long as her mum is agreeable to it. I got a present for you to give her and a card, so you can wrap it up tonight if you like.'

'Thanks, Mum.' Jo hummed along to the Christmas songs on the radio while Mel stared glumly out of the window.

'And did you decide if you're going to the Christmas disco at school tonight?' Jess asked her.

Mel shook her head. 'No, I reckon I'll give it a miss.'

'That's a shame, because I got you a new top and those jeans from Monsoon that you've had your eye on,' Jess said, handing her a carrier bag. 'Why don't you just try them on? It might get you in the mood, and we can always change the top if you don't like it or if it doesn't fit. We've just about got time to get back to the shop before it shuts.'

'Thanks,' Mel mumbled ungraciously, and snatching the bag from her mother she disappeared off up the stairs.

Jess shook her head despairingly. There was just no pleasing Mel nowadays no matter what she did, and it was seriously getting her down. The girl was becoming more and more reclusive.

Jess slipped upstairs to change into the new, bigger trousers she had bought for herself. She sighed with relief when she took off the pair she had been wearing, and then reaching into the bedside drawer, she took out a band to tie her hair back while she cooked the dinner. It was then that her eyes settled on the journal and almost instantly the whispers started up again. She hadn't read a word of it for weeks, but promised herself that tonight, after they'd put the Christmas tree up, she would have an early night and catch up on the next chapter of Martha's life. Then in a happy mood, she went downstairs to prepare the evening meal.

Simon was home early. The weather was playing havoc with his outdoor jobs and he was beginning to wonder if the rain was ever going to stop; however, he had called into the marketplace and remembered the Christmas tree.

It towered above Jess and she chuckled as he dragged it into the kitchen. 'Is it big enough?' she teased.

'Well, you didn't say what size you wanted,' he said lamely as he leaned it against the wall. 'I'll fetch a bucket in and set it up for you after dinner. Where are you going to put it?'

'I thought we'd put it in the formal lounge.' Jess could just picture it against the ornate marble fireplace but Jo had other ideas.

'Oh Mum, please don't put it in there,' she said. 'We never get to go in there so we won't see it. And Alfie isn't allowed in there either because of the new carpet. Can't we put it into the small lounge where we sit every night?'

'She does have a point,' Simon agreed. Jess was very house-proud when it came to the rooms that had been decorated, which was most of the downstairs ones now.

'But I thought we might use the formal lounge seeing as it's Christmas,' Jess answered.

'Nah, let's stick to the small one, it's cosier,' Jo insisted, and when Jess saw Simon wink at her she sighed. She knew when she was out-voted.

'I suppose you're right but let's have dinner first, eh?' She had made a large pan of beef stew with fluffy dumplings floating in it, and the smell was making Jo's stomach rumble in anticipation.

When the meal was over Jo went off to wrap her friend's birthday present ready for the next day and Mel slouched off to her room to play on her computer.

It was then that Simon became serious as he told Mel, 'Bill had to leave work this morning. His wife called him on his mobile to tell him that his dad has passed away unexpectedly. It looks like it was a massive heart-attack, from what we can gather. And he only lost his mum last year so it's hit him pretty hard.'

'Oh, how awful and just before Christmas too. Not that there's ever a good time to lose someone you love,' Jo said, thinking back to the time when she had lost her gran. 'The poor chap must be devastated.' She was very fond of Bill, who had turned out to be Simon's right-hand man over the years.

'He is, I've told him to have as long off as he needs. He'll have to organise the funeral and everything now, and it's not as if we're inundated with work at this time of year. In fact, things are pretty grim at the moment. I've got enough booked until the end of January but then nothing.'

Jess smiled at him. 'Try not to worry about it. It's early days yet, and it's not as if we're starving, is it? Something will turn up. It usually does and then by the time spring arrives you'll be working all the hours God sends again.'

'You're probably right,' Simon admitted, then shot off to the outbuildings to find a bucket sturdy enough to house the Christmas tree.

Once he had gone off for his weekly game of darts Jess and Jo set to and decorated the tree. Jess had chosen to store the baubles and lights for it down in the cellar instead of all the way up in the attic, and she wasn't at all keen on going down there. There was only one single light bulb to illuminate the whole massive space and the steps were slippery with damp and mould. She'd been intending to get down there and give the whole place a thorough clean ever since they'd

210

moved in, but as yet she hadn't found the time. Now she couldn't envisage it getting done until well after the baby was born. Not that there was any panic.

Later when the tree was dressed, Jess switched on the lights.

'Oh, it looks lovely,' Jo gasped with childish pleasure.

Jess grinned, pleased with her response. 'Yes, it does, but now it's bedtime for you, young lady. I've promised myself an early night as I'm worn out.'

'You're not ill, are you, Mum?' Jo looked at her anxiously.

Jess ruffled her hair. 'Of course I'm not. But I'm lumping this around with me now and I get tired.' She rubbed her expanding stomach and Jo was all smiles again as she pecked her on the cheek and skipped happily out of the room.

An hour later, Jess settled contentedly back on her pillows and opened Martha's journal and as she began to read, she forgot everything.

*27 December*

Oh, it's been a wonderful Christmas but so busy that it has passed in a blur. The Master and the young Master and Mistress all had their Christmas dinner in the dining room and it looked so grand that I could hardly believe it. The table was covered in a snow-white cloth and laid with the best silver cutlery and the finest china, and the guests all drank out of crystal goblets. The meal consisted of five courses and I had never seen so much food all at one time in my life before . . .

The panic was over and Mrs Bloom sighed with relief as she dropped exhausted into Granny's old rocking chair. 'Eeh, I don't mind admittin' I were panickin' there fer a time,' she said, wiping the sweat from her brow. 'That goose the Mistress ordered was so enormous I'd feared it would never go in the oven, but all's well that ends well. I wonder if they all enjoyed it?'

Martha was at the sink rubbing salt into the bottom of the great sooty cooking pots when the door opened minutes later and the cook's question was answered when Miss Melody appeared looking beautiful in a pale green silk gown with pearls about her throat and dangling from her ears.

'Oh Cook, I just had to come and thank you personally for such a lovely meal,' she smiled. 'The goose and vegetables were cooked to perfection and so were the plum puddings.'

Cook beamed with satisfaction and suddenly all the hard work they had put in was worthwhile.

'I had them puddin's soakin' in brandy fer days,' she told Miss Melody proudly, and the kindly young woman nodded.

'Well, everyone enjoyed them, so thank you again, but I also came to ask if the staff would mind lining up in the hall mid-afternoon? Master Leonard and I have a few little gifts for you all.'

Grace and Martha's mouth gaped open. They had never been given a present by Master Fenton in all the time they had worked there.

'That's right kind o' you, Miss Melody. We'll be there,' Cook told her and with a satisfied nod to them all and a final friendly smile, the young woman left the room to rejoin her guests.

As promised, the servants formed an orderly queue in the entrance hall later that afternoon and Miss Melody and Master Leonard worked their way along the line forgetting no one. She gave Grace and Bertie a beautiful counterpane to put on their bed when they moved into their new cottage and Grace was so speechless with pleasure that she could not find the words to thank her, so she merely bobbed her knee.

Martha received a selection of some beautiful ribbons that had been woven in his ribbon factory in the town. They were all the colours of the rainbow and Martha knew that it would be hard to decide which one to wear first. The Mistress had even remembered Granny Reid, who was still confined to bed, and gave Martha a thick pair of woollen bedsocks that had Granny crowing with delight when the girl took them up to her. And so the young Master and his wife spoke to each servant until all the presents were given out and then the staff returned to their duties in a happy frame of mind.

Grace and Martha, with Polly giving a hand, set to to get the dining room ready for the afternoon tea, fearful that they would never manage all that needed to be done in time. Everyone was fluttering about in a panic but thankfully they managed it and once the guests had finished, the staff were then given permission to have their own Christmas dinner. Cook had prepared and cooked a slightly smaller bird for them and everyone attended, even the Tolleys and their brood. They were all tired but even so they all enjoyed it and the atmosphere was gay. Along with the goose they were served with crispy roast potatoes, vegetables and all the trimmings. Little Joey's eyes almost popped out of his head when he saw so much food and he ate so much that Phoebe feared he would make himself sick. The main course was followed by yet another of Cook's delicious plum puddings. Bertie had two helpings and then collapsed into a chair and was unable to move for half an hour. Miss Melody had supplied wine and ale to serve with the meal and some of the servants were more than a little tipsy by the time the meal was over but it was Christmas, after all.

'Right, that's it then, you lot,' Cook barked eventually. 'The party's over now and we all 'ave to get back to work.'

They prepared the dining room and the meal ready to cook for breakfast the next morning and then at last, tired but happy, Martha was able to go and sit with her granny for a while.

'Ah, Granny,' she scolded on entering the old woman's room. 'You've scarcely touched the tray I brought up fer you earlier.'

'Well, I ain't got much of an appetite at present, pet. But I enjoyed what I had,' Granny placated her.

The dear old woman looked so frail that suddenly all the pleasure was wiped out from the day. What would she do if anything should happen to her gran? Martha couldn't envisage her life without her in it. But then she shook off her sad thoughts. Miss Melody was paying for the doctor to visit Granny regularly now and she could only hope that soon she would start to improve. She spent some time talking to her and holding her hand, but then Granny chuckled when Martha yawned widely.

'Get yerself off to bed, pet,' she urged. 'Yer look done in.'

'I think I will,' Martha agreed, and kissing the old woman's head she then tucked the blankets beneath her chin and headed off to her own room. It had been such a wonderful day that Martha was sure she would never be able to sleep, but all the same she dropped off the instant her head hit the pillow and didn't wake till first light the next day.

Boxing Day soon proved to be as hectic as Christmas Day. Master Leonard had arranged a shoot in the grounds for the men in the morning, and the women stayed in the drawing room watching from the window. Bertie had been out since the crack of dawn beating the bushes to disturb the pheasants, and the whole event was a huge success. Maids took glasses of hot punch out to the men on silver trays, and when the men eventually came in they rushed away to get changed before going in to lunch.

In the evening the ladies played the piano and sang in the drawing room, and there was a party atmosphere once again throughout the whole house. Martha was clearing the dirty pots from the dining room when she ran into Master Fenton in the hallway, and suddenly the mood was gone.

He stared at her thoughtfully as Martha lowered her head and made to pass him, laden down with the heavy tray she was carrying, but he extended his arm and placed it against the wall, effectively blocking her path.

'Excuse me, sir,' Martha said politely but he merely leered at her as he asked, 'Is it right what I'm hearin' – that you're walking out with young Billy who works for Farmer Codd on Leathermill Farm?'

'Yes, sir, it is.' Martha's cheeks flamed as she kept her eyes averted from his face, afraid of what she might see there.

'Mm, so I dare say you'll be thinking of marriage in the not too distant future, eh?' he went on.

Martha shook her head in quick denial. 'Marriage hasn't been mentioned yet, sir,' she gasped, praying that someone would come to find her.

'Well, perhaps I should start to show you what will be expected of you,' he murmured, and without warning his hand snaked out and gave her breast a vicious squeeze. Martha was so shocked that she cried out and the tray of dishes she was carrying crashed to the floor, sending splinters of china shooting in every direction. Seconds later, the green baize door was flung open and Bertie appeared.

Seeing what was happening, he roared like a bull – and as Martha looked helplessly on he raced along the passageway and caught the Master by the scruff of the neck, shaking him as a dog would a rat.

'Why, you dirty low-down bastard,' he cried. 'Ain't it enough that you raped me wife an' made her with child? Must you now try to take her young sister's innocence too?'

With tears flowing freely down her cheeks, Martha looked around and was horrified to see the young Master and Mistress standing in the open door of the drawing room with shocked expressions on their faces.

Grace had run from the kitchen too now and she was also crying as she hung her head in shame and wrung her hands together.

The young Master suddenly strode forward and with a strength Martha would never have given him credit for, he dragged Bertie off his uncle and held him at arm's length.

'Bertie, you go about your business and leave this to me now,' he ordered.

'But—' Bertie protested.

'I said *leave it to me*, man.'

Bertie's arms dropped helplessly to his sides and he allowed Grace to lead him away, still glaring at Master Fenton.

'And you, Martha, clear up these broken pots and take them to the kitchen, would you?' the young Master now said in a kindlier tone.

Shaking like a leaf, Martha stooped to do as she was told as the young man then grabbed the Master's elbow and forced him towards the study. The Master was swaying and obviously the worse for drink, but his young nephew showed him no mercy.

When Martha had all the broken crockery collected together on the tray she scuttled away to the kitchen with tears still raining down her cheeks, and the second she entered the room, Cook caught her to her ample bosom in a hug.

'There, there, pet,' she soothed. 'Never you fear. The young Master will sort that tyrant out, now that he knows what's been goin' on, you just mark me words.'

Martha truly wished that she could believe her, but she could not shake the sense of foreboding that had settled about her like a shroud. And there was poor Grace who was now sobbing brokenly as Bertie paced up and down the kitchen in a blind rage. Their dreadful secret was out in the open now for all and sundry to hear about, and they both wondered how they would bear it.

Martha prayed this was not the end of the happier times they had lately enjoyed.

Jess closed the journal with tears in her eyes as she tried to imagine the humiliation poor Grace must have felt when Bertie broke down and shouted her shame for all to hear. She supposed he must have loved her very much indeed to marry her, knowing that she was carrying another man's child, even if it had been forced upon her. But it seemed as she read on and became increasingly entwined in their lives that Bertie was finding it more and more difficult to deal with, and that his hatred of his Master was growing by the day. Where would it end, Jess wondered – and why was Martha still here, waiting for her? And she *was* here . . . Jess knew that now as surely as night followed day, and somehow she had to figure out why.

# Chapter Twenty-Eight

'How was Bill today?' Jess asked the next afternoon when Simon arrived home early yet again. The rain was falling with a vengeance and now the River Anker had burst its banks and the bottom of the lawn was severely flooded. It wasn't really a problem apart from the mess the water left behind when it subsided. The lawn sloped sharply so there was little or no fear of the house itself ever being affected.

'He only popped into work briefly,' Simon told her with a shake of his head. 'The poor chap is up to his neck in funeral arrangements. But worse than that, it seems that his father didn't leave a will, which will cause all sorts of problems now. You know, Jess, it got me to thinking . . . we ought to make a will.'

'Us?' She swivelled on her heel to stare at him, appalled. 'But . . . we're not *that* old.'

'It has nothing to do with age,' Simon stated sensibly. 'What if I had an accident? Or what if, God forbid, anything happened to you? We need to know that the children are going to be seen to.'

'I suppose there is that in it,' Jess agreed hesitantly, although the very thought of making a will seemed so final. As if one of them might keel over at any minute. 'But how do we go about it?'

'Easily,' he assured her. 'I make a quick phone call, a solicitor comes out to see us, we tell him who we want everything left to in the event of anything happening to either of us, and Bob's your uncle.'

'Is it really as simple as that?'

He nodded. 'It certainly is, and there's no time like the present so I'll go through the *Yellow Pages* this afternoon and make the call.'

'I suppose we could use the same solicitor who dealt with the house sale for us,' Jess said musingly.

'That makes sense,' Simon agreed. 'Just leave it with me. When would you like them to come out?'

'Could we wait until the New Year now?' she asked, still uncomfortable with the idea.

'To tell you the truth, I'd sooner get it out of the way this week. I might be too busy after Christmas, and then it would mean taking time off work,' he pointed out.

Jess nodded reluctantly, supposing that he was right.

He smiled and after dropping a kiss on her forehead he went off to the outbuildings to sort his tools out before ringing the solicitor.

The solicitor called to see them the following day, and just as Simon had promised, everything was surprisingly easy – so much so that by the time he left, Jess wondered what she had been so worried about.

The first Christmas in their new home went surprisingly well. Both the girls were given new computers each on Christmas morning, along with numerous other smaller gifts, and even Mel managed to raise a smile. They celebrated it quietly and uneventfully. Jess had started to be quite sick in the morning again and there was no one other than her close family that she particularly wanted there. She cooked them all a traditional Christmas dinner with all the trimmings, and as she prepared it she couldn't help but think back to the Christmas Martha and her family had spent in Stonebridge House. Everything was so much easier now, thanks to all the modern labour-saving devices. She found that she was viewing the house through different eyes, so much so that she could picture the rooms as they would have been back then. It wasn't difficult; Martha's descriptions of the place were so explicit. She could imagine Miss Melody drifting down the staircase in her beautiful gowns and the maids scuttling from one room to another as they did their chores in starched white aprons and mobcaps. She could also sense Martha's fear of Master Fenton, so tangibly that she could have reached out and touched it.

Simon continued to be in a good mood and apart from two nights a week when he went out for a drink or a game of darts with his workmates, he stayed in and was attentive and caring. Jess could hardly believe the change in him and prayed that it would continue.

On Boxing Day they all wrapped up warmly and went for a walk along the swollen banks of the River Anker as far as the stone bridge. It was almost completely under water and the arches were clogged with debris that the swirling current had carried there. For no reason that Jess could explain, a cold finger played up her spine as she looked at it – and she somehow knew that something bad had once happened there, although as yet she could have no idea what it was.

'Come on, let's go back and have a warm drink,' she suggested, turning the collar of her coat up. 'I'm frozen and I've had enough walking for one day.'

Simon nodded affably as he skimmed a stone across the heaving water and called Alfie to heel. The dog seemed to have rolled in every mud puddle they had passed and now looked more like a black Labrador than a golden one.

Jo was skipping along merrily in front of them whilst Mel walked behind them with a closed expression on her face. It didn't much trouble Jess; it had taken her all her powers of persuasion to get her eldest daughter to come with them in the first place and she hadn't really expected much else.

'Ouch!' Jess suddenly stopped and put her hand to her stomach.

'What's wrong, love?' Simon asked as he took her elbow.

'Nothing,' she said a little breathlessly. 'The baby just gave me its first proper kick, that's all, and I wasn't expecting it.' She knew that soon, she would have to go into proper maternity clothes. 'I feel really fat,' she said glumly. 'And I'm not sure if it's all I've eaten over Christmas or the baby growing.'

Simon chuckled. 'I dare say it's a combination of both. But then you can't expect to have a baby without putting weight on.'

At the mention of the baby, Mel's expression darkened and now she overtook them and headed for the house.

'Do you think she'll accept the baby when it comes?' Jess murmured with a worried expression on her face.

'Of course she will.' Simon kept his eyes fixed on Mel's back. 'She'll have to, won't she?'

'I suppose so.' Jess wished that Mel could be just a little excited about the prospect of a new brother or sister. Jo certainly was and went on about it all the time, but Jess hoped that once Mel actually saw the baby, and realised that it was a real little person, she would be more tolerant.

'When are you going to get the paper for the nursery?' Jo suddenly asked, as if she had been able to read her mother's mind.

'I thought we might pop down and get it sometime this week. The decorators will be coming in to start on it as soon as we've got the New Year over, so I can't wait for much longer.' Seeing as Simon didn't have a lot of work on, Jess had hoped that he would do the decorating, but she was fed up of dropping hints. 'Are you quite sure you've decided on the one with Winnie the Pooh on?'

Jo nodded. 'Yep! That's the one I like.'

'Then that's the one it shall be.' Jess smiled at her fondly, hoping that the new baby would inherit its sister's sunny nature. Jo was shooting up now and was at that curious stage where she seemed to be all arms and legs, neither a child nor yet a young woman. She was already taller than her older sister and Jess guessed that she was going to take after her father for her height.

She remarked on it now to Simon as they strolled along. 'I reckon she could be a model if she keeps on growing the way she is and stays as skinny.'

'You could be right,' he said. 'She's turning into a little stunner, isn't she?'

As soon as they got in Jo went off to log onto Facebook and Mel went to her room to play her new CDs, leaving Jess and Simon to enjoy a leisurely afternoon cuppa together.

'Ah, this is the life,' Jess sighed contentedly as she wriggled her bare toes and held them out towards the fire that was blazing in the grate. Simon had offered to fit a living flame gas fire in this room for her but Jess had decided to keep the coal one. It was so much cosier somehow and worth all the mess of having to clear out the ashes each morning and bring the coal in.

The following morning, Simon ran Jo into Weddington to pick up her friend, Molly, who was coming for a sleepover, and Jess decided that once he was back, she would pop into town and pick up the wallpaper for the nursery while she was in the mood. She had no doubt the town centre would be heaving with people shopping in the sales but she wanted to get it out of the way while Simon was at home to keep his eye on the girls.

As soon as they were back, she picked up her car keys. 'I'm going into town,' she told Simon. 'I don't suppose I can tempt you to come with me, can I?' She grinned, knowing the answer to the question before she even asked. Simon hated shopping and only ever went when he absolutely had to.

'No, thanks,' he said hastily. 'It's hardly my favourite pastime, as you know.'

She chuckled. 'I guessed you'd say that. I just want to pick the wallpaper up from town and call in to Asda on my way home, so I shouldn't be too long.'

It was just beginning to rain as she pulled out of the courtyard, and by the time she got to the end of the drive it was pelting down. Switching the windscreen wipers on full she leaned forward and peered through the screen as she turned into the lane that led to the main road.

Lorries were thundering past with a constant stream of cars and vans between them. Jess changed down to third gear and gently touched the brake, but nothing happened. Pressing her foot down harder, she applied more pressure and it was then that it hit her like a douse of cold water: she had no brakes and she was heading towards the main road. Sobbing with fear and frustration she pumped the brakes again and again, as the main road loomed closer, and then from the corner of her eye she saw a farm gate that had been left open and she swerved the car towards it, narrowly missing the wooden posts by inches as she careered past them out of control. With shaking fingers she switched off the engine and immediately the car lost speed and bumped across the uneven grass before coming to a stop in the middle of the field. Badly shaken, Jess leaned over the steering wheel and began to cry as shock coursed through her. Had the gate not been open she would have had no option but to career into the main road, and then God knows what might have happened.

Minutes later there was a rap on the car window.

'Are you all right, love?' A middle-aged gentleman with a bald head and a nose that looked as if it had done ten rounds with Mike Tyson was peering in at her with concern. 'I was following you back there on the lane when I saw you suddenly swerve through the gates. What happened?'

'M-my brakes failed,' Jess sobbed.

'My God.' He tutted as he stood there in the rain. 'It's a good job that you spotted the gate open then.' Looking towards the traffic that was flying past on the main road just metres away from them, he asked kindly, 'Where do you live? You look a bit shaken up. I'll give you a lift home. Come on.'

Jess unfastened her seat belt and climbed from the car on unsteady legs. 'I er . . . live just back there in Stonebridge House. Thank you, it's very kind of you, but I can't understand it. The car is less than a year old.'

'Unfortunately these things happen sometimes. But luckily for you you've lived to walk away from it,' he said as he gently took her elbow. 'Best leave the car here and get your husband to come and look at it, eh? Come on – let's get you out of the rain. You look as if a good stiff drink might do you the world of good.'

He helped her back to the lane where he had parked his car and after reversing it he headed back the way she had come. When they pulled into the courtyard she thanked him profusely.

Simon was standing in the kitchen window and he rushed outside immediately.

'What's happened?' he asked as he stared at Jess's pale face. 'And where's the car?'

'I had an accident,' Jess stuttered, still visibly shaken. 'Or should I say I almost had an accident. I was heading for the main road when I realised that the brakes weren't working and I couldn't slow down. Luckily I noticed a farm gate was open and I managed to steer the car into a field where I turned the engine off and waited for the car to stop. This gentleman saw what was happening and very kindly gave me a lift home.'

'My God.' Simon wrenched the car door open and helped her out as he nodded at the man. 'Thanks for bringing her home, mate. Thank goodness you were there.'

'You're welcome,' the man replied. 'But she's had a nasty shock. I should get her checked over by a doctor, if I were you.'

Simon nodded grimly as he led Jess towards the house and once inside he pressed her into a chair.

'Are you hurt?' he asked anxiously. 'Did you injure yourself?'

Jess shook her head. 'No, I didn't even have a bang. I'll be right as rain once I stop shaking.'

'And where's the car?'

'Still in the field leading down to the main road. I couldn't drive it home without any brakes, could I? I'm going to ring the garage where I bought it from and give them hell. It's not even a year old yet, for Christ's sake, and it's still under warranty! I could have been killed.'

'Don't do that,' Simon told her hastily. 'I'll give Dan a ring and he can come with me and we'll tow it back here.'

Dan was the young man that worked for Simon as his labourer. He was a nice young chap and engaged to be married, and Jess knew that Simon set a lot of store by him because he was a good worker.

'But you shouldn't have to do that when it's still under warranty,' she protested.

'There's not much Dan doesn't know about cars, and I want to find out what caused the brakes to fail before I contact the garage,' Simon told her with a frown.

'All right then, if you think that's best,' Jess conceded, just grateful that she had come out of it unscathed. 'I reckon I might go and put my feet up for a bit while you ring him, if you don't mind. My heart is going fifteen to the dozen.'

'Of course you should. Come on, let me help you upstairs.' Simon promptly hauled her to her feet again and led her away.

Once Jess was settled against the pillow on her bed, tears coursed down her cheeks as she allowed herself to think of what might have happened. Had she not spotted the open farm gate when she did, she would have shot straight out into the path of the ongoing traffic and she wouldn't have stood a chance. She and her unborn baby would probably have been killed outright, and suddenly she realised just how much she did want the child now. Her hand dropped to protectively stroke her stomach. There was no doubt about it, a guardian angel must have been watching over them today.

Eventually she fell asleep with the sound of whispering in her ears.

# Chapter Twenty-Nine

The following morning at breakfast, Simon tossed Jess her car keys across the table. He had towed it back from the field the day before.

'Why are you giving me these?' she asked. 'Shouldn't it be going into the garage?'

'It's all mended,' he assured her. 'Dan had a look at it: somehow the brake cable had snapped, but he's fixed it now.'

'But how could that have happened?'

Simon shrugged as he tucked into his Weetabix. 'Just one of those things, I suppose. Perhaps it was faulty. But all's well that ends well. There's no point in taking it any further.'

Jess dropped the keys into her handbag as if they might bite her. Somehow the thought of having her own car wasn't quite so attractive any more and she wondered if she would ever find the nerve to get behind the wheel again. The incident the day before had badly shaken her.

'I shall be out for most of today,' Simon informed her, and when her face fell he said, 'Sorry, love, but I've got some quotes to do, and with work being as it is I can't afford not to do them.'

He had promised to have two whole weeks off work over Christmas and the New Year, but Jess could understand that he couldn't turn possible work down. There were lots of good programmes on the TV and she decided that she might even find time to read a little more of Martha's journal too.

'Of course you should go,' she agreed. 'Is Bill coming with you?'

Simon nodded. 'Yes, I've got to pick him up at ten.' Glancing at his wrist-watch, he hastily finished his last mouthful and got up from the table. 'I'd better get a move on else I'm going to be late.' He then kissed her before asking, 'You are feeling all right, aren't you? I know you were pretty shook up after what happened yesterday. Do you think I should get the doctor to check you out?'

'No, I'm feeling absolutely fine now I've had a good sleep,' she said. 'You just get off and I'll see you later.'

Once he'd gone she had a leisurely shower and got dressed, toying with the idea of going to see Laura.

Laura was becoming a little reclusive since she had found out about Beth's unplanned pregnancy, and Jess was concerned about her. But then Den might be off work and she didn't wish to intrude. She decided she would take a leisurely walk down the drive and if his car was there she would come back. It wasn't, and seconds later she was sitting with Laura in her kitchen telling her all about the accident the day before.

Beth was sitting in the chair at the side of the inglenook fireplace again, rocking to and fro, locked in a world of her own more than ever now.

'Good lord.' Laura looked horrified. 'Just imagine what might have happened. You must have had someone watching over you yesterday.'

'That's what I thought,' Jess chuckled. 'I have to admit I've never believed in guardian angels before but I'm beginning to now.' As she glanced towards Beth her eyes became sad and she whispered, 'How is she?'

'Not good.' Laura folded her arms tightly across her chest and Jess was shocked to see how much weight she had lost.

'She hardly ever speaks now,' Laura continued, her eyes locked on her daughter. 'Den and I are seriously worried about her but the doctor says there's nothing we can do. The trouble is, she doesn't really understand what's happening to her and I know she desperately misses going to the youth club. She keeps pointing to the door and saying "Simon". She misses him picking her up and taking her there.'

'It's so sad,' Jess said as sympathetic tears burned at the back of her eyes. 'I reckon if Simon could get his hands on whichever lad did this to her, he'd strangle him with his bare hands.'

Changing the subject slightly, Laura asked, 'And how are things with you now?'

'Unbelievably good, apart from the fact that Mel is still having her moods,' Jess replied. 'Simon has suddenly had a complete change of heart about the baby and actually seems to be looking forward to it now. He was devastated when I had the accident yesterday and couldn't do enough for me. He isn't going out so much either, so all in all things are looking up.'

'Good.' Laura looked pleased for her and once more, Jess felt guilty as she remembered that she had once suspected Laura of having an affair with her husband.

'And how is your family tree progressing?' she asked.

Laura looked slightly more cheerful. 'Very well actually. I've almost completed mine and Den's, and I'm well on the way with the Fenton one too. It makes very interesting reading, believe you me. I wondered how you'd feel about me tracing yours and Simon's? It gives me something to do now that I can't go out so much, and I really enjoy it. All I'd need to know is your dates of birth and the places where you were both born and then I could take it from there.'

'Feel free,' Jess laughed and promptly gave her the information she had asked for before standing up. 'Right – I'd better get back else the girls will wonder where I've disappeared to,' she said. 'Planning anything special for New Year's Eve, are you?'

'No, just a quiet night in with a bottle of wine and the TV.'

'Same here,' Jess told her, and minutes later she was on her way back up the sweeping drive. There had been a severe frost the night before and the trees looked pretty with it glistening on their bare branches. She paused to watch a rabbit hopping across the frozen grass before proceeding at a leisurely pace. It was moments like this that made her glad to be alive and to count her blessings – particularly after what had happened the day before. Jess knew that it would be a very long time before she felt confident driving the car again, even though Simon had assured her that it was now as safe as houses.

Pushing the gloomy thoughts aside, she moved on, determined to hold on to her optimistic mood.

She was pleasantly surprised when Simon chose to stay in with her on New Year's Eve. They curled up on the settee with a big box of chocolates and it reminded Jess of the days when they had first been married. They hadn't been able to afford to go out much back then and had been perfectly content in each other's company.

It was when she went to make a cup of cocoa during a break in the film they were watching that he followed her into the kitchen looking slightly sheepish as he leaned on the kitchen table.

'All right, out with it,' she said. 'I know that look: what do you want to ask me?'

'Well, I'm not sure how you're going to feel about this,' he said hesitantly. 'But the thing is, young Dan is getting married at the end of January.'

'I already know that,' Jess replied.

'He's decided to have a stag weekend and he's asked me and some of the other blokes from the darts team if we'd like to go.'

'A stag *weekend*?' Jess grinned. When she and Simon had got married, a stag night and hen do had consisted of nothing more than a pub crawl with a few of your mates, but things had moved on since then.

'Yes, normally I wouldn't dream of going if I had work on, but jobs are a bit sparse at the moment, as you know, so I thought you might not mind me going?'

'Of course I don't mind,' Jess told him. 'Where is he thinking of? Blackpool?'

'Actually, it's a bit further afield than that. He's going to London.'

'London!' Jess's eyes almost popped out of her head. 'That's an awful long way to go just for a weekend, isn't it?'

'As a matter of fact it's Monday to Friday. And the thing is . . . if you're sure you wouldn't mind me tagging along, I might need another small loan.' He watched her face closely for a reaction before hurrying on, 'It wouldn't need to be as much as I borrowed last time. Five grand should do it. I've had to pay the men's wages you see, and what with work being a bit sparse . . .'

'You don't have to explain.' Jess smiled at him, sensing his discomfort. 'A break would do you good right now. You've worked flat out all through the summer. After all, me and the girls went to Paris, didn't we?' And what a disaster that nearly turned into, she thought.

'Of course, the money wouldn't be all for the break,' he went on to explain. 'I've got suppliers banging on the door for payment at the moment and I need to keep them happy.'

'It's not a problem,' Jess said. 'The banks won't be open tomorrow because it's New Year's Day, but as soon as they are I'll pop into town and get the money out for you. I might even get you a few new clothes while I'm at it. If you're going to London you'll need some new togs to go in.'

'Thanks, love. I don't know what I did to deserve you.' He kissed her cheek and disappeared off back into the lounge as Jess went about making their cocoa and the subject wasn't mentioned again that evening.

With January came heavy frosts and bitterly cold winds. Simon's work continued to be spasmodic but to his credit he worked whenever he could. Jess still wasn't overly concerned. This had happened many times before. Once spring arrived he would be inundated with work again and she still had a very tidy sum in the bank to tide them over.

The decorators had been in and the nursery for the new baby was now finished and she and Jo had been shopping for furniture for it. There was a small white swinging crib with lace drapes that Jo had fallen in love with. Jess had considered using the crib she had found in the attic, but Jo loved this one so much she had decided to indulge her. A white wardrobe and a chest of drawers were slowly being filled with baby clothes. A cream carpet covered the floor wall to wall, and Winnie the Pooh curtains that matched the wallpaper that Jo had chosen hung at the windows. Jess had been to the hospital for her scan where they had asked her if she would like to know the sex of the baby. She had promised herself beforehand that she wouldn't ask, but at the last minute the temptation was too much for her to resist. After all, she told herself, it's not as if it's my first baby, is it? And at least if I know what sex it is I can begin to buy clothes in the appropriate colour. And so she had nodded mutely as the midwife stared at the screen where Jess could see her baby's hearbeat, strong and steady.

'It's a little boy,' the woman told her and Jess's mouth gaped open. She could hardly believe her luck and couldn't wait to get home and tell Simon and the girls. She was going to have a son, and so now the majority of the clothes she bought would be blue and she began to try and imagine what he would be like. Would he be tall and dark-haired like his father, or would he take after her?

Simon was ecstatic when she told him that he was going to have a son and so was Jo, although Mel took the news in her usual disinterested way with a shrug of her shoulders. She still really didn't want the baby, whatever sex it was, and made no secret of the fact.

The following week, Laura took Beth to the hospital for her scan and they found out that she was carrying a little boy too.

'They'll be good company for each other as they get a little older,' Laura enthused. Beth was over the worst of her sickness now and although she was very pale she was coping better.

And then almost before they knew it, it was time for Simon to leave for his break in London.

'I hope I haven't put too much in your case,' Jess said worriedly as she stared at the mountain of clothes she had packed for him.

'I'm only going for five days, you know,' he teased. 'There are enough togs in there to last me for a month with two changes a day.'

'I suppose I could take a couple of T-shirts and a pair of jeans out,' Jess mused. Now that his departure was imminent she was glad that he was going because he had earned a rest, but the selfish side of her knew that she would miss him. *Still, he'll be back before I know it*, she consoled herself, *and it will be nice for me and the girls to have some quality time together –* if *I can lever Mel out of her room.*

The house seemed strangely empty the next day. The girls were both at school and she wandered from room to room aimlessly, looking at what still needed to be done and trying to assess how much it might cost. With the birth of the baby looming nearer, her plans for opening a B and B had been put on hold for the time being, which was quite worrying as the money in the bank was dwindling faster than she had expected it to. The cost of keeping such a large house running was astronomical and Simon had almost fainted when the gas and electric bills had popped through the letterbox.

'*Jesus!*' he'd exclaimed. 'I bet it doesn't cost this much to heat Buckingham Palace.'

'Well, we've had to keep the heating on and keep the place warm,' Jess had countered defensively. 'Everyone's heating bills have gone up this year. Just stop worrying about it, I'll sort it.'

'Oh yes, of course, I forgot – *you're* the one with the money and controlling the purse-strings now, aren't you?'

It was the first time they had had a cross word for weeks, and Jess had been bitterly hurt – but ever the peacemaker she had chosen to let it go and in no time at all he'd forgotten all about it even if she hadn't.

Once her little tour of inspection was completed she passed a leisurely half an hour in a nice warm bath. She then hurried off to the bedroom and slipped into clean clothes before getting her hairdryer out.

I'll go and have a cuppa with Laura when I've dried this mop, she thought to herself, and leaned down to plug the dryer in.

And then everything seemed to happen in slow motion as a pain ripped up her arm and she was flung across the room. Good God, I've been electrocuted, she thought to herself as darkness rushed to meet her and she sank into it gratefully as someone whispered urgently in her ear.

# Chapter Thirty

'Mum, Mum – *please* talk to me!'

There was a voice that seemed to be coming from a long, long way away as Jess struggled to open her eyes. Eventually she managed it and found herself peering up at Jo. Laura and Mel were standing right behind her and now that Laura saw she was conscious she soothed, 'Don't try and talk, there's an ambulance on its way. Just lie quiet . . . it should be here any minute now.'

Even as she spoke the sound of sirens penetrated the fog that seemed to be surrounding Jess and she nodded numbly as she tried to think what had happened. She appeared to be lying on the bedroom floor, but why? And then slowly as the fog cleared it came back to her. She had been about to dry her hair. She had bent and plugged the hairdryer in and then there was nothing until now.

'Wh . . . what happened?' she asked groggily as she tried to lift her head. It felt too heavy for her neck and she flopped back like a rag doll.

'It looks to me like you've had an electric shock,' Laura told her. 'One of the wires is sticking out of the back of your hairdryer and you must have touched it as you plugged it in. Thank God you had slippers with rubber soles on, eh? It might have been a different story altogether if you hadn't.' All the time she was talking she was stroking Jess's hand reassuringly and seconds later two paramedics burst into the room.

'Stand aside,' the taller of the two men said as he dropped to his knees beside Jess. 'What happened here?'

Laura quickly explained what she thought had happened. 'I don't know how long she may have been lying there,' she finished breathlessly. 'Young Jo here ran to fetch me when she found her like this. Jo had come home from school and she didn't know what to do.'

'You did absolutely right,' the paramedic told Jo, who was deathly pale with shock and fear. 'And your mum is going to be fine, so don't look so worried.'

'B-but she's going to have a baby,' Jo told him tremulously. 'Will it be all right?'

'I'm sure it will, but we're going to take her into hospital and have her checked out just to be on the safe side,' the man replied. 'Now is there someone here to keep an eye on you two? Where is your dad?'

'He went to London this morning,' Jo whimpered in a small voice as tears streamed down her waxen cheeks.

'Don't worry. I'll stay with you girls until we know what's happening,' Laura told her. 'You can come back to the cottage with me, and bring Alfie the dog with you.'

They all watched as Jess was carefully lifted on to a stretcher, protesting, 'I'm fine now, honestly. Really, there's no need for this.'

'There probably isn't,' the paramedic placated her. 'But you've had a nasty shock and it's better to be safe than sorry, eh? Once a doctor at the hospital has checked you and the baby out he or she will probably let you out later this evening, so there's nothing to get upset about. Just lie back and relax and you'll be back here before you know it. I should treat yourself to a new hairdryer though if I were you,' he finished with a cheeky wink.

Just as the paramedic had promised, Jess was discharged that evening after the doctor had done tests on herself and the baby, and assured her that all was well. Den came in his car to fetch her home and when she got there, Mel, Jo, Laura and Beth were all waiting for her in the kitchen.

'I'm absolutely fine,' she told them as they all stood there anxiously watching.

'The doctor says as long as I rest for a couple of days I'll be hunky dory.'

'Yes – and that's exactly what you're going to do,' said Laura. 'I shall see to that, young lady. Den has thrown the hairdryer away and the first time you go out, you can treat yourself to a new one.'

'But I can't understand how it happened. It was fine the last time I used it,' Jess murmured.

'It looked pretty old, and the wire probably just worked its way out of the casing with use,' Den said. 'Nothing lasts for ever, especially electrical equipment. They don't make things like they used to nowadays. Just think yourself lucky you got away with it as you did.'

It was the most Jess had ever heard Den say all in one go in all the time she had known him, and she found herself grinning despite what had happened.

'I don't know. You're not to be trusted on your own just lately,' Laura teased as she put the kettle on to make Jess a hot drink. 'I reckon you're getting accident prone, what with this and the car brakes.'

'I think you may be right.' Jess leaned back in the comfy chair and enjoyed being waited on. 'I shall have to make myself a sign, Danger Hazard. Keep away!'

On a more serious note now, Laura asked, 'Do you want me to ring Simon on his mobile and tell him what's happened?'

'Oh no,' Jess said hastily. 'He'd only worry and there's nothing he can do. I'm fine now and I don't want to spoil his holiday.'

'Have it your own way,' Laura said, as she poured boiling water into the teapot. Personally she didn't think much of Simon for clearing off and leaving Jess when she was pregnant, but, it was none of her business and she had enough on her own plate to worry about at present.

The following morning, Jess felt much better although the girls still insisted on walking to school themselves.

'To be honest, Mum, I'd rather,' Jo admitted. 'I'm getting a bit old now for my mum to be taking me, and my mates are beginning to take the mickey about it and calling me a sissy.'

'Oh!' Jess had forgotten that both of the girls were growing up now and becoming more independent. 'But isn't it rather a long way? And won't you get cold?' she muttered lamely.

Jo chuckled. 'Mum – it's no further than when we walk back every afternoon.'

'All right then, if that's what you want.' Jess kissed Jo and Mel and walked to the door with them. 'Now you will mind how you cross the roads, won't you? And be sure not to talk to any strangers.'

Jo raised her eyes to the heavens and giggled. 'There you go again. We're not babies, you know. Now why don't you go back to bed and have a good rest? And don't get trying to do anything either. Mel and I can do the cleaning up when we get home.'

'Now who am I to refuse an offer like that?' Jess said with a twinkle in her eye. 'See you later then, girls.' But inside she felt like crying. Jo's statement had brought home to her the fact that neither of the girls needed her quite so much any more, and she felt as if she'd been made redundant. The school runs had been part of her life for so long now that she wouldn't know what to do with her spare time.

But then she supposed it did have its plus side. Actually the thought of another hour in bed was quite attractive so she climbed the stairs and hopped back under the duvet with a contented sigh. She would have a new baby to contend with soon and she had no doubt she would be glad of the extra time then. She lay there for a while wondering what Simon was doing and what his hotel was like. He had done all the organising for the trip himself so she had no idea even what hotel he was staying in, but at least she could still reach him on his mobile if there was an emergency, which she seriously hoped there wouldn't be, after what had happened the day before.

Rather than dwell on that she decided to read a little more of Martha's journal so she lifted it from the drawer, snuggled down and began.

*31 December*
It is hard to believe that it will be a brand new year tomorrow. The week has passed in a flash but all the guests have left now and so no doubt tomorrow the house will return to some sort of normality. I fear the extra work has taken its toll on Grace and I wonder if she will carry her baby to full term now. Her ankles are very puffed up, and today I caught her leaning heavily on the side of the horse trough near the stables. She insisted that she was all right, but I have my doubts . . .

'Are you all right, Grace?'

The young woman straightened, and rubbing her aching back, she raised a wobbly smile for her sister. 'I'm fine, love. I reckon it's all the extra work just catchin' up on me. I might try an' get a couple of hours' rest this afternoon so as I can enjoy the party tonight.'

'See as yer do then,' Martha replied bossily as she headed for the dairy. She was in fine spirits at the prospect of the party that was planned for that evening. Jimmy would be coming and she intended to find time to wash her hair before it began so that she looked her best, not that she would have much spare time. Cook was busily preparing the food in the kitchen for it even now, and once it was all done Martha knew she would be kept on the run transporting it over to the two big trestle tables that had been set up next to the hay bales. Grace wouldn't be able to help much, that was for sure, but then she hoped that Bertie and the Tolleys would give her a hand. She hummed away happily to herself as she worked, and once she was done she headed back to the warmth of the kitchen.

'Ah, there you are,' Cook commented as she transferred a steak and kidney pie from the oven to the table. The aroma filled the air and Martha sniffed appreciatively.

'Cor, there looks to be enough food here to feed an army,' Martha joked, and the large woman smiled.

'Better too much than not enough, an' yer know how the men can put it away when they've had a skinful. Now, you take that tray up to yer granny, would yer, before we start to get this lot over to the barn.'

Martha obediently lifted the tray that was covered in a snow-white cloth and minutes later she carried it into her granny's room. The old woman was sitting up in bed propped up by pillows and Martha was pleased to see that she looked a little better today.

'How are all the preparations goin', pet?' she asked as Martha placed the tray on her lap.

'Oh, I reckon Cook has everythin' in hand and the barn looks lovely. Bertie and Hal have strung lanterns everywhere and swept the floor so it will look grand tonight, but I think Cook wants you to eat somethin' today, do yer hear me?'

'I hear yer.' Granny smiled. She knew that the girl worried about her and felt so useless stuck away in her room, although she was forced to admit she would have been neither use nor ornament had she gone down to the kitchen.

Martha set about tidying the room as Granny lifted the spoon and tasted the chicken broth before asking, 'His lordship still away, is he?'

'Yes, he left to spend the New Year in London the day after he caught me in the hall,' Martha said.

Granny nodded with satisfaction. 'Best bloody place fer him,' she muttered. 'An' fair dos to Master Leonard fer clearin' him off. It's only a shame that the wicked bugger 'as to come back. But when he does, you just be sure an' keep out of 'is way as much as yer can.'

Martha hardly needed telling that but she nodded anyway.

'An' how is our Grace bearin' up now?' the old woman asked.

'Oh, she seems to be all right, though I know she was mortified fer the staff to learn what the Master had done to her. Do yer reckon she'll take to this baby, Granny? I mean, knowin' how it was conceived?'

'I think so.' Granny gazed towards the window. 'I had a good talk to her just last night an' she told me that at the end o' the day it ain't the baby's fault so she'll try her best to love it. I mean, it didn't ask to be born, did it? It's Bertie I'm more worried about. I'm convinced that if he could kill the Master an' get away wi' it, he would wi'out givin' it a second thought. But I ain't sure that he won't see the Master every time he looks at the poor little mite once it arrives. Still, we'll just have to wait an' see, won't we? But now let's talk o' happier things. What were yer plannin' on wearin' tonight, an' is young Jimmy comin'?'

Martha flushed. 'Yes, Jimmy is coming. An' I've altered the gown that Miss Melody gave me to wear. I'm worried that it might be a bit too grand for a party in a barn though.'

'Rubbish. I've no doubt you'll look beautiful, an' it'll do yer good to 'ave a chance to dress up fer a change. But just make sure as yer come up here so I can see yer in all yer finery, won't yer?'

'I will,' Martha promised. 'But I'd best get on now, else Cook will be screamin' for me. Bye for now, Granny.'

She skipped from the room as the old woman watched her go with an affectionate smile on her face. She was a good girl, was her Martha. None better. An' if that whorin' old bastard so much as laid hands on her again it wouldn't be Bertie who would be committin' murder but herself, 'cos she'd run him through wi' a knife without givin' it a second thought.

The party was in full swing within minutes of it starting. It was a bitterly cold evening and so everyone decided to dance to keep themselves warm, all apart from Grace that was, and she was so big now that she could scarcely wobble about, let alone dance. Jimmy's eyes almost started from his head when he arrived and saw Martha dressed in the gown that Miss Melody had given her. It was a lovely shade of cornflower blue, fitted tight into the waist with a billowing skirt. Martha had tied her hair high onto the top of her head with one of the ribbons that the young Master and Mistress had given her for Christmas, and as he took her hands, he said, 'By, lass, yer look all grown up. An' yer could be taken fer gentry in that get-up.'

Martha blushed prettily. Granny had said much the same thing when Martha had gone to visit her in her finery and the girl felt wonderful. It wasn't often she got to dress up, and she had never owned a gown the like of this one before.

The party had been going on for some time when Miss Melody and Master Leonard put in an appearance, and Hal instantly stopped fiddling and everyone halted the dancing.

'Oh, please don't stop,' Miss Melody implored. 'We only popped across to make sure you had enough ale and wine.' She and her husband had donated two barrels of ale plus numerous bottles of wine to them all as a New Year present, and it was Hal who chuckled now before saying, 'Thank yer kindly, ma'am, but I reckon if we were to drink all that lot tonight there'd be none of us fit enough to do any work tomorrow.'

Miss Melody smiled. She was draped in a warm cloak and she told him, 'Good, then we'll leave you to it. I don't mind telling you, if I wasn't so huge I would have liked to stay and have a dance myself.'

'And it's right welcome you'd have been,' Bertie responded warmly.

The young Mistress looked towards the trestle table that was weighted down with food and grinned approvingly. Young Joey, who hadn't stopped eating since he'd arrived, was tucking into yet another slice of Cook's delicious pies, and spread across the table were various pickles, fresh baked crusty loaves and sweetmeats along with a variety of other things.

'Then if you are quite sure that you have everything you need, we shall leave you to it, and please don't worry if you're a little late going about your chores tomorrow. I'm sure we shall survive if breakfast is not exactly on time.' She slipped the hood of her cloak over her shining hair and glancing towards the barn door, she said, 'It's very cold. Do you think we might be in for some snow?'

'No doubt about it,' Hal replied with certainty. 'An' before the night is out, if I'm any judge. Goodnight, sir, madam.'

The young couple slipped away and in no time at all the party was in full swing again.

At some point Jimmy took Martha's hand and led her towards the barn door, and once outside they stared into each other's eyes.

'I can't get over how lovely yer look tonight, pet,' he said with a small catch in his voice. 'An' I've been waitin' to get yer on yer own 'cos there's somethin' I've been wantin' to ask yer.'

When Martha stared up at him expectantly, he cleared his throat nervously and stumbled on, 'Well, the thing is . . . I love yer . . . an' I were wonderin', would yer consider settin' a date fer the weddin'? I mean I know I ain't much of a catch, but—'

Martha quickly laid a finger across his lips. They had both known for some time that their feelings for each other would lead to this, but this was the official proposal that Martha had been waiting for.

'Don't say any more, Jimmy.' Her eyes were shining and she felt that she might burst with happiness. 'You would be the best catch in the world to me, an' I'd be right proud to be yer wife.'

Jimmy's chest seemed to swell to twice its size. 'In that case I'll ask the Mistress fer permission to wed yer, the first chance I get.' And then he kissed her and a thousand fireworks exploded behind her eyes. It was as they were standing there locked in an embrace that the first flakes of snow began to flutter down and Martha laughed. Eeh, this looked set to be the best New Year ever.

They joined the rest of the staff in the barn then and Jimmy did not return to Leathermill Farm until the early hours of the morning when they had all seen the New Year in together. By then the snow was already inches deep underfoot and coming down with a vengeance, but all of them were in too high spirits to care.

Although she was tired, Martha was far too excited to sleep when she first went to bed and she lay reliving every moment of the wonderful evening she had just spent before writing in her journal until the candle burned low. This would be an entry to show her grandchildren one day.

*3 January 1838*
My feelings that this year was going to be a good one were as wrong as they could be. What a terrible few days it has been.

  I had scarcely fallen asleep in the early hours of New Year's Day when Grace woke me in a panic and told me to get up immediately. Miss Melody had been taken poorly and Grace had sent Bertie to fetch the doctor. But because the snow is so thick on the ground he was struggling to get the horse to go beyond the end of the lane . . .

'I tell yer, Prince won't budge another step,' Bertie said in alarm as he came back into the kitchen after trying to urge the Master's horse on. 'Should I set out on foot to fetch the doctor?'

'No, that won't be necessary just yet,' Miss Prim said, taking control of the situation. 'There are quite enough of us here to care for the dear girl, though I am fearful that she may be going into early labour. I pray that I am wrong, for she has some weeks to go yet, but for now all we can do is take one step at a time. Grace, come with me.' And with that she swept from the room and headed to the young Mistress's room whilst everyone sat there in the kitchen feeling totally useless.

Throughout the night, Martha and Grace took turns sitting with Miss Prim as she mopped the poor Mistress's brow and spoke soothingly to her. She was obviously in a great deal of discomfort and complained of severe pains in her back.

236

It was the afternoon of the following day, as Martha lifted the young woman's head from the pillows to give her a sip of water that she noticed that the bedsheets were wet. Her waters had broken.

She quickly informed Miss Prim and Grace of the fact, and they exchanged a worried glance. Miss Prim then headed to the kitchen where she found Bertie sitting with his head in his hands.

'Ah, Bertie . . .' He was instantly on his feet. 'Do you think there is any chance at all that you could make it to Caldecote village? I know the weather is appalling but I fear that Miss Melody's baby is coming now, and as we cannot get the doctor, Grace tells me that a woman she called Mother Dickinson who lives there may be able to help?'

'Aye, she would,' Bertie instantly agreed. 'Mother Dickinson 'as been deliverin' babies around these parts fer as far back as I can remember. I'll get off straight away an' I'm sure I'll be able to get there if I go on foot. Just leave it wi' me.'

Miss Prim nodded her thanks before then turning her attention back to Polly and Cook. 'Do you two think you might be able to get some water boiled, as much as you can, please? Oh, and I'll need clean towels too – lots of them.'

'I'll go an' get the towels,' Polly volunteered and she shot away as Cook began to fill everything she could find with water and put it on to boil.

Once back upstairs Miss Prim found Master Leonard pacing up and down the landing like a man demented. Beyond the bedroom door he could hear his wife groaning with pain and he could hardly bear it.

'I'm going in to Melody, she needs me,' he informed Miss Prim, but she stayed him with a hand on his arm.

'I'm sorry, dear, but I'm afraid I cannot allow that,' she told him in a firm voice. 'The birth room is no place for a man to be, but if you want to help you could perhaps go to the Tolleys' cottage and tell Phoebe that we may have need of her?'

'Of course.' He sprang away to do as he was told, grateful to think that he was doing something useful. And then the waiting began, and as the minutes on the fine gilt clock on the mantelpiece in the bedroom ticked away, Miss Melody's agony went on.

After what seemed like an eternity but was in fact only two hours, Bertie returned and they were all thankful to see that he had old Mother Dickinson with him.

The old woman shook the snow from her shawl and instantly taking control of the situation began to gently probe about the mistress's swollen stomach.

After a while she looked up and informed them in her usual forthright way, 'This babby be breech. An' I'm fearin' the young Mistress ain't goin' to be havin' a good time of it. But still, we can only do what we can do, so I'll wash me 'ands now while yer get me some o' them towels ready.'

Miss Prim wrung her hands as Grace patted her comfortingly on the back. They had all very quickly realised how much the young Mistress meant to the woman, and Grace knew that Miss Prim would be feeling her pain.

Once Mother Dickinson's hands had been thoroughly washed she rolled up her sleeves and approached the bed again to address the young Mistress, 'Right, dearie, I want yer to do as I tell yer when I tell yer to. Do yer hear me?'

Miss Melody nodded and groaned as her head thrashed from side to side on the pillow.

Mother Dickinson then turned to them all and asked, 'Now who's stayin' an' who's goin'? This bain't gonna be no peepshow an' it won't be fer the faint-hearted.'

'I think Phoebe and I should stay,' Miss Prim answered. 'Perhaps Grace and Martha could supply us with hot water?'

'An' are yer quite sure that yer want to see this, missus?' Mother Dickinson said sternly, looking Miss Prim straight in the eye. 'This ain't goin' to be very nice, so I'm givin' yer fair warnin'.'

Miss Prim raised herself up to her full height before answering imperiously, 'I have cared for Miss Melody since the day she drew her first breath, so I have no intentions of deserting her now when she needs me most.'

''Ave it yer own way then, but don't say as yer hadn't been warned.' Mother Dickinson leaned down to Miss Melody and told her gently, 'I'm goin' to 'ave to try an' turn this babby, me love.'

Miss Melody smiled bravely, but as Martha and Grace scurried from the room, she let out a cry like that of a wounded animal. Grace quickly made the sign of the cross on her chest as they paused outside the bedroom door in case they should be needed.

'I might as well go and start fetching the hot water up,' Martha volunteered. 'You stay there. It'll be too much for you, humping it up an' down the stairs.'

As the afternoon turned to evening the snow continued to fall like a thick dense blanket and Miss Melody's suffering was unabated. Downstairs, Master Leonard refused all offers of food and drink and continued to pace up and down the study like a caged animal, with one eye forever on the clock whilst the rest of the staff flitted soundlessly about the house like ghosts.

It seemed that Mother Dickinson had done all in her power to shift the unborn child into a favourable position to be born, but twenty-four hours later the birth seemed to be no nearer, and now Miss Melody's cries had dulled to soft hiccuping sobs. Grace and Martha managed to snatch a few hours' sleep on the chairs spaced along the landing but eventually Grace rose and rubbed her aching back. 'I shan't be long, pet. I need to go to the closet,' she told her sister. Martha's small white teeth nipped at her lower lip. Grace looked awful and now she began to fear for her too.

'Why don't you go and lie down. I'll fetch you if you're needed,' Martha urged, but Grace merely shook her head and set off unsteadily down the stairs.

Shortly afterwards, Phoebe briefly left the bedroom to give her an update.

'The mistress is bleeding badly. I fear for both her and the child if something doesn't happen soon. Mother Dickinson is doing all she can, but nothing seems to be helping.' Then chewing on her knuckles, Phoebe went back into the bedroom and the vigil continued.

Finally, as day gave way to night again, Mother Dickinson turned to Miss Prim and told her gravely, 'I'm goin' to have to cut her to get the child out.'

Miss Prim, who by now was almost beside herself with fear, said hoarsely, 'Oh no, surely not?'

The old woman waved a gnarled finger in Miss Melody's direction. 'Look at 'er!' she ordered. 'Do you 'ave any better ideas? The poor soul is bleedin' like a stuck pig, an' if I don't do sommat soon now we'll be losin' the pair of 'em!'

Composing herself with a great effort, Miss Prim nodded. 'In that case you must do what needs to be done. Thanks be to the Lord that the dear soul is so far out of it now that she will not know what you are doing.'

Seconds later, Mother Dickinson appeared in the bedroom doorway and told Martha, 'Run to the kitchen, lass, an' ask Cook fer the sharpest knife she 'as. An' be quick about it, mind.'

239

In no time at all Martha was back up the stairs with what she had been asked for, and after taking the knife from her without a word the old woman shuffled back into the bedroom. Grace had joined Martha again by then and they waited fearfully to see what might happen next.

Suddenly a wail of such agony sounded from the bedroom that their blood turned to water. Master Leonard must have heard it downstairs too, for now they saw him racing towards them, taking the stairs two at a time as the tails of his frockcoat flew out behind him.

'In the name of God, what's happening?' he demanded as he joined them on the landing. He looked beside himself and Grace tried to calm him as best she could as she explained what Mother Dickinson was going to do.

'Damn and *blast* the weather,' he cursed as he looked towards the landing window where the snow was still falling thickly. 'If it weren't for the snow, the doctor would have been here hours ago!'

Grace placed a comforting arm about him, forgetting for now that he was gentry and she was a mere servant. This was no time to be concerned about class distinction. He was just a man who was in mortal fear of losing his wife and unborn child.

'Hush now,' she soothed. 'Mother Dickinson has brought more souls into this world than I've had hot dinners. Miss Melody is in good hands.'

Everything seemed to have gone unnaturally quiet in the room beyond and they all eyed the door with trepidation until it suddenly opened and Miss Prim appeared, looking more like a waxwork doll than a living woman.

'Mother Dickinson had delivered the child,' she told the young Master as tears trickled down her cheeks. 'It was a boy . . . but he did not survive.'

'And Melody?' Master Leonard's hands were clenched into fists and he looked tormented as he received the news about his son.

'She is very weak and she has lost a lot of blood,' Miss Prim informed him. 'Mother Dickinson is still trying to stem the bleeding.'

'But . . . she will survive . . . *won't she*?' The last words were said more as a plea than a question but Miss Prim could not truthfully tell him what he wanted to hear.

'It is too soon to tell.' She turned her head from the torment in his eyes. 'She is in God's hands now.'

Master Leonard suddenly barged past her and entered the bedroom.

240

Whether it was a gentleman's place to be in a birthing room or not, he needed to be with his wife now.

As word spread about the house, a great dark shadow seemed to fall across it. Cook threw her apron over her head and sobbed shamelessly for the little soul who had lost his battle for life, and the rest of the servants hung their heads. They had all grown fond of the young Master and Mistress, and knew how much they had been looking forward to the birth of their firstborn.

Bertie arrived on the landing and, gravely concerned for his own wife led Grace away to get some rest, whilst Martha headed for her room. It had been a terrible day, one none of them would ever forget.

# Chapter Thirty-One

Tears were pouring down Jess's face now but she was so gripped by the drama that she forced herself to read on.

*4 January*
Miss Melody is hovering between life and death but the snow is still coming down thicker than ever and so there is no chance of getting a doctor to her. Miss Prim and Master Leonard have not left her side and the whole house is in mourning . . .

'Why don't you go and rest for a while?' Miss Prim suggested as she looked towards Mother Dickinson who was still leaning over Miss Melody. 'You could have a sleep in one of the guest rooms and I will watch over her whilst you are gone.'

'I suppose it would make sense.' The old woman swiped a stray lock of grey hair from her forehead. They were all dropping with fatigue now, but at least she had managed to slow Miss Melody's bleeding. Not that the poor lamb was out of the woods yet, not by a long way. She had developed a high fever, which was something else for them to be fearful about.

Master Leonard, who had refused to leave the room, now urged her, 'Yes, do go and rest. You have been marvellous but you'll be no good to Melody if you make yourself ill too.'

'Very well, sir. But only fer a little while, mind,' the old woman reluctantly agreed, and Polly led her away to one of the spare bedrooms whilst Miss Prim placed yet another load of bloodied bedding into the basket ready for it to be put into soak in the laundry. Polly had been carting it down with frightening regularity all day and was wondering how so much blood could come out of one person.

'Why don't you try to get a rest too, sir?' Miss Prim suggested as she looked towards Leonard who was clutching his wife's hand.

'Thank you, but no. I prefer to stay here.'

Miss Prim knew that he was thinking along exactly the same lines as herself. If the blood loss didn't kill Miss Melody, the fever well might. It was a daunting thought. She then looked towards the small crib that held the child and said in a low voice to Grace, 'We should think of washing and dressing the child, poor little mite.'

'I'll do it,' Grace volunteered, and without a word she lifted the child from the crib and slipped away with him clutched tight to her wrapped in a fine white shawl.

She carried him down to the kitchen and when Cook had fetched her a bowl of warm water she washed the little soul from head to toe and dressed him in one of the soft lawn nightdresses the young Mistress had bought in readiness for his birth.

Cook sobbed unashamedly as they looked down onto his tranquil face.

'Eeh, it's a cruel life,' she wept. 'He's so beautiful, like a little angel – an' had he lived, he would have led a charmed wife. The young Master and Mistress were so lookin' forward to his comin'.'

'I know,' Grace answered chokily. 'I just thank God that Miss Melody doesn't know of his passin' yet. If she did, I fear it would finish her off in her weakened state. But what should I do wi' him now? I mean, until we know where the Master wants him to be buried?'

'Happen yer could place him in the bedroom next to his mother,' Cook said wisely. 'It ain't the time to be askin' the master such things while he's so worried about the mistress.'

Grace lifted the infant and nodded, then set off up the stairs again. Like everyone else she was exhausted, but even so she needed to be there for the young Mistress.

She carried him into the empty bedroom next to the one where Miss Melody lay fighting for her life, and after laying him on the bed she hurried away to fetch his crib, and when she had placed him in it, she crept away.

Mother Dickinson was back in Miss Melody's room within the hour and finally at tea-time she managed to slow the flow of blood.

'Will she be all right now?' Mr Leonard's eyes were full of hope as he looked at her.

The old woman paused before answering, having no wish to lie to him. 'I can't say yet, sir. She's slipped into a stupor an' until the fever breaks she could go either way. But never fear, I shall do all I can, I promise yer.'

And so the terrible waiting continued as the young Master tried to contemplate life without his beautiful young wife. It had hurt him deeply to lose his much longed-for son, but should he lose Melody too, he would have nothing left to live for.

Jess slowly closed the journal, unable to bear to read another page right now. And it was then that the sound of soft sobs floated to her from above, and she knew that it was Martha crying.

'How awful it must have been for you all,' she whispered, wondering if this was the room where the unfortunate mother had given birth. And as she lay there thinking back over what she had just read, she stroked her stomach absently.

Sometime later she drove into town to do a little shopping. Jo was desperate for a new pair of school shoes, and as time was on her hands, Jess decided that now was as good a time as any to go and get them. She still wasn't too confident about driving after the incident with the brakes before Christmas, but she could be stubborn when she wanted to be and wouldn't let the fear beat her.

She was just coming out of the Co-op shoe shop in Abbey Street when she spotted a familiar face on the other side of the road and crossed over. It was Dan's fiancée, Abigail. Jess had only met her a couple of times but she had taken a shine to the girl and now she called out, 'Hi, Abigail! All ready for the wedding, are you?'

'Just about.' Abigail tossed her long blonde hair across her shoulders. A petite lass, she looked much younger than her twenty years and certainly didn't look old enough to be getting married.

'I wonder if the chaps are enjoying themselves?' Jess said as they fell into step and strolled along.

Abigail peeped at her out of the corner of her eye before replying, 'Er . . . hopefully. But it will be nice when a bit more regular work comes in, won't it?'

'Yes, it will. What are *you* planning on doing for your hen do?'

'Well, to be honest I haven't given it a lot of thought,' Abigail replied, looking at her a little strangely. 'The wedding isn't for another few weeks yet.'

Jess was just about to ask her if she was missing Dan when a larger lady then approached them and instantly started to chat to Abigail. It was obvious that they knew each other well and so feeling rather in the way Jess bade them a hasty goodbye and hurried back to the car.

On the way home she called in to see Karen, and when she told her about what had happened with the hairdryer, Karen rolled her eyes.

'I think we're going to have to employ a keeper to watch out for you,' she said jokingly as she carried the coffee pot to the table and swiped aside a pile of magazines. As usual, Karen's home was organised chaos. There was a huge pile of ironing waiting to be done teetering on one of the chairs and the sink was full of dirty pots waiting to be washed. And yet for all its untidiness the place had a homely air about it; it was lived in and it showed. Jess sometimes wished she could be more like her friend and not fret so much about everywhere being spick and span, but she had never been able to abide untidiness in her own home and she supposed that she was too old to change now. It was just part of her make-up.

When the girls got home from school that afternoon, Mel told her mother casually, 'I thought I saw Dad this afternoon. He passed me in a car as I was walking home. There was a lady driving it.'

'You'd have a job,' Jess chuckled. 'He's in London right at this minute and probably having the time of his life.'

'Well, he must have a double then,' Mel muttered, and the subject was dropped.

It was strange not to have Simon there at the house that evening, and once the girls had gone to bed Jess checked and double-checked that all the doors and windows were locked, suddenly conscious of how isolated they were at Stonebridge House. Funnily enough, she had never felt that way before, but then she supposed that was because she'd always had a man in the house. She had expected Simon to phone but so far he hadn't. But then she wasn't overly concerned, and in actual fact it was quite nice to have the bed all to herself and to be able to stretch out. Snuggling down under the duvet with a large mug of cocoa and a *Take a Break* magazine, she sighed contentedly. The wind outside had died down some time ago and everywhere was strangely still. I wouldn't be surprised if we weren't in for a thunderstorm, Jess thought, glancing towards the window. The sky was a curious grey colour and there was not a sound to be heard until suddenly the dark was illuminated with a flash of lightning. Here it comes, Jess thought, feeling nervous. She had never liked thunderstorms. The bedroom door was then flung open and Jo appeared, clutching the teddy she still took to bed each night under her arm.

'Can I get in with you, Mum?' she asked, just as a crash of thunder sounded in the distance. Before Jess could answer her, Jo had covered the distance between the door and the bed and was cowering under the duvet.

'It's all right, love. It can't hurt us in here,' Jess said soothingly as another flash of lightning lit the room.

Jo hotched closer to her and Jess put her arm about her protectively. It was then that the bedside light flickered and dimmed before going out completely.

'Shit!' Jess muttered. 'It looks like the fuse has tripped on the lights.'

'Can you fix it?' a little voice came to her from under the covers.

'Of course I can,' Jess said far more brightly than she was feeling. 'But the fuse box is down in the cellar. Will you be all right while I go down and fix it?'

'Y . . . yes,' Jo whimpered as Jess swung her legs out of the bed. The thunder was growling ominously now and becoming louder by the second. A sure sign that it was coming closer.

'Now where does your dad keep his torch?' Jess tried to think and then remembered that he kept it in a drawer in the kitchen.

Damn, that would mean she had to find her way down the stairs in the dark, but what alternative was there?

The baby began to kick as if he had picked up on her nervousness, and fumbling round in the dark she found her dressing-gown and slid it on before groping her way to the door with her hand held out in front of her.

'Mum, what's happening?' Mel's voice wafted along the passage to her.

'It's all right, love, the lights have tripped, that's all. Just sit tight and I'll have them back on in no time,' Jess shouted back to her.

She inched her way along the landing, keeping close to the wall, and when she came to the staircase she gripped the banister and tentatively began to descend the stairs. Everything looked completely different in the darkness and Jess's heart thumped uncomfortably as the shadows seemed to jump out at her.

Keep a grip on yourself, girl, she chided herself. You're a bit old to be frightened of bogey men.

It was as she was stumbling blindly along the hall that the sleeve of her dressing-gown caught the vase of flowers she had on the hall table and instantly it overturned and ice-cold water cascaded all down her leg as the vase crashed to the floor.

246

'Bugger it!' Jess cursed as she moved doggedly on. There was no point in trying to pick everything up until the lights were back on.

As she stumbled into the kitchen she stopped dead as a flash of lightning illuminated the room. The back door was swinging open but she could have sworn she had locked it before going to bed. She glanced down at Alfie, who was cowering in his basket, then clutching the front of her dressing-gown she said as calmly as she could, 'Is anyone here?'

There was nothing but the crash of thunder overhead as she stood there trembling. Her mind was working overtime. What if someone had broken in? Reaching out to the knife block that she kept on the nearest worktop she snatched the largest cleaver from it and advanced towards the door with it held out in front of her. The key was still in the lock and there was no sign of a forced entry.

Sighing with relief, she slammed it shut and hastily locked it, cursing herself as she did so. And it was then that the whispering started, urgent and close by. She whirled about but there was no one there. Now she began to throw the drawers open and when her hand finally closed around the handle of Simon's torch she sobbed with relief and quickly switched it on before shining it all around the room. She was alone as she had somehow known she would be. The beam of bright light sliced through the shadows as her heart slowly returned to a steadier rhythm. Straightening her shoulders in a determined way she then headed for the cellar door. She hated the thought of having to go down into that damp dismal space, but as things stood she really didn't have a lot of choice. The girls were frightened and they were relying on her.

Feeling her way down the slimy steps she made a mental note to clean them properly the first chance she got. She had been promising herself that she'd do it since the day they'd moved in, but there was something about the cellar that frightened her and she'd always put it off. *It's probably all the scary films I've watched*, she comforted herself as she slowly moved on, placing one foot gingerly in front of another. She knew roughly where the fuse box was, and now she shone the torch around until she'd located it. The new fuse box the electrician had installed was very sensitive, and this was not the first time the lights had tripped since it had been put in. It only needed a bulb to blow and the whole lot would go out. Jess saw the problem instantly, once she had managed to open the door of it, and she quickly flicked the switch up and down again. The lights instantly came back on but

247

just as they did she heard a noise behind her and as she made to turn, something came crashing down on her head and she dropped to the floor like a stone.

'It seems likely that someone had broken in,' the police officer informed her the next day, snapping his notebook shut. 'That's probably why you found the door open in the kitchen when you first came downstairs. You must have disturbed them. Hadn't you got your house alarm on?'

Jess shook her head miserably, feeling like a complete idiot. 'No, I don't always bother because it's so quiet here,' she said sheepishly.

'Then you should,' the officer said sternly. 'It's these quiet, out-of-the-way places that are the biggest targets for thieves.' The house had been crawling with police until half an hour ago and Jess's head was spinning at all the questions they had asked her. But now there was just the officer standing before her and one other left.

Laura was standing with her hand protectively on Jess's shoulder and she glared at the man.

'I don't think she needs to hear that right now,' she said briskly. 'She's shaken up enough as it is.'

'I'm sorry, but I'm only doing my job,' he pointed out, then turning to Jess again, he asked, 'Are you quite sure that you didn't get a look at who did this to you?'

Jess sighed. She had already answered the same question at least a dozen times. 'No, I didn't. It all happened so quickly, and then all I saw was stars for a few minutes and when I'd pulled myself together, whoever it was had run off.'

'And you're quite sure that nothing's been taken?'

'Not that I can see.'

The officer shook his head. 'Well, there are no fingerprints on the bottle that was used as the weapon on you, unfortunately, so I fear there isn't a lot we can do for now, unless anything else occurs to you, so I'll leave you to rest now. Are you quite sure that you don't want to go to the hospital?'

'No way,' Jess said quickly. 'They'll know me there soon at this rate and I'm perfectly all right apart from an egg on my head.'

'Very well. But do make sure that you put your burglar alarm on in future and if you need us, don't hesitate to give us a call. Good day.'

Once the police officers had finally left, Laura said, 'You're not having much luck at the minute, what with one thing or another are you, love?'

'You can say that again.' Jess tentatively touched the lump on the back of her head.

'What I can't understand is why Alfie didn't bark when a stranger came in,' Laura said thoughtfully.

'I hadn't thought of that, but then you know what a big softie he is and he's terrified of thunder,' Jess grinned. 'He'd wag his tail for anybody who made a bit of fuss of him. One thing is for certain: after this, he certainly won't qualify for Guard Dog of the Year.'

'No, he won't, and I think we can safely say Simon won't be too keen to leave you on your own again when he comes back and you tell him everything that's happened,' Laura said ruefully. 'But then I suppose we should look on the bright side. You've come out of it with nothing worse than a thumping headache and a lump on your head. They say everything comes in threes, and what with the car incident, the hairdryer and now this, you've hopefully had your lot of bad luck.' She then made her friend a nice strong cup of tea with lots of sugar in it and insisted that she put her feet up for an hour. After all, as she pointed out, surely nothing could go amiss if Jess was just sitting there and she was keeping her beady eye on her?

# Chapter Thirty-Two

The rest of the week passed uneventfully and Simon arrived home at four o'clock on Friday afternoon. He listened with amazement as Jo told him all about what had happened since he'd been gone. Jess couldn't get a word in edgeways.

She was feeling a little cross with him, if truth be known, because as yet he hadn't even given the girls a small present, which she considered was the least he could have done after a few days gallivanting down in London. Not that Mel seemed much bothered. She'd been in a slightly better mood while her dad was away but the second he set foot through the door she disappeared like a cat with its tail on fire.

'I bet you won't be leaving the back door open again,' he said caustically when Jo had finished her tale, and Jess bristled.

'As it happens I would have staked my life that I'd locked it,' she snapped.

'But you couldn't have done, could you?' he argued. 'Otherwise they would have had to break in and the police said there was no sign of a forced entry.'

'I suppose so,' she admitted grudgingly, with an awful feeling that she was never going to hear the last of this. Simon could be very self-righteous when he wanted to be. She was bristling like a porcupine by now but she softened slightly when he put his arm around her. 'Are you quite sure that you're all right?'

'I'm absolutely fine,' she told him. 'Just a lump on the back of my head and dented pride.'

'Then let's hope that's the end of it,' he said. 'You obviously disturbed whoever it was, and hopefully they won't risk coming back.'

Within days their life had slipped back into its normal pattern, apart from the fact that Jess no longer ran the girls to school.

She was heavily pregnant now, and had less than two months to go until the birth. She tired easily and had taken to having a rest for an

250

hour each afternoon with a good book or a magazine. She quite enjoyed it because she knew that this new-found space would be very short-lived. Before she knew it she would be running around after the baby – and she found that she was really looking forward to it now. There were were still periods when she fretted about how Mel and Simon would cope, but for the majority of the time she was content.

Beth was getting large too now – in fact, Laura told her that she was eating her out of house and home, gobbling up everything edible in sight. The girl still had absolutely no notion of what lay ahead of her and Jess cursed the boy who had got her into this condition.

February came in with driving winds and pelting rain, and once more the river at the bottom of the garden burst its banks to such an extent that Blue Brick Cottage was at risk of being flooded. The water crept up the garden at an alarming rate and came dangerously near to the front door, but thankfully up to now it had come no closer, although Laura feared it would if the rain continued.

Jess fretted about the girls walking to and from school in such appalling conditions but they simply took their umbrellas each day and assured her that they were fine. They were obviously enjoying their new independence. Simon worked whenever he could, but weather conditions ensured that some days he was unable to do anything. Jess sensed that he was concerned about money and she was proved to be right when he approached her one day after the postman had been and said tentatively, 'Jess, I know it must seem as if I'm always holding my hand out nowadays but all the insurances are due this month. Both the cars, the house insurance and our life insurances.' He looked terribly uncomfortable, and knowing what a proud man he was, Jess instantly felt sorry for him.

'So,' he went on, waving the letter that had just arrived in the air, 'I was wondering if I could perhaps have another temporary loan? I know I haven't paid back any of the rest of what I owe you yet, but I will as soon as I get back on my feet again.'

Seeing as the insurances were the only bills Simon ever paid now, Jess couldn't see why he was making such a big thing of it, but all the same she told him, 'Of course you can. How much do you need?'

'Three thousand should do it.'

'Three thousand pounds?' she gasped incredulously.

He coloured slightly as he nodded. 'Yes, three thousand. Do you have any idea at all, how much the insurance on this place is? It's like a second bloody mortgage.'

'All right, all right, of course you can have it,' she said hastily, 'I'll write the cheques out so you can send them off today,' and keen to avoid an argument she made an excuse to leave him to it and hurried away.

On the days when he was unable to work, Simon took to clearing out the attics. He had always intended to turn the large attic into an office but as yet he hadn't tackled Martha's room or any of the other smaller rooms on that landing. Jess was pleased about that. Somehow it didn't seem right to touch the girl's room.

Today, as soon as she had seen her daughters off to school, she went back to bed for half an hour. She had been up half the night with heartburn and smiled as she thought back to what her gran had used to tell her: 'If a woman has heartburn during the last part of her pregnancy, it means that the baby will be born with a lot of hair.' Her gran had been full of old wives' tales and now as the birth approached, Jess missed her more than ever.

Settling herself comfortably back against the headboard, Jess took Martha's journal from the drawer. She hadn't touched it since learning of poor Miss Melody's baby dying, but now she felt ready to read on and so she opened it to the next page.

*5 January*
Poor Master Leonard has been beside himself with grief and fear today, and has barely left Miss Melody's side. Cook kept sending up treats to tempt him to eat, but they were all returned to the kitchen untouched. Miss Prim and Grace have been in there all day with her too, taking it in turns to sponge her with cool water and praying for her temperature to break.

'I really think you should return to your cottage now, Mother Dickinson,' Miss Prim told the old woman late that afternoon. 'By your own admission there is nothing more that you can do. And now that the snow has stopped, Bertie could escort you home. He will then try to get into Nuneaton to fetch the doctor.'

'I dare say yer right.' Mother Dickinson rose wearily and rubbed her aching old back. She could never remember being so tired in her whole life and would be happy now to return to her own fireside and her cosy little cottage in Caldecote.

Master Leonard rose from his seat at the side of the bed and crossing to the old woman, he took both her hands in his. 'May God bless you for what you've done for my wife,' he told her sincerely.

252

She shrugged. 'I just wish I could 'ave done more, sir,' she mumbled.

Master Leonard then fumbled in the pocket of his creased breeches and withdrew a number of gold sovereigns as the old woman's eyes almost popped out of her head.

'Please take this as a sign of my appreciation.'

Her head wagged from side to side, setting her grey hair dancing about her head like snakes. During the vigil none of them had had time to wash or set a brush through their hair.

'That's too much,' she protested.

He smiled sadly. 'If anything, it is not enough – so take it, I beg you.'

She cautiously took the heavy coins in her hand and felt the weight of them before dropping them into the pocket of her old grey serge dress.

'Thank yer kindly, sir.' She lifted her shawl and Polly then led her from the room and they went in search of Bertie, whilst Leonard and Miss Prim turned their attentions back to the poor woman lying in the enormous brass bed.

Grace and Martha had retired to the kitchen to snatch a well-earned cup of tea with Bertie and Cook. Phoebe was there too, and once they had seen old Mother Dickinson and Bertie on their way they all returned to sit at the large scrubbed table.

'Eeh, I still can't take it in,' Cook shook her head, setting her chins wobbling. 'Only a matter o' days ago we were all lookin' forward to havin' a couple o' children runnin' around the place. Now there'll only be the one.'

'Huh! There will be if Grace will slow up a bit,' Martha remarked, then addressing her sister directly she pleaded, 'Why don't yer go an' get some rest, Grace? There are more than enough of us to look after Miss Melody. Yer look dead on yer feet, an' if yer don't rest soon there'll be two of youse we're all lookin' after.'

'I'm fine,' Grace assured her, although her back was aching alarmingly.

'Right, well, I'd best go an' get the slop bucket from Miss Melody's room,' Polly said, after draining her mug, and she walked wearily from the room. Polly usually skipped everywhere, but none of them had any energy left.

Whilst Polly was collecting the bucket Miss Prim slipped from the room to visit the latrine and it was as she was returning that she met Polly on the stairs. Polly suddenly slipped and the bucket clattered

253

down the steps, spilling its contents. Before the girl knew what was happening, Miss Prim had boxed her soundly round the ears. For a moment it would have been hard to say who was the more shocked of the two of them, but Polly then burst into tears, closely followed by Miss Prim.

'Oh, my dear girl, I am *so* sorry,' the older woman sobbed. 'I'm so tired I scarcely know what I am doing. Do forgive me!'

'S'all right,' Polly gulped, but somehow she couldn't seem to stop the tears from flowing.

It was then that Grace, who was returning to Miss Melody's room, reached them on the stairs, and nearby slipped.

'Is everythin' all right?' she asked.

'No, dear, everything is very *far* from all right,' Miss Prim cried. 'And I have the most fearful feeling that things will never be all right again. If only the doctor would come . . .' She then lifted her skirts and ran back up the stairs.

Eeh, Grace thought, the world has gone mad. This has been such a happy house since the young Master and Mistress arrived. How quickly things could change, and now she wondered if it would ever be a happy house again as she comforted young Polly as best she could.

Jess closed the book with a large lump in her throat as she stared at the sketch of Martha hanging on the wall. To look at that, no one would have believed the heartache she had in store for her when Bertie had sketched it. The field she was in was covered in wild flowers, and although her face was not visible as she bent to pick them, because of the curtain of hair that covered it, Jess could somehow sense that she was smiling. Heaving herself off the bed, she left the journal on the duvet and slowly climbed the stair to the attics. At the end of the long landing leading to the largest storage room was a pile of trunks and old furniture that Simon had placed there. Lifting the lid of the first trunk, she began to sift through it, to check that these were the ones she wanted to dispose of. It was as she was sifting through the last one that her eyes grew round with interest as she saw a number of sheets of paper in the bottom. They were yet more of Bertie's sketches – and Jess felt as if she had happened on buried treasure!

There was one of the house and another of an old lady chopping vegetables who Jess assumed must have been Granny Reid. And yet another of a younger woman with a sweet face – possibly Grace? And then Jess's heart raced as she studied the final sketch. It appeared to be of the same girl as the one in the sketch she had hanging in the bedroom, but this time her face was visible. Somehow actually seeing her face made her seem all the more real. Trembling, she stumbled down the stairs clutching the sketch in her hand. She would show it to Laura. In no time at all she was heading down the drive and minutes later she barged into Laura's cottage without knocking.

Laura was tackling a large pile of ironing and glanced up, startled. 'Crikey, where's the fire?' she teased, then seeing Jess's chalk-white face she pressed her down onto the nearest chair. 'Whatever's the matter?' she asked. 'You look as if you've just seen a ghost.'

'I think I have,' Jess said shakily, as she pushed the sketch towards Laura.

The woman studied it for a second and then let out a long breath. 'Where did you get this?'

'I just found it up in one of the trunks in the attic,' Jess explained. 'It's made her feel more real, seeing her face like this.'

She fidgeted with the button on her cardigan. 'Do you think it might be this girl Martha who is still in the house?'

Laura nodded. 'I should imagine it's her, yes. And if it is, that might explain why you felt drawn to the house when you first came to view it, and why she stayed behind, knowing that you would come to live there one day.'

But what was she trying to tell her? Jess thought. It was all very worrying and frustrating.

Laura stared at her solemnly. She must have wanted you to find her journal for a reason.'

Jess was obviously severely shaken. 'So what shall I do now?'

'Nothing,' Laura advised her simply. 'You just wait until Martha decides to reveal her purpose or her intentions. There's nothing else you can do.'

'It's a bit nerve-wracking,' Jess muttered as the button finally pinged off her cardigan and rolled across the floor. Beth instantly bent from her seat at the side of the fire and snatched it up, clutching it possessively in her hand as the two women looked towards her.

'She's not too good today,' Laura murmured.

Jess could see that; the girl's eyes were blank and staring as she rocked to and fro in her chair.

Poor soul, she thought. This pregnancy was an awful lot for her to endure. Beth had piled weight on and was still devouring everything in sight, to the point that the midwife was seriously concerned about her. As ever, Jess felt guilty about burdening Laura with her problems when she had enough on her plate, but she was still impressed with Laura's knowledge of things that she herself didn't understand.

Hoping to lighten the mood she asked, 'And how are the family trees coming along? Have you managed to find time to work on them?'

'Oh yes.' Laura brightened instantly. 'As soon as Beth goes to bed each night I'm straight onto the computer. I think it's only that which is keeping me sane at the minute, and I finished yours last night. I managed to trace your family back as far as 1732. As soon as I get a chance I'll print it all off for you – I think you'll find it really interesting. One of your ancestors was actually a vicar and your family moved here originally from Wales.'

'Really? I never knew that,' Jess said. A sudden thought occurred to her and she asked, 'Did you find any link with my ancestors to Stonebridge Hall?'

Laura shook her head. 'Not a thing.'

'Well, that's *that* theory out of the window then.' Jess grinned ruefully. 'I thought you were going to tell me that my family had once owned the Hall or were servants there in times gone by. That would have explained a few things, wouldn't it?'

'I suppose it would, but as far as I can see there's nothing to link you to the place at all.'

Feeling much calmer now, Jess stood up.

'Thanks for the chat, Laura, but I think I've taken up more than enough of your time now, so I'll be off.'

Crossing to Beth she pecked her cheek affectionately then set off up the drive towards the house. Finding the sketch had been a great shock to her, but now she was thinking more sensibly again, she realised that things were no different now from what they had been before. If Martha was there for a reason she would reveal what it was in her own good time. Once she entered the welcome warmth of her own kitchen she stood there for a few seconds letting the peace of the place wash over her as Alfie bounded out of his basket and came to greet her. And then, just as she had known they would, the whispers started up again. They were becoming louder and more urgent by the day, but all she could do was be patient until she discovered what it was they were trying to tell her.

# Chapter Thirty-Three

That evening after dinner Jess slapped the sketch down on the table in front of Simon and asked him bluntly, 'What do you think of that?'

He lifted it and studied it intently.

'Who's this?' he asked.

'I think it's the girl whose journal I found. It was in one of the old trunks up in the attic.'

'Really? She was a nice-looking girl, wasn't she?' he commented.

'I'm more convinced than ever now that that girl – or at least her ghost – is still here in this house,' Jess told him. 'I also believe she is trying to tell me something.'

'I reckon you should be an author with an imagination like that,' Simon smirked.

Simon didn't believe in God, ghosts, angels or anything that he could not see or touch, and Jess knew of old that nothing she said was going to change his mind now.

'Think what you like,' she sighed, 'but I *know* she's here.'

He patted her hand indulgently. 'Of course you do, love. It's quite normal for pregnant women to behave a little oddly. It's something to do with the hormones.'

Biting down on her lip, Jess stamped off into the lounge where Jo was watching the television.

'Do you fancy coming for a ride to see Karen with me tonight?' she asked, forcing herself to sound normal although she felt far from it.

Dragging her eyes away from *Emmerdale Farm* just long enough to flash a smile, Jo nodded. 'Yes, please, but can you wait until this has finished?'

'All right, but if you're not ready to go the second it does, I'm off without you otherwise it won't be worth going.'

Jess pottered off back to the kitchen to clear the pots from the table, relieved to see that Simon had taken himself off to the shower. She then lifted the sketch and popped it into her bag to take with her before busying herself until it was time to go.

Karen was just as sceptical as Simon had been when she showed her the sketch later that evening. 'I tell you, Jess, I'm getting really worried about you,' she said frankly. 'This girl is nothing at all to do with you. She could have been anyone!'

Jess kept her smile firmly fixed in place. Just like Simon, Karen could be very stubborn, and she knew that it would be useless trying to convince her that Martha was still in her house. Without a word she hastily shoved the sketch back into her bag and changed the subject, and for the rest of the evening it wasn't mentioned again.

Jess left a little earlier than usual that night. Her ankles were puffy and she got tired easily.

'Is everything all right, Mum?' Jo asked on the way home, picking up on how quiet Jess was.

'Everything is fine, sweetheart,' Jess assured her. 'I'm just a bit tired, that's all. It's lumping all this lot around in front of me. I shall be glad when your brother is here.'

Jo was instantly all smiles. 'Less than two months to go now,' she said happily.

The downstairs was in darkness when they got home and Jess fumbled her hand along the wall to locate the light switch in the kitchen.

'Night, Mum.' Jo patted Alfie and kissed her mother before skipping away to bed as Jess began to check that all the doors were firmly locked and bolted. She always made doubly sure ever since the break-in.

It was as she approached the landing that she saw Mel coming out of the bathroom. She was clutching her dressing-gown around her and had obviously been crying, but she didn't even acknowledge her mother.

'What's wrong, love?' As the girl approached her, Jess put her hand out to her but Mel slapped it away furiously.

'What do *you* care?' she screamed, obviously very close to hysteria. 'Why don't you just *leave* me alone? I *hate* you . . . do you hear me? *I hate you*.' With that she tore along the landing and disappeared into her bedroom, slamming the door resoundingly behind her, leaving Jess to stare after her in amazement.

I wonder what the hell brought that on? Jess thought, but she knew better than to go and try to find out. When Mel was in this mood it was best to leave her well alone to come out of it.

Feeling deeply hurt, she stared from the landing window out over

258

the gardens. They looked beautiful bathed in moonlight and she wished that the inside of the house could be as serene as the outside appeared to be.

Eventually she made for the staircase that led to the attics. She was out of breath by the time she reached the top. Soon she was standing in Martha's room. The smell of roses was overpowering and now the whispers began again.

'What *is* it you're trying to tell me?' she pleaded to the empty room and as she stood there praying for an answer she thought she heard soft footsteps on the stairs.

Hurrying to the door she peered up and down the narrow passageway but there was no one in sight.

Maybe I *am* going barmy, she thought to herself as she headed back towards the stairs. I reckon the best thing I could do is get myself off to bed. She was desperately tired now and looking forward to sinking into her comfortable mattress.

After clicking off the bare bulb that illuminated the landing she had just put her foot on the first step when she heard a scuffle behind her. Partially turning, she peered into the murk, but it was too dark to see anything other than a figure advancing on her – then suddenly she felt something shove her hard in the back. Her arms flailed as she tried to stay upright, but it was no good. She could feel herself falling and the next thing she knew she was toppling headlong down the steep staircase. She vaguely remembered wrapping her arms around her stomach to protect her unborn child, then she hit the floor at the bottom of the stairs with a sickening thud and pain flooded though her.

'*Help!*' she cried out feebly as she felt something warm and sticky gush from between her legs. And then she knew nothing more.

'It's all right, Jess. Just lie still now.'

Jess blinked in the bright light and then she groaned with pain and tried to roll herself into a ball.

'You must lie still,' the voice told her and Jess gazed up at a solemn-faced paramedic.

'Where am I? What's happened?' She seemed to be looking at everything through a haze, and in that moment she wished that she could die. This was pain like she had never known before. All-consuming and agonising.

'You're in an ambulance on your way to the George Eliot Hospital.

You've had an accident, but you'll be all right if you just do as you're told,' the paramedic soothed her. 'Your husband is following on in his car.'

Jess gasped as a fresh contraction ripped through her. She was in labour – it was a pain she would never forget – but it was too early. Would the baby survive being born this soon? Tears squeezed out of the corners of her eyes as she gritted her teeth.

'I . . . I was on the attic stairs,' she told him as everything came rushing back. 'And then somebody pushed me.'

'Shush now,' the man said urgently. 'You're haemorrhaging badly and I don't want you to talk. Save your strength.'

She flopped back on the pillows, the sound of the ambulance's siren loud in her ears, and prayed that they would be able to save her child.

When they arrived at the hospital the paramedic leaped up and swung the back doors open, and instantly two male nurses climbed in and began to manoeuvre her onto a wheeled stretcher. She could feel herself drifting in and out of consciousness; felt as if she was caught in the grip of a nightmare and prayed for it to end.

They had barely reached the doors to the hospital when Simon appeared at her side breathless and panting.

'How is she?' he asked the doctor who was waiting at the door for her.

'We'll know more when we've examined her,' he replied shortly. 'Now go into the waiting room, would you, sir, and leave us to do our job.'

Simon's face faded away then Jess found herself staring up at the striplights set at intervals all along the hospital corridor as they rushed her along. Before she knew it she was wheeled into a room and the doctor was examining her.

'C-can you stop the labour?' she choked out, writhing in pain.

He prodded gently around her abdomen. 'I'm afraid not, Mrs Beddows. You've gone too far for that.'

A nurse was attaching a monitor to her that was recording the baby's heartbeats, and as she looked towards the screen, Jess's own heart contracted with terror. She had very little medical knowledge, but even she could see that the baby was in distress.

'We're going to perform an emergency caesarean,' the doctor told her. 'It will give the baby a better chance.'

'No!' Jess whimpered. But at that moment she felt a stinging pain in the back of her hand as the nurse administered an injection, and she felt as if she was floating.

The trolley she was lying on was moving again now as they rushed her off to theatre. People were waiting there for her, but all she could see of them were their eyes because they were wearing masks.

'Now just try to relax,' a voice encouraged.

She vaguely wondered where Simon was. And then suddenly memories came flooding back. She was standing at the top of the stairs and there was a dark shape behind her. Someone had pushed her. But who?

She opened her mouth, frantic for an answer but it was too hard to try and form words. Even as she struggled against it, her eyelids drooped and she fell into a drug-induced sleep.

# Chapter Thirty-Four

When Jess woke up, there was a watery sun shining through the window at the side of the bed. She was in a small side room and beyond the door she could faintly hear the sound of babies crying. She prayed that one of them was hers.

She rubbed at her eyes for a second and when she opened them again she saw a nurse and a doctor in a starched white coat standing at the end of the bed as if they had appeared by magic.

'My baby?' she managed to choke out. Her throat was dry.

The doctor was a tall man with a mop of unruly fair hair and eyes that were red-rimmed from lack of sleep. Jess supposed that he was somewhere in his early thirties although the weary stoop of his shoulders made him appear at first glance to be much older.

He smiled at her sadly. 'There's no easy way for me to say this, so I'm just going to come right out with it. I'm so sorry, Mrs Beddows . . . but I'm afraid we lost the baby. The shock of the fall and the birth was just too much for him. He lived for ten minutes, although we did all we could to save him, I assure you.'

Jess stared at him in wide-eyed disbelief. 'No, there must be some mistake. You must have my baby mixed up with someone else's.'

The doctor and the nurse exchanged a glance before he told her softly, 'I'm afraid there has been no mistake. Would you like to see him, Mrs Beddows?'

'*No!*' Jess was struggling to take in what he had just told her. She didn't want to believe it yet something in his sad eyes told her that it was true. Her baby – her *son* was dead. Guilt stabbed at her sharp as a knife. *This must be my punishment for not being sure if I wanted him when I found out I was pregnant,* she told herself. The nurse came to hold her hand now but Jess shook her off roughly. She knew that she should be crying as she thought of the baby's nursery back at home, but she felt numb inside, as if she was no longer capable of feelings.

'Where is my husband?' she asked dully.

'He was here with you for most of the night after you came out of theatre,' the nurse assured her. 'But he left a while ago. He said he had to see to breakfast for your daughters. I'm sure he'll be back soon.'

'I have to continue with my rounds now, Mrs Beddows,' the doctor said gently, 'but if you need me, just tell the nurse here and she'll page me. Thankfully, you've come out of the accident far better than you might have, and all being well, you'll be able to go home tomorrow.'

*Home* . . . the word rattled round and round in Jess's head. She would be going home – without her baby. For months she had pictured leaving the hospital with him all wrapped snugly in a blue shawl, cradled in her arms, but that would never happen now. He would never wear the mountain of baby clothes she and Jo had chosen so lovingly, never ride on the beautiful rocking horse that she had made Simon carry down from the attic, or lie kicking in his cot as he watched the mobile of all the *Winnie the Pooh* characters dangling above it. She tentatively fingered the flabby stomach beneath the sheets, devoid of the life that had been growing there. And then her thoughts shifted, and once again she was at the top of the attic stairs. There *had* been someone standing behind her, a dark shadow, and they had pushed her. She could remember clearly the awful feeling as she had pitched head-first down the steep stairs. But who could it have been?

A picture of Mel's face flashed before her eyes but she rejected it immediately. *I'm being irrational*, she told herself. *Mel might not have wanted the baby, she never made a secret of the fact, but she would never have done anything to harm me.*

As the sounds of babies crying wafted to her from the main ward beyond the door, instead of mourning for the little boy that she would never know now, she felt dead inside, as if her tears had been locked away in some dark and secret place from which they could not escape. *It's perhaps as well*, she tried to convince herself. *If I start crying now I might never stop.*

A young woman in a voluminous dressing-gown carrying a new baby wrapped in a pink blanket pottered past the door then, her pride coming off her in bright rays as she stared down at the infant in her arms. She paused briefly when she felt Jess's eyes on her, but then scuttled on when she noticed the empty crib that had been pushed into a corner of the room.

Jess stared at the ceiling. Where was Simon? He should be here. This had been his baby too and she wondered how he was feeling. He hadn't wanted the baby either in the early days of her pregnancy,

263

but he seemed to have come round to the idea over the last couple of months. And Jo . . . poor Jo. Jess knew that of all of them, she would be the worst affected by this latest accident. She had been so looking forward to having a baby brother.

A nurse came in then and Jess's thoughts were distracted as the young woman fiddled with the IV drip that fed into the back of her hand. She took her temperature and her blood pressure before making notes on the chart that was hooked on the end of the bed then slipped away without a word. It seemed that no one quite knew what to say to her, but then what *could* they say? *I'm so sorry that your baby has died?* It sounded so ineffectual.

At lunch-time a nurse brought her an unappetising-looking meal on a tray but Jess ignored it and eventually it was taken away untouched. Mid-afternoon, another woman came into the room and introduced herself as the hospital's social worker. She looked to be little older than Mel, and Jess gazed at her blankly. She was a pretty young woman with soulful brown eyes and shoulder-length fair hair, dressed in a checked shirt and jeans, and as she pulled a chair up to the side of the bed and sat down, Jess suddenly felt very old.

'I'm Christie Best,' she told Jess solemnly, then went on to ask if Jess would like to see a counsellor. 'It does help sometimes to talk about it,' she told her softly.

Jess shook her head. What good could it do? It wouldn't miraculously bring her baby back to life, would it?

Eventually the girl sighed and rose to her feet. It was very clear that Jess wasn't ready to talk about anything just yet. 'If you don't want to talk about it, how about seeing your baby?' she asked as she slipped a photo into Jess's hand. 'This is your son. I er . . . thought you might like to keep it.'

Jess didn't even attempt to look at it, but now the tears that were locked inside had risen into her throat and she was afraid that they might choke her.

'I'm going to leave you now.' The young woman's voice was heavy with sympathy. 'I think you need some time to get your head around what's happened. But if you should decide that you want to see him, just ring the bell and someone will bring him to you. At some stage we have to arrange the funeral, but think about if for now. There's no rush.'

As she left the room, shock settled around Jess like a wet blanket. A funeral! She hadn't thought that far ahead, but of course the child would need to be laid to rest.

Slowly she lifted the photo, and as her eyes settled on a tiny baby wrapped in a blue blanket the lump in her throat grew even larger. This small slip of paper was all she had of her son now; she would be taking this measly reminder home rather than him. And yet still the tears remained trapped inside as she gazed at the picture. A few moments later yet another nurse entered the room and now Jess told her, 'I . . . I want to see my baby.' She had no idea where the words had come from. She hadn't meant to say them but now there was no going back.

'I'll go and tell Sister right away.' The young nurse left as Jess lay still, her mind in turmoil. It seemed like a lifetime until a shadow appeared in the doorway again, and this time Jess saw that it was the Sister and she was holding a white broderie anglaise Moses basket in her arms. Closing the door quietly behind her, she approached the bed with a sympathetic smile on her face.

'Would you like me to stay with you?' she asked. 'Or would you rather spend some time on your own with him?'

Jess gulped. 'I think I'd rather be alone, please.'

'Of course. Just ring your bell if you need me. And do pick him up if you wish to.' The woman laid the basket on the end of the bed then turned and quietly left the room.

Jess took a deep breath and slowly sat up, clutching the dressing on her stomach as she did so. She felt as weak as a lamb, but forced herself to swing her legs out of the bed and then sat there for a moment until the wave of dizziness that swept over her had passed.

Very cautiously she walked to the end of the bed, holding on to the mattress for support and after another deep breath she made herself look down into the basket. The sight that met her eyes made her gasp with pain. The child looked absolutely perfect and was like a miniature clone of his father. The nurses had dressed him in a little blue Babygro and he looked so peaceful that Jess expected him to wake up at any minute and cry for a feed. His long lashes were curled on his soft cheeks and his head was covered in thick dark hair that was exactly the same colour as his father's. His tiny hands were curled into fists and now she gently stroked his fingers, revelling in the feel of his satiny skin. She had promised herself she would only look at him, but now the desire to hold him in her arms took over and she gently lifted him from his crib and cradled him against her chest, suddenly forgetting all about the stitches in her stomach.

And then the tears finally fell, running in rivers down her face and dropping onto his pale, cold cheeks.

'Hello, sweetheart,' she mumbled brokenly. 'I'm your mummy and I love you so *very* much.' And in that moment she realised that she really *did* love him. She would always love him and remember this brief precious time when she had been able to hold him.

She was still sitting there gently rocking him to and fro when the door opened and glancing up, she saw Simon standing there with a look of pure horror on his face.

'Is that . . .' His voice trailed away as he stared at the baby.

'It's our son, Simon, and he's truly beautiful. Do you want to hold him?'

He pressed himself against the wall. 'No,' he choked out. 'He's *dead*, isn't he?'

'Yes, sadly he is, but he's still our son and this will be the only chance you'll ever get to touch him. Are you quite sure that you don't want to?'

The look of disgust on his face cut into her like a knife. 'Yes, I *am* sure,' he ground out. 'It's unhealthy to sit there nursing a dead baby. Get the nurse to take it away.'

'He isn't an *it!*' Jess stared at him, all the hurt she was feeling mirrored in her eyes, and in that moment it hit her that Simon had never truly wanted this child. The last couple of months he had just pretended to, in order to appease her.

'He would be alive if someone hadn't pushed me down the stairs,' she said bitterly.

Simon looked at her as if she had totally taken leave of her senses but he kept his voice calm as he told her, 'Look, love, you've had a terrible accident. It was no one's fault and no one pushed you. You're just distraught at the moment and your imagination is running away with you.'

'Someone *did* push me,' she declared, and stared at him defiantly.

He held up his hands in an effort to placate her. 'All right, all right. Let's talk about this when we get you home. But for now, how about we ask the nurse to take . . . him away.'

He hurriedly opened the door and seconds later the Sister reappeared and waited while Jess gently laid the baby back in his crib after kissing him for the last time. And as she watched the kindly woman carry him away, she felt as if a little part of her heart was going with him.

'I'm coming home,' she told Simon dully when the nurse had disappeared from sight.

'Oh good. When?'

'In the morning, all being well. Will you be able to fetch me?'

'Well, I was planning on going to work,' he said uncertainly, but seeing the look on Jess's face he quickly ended with, 'but of course I'll break off to come and get you.'

'How *good* of you.' Jess could not keep the sarcasm from her voice. She felt as if she was dying inside and yet not once had Simon even said how sorry he was about losing the baby. It was as if their son had never existed. As if they had never even been expecting a baby.

He shuffled from foot to foot looking more uncomfortable by the minute as he watched Jess's devastated face, but then a gentleman in a dark suit entered the room telling them that he had come to organise the baby's funeral with them.

'Funeral?' Simon scratched his head. 'I didn't think we'd have to have one of those.'

'Oh, did you think we were just going to dig a hole in the back lawn for him then?' Jess said. At that moment, she hated her husband.

'Look, I er . . . reckon I'm going to leave this to you,' he muttered now as he tugged at his collar and inched towards the door. 'Ring me tomorrow when you're ready to come home, eh?' And with that he beat a hasty retreat, leaving Jess to talk to the undertaker alone.

Later that evening, a nurse removed the drips from the side of Jess's bed and told her that she was doing well. Jess managed to raise a smile even though she felt as if she might never 'do well' again. It had been a long gruelling day and eventually she slept from pure exhaustion.

The following morning, when the doctors had done their rounds and pronounced her well enough to go home, Jess slowly made her way to the pay phone at the top of the ward and dialled the house. She could hardly wait to get away from the maternity ward, as each time one of the newborn babies cried it was like a knife stabbing into her heart. After a while when there was no reply, she rang Simon's mobile, but again she was forwarded to his answer machine and she gritted her teeth with annoyance. He had known she was coming home today, so *why* didn't he answer? She briefly thought of ringing Laura and asking her to fetch her, but then swiftly changed her mind and rang a taxi instead. She would have to go home in the nightdress and the gown that the hospital had loaned her, and pay the taxi when they got to Stonebridge House, but anything was better than having to stay in this place another second. The Ward Sister was not at all happy about her going home in a taxi on her own, but Jess stood her ground, insisting that she would be fine and promising to return the nightclothes at the earliest opportunity.

And so she left the hospital with empty arms and an even emptier heart, and as the taxi pulled away from it she tried not to think of what should have been.

When the taxi pulled into the courtyard at Stonebridge House, Jess was surprised to see Laura just storming out of the kitchen door with Simon hot on her heels. Laura looked momentarily stunned when she saw Jess but quickly regained her composure as she opened the car door for her, whilst Simon watched from the kitchen doorway, clearly agitated.

'I er . . . I'm so sorry to hear about the baby,' Laura stammered, then without another word she strode away, her coat flapping behind her in the wind as Simon hurried forward to help Jess out of the taxi and pay the driver.

'What was all that about?' Jess questioned as she leaned heavily on Simon's arm.

'Oh . . . she seems to think that I should have been taking better care of you,' he muttered.

Jess shrugged. She appreciated Laura's concern but at that moment in time she had more things to worry about than Laura's feelings, so she merely nodded as he gently helped her inside.

# Chapter Thirty-Five

Baby James Beddows was buried the following week in a simple ceremony at the church where Jess's grandmother had been buried. Her grandmother's grave had been opened and his tiny coffin was laid in with hers. Somehow it gave Jess a measure of comfort to know that her gran was watching over him and keeping him safe until they met again one day. There were few mourners, just Jess and Simon and the two girls, and Karen and her husband, Geoff, who stood white-faced as they tried to come to terms with what had happened. Surprisingly, Mel had taken it as badly as Jo, which completely shocked Jess, seeing as Mel had never seemed to want the baby.

As soon as the service was over, Karen and Geoff quietly offered their condolences and slipped away, correctly guessing that the family would wish to be by themselves.

Jess was quite hurt that Laura hadn't put in an appearance. In fact, she hadn't seen her at all since the day she had returned home from the hospital, but she surmised that Laura didn't know what to say to her and so had chosen to stay away for the time being.

Jo was inconsolable on the way back to the house and sobbed into Jess's shoulder in the back seat. The girls had both had a day off school to attend the funeral, and once they were all home again, Simon insisted that Jess should go for a lie-down. She went quietly. It didn't really matter where she was or what she did; the hurt was never far away as she pictured her baby's perfect little face.

After changing out of the black coat she had bought for her grandmother's funeral, Jess slipped into bed. Soon afterwards, Simon brought her a cup of tea and placed it down on the bedside table, asking, 'Would you mind very much if I went back to work? The girls are here if you need anything and I think I'd like to be doing something rather than just sitting about.'

Jess nodded, not really caring what he did or where he went at that moment in time. He stood uncertainly for a second staring down at her pale face on the pillow before turning abruptly and leaving the room.

She lay for a long time staring at the ceiling until eventually she took Martha's journal from the drawer. She desperately needed something to distract her and hoped that reading a little more might do the trick as she opened it to the page she had carefully marked.

*6 January*

The day started well, for Miss Melody's fever broke during the night and now the doctor thinks she may come through this after all. The whole household offered up prayers of thanks although we are all gravely concerned about how she will take the news of her baby's death when she is well enough to be told.

'Eeh, thank the Lord!' Cook exclaimed when Miss Prim entered the kitchen to tell them that the young Mistress's fever had broken.

'She is still very weak, of course,' Miss Prim went on, 'but the doctor is hopeful now that she will pull through with constant nursing. I really don't know how I shall ever be able to thank you all enough for the diligent care you have shown her,' Miss Prim went on. 'Dear Grace is still up there with her now, although I have pleaded with her to come away. The dear girl has been like Melody's guardian angel but she must be totally exhausted by now.'

'That's Grace fer yer,' Cook replied philosophically. 'Got a heart o' pure gold, that one has, so 'as that sister of 'ers. Young Martha is tendin' to her gran at present.'

'Yes, well, I must get back upstairs now, but I thought I would let you all know the good news. The doctor will be staying, at least until this evening, so perhaps we shall all be able to get some rest soon.'

The mood in the house seemed to lift a little as the day progressed, but then as night fell they were all too soon presented with yet another tragedy.

Lifting the jug from the small table at the side of Miss Melody's bed, Grace whispered, 'I'll just pop down to the kitchen an' get 'er some fresh water whilst she's restin' easy.'

'Very well, dear.' Miss Prim smiled and settled further down into the comfortable chair that Leonard had had brought into the room for her. But she had barely laid her head back when a loud bang on the landing outside had her jumping upright.

'Whatever was that?' she asked the young Master but he was already on his way to the door.

The second he threw the door open they found Grace in a heap on the landing carpet, doubled up with pain, and without wasting a second he snapped at Miss Prim, 'Run down to the kitchen and get the doctor, would you? I'll carry her into that bedroom there. And get Bertie too whilst you're at it.'

The two men were racing up the stairs in a second and while the Master took the doctor into Grace, Miss Prim tried to comfort Bertie on the landing. 'I'm sure she is just exhausted,' she soothed, but seconds later she was proven to be wrong.

'It seems that your baby is on the way, Bertie,' Leonard told the anxious young man, and the colour drained from Bertie's face. Then: 'Miss Prim, could you organise towels and hot water, please, and perhaps send for Phoebe in case the doctor needs any help?'

Poor Phoebe had only just gone home, but they all knew that she wouldn't mind coming back to help Grace.

'Right away, sir.' Miss Prim hurried away to do as she was told, hardly able to take in that soon she was going to be witness to yet another birth. Now all they could do was pray that this one would go more smoothly than the last.

Poor Bertie was almost beside himself with worry as he paced up and down the landing under the watchful eye of the young Master, who felt powerless to help him. Grace's screams echoed around the house as the doctor battled to deliver the baby. But then after an hour, the screams stopped abruptly – and the sound of a newborn baby's wail filled the air.

Martha, who was holding fast to Bertie's hand, smiled widely, but the smile was wiped away when the doctor appeared in the doorway some minutes later, his face set in grim lines.

'Miss Prim, would you kindly go in and help Phoebe attend to the infant?' he asked, and as the woman sprang forward and disappeared into the room he had just left, the doctor turned his attention to Bertie and Martha.

'I'm so sorry,' he began, spreading his hands helplessly, 'but I am afraid Grace has gone. There were complications and I could not save her.'

'What do you mean, she's *gone*?' Bertie's whole body was trembling as Martha clung to his arm.

'I fear her heart gave out,' the doctor said gravely. 'She was exhausted and then with the strain of the birth on top . . . I'm so sorry. This house has seen more than its fair share of heartaches over the last few days.'

271

Bertie and Martha stared at the doctor, unable and unwilling to take in what he was telling them. It couldn't be true, Martha thought: her beautiful, kind sister was dead. But Grace was only a young woman, and had her whole life stretching before her!

'Would you like to see her?' the doctor asked kindly, realising that neither of them would believe it until they saw the evidence of what he was saying with their own eyes.

Martha nodded as she nudged Bertie forward. The fire that Polly had set was roaring up the chimney now, and the warmth met them as the doctor ushered them into the room. Miss Prim was sitting with her head bowed in a chair with a newborn infant cradled close to her chest. Neither Bertie nor Martha even glanced at the child. It was the woman in the carved four-poster bed that held their attention. Grace's hair was spread across the pillow like a shining halo and she was even more beautiful in death than she had been in life.

It was then that a cry of such torment erupted from Bertie's throat that Martha knew she would never forget it for as long as she lived.

Bertie fell across his wife, tenderly kissing her face and murmuring words of endearment as Martha looked helplessly on as if she was in a trance. And then the doctor gently touched Bertie's back and told him, 'Look – you have a fine son.'

Bertie's cries were halted as he glanced towards the infant with contempt. 'That bastard is no son of mine!' he said savagely and with that he turned and slammed out of the room as they all watched with their mouths hanging slackly open.

'The poor soul is in shock,' Miss Prim muttered through her tears. 'But won't *you* come and look at him, Martha?'

Martha slowly crossed the room until she was standing in front of the child and as she gazed down upon his tiny face, the tears that she had held back suddenly ran in rivers down her pale cheeks. He was still Grace's child, after all. Her nephew.

'What will become of him now that his mother is dead if Bertie doesn't want him?' she asked fearfully.

Miss Prim shrugged her slight shoulders. 'That is in God's hands now,' she said solemnly. 'But for now you must ask Polly to run to the village and fetch the wetnurse who was going to feed Miss Melody's baby. The child will be hungry soon.'

Martha stumbled away to do as she was told, but first she knew that she must visit Granny Reid to break the news to her.

As she related the tragedy to Granny, the old woman screwed her eyes tight shut and pressed a clenched fist to her heart. But then she composed herself and croaked, 'Go an' tell Miss Prim I wish to see 'er, lass. We must do what is in the child's best interests now. It is what Grace would have wanted.' Her gnarled old fingers plucked at the bedcovers as her faded old eyes brimmed with tears and Martha turned blindly away.

Minutes later, Miss Prim entered Granny's room whilst Martha ran to the village to fetch the wetnurse.

When she returned she found Miss Prim still closeted in Granny's room, and as she entered they both looked towards her.

'Ah, Martha, I'm glad yer back. There is somethin' we want yer to hear,' Granny said. 'We 'ave decided what must be done. The child will be dressed an' placed beside Miss Melody ready fer when she properly wakens. And from this day on she must believe that the child is hers. It will be the best all round if Master Leonard is willin' to go along wi' the idea. We have a child wi'out a mother an' a mother wi'out a child, so it makes sense, an' there is Fenton blood runnin' through the infant's veins, after all. Miss Melody need never be any the wiser an' she will love him as if he were her own. Her child can then be buried in the coffin wi' Grace. All the staff here are trustworthy. They will hold their tongues and keep the secret fer love o' Miss Melody when we explains it to 'em.'

Deep down, Martha knew that this would be for the best, so she nodded as Miss Prim bustled away to put the idea to the young Master.

Master Leonard agreed wholeheartedly with the plan and within an hour Grace's baby was dressed in the finest clothes that money could buy and was sleeping contentedly in a crib at the side of Miss Melody's bed. Meanwhile Phoebe reverently laid Grace out and placed two shining pennies on her closed eyes before laying Miss Melody's dead baby in her arms.

That night for the first time since she had been a tiny girl, Martha slept with her Granny. She could not face the thought of being alone as she struggled to picture a life without her beloved sister.

Jess closed the book as tears streamed down her face, and in that moment she wasn't sure who she was crying for: was it for Grace, or Martha? Or was it for Bertie, the baby who had died, or her own baby? At that precise time she had no way of knowing; the hurts were all intermixed, and she eventually fell into an exhausted sleep.

It was dark when she woke and she started as she saw Simon standing there with a tray in his hands.

'I thought you might be hungry,' he told her, 'so the girls and I have rustled up a meal. It's not posh, I'm afraid, but at least it will fill a hole.'

'Thanks, but I'm not hungry,' Jess told him dully as she struggled up onto the pillows. 'What time is it?'

'It's gone eight,' he replied, hurrying to close the curtains against the freezing cold weather. Jess stared down at the poached eggs on toast. She knew she was being ungrateful, but couldn't seem to help herself as she pushed the tray away.

'Where are the girls? Are they both all right?'

He nodded. 'They're fine and downstairs watching the telly. But you've got to eat, Jess.'

'Perhaps tomorrow,' she whispered as she turned on her side with her back to him. She heard him sigh before lifting the tray and leaving the room again; and as she thought of her baby spending his first night all alone beneath the frozen soil in the churchyard. she started to cry again and wondered if she was ever going to be able to stop.

# Chapter Thirty-Six

The next two weeks passed in a blur of misery and pain for Jess. She would wander into the nursery that she and Jo had so lovingly prepared for the new arrival and break into a fresh torrent of tears. She knew that she was torturing herself needlessly but didn't seem able to stop it. But even if her heart felt as if it was broken, her body was slowly beginning to mend. She had had her stitches out, which was a huge relief, and the bruises she had got during the fall had all but faded away now. And all the time the whispers were there in the background. Once or twice she had thought she had seen someone in the mirror behind her, but each time she turned there was no one there, although she could feel the presence of Martha, who never seemed to be very far away now.

Laura had still not put in an appearance and Jess could only suppose that Beth was unwell, although it did seem strange that she hadn't even popped in to see her of an evening when Den was at home to keep his eye on their daughter. Stranger still, Mel seemed to be spending a fair bit of time at the cottage now, but Jess supposed that this was better than shutting herself away in her room all the time and so wisely didn't comment on the fact.

Karen, on the other hand, had been wonderful. She had called in regularly and done any shopping Jess needed doing, as well as helping the girls with the housework. But now Jess was beginning to feel a little bored, being housebound. It seemed a long day when Simon was at work and the girls were at school, and she wandered around the house aimlessly looking at the jobs that needed doing and feeling frustrated because she wasn't well enough to tackle them yet.

She longed to talk about what had happened to someone, but everyone seemed to be tiptoeing around her because they were afraid of upsetting her further, and she felt like screaming at them, 'Let me talk about my baby! Let me talk about who it was that pushed me down the stairs!' But she didn't; she kept the hurt trapped inside where it festered like an enormous boil that must eventually burst. Today was no different, and after attempting to read a book and watch a little TV she went to her room and again took Martha's journal from her drawer.

*9 January*
Grace and Miss Melody's baby were laid to rest beneath an old oak tree in the churchyard yesterday morning following a simple ceremony in St Theobald and St Chad's Church in Caldecote. It was a bitterly cold day and the grass was still stiff with hoar frost as the coffin was lowered into the ground. Almost every villager turned out to pay their respects, as well as all the staff from the House, and the tiny church was full to capacity. Bertie was beside himself with grief and I think he would have fallen into the grave, had it not been for Hall Tolley's strong arm to support him . . .

'How did it go?' Granny asked, the instant Martha returned from the funeral.

'It went as well as a funeral could go,' Martha assured her. 'Master Leonard led the procession an' the church were packed.'

Granny wiped her wrinkled cheeks as she tried to picture her sweet Grace lying beneath the cold earth.

'But I shall 'ave to go now.' Martha tucked the blankets beneath Granny's chin. 'The Master 'as laid on a feast fit fer a queen down-stairs, an' 'alf o' the village 'ave come back to take advantage o' the fact, so happen they'll need a hand. Is there anythin' I can get yer?'

When Granny's head wagged, Martha sighed. The old woman had refused all offers of food, drink and even her medicine since Grace had died, and seemed to be visibly shrinking by the day.

Bertie was another one who was giving her grave cause for concern, for since Grace's passing he had not been sober. Now as she headed off to the funeral feast she could only hope that he would conduct himself properly.

Martha's hopes were dashed the second she set foot in the dining room, where the meal had been laid the whole length of the table. It was instantly obvious that Bertie had already had more than a few glasses of ale and wine, and Martha gave the Master a worried look. He nodded imperceptibly, as if he was silently telling her that he understood, and for the next two hours they both kept a close eye on Bertie. As the time wore on, Bertie got steadily louder until eventually the Master had a word in Hal Tolley's ear following which, Hal led

Bertie from the house and back to his rooms above the stables. It had been a dark day indeed, saved only by the fact that Miss Melody was finally improving and was totally besotted with her new son. All they could do was pray that she might never discover that he was, in fact, Grace's child.

*12 January*
I had thought that the worst must surely be behind us all now but I was wrong, for today Master Leonard gathered the staff together and informed us that as soon as his wife was well enough to travel, they intended to return to their country estate so that Miss Melody could be closer to her parents until the baby is a little older. This means, of course, that we will once again be at the mercy of Master Fenton . . . A dark shadow has fallen across our already grieving household.

'Don't you think he is just the *most* beautiful baby you have ever seen, Martha?' Miss Melody asked as the girl straightened the bedcovers. Martha swallowed the lump that rose in her throat. 'I'm sure that he has a look of his father about him,' Miss Melody mused as she studied his face intently, but all Martha could see when she looked at him was her beloved sister.

Already she knew that her nephew would never want for anything, least of all love, but it did nothing to ease her heartache. And each time she saw Miss Melody cradling him to her and crooning at him, she had to look away.

Gathering up his dirty linen, Martha now asked, 'Is there anythin' I can get fer yer, Miss Melody?'

'No, thank you, dear.' Miss Melody smiled at her kindly. She had been told that both Grace and her infant had died at the birth and wished there was something she could do to ease poor Martha's pain.

Martha now bobbed her knee and scuttled away, and her last sight as she closed the bedroom door was of Miss Melody rocking the baby as she sang him a lullaby.

Downstairs, the mood in the kitchen was sombre.

'Bertie ain't got up fer work again today,' Phoebe informed Martha. 'An' whilst I know the young Master will make allowances fer him 'cos of all that's happened, I can't see the old 'un doin' the same.'

Cook sucked in her breath and sighed. 'Bless 'is soul, he ain't been

277

sober since the day Grace passed away,' she said worriedly. 'No doubt he'll rousle 'isself round soon.'

Martha wasn't so sure. Knowing how intently Bertie hated Master Fenton, she could see trouble ahead but felt powerless to prevent it. The only bright spot on the horizon at present was Jimmy, who had been her rock throughout that terrible time. Only the day before, he had promised that, as soon as the right opportunity arose, he would ask permission for them to be wed in the summer. It could not come quickly enough for Martha, but this led to yet another worry. What about her granny? Would she come with them? And where would they all live? She pushed these thoughts to the back of her mind; after all that had happened, anywhere would be preferable to living here – and she now had no wish to stay in the house a day longer than was necessary.

*1 February*
It has been a sad day indeed, for Master Leonard and Miss Melody left this morning for their other home, and now Master Fenton is once more in charge. This can only mean trouble for all of us . . .

The house seemed suddenly half-empty with the departure of the young Master and Mistress, for their staff had gone with them too.

'I shall miss that Miss Prim,' Phoebe sniffed as they sat at the kitchen table.

'An' I shall miss Polly too,' said Martha.

'Aye, well, it ain't all doom an' gloom. At least yer in charge o' the kitchen again, Phoebe.'

'Hmm.' The young woman glanced around at the rows of gleaming pots and pans. 'Funny thing was, I got to quite like Cook once I got used to her. She were as soft as butter 'neath all that shoutin'. But hadn't you best get off to the mill, Hal Tolley? The Master won't be as tolerant wi' us as the young 'un was.'

'I was asked to stay here to help load all the luggage onto the carriages,' he pointed out.

'So yer were, but they've been gone this half-hour since so get yerself away.'

Hal grinned as he rose and pecked his wife on the cheek – and then he was gone and they were left to try and get back into some sort of a routine.

'Checked on Bertie yet today, 'ave yer, love?' Phoebe now asked Martha.

The girl shook her head. 'I'm really worried about him,' she confided. 'An' I wonder if he ain't losin' his mind. I'm afraid of what he might do to the Master – 'specially now Master Leonard ain't here to stop him. When I helped him across to his rooms last night he swore to me that he'd have his revenge on him, an' I don't know what to do.'

'Ain't nothin' a slip of a girl like you *can* do,' Phoebe said sensibly. 'But happen he'll come round. He's still grievin' fer Grace really bad. He'll settle back down in time.'

But would he? Martha wondered.

As Jess gently closed the book, her throat was full. Poor Martha, she had suffered so much in her young life. She was almost at the end of the journal now and hoped that it would have a happy ending. God knows, the girl deserved it after all she had been through. At times, Jess had been sorely tempted to cheat and read the last page, but had so far managed to resist doing so. Each time she read an extract it seemed to bring her closer to Martha – so close that she could picture her now if she closed her eyes or even looked into a mirror.

She had not been up to the attic since coming out of hospital, but today she felt the need to and slowly headed in that direction. At the foot of the steep staircase she stared up, picturing herself tumbling the whole length of them. But who had pushed her? No matter what Simon said, she *knew* that someone had been there. She could still remember the feel of their hand on her back before she fell.

Taking a deep breath, she slowly started upward, and once at the top she headed straight for Martha's room. Again the overpowering smell of roses met her and she clasped her hands in consternation. *Why* was Martha still here? And *what* was she trying to tell her? Eventually she went out, closed the door and made her way into the large storage attic where she peered aimlessly out of the window, which overlooked the drive and Blue Brick Cottage. What she saw made her frown: Simon's Land Rover was parked at the end of the drive and she could see him talking to Laura. Of course, they were too far away for her to see their faces, but by the way Laura was waving her arms about, it looked like they were having a heated argument. After a few minutes she saw Simon climb into his vehicle and roar up the drive, so she hastily went back down the stairs to see what was wrong.

He was already in the kitchen by the time she got there, looking none too pleased with himself.

'I thought you might be back early with the weather being as it is,' she said, before adding, 'Is everything all right? You've got a face like a slapped arse on you.'

'Oh, I'm just having a bad day, that's all,' he retorted.

Jess waited for him to tell her that he had been speaking to Laura, and when he didn't, she asked tentatively, 'Didn't I see you speaking to Laura at the end of the drive just now?'

'What! Oh, er . . . yes. She was just asking how you were,' he replied, looking distinctly uncomfortable.

'Really? I'm surprised she hasn't been up to see me. Beth never comes here either now, which is strange because until a few months ago she couldn't keep away. I thought I might take a gentle wander down to see them when I feel up to it.'

'I shouldn't advise that,' he said, a little too quickly. 'You've got enough troubles of your own without having to listen to hers. I just want you to concentrate on getting well.'

Simon obviously wasn't in the best of moods and Jess didn't want to make things worse. It was hard enough just getting through each day at the moment without adding to her worries.

'I think I might go up and have a lie-down for a while,' she said now, not that keen on staying to look at Simon's frowning face.

'What? Oh, yes . . . right you are. It will do you good. I might go and pick the girls up from school in a while. It's started to rain again and the wind out there is enough to cut you in two.'

Jess didn't say a thing although she guessed that Mel would rather walk a marathon in a gale than have her dad pick her up. Things were no better between them – in fact, they had deteriorated to the point that Mel could barely bring herself to be civil to him.

Jess plodded painfully upstairs and was sound asleep before her head had scarcely had time to hit the pillow. Some time later, she awoke to the sound of someone crying. She slithered off the bed and padded along the landing towards Jo's room, cursing softly. Just what the hell was happening to this family? If it wasn't one of the girls crying it was the other – and they seemed to be lurching from one crisis to another.

'What's wrong *now*?' she snapped, when she saw Jo huddled in a miserable heap on the bed.

'It's Dad and Mel . . . they're arguing again,' Jo whimpered. Jess's anger dissolved as she placed a comforting arm about her daughter's shoulders. None of what had happened was her fault after all.

'Then I suggest we leave them to it.' Tilting Jo's chin she smiled at her younger daughter reassuringly. 'It's high time they sorted themselves out, don't you agree? I'm sick and tired of the way they behave towards each other, and just for tonight they can bloody well get on with it. They can tear each other limb from limb, for all I care!'

Jo giggled. Her mum didn't swear often, at least not in front of her and Mel, and when she did she always found it amusing. It was then they heard footsteps pounding up the stairs and seconds later Mel skimmed past the open bedroom door as if Lucifer himself were after her.

'Right, now *she's* gone off to sulk in her room and Dad will be sulking downstairs,' Jess told Jo matter-of-factly. 'So *I* am going to take full advantage of the peace and quiet and go for a nice long soak in the bath. And *you*, young lady, can listen to your CDs or watch telly, eh?'

Jo nodded vigorously as Jess planted a kiss on her cheek before heading off to the bathroom for the promised soak.

Half an hour later Jess was tucked back up in bed again with Martha's journal on her lap and the bedroom nice and cosy. She was eager to find out what happened to Martha now and so she opened the journal with anticipation and settled down to read.

*10 February*
The house has not been the same since Master Leonard and Miss Melody left, and all of us are missing them sorely. The Master had Bertie into his study shortly after they left and told him in a voice that we could all hear that if he did not pull himself together and get back to work, he would be dismissed. Bertie slammed out of the Master's study when the lecture was over and I could see the hatred burning in his eyes . . .

As Phoebe carried Granny's tray back into the kitchen, Martha looked at it and asked, 'Has she eaten anythin', Phoebe?'

Phoebe shook her head as she poured the untouched soup into the swill bucket for the pig.

'Not so much as a mouthful.' The older woman sighed. Since Grace had died, Granny Reid seemed to have lost the will to live and just lay there in bed staring at the ceiling.

'Perhaps the doctor will be able to prescribe a stronger tonic when he calls to see her tomorrow?' Martha suggested hopefully.

'Ah, the thing is . . . the Master came in 'ere earlier on an' told me that the doctor won't be callin' again.' Phoebe looked at Martha apologetically, as if it was her fault. 'He reckons there ain't no point, but between you an' me I don't think he wants to 'ave to carry on payin' the bills.'

Martha opened her mouth to protest but the words were checked when Bertie suddenly appeared from the open cellar door at the end of the kitchen. He was in the process of taking all the crates of wine that had been delivered earlier in the afternoon down to the wine-racks below. 'Would yer just look at this lot,' he snorted in disgust. 'I know I've been hittin' the hard stuff more than I should, but this tells me the wicked old bastard is goin' to be startin' 'is tricks again – yer know? Drunken parties an' what not.'

'Now that the young Master an' Mistress 'ave gone, yer could well be right,' Phoebe agreed. 'But there ain't much we can do about it.'

Bertie grunted before hoisting another crate and disappeared back down into the cellar.

'Try not to worry about yer Granny, love,' Phoebe told Martha. 'Grief takes different folks different ways, an' yer do have Jimmy's visit to look forward to. When is he comin' to see the Master?'

'Friday night,' Martha told her, as she dried her hands on a piece of huckaback. 'But I wish he could have asked Miss Melody permission fer us to wed instead of havin' to ask *him*.'

'Well, in all fairness they'd no sooner decided to go than they'd upped an' gone, an' the Master does know that Jimmy had asked permission to walk out wi' you, so it won't come as no surprise to him.'

'I know that, but I feel nervous about it all the same,' Martha muttered. But there was nothing to be done now but wait and see what the outcome of Jimmy's visit would be.

*14 February*
I am to be married in June! Jimmy and I will live in a cottage within the grounds of Leathermill Farm and Granny will come with us . . .

'What? Yer mean he's *agreed* to it?' Martha's eyes stretched wide as she stared up at Jimmy, who was grinning from ear to ear.

'Aye, he has that, and he even allowed me to suggest a date. I said the sixth o' June. Will that suit yer?'

'Oh, *yes!*' Martha laughed for the first time since Grace had died as Jimmy lifted her off her feet and swung her about.

'We're goin' to live in a little cottage in the grounds of Leathermill Farm. I've already cleared it wi' Farmer Codd, an' yer Granny can come too. What do yer think o' that? You'll not have far to come to work each day, will yer?'

Jimmy's happiness was infectious but suddenly the smile slid from Martha's face as she asked, 'But what about Bertie?'

Jimmy shrugged. 'There ain't much we can do for him, I'm afraid,' he admitted. 'But at least you'll still get to see him each day, an' Phoebe and Hal will keep their eye on him.'

'But he *hates* the Master so.' Martha looked up into Jimmy's eyes. 'I'm fearful what he might do to him, given half a chance.'

'Now he's come off the booze he'll be more sensible,' Jimmy assured her, but deep down he too had concerns, for every time Bertie so much as looked at the Master his loathing for the man was writ there on his face for all to see. Even so, they had wedding plans to make, so for now their talk turned to happier things as they began to plan their future. One thing was for sure: now that Martha knew she would not have to sleep under this roof for much longer, she felt a lot happier.

*16 February*
Last night, as I went from room to room checking that all was well before retiring to bed, the Master came out of his study and waylaid me in the hallway. I was shaking so much that I could scarcely hold the lamp I was carrying. And yet he seemed reasonable and sober when he asked to speak to me and so I followed him into his study. What a terrible mistake that was . . .

'So, did Jimmy tell you that I have given my permission for you to marry in June?' Lifting a heavy cut glass tumbler full of whisky, the Master eyed Martha as she nodded slowly.

'Yes, he did, and thank you kindly, sir.'

'Hm, and how do you think you will enjoy being a married woman? Are you aware of all that being wedded entails?'

'I er . . . yes, I think so, sir.' The first flames of fear were beginning to flicker in Martha's stomach as colour rose in her cheeks, and without even being conscious of what she was doing, she began to slowly back towards the door.

'I just wonder if you do.' The Master slammed his glass down, sending sprays of amber-coloured liquid all over the beautiful silk-fringed rugs Miss Melody had chosen, and then he began to slowly unbutton the fine satin waistcoat beneath his frockcoat as Martha looked on in horror.

'There's more to looking after a man than putting his meals on the table and keeping a clean house,' the Master told her now with a strange glint in his eye, and terror suddenly ripped through Martha as she realised his intentions. He had taken Grace down before her wedding to Bertie, and now he intended to do the same to her – and she knew that she would not be able to bear it. She turned in such haste that she tripped on her skirt and the lamp she was holding crashed to the floor. Oblivious to the mess, she struggled to her feet and began to run, but she had not even reached the door when his arm suddenly came about her waist from behind, and he flipped her onto her back. Then like a wild animal, he began to tear at her skirts and the buttons on her blouse as she struggled against him. At last she was able to catch her breath again and began to scream at the top of her lungs.

Somehow he had managed to undo his trousers and now they flapped about his ankles as he positioned himself above her, panting, ''Tis my right to break in any virgin that works for me before she goes to her husband. This is what you must expect, once you are married. Lie still and you might even enjoy it!'

'*NO!*' Martha howled as she tried to tear at his face with her finger-nails, but her strength was no match for his, and suddenly a pain the like of which she had never imagined tore through her as he entered her roughly. Martha felt as if she was caught in the grip of a nightmare as he bucked above her, and she continued to sob. The pain seemed to go on for ever but then the Master suddenly let out a deep groan and dropped his full weight on her as she felt something sticky and hot between her legs.

Just then, the door was suddenly thrown wide open and Bertie stood there. He took in the situation at a glance and before Martha had time to realise what was happening, he had covered the distance between them and the Master's weight was suddenly shifted off her. Cringing with shame and embarrassment, Martha tried to cover her nakedness but Bertie had eyes only for the Master.

'You dirty stinkin' *bastard*!' he roared, shaking the Master like a dog might shake a rabbit. 'You'll not take any more young lasses down after I've finished wi' yer. Enough is enough.' He then proceeded to flay the Master as Martha looked on helplessly, shaking with terror.

By now, Phoebe also appeared in the open doorway, one hand flying to her mouth as she made the sign of the cross on her chest with the other.

'Bertie, fer God's sake stop! You'll kill 'im.' She tried to pull Bertie away from the Master but the young man was beyond reason now and his clenched fists and feet continued to slam into him.

After what seemed like an eternity, as Phoebe added her screams to Martha's, the Master went limp and collapsed in a pool of blood as Bertie stood looking down on him. It was then that Granny appeared with a thin shawl wrapped about her nightdress. She had heard all the commotion even up in the servants' quarters and had somehow found the strength to come and see what was happening.

Leaning heavily against the doorframe with her breath coming in shuddering gasps, her gaze settled on Martha, and the light went out of her eyes

'Oh no, not you too, lass,' she whimpered, and then she too collapsed as Martha began to rock to and fro, weeping hysterically.

'I shall have to send Hal fer the doctor,' Phoebe said, distraught, and she sped from the room.

Both Granny and the Master appeared to be dead, Martha thought numbly, and what would become of poor Bertie now?

Somehow she managed to haul herself to her feet, and Bertie lifted Granny into his arms as if she weighed no more than a feather and carried her back to her bed. Martha followed, unwilling to be left alone with the Master.

The doctor arrived almost an hour later, and shook his head gravely as he examined the Master. 'He's in a bad way,' he informed them, then to Hal, 'Get the horse and carriage ready, would you, Hal? We need to get him into hospital. He may have internal bleeding. I'm afraid we shall need to fetch the Constable, too. Perhaps young Jimmy would go for him?'

Within no time at all Hal had the carriage at the front door and he and the doctor lifted the Master into the carriage and set off for the hospital. Shortly after they had gone the Constable arrived and started to question Bertie and Martha.

'So what started all this then?' The man really had no need to ask as he looked at the state of Martha's clothing, but rules had to be followed.

'The Master . . . he . . .' Martha broke into a fresh torrent of sobbing. 'He called me in here an' he . . .'

Phoebe hugged her protectively as the girl squirmed with humiliation in her arms.

'Ain't it more than clear what 'appened?' she snapped. 'The Master raped the girl, an' when Bertie 'eard her screams he ran in here to 'elp her.'

'Aye, it were me as battered him,' Bertie admitted now. 'An' I'd do the same again, given 'alf a chance, so don't expect no apologies from me, man! The dirty swine got no more than was comin' to 'im an' I just wish I'd done it sooner. He took me own wife down afore we were wed an' left her wi' a bellyful, an' if I'd done it then I could have saved Martha from havin' to go through the same thing. He's a sick, rotten bastard, an' I hope he dies a slow painful death, so I do!'

'Aw Bertie, man.' There was a measure of sympathy in the Constable's voice, for Bertie was a well-respected member of the community, but even so he was there to enforce the law. 'You know I'm goin' to have to take you in fer this, don't you? An' if the Master should die . . . Well, you'll be up for murder an' you could well face the noose.'

'*No!*' Martha whispered, appalled. The nightmare seemed set to continue and it was so unfair.

The Constable said to her, 'I'm right sorry for what's happened, miss. Would you like me to send the doctor back to look you over once he's got the Master to hospital?'

When Martha shook her head he nodded and strode from the room and she watched helplessly as Bertie was taken away.

'It's wrong,' she sobbed into Phoebe's shoulder. 'Bertie was only tryin' to help me. An' what if the Master has planted his seed in me?' The very thought of that was terrifying.

'Let's face each problem as we come to it, eh, pet?' Phoebe soothed. 'Fer now we need to go an' check on yer granny. She's had a terrible shock, an' in her state o' health it ain't goin' to do her no good at all. Then we'll get you cleaned up again.' She led Martha from the room by the hand as if she was a small child and as Martha limped along with her, she felt as if her whole world was crashing about her ears.

*18 February*
Word has reached us that the Master is rallying round. He has three broken ribs and is covered in cuts and bruises, but the doctor brought word that he will live. Even so, Bertie will face a long

prison sentence for inflicting his injuries and I cannot help but feel it is all my fault. Jimmy has called twice, but each time I have made an excuse not to see him . . .

'Young Jimmy's downstairs again. Won't yer just come an' have a quick word wi' him? The poor lad is worried sick,' Phoebe told Martha, who was sitting at the side of her granny's bed gripping her frail hand. She had scarcely moved from there since the night of the incident.

'No – I don't want to see him,' Martha said flatly, never once taking her eyes from her granny's face. The doctor had gravely informed them that the old woman was slipping away. It was only a matter of time now.

Martha was still dressed in the same clothes she had been wearing when the Master raped her, and she had neither eaten nor drunk since that night. Now she looked almost as ill as the old woman did. Sighing heavily, Phoebe bunched her skirts into her hand and quietly left the room.

Alone with her own thoughts, Martha's mind raced. How could she ever face Jimmy again? She felt used and dirty, and knew that she would never feel clean again. It would be as well if she cancelled the wedding.

Her eyes strayed back to her beloved granny's face and the tears began to rain down her cheeks. Granny's every breath was laboured now and her passing would be almost a blessing. Martha could only pray that when it came, it would be peaceful.

*20 February*
I am all alone in the world now. Granny passed away during the night . . .

'Aw lass, I'm so sorry,' Phoebe murmured as Martha pulled the sheet across her granny's face. Strangely enough, a lot of the pain had gone from the old lady's face now, and Martha could see that she was finally at peace.

'Come on, it's time you got something inside you. I'll come back and lay her out later.' Phoebe gently took Martha's elbow and led her towards the stairs, and it was as they were descending them that Martha asked, 'What time is Bertie in front of the magistrates?'

'Any time now,' Phoebe answered with a glance towards the clock. 'But don't fret. Hal is there an' he'll be back to tell us what's gone on.

At least the Master ain't died.' She then helped Martha to wash and change her clothes, brushing her hair for her and watching over her as she ate her soup and a small slice of apple pie.

It was almost two hours later when Hal did arrive home and they knew instantly by the stoop of his shoulders that he was not bringing good news.

'He got eight years' hard labour fer assault,' he informed them as he sank down wearily onto a chair at the side of the table.

Martha's hand flew to her mouth. *Eight years' hard labour*. Poor Bertie, and all because he had tried to help her. Martha was truly alone now, apart from Jimmy, and she now knew what she must do in that direction.

That evening, when a tap came on the kitchen door, Phoebe answered it to find Jimmy standing there again.

She had no need to say anything, for Martha instantly rose from her place by the fire, picked up her shawl and joined Jimmy in the courtyard.

As soon as they were alone, he grabbed her hand and shook it up and down, his face full of distress. 'Aw *lass*,' he gabbled. 'Why wouldn't yer see me afore? I've been out o' me mind wi' worry about yer.'

Martha looked at him sorrowfully as she slowly extricated her hand from his.

'I'm sorry about that, Jimmy, but what wi' Granny an' everythin' . . .'

'It's all right. I understand, an' I can't tell yer how bad I feel about what's happened. I should have set the weddin' fer sooner. In fact, I still can. I'll go an' see the parson this very night an' tell him—'

'There'll be no weddin' now,' Martha interrupted, her voice flat and dull. 'That's what I came out here to tell yer.'

'What do yer mean?' Jimmy looked shocked.

'How could I marry any man now?' Martha looked at him with dead eyes and he saw no trace of the girl he had fallen in love with. 'I'm soiled goods, Jimmy. Can you understand that? The Master *raped* me.'

'Aye, I know he did, but that weren't your fault,' he choked. 'It don't make no difference to how we feel about each other.'

'Oh, but it does. I saw what the Master did to Grace an' the way it affected her an' Bertie, an' what if I have the Master's seed growin' in me?'

'Then I'll take the child an' bring it up as me own.'

'No, Jimmy.' Martha spoke firmly. 'I've made me mind up, an' there'll be no swayin' me. It's over an' I'll thank yer kindly not to call on me again.'

And with that she turned and walked back to the house as Jimmy's dreams turned to ashes.

*5 March*

The Master returned from the hospital today and within an hour of being home he ordered me into his study to gloat at dear Bertie's sentence. He told me that from now on, I shall do as he orders or he will tell Miss Melody that the child she has taken as her own is actually *his* child . . .

'What did he say?' Phoebe asked fearfully when Martha returned to the kitchen.

'First of all he wanted to gloat about Bertie's sentence,' Martha replied remarkably calmly. 'Secondly, he told me that from now on I will do as he pleases when he pleases, or it will be the worse for me. He also threatened to tell Miss Melody that the baby is his if I don't comply with his wishes. As he quite rightly pointed out, I have no one to watch out fer me now.'

Phoebe visibly bristled. 'Yer still have me an' Hal – we'll watch out fer yer, lass. An' we're as close to family as you'll get.'

Martha shook her head. 'I thank you right kindly, Phoebe, but I think enough people have suffered at the Master's hand now, don't you? I wouldn't want you an' Hal gettin' into trouble too.'

'Just what is that supposed to mean?' Phoebe was finding Martha's state of mind highly disturbing. The girl hadn't shed so much as a tear since her gran had passed away, and she seemed to have grown up overnight. Not that this was surprising after what she had been through. This morning Bill Capener, the local coffinmaker, had delivered a plain pine box for her gran to lie in, but even the task of transferring the dear soul into it hadn't moved Martha. She might have been handling a stranger for all the emotion she had shown. To Pheobe, it was as if she had no feelings left any more. Sighing heavily, she turned her attentions back to the herbs she was grinding in the pestle and mortar.

It was much later that afternoon when Phoebe had lost track of Martha that her feet guided her to the old woman's bedroom – and there was the girl standing at the side of the open coffin.

'Ah, I thought I might find you 'ere,' Phoebe said gently, moving to stand at Martha's side.

'You will see that she's laid to rest properly, won't yer?' Martha suddenly asked, and Phoebe frowned.

'Well, of course I will! But the parson will be 'ere tomorrow night to make the arrangements fer the service, so you'll be able to tell him yourself what yer want fer her.'

Martha nodded, and then left the room without another word as Phoebe scratched her head in consternation and watched her go.

It was as Martha was serving the Master his dinner that evening that she smiled at him coquettishly and said, 'I were wonderin' if yer might like to take a walk along the river wi' me tomorrow, sir?'

Jake Fenton was so shocked that he almost choked on his mouthful of potato, but then composing himself he looked at her suspiciously.

'And why would you want to walk with me?'

''Cos if I'm to be *nice* to yer, sir, I'm thinkin' it would be better if we got to know each other a little better.'

Jake Fenton frowned. Why would he want to be seen walking with a maid? But then . . . she *was* a comely little piece and it would be nice to have her 'on tap', so to speak.

'We could walk down to the stone bridge,' Martha went on suggestively. 'The river is high an' it's a pretty sight along there.'

'Well, I dare say it would do no harm,' he conceded, and he then sat back to allow Martha to serve him more hare pie. It could be that he hadn't lost his looks and his way with women, after all.

Once alone in her room that evening, Martha lay fully dressed with Jimmy's treasured brooch pinned to her blouse, thinking and making her final plan. There seemed to be no other road left to her now.

*6 March*

This will be the last entry I will ever make in my diary. Today, I shall walk with the Master to the stone bridge and once there, I intend to kill him. The knife I shall use is already in my apron pocket. It is one of Phoebe's sharpest and I took it from the kitchen earlier today whilst she wasn't looking. I shall stab him when we are standing on the bridge and then I shall push him in. The water is high and raging there at the moment, and he will stand no chance of survival in his weakened state. It is the only way I know that will stop him from ever ruining another girl's life as he has ruined mine and my dear Grace's. I shall then throw myself into the river. I have nothing and no one left to live for now, so my life will be a small price to pay to know that the world will be rid of this evil, depraved man. I only pray now that I will have the physical strength to carry out my plan, for my one purpose in life now is to have revenge on the Master. Once he is gone, the Tolleys, my dear friends, will then be able to live here in peace. And Jimmy, my dear wonderful Jimmy, will some day soon meet another girl who will make him happy. I know that if I lived, I could never be the same again. I am not the same person I was but am now consumed with hatred and bitterness. It may be that Our Dear Lord will not allow me access to His heavenly kingdom after committing murder and suicide, but I am prepared for my spirit to roam the earth forever if I have cleansed this world of the Master.

Now I have but one last thing to do before going to meet the Master. I must make my curse and it is this: May every male Fenton who mistreats his fellow men and women, from this day forward never know a moment's peace, and may the wrongdoers with bad blood all die a slow and terrible death.

Martha Reid

Jess gasped as she read Martha's final words and furiously turned the page, but there was no more. The journal was finished. *Surely* there must be another journal somewhere that would carry on from this one? She could not bear the thought of Martha meeting such a terrible end, and promised herself that she would look around the attics the very next day.

# Chapter Thirty-Seven

Two days later, Karen called to take Jess shopping. Jess still didn't feel strong enough to drive, and welcomed the treat. She had been searching the attics ever since finishing Martha's journal but as yet had not found another one, which could mean only one thing. Martha must have carried out her threat and perished with the Master. That would account for her clothes still hanging in the wardrobe. But why would her spirit have stayed behind all this time? It was a puzzle, and one to which Jess could find no solution as yet.

'You're very quiet today,' Karen commented as they made their way home after a brief tour of the shops.

Jess was shocked at how quickly she had tired and was longing to get home. She hadn't slept well for the last couple of nights thinking of Martha, and that, added to the constant bickering between Mel and Simon, was wearing her down.

'Oh, I'm still just a bit tired.' Jess tugged her fingers through her hair. 'I tend to think I can do a lot more than I can, and then I get all frustrated when I have to stop.'

'It's early days yet,' Karen pointed out. She could only guess at how heartbroken Jess must be feeling at losing her baby boy, and up to now had carefully avoided mentioning what had happened, although she knew she would have to address it at some stage. Jess would be living with her loss for ever, and Karen knew that her friend would need a shoulder to cry on in the days and months ahead.

They were almost at the end of the lane now, and as Blue Brick Cottage came into sight, Jess spotted Laura outside.

'Pull up for a moment, would you?' she asked and Karen obligingly drew up alongside Laura, who had just put the rubbish bin out for collection.

'Oh, hello, Jess.' Laura looked decidedly uncomfortable. 'Er . . . how are you feeling?'

'I'm getting there. But I've missed you popping in for a cuppa. Is everything all right?'

Laura nodded hastily. 'Yes, thanks. But I've been busy – you know, looking after Beth and whatnot.'

Jess found this a poor excuse. It had never stopped Laura from visiting before, but she tactfully told her, 'Well, do call in if you get the chance. I'm still a bit housebound at the minute and I'd welcome the company.' She had the distinct impression that Laura was keen to get away and she was proved to be right when her neighbour shot away towards the back door of the cottage without another word.

'So what have you done to her then?' Karen asked in her usual forthright way. 'It seemed like it was taking her all her time to even speak to you.'

'It did, didn't it?' Jess tried to think what she might have done to upset her neighbour, but could come up with nothing – unless Simon or one of the girls had upset her, that was. She decided she would ask them that evening.

When Karen left an hour later Jess lay down for a while and had a rest before resuming her search of the big attic. She was still there when Simon arrived home mid-afternoon and she jumped when he suddenly appeared in the doorway.

'What are you doing in here again?' he questioned. 'Don't tell me you're still looking for another bloody journal?'

When Jess flushed guiltily, his lips tightened. 'This is getting unhealthy. You're damn well *obsessed*, woman! I'm beginning to worry about you – especially with all these so-called accidents you're having.'

'What is *that* supposed to mean?' Jess straightened from the trunk she had been going through. 'Are you trying to say that I'm going mad?'

He looked at her for a long moment before turning and striding away down stairs as Jess sagged against the wall. He hadn't uttered a single word but his look had said it all. Perhaps he was right. Perhaps she *was* going mad. After all, when she had first moved in she had laughed at Laura for telling her there was a presence in the house, and now here she was searching for another journal that had belonged to the girl, and even talking to her sometimes. It was a sobering thought, and as she snapped off the light and carefully made her way down-stairs, her hands were shaking.

It was the following week when Simon unexpectedly suggested one evening over dinner, 'Why don't you get yourself off to see Karen for a while? You should be OK to drive now, and if you don't get back behind the wheel soon you're going to lose your confidence.'

293

Jess paused to look at him. She had to admit that she was sick to death of staring at the same four walls.

'I suppose you're right, and it would be nice to get back into some sort of routine,' she admitted.

'Can I come with you?' Jo piped up and Jess grinned.

'I don't see why not. But I won't be late – you've got school in the morning. Would you like to come too, Mel?'

Before the girl had time to answer her, Simon scowled. 'I think it would be best if she stayed behind to catch up on some homework, don't you? Her last school report was appalling and she needs to pull her socks up good and proper.'

Mel scraped her chair across the tiles as colour suffused her pale cheeks. But she didn't contradict her dad; she merely ran upstairs.

'That was a bit harsh, wasn't it?' Jess said. 'You could try praise and encouragement instead of barking at the poor kid all the time. No wonder she hasn't got a good word to say to you.'

'Spare the rod and spoil the child,' Simon snapped back. 'The trouble with you is you're too soft on the pair of them. It wouldn't hurt Jo to stay behind and do some homework too.'

Realising that this was in danger of turning into a flaming row, Jess took a deep breath before saying, 'I suppose your dad is right, Jo. It wouldn't hurt you to do a bit of homework too. And it's not as if I'm going to be gone for long.'

Jo's face fell a foot but she didn't argue. She simply called Alfie to heel and disappeared off into the lounge with him.

'*Happy* now, are you?' Jess said caustically, and before Simon could reply she turned and went to get changed before she said something she might regret. A few hours away from Simon seemed like a very good idea indeed.

Once in the car, Jess broke out in a cold sweat. Simon had been right about one thing. It was hard to drive again after such a long time. Even so she turned the key in the ignition and cautiously reversed before steering the car onto the drive, testing the brakes every few seconds. Her heart was in her throat but she forced herself to go on, afraid that if she gave up now she might never have the nerve to get behind the wheel again.

The journey to Karen's seemed endless but at last she arrived. Her friend was pleased to see her and instantly made her a nice cup of hot sweet tea. But somehow Jess could not rest or relax. Every instinct she had was screaming to her that something wasn't right, and the familiar whispers were loud in her ear. Within minutes of being there she picked up the car keys and told Karen apologetically, 'I'm sorry, love. But I have to go.'

'Bloody hell, you've only just got here,' Karen objected. 'You haven't even finished your drink yet!'

'I know and I'm sorry. But really I can't stay. I'll call you in the week.' Before Karen's bemused eyes Jess found her coat and seconds later was back in the car and heading towards home.

All the nervousness she had felt earlier in the evening about driving had fled now and she just wanted to be home. Pressing her foot down hard on the accelerator she went as fast as she dared as the feeling of foreboding that had settled on her grew worse by the second. The streetlights flashed past, and by the time she turned into the drive leading to Stonebridge House her heart was pounding. The river was high and raging, even as far as over the road in places, and Jess had to temporarily slow down as the car ploughed through it, throwing up a spray of icy water. The first thing she saw when she screeched to a halt was the back door banging open in the wind and she almost fell out of the car, leaving that door to flap open too as she sped into the kitchen.

Jo was sitting at the kitchen table with her head in her hands sobbing uncontrollably and Jess rushed across to her.

'Whatever is the matter?' she asked in a shaky voice as she hugged the girl to her. 'What's happened?'

Jo gulped and drew air into her lungs before she could speak as she raised her tear-stained face to her mother's. 'It . . . it's Dad and Mel. I heard them having a terrible row in her room so I came downstairs out of the way. Th . . . then Mel shot past me and ran outside and Dad chased after her.'

'And where are they now?' Jess was fighting to stay calm.

'I d-don't know,' Jo stuttered. 'They've been gone for ages.'

'Well, they can't have gone far. Your dad's car and his van are still in the courtyard.' Jess looked towards the dark window. The wind was howling and it had started to rain. It certainly wasn't a night for being outside.

'What shall we do?' Jo asked in a small voice.

'We'll wait for a while and see if they come back. If they haven't, after an hour I'm going to phone the police.' Jess could see no alternative although she hated to go to such drastic measures.

They sat huddled together watching the hands of the clock ticking the minutes away until Jess could stand it no more.

'Look, you get yourself off to bed, pet,' she suggested. 'I'll go out with Alfie and see if I can find them.'

'I want to come with you,' Jo replied imploringly, but Jess shook her head as she pulled her outdoor coat on.

'You certainly won't. It's awful out there. I need to know that you are safe at least, so run along and do as I say, there's a good girl now.'

Jo pouted but meekly walked towards the stairs as Jess tugged the back door open. The force of the wind took her breath away, but with Alfie bounding along at the side of her she set off across the lawn towards the copse.

'*Mel! Simon!*' she screamed into the deep night, but the wind snatched the words away. The rain was coming down faster now and she wished that she had thought to bring the torch with her. Within seconds her hair was plastered to her head and icy drops of rain were running down the neck of her coat. The inside of the copse was as dark as the grave, and the wind was whistling eerily through the leafless branches. With her hands stretched out in front of her she ventured a few yards in, but she had taken no more than a few steps when she went sprawling over a fallen branch to land in a muddy heap on the ground.

'Damn and blast!' she cursed as she struggled to her feet and then forced herself to stand still and listen as she clutched her still tender stomach. There was nothing but the sound of the wind. Even the night creatures had taken cover on such a wicked evening. Knowing that it would be pointless to venture any further without a light of some kind she cautiously picked her way back amongst the trees until she was on the lawn once more.

'Which way now, Alfie?' she mused, more to herself than the dog. He barked and started across the lawn in the direction of the river, and not knowing what else to do, Jess followed him. The Anker had burst its banks and was creeping its way up the lawn, and the grass that ran alongside it was treacherously slippery. Jess tried to keep up with Alfie who was leaping ahead, yapping as if his very life depended upon it. What seemed like a lifetime later they came to the stone bridge, or what remained of it. The river was heaving and swirling here, as it struggled to find its way beneath what was left of the three stone arches. Floating debris had collected there, which made the passage of the water even more difficult. Jess shivered as she looked into the black inky depths. Anyone falling into that would stand no chance of survival and she could only pray that Simon and Mel had not come this way.

There was no sign of either her husband or her daughter. It was too dark to see much, and Jess suddenly acknowledged the futility of what she was doing. Simon and Mel would probably be safely back at home by now, so she decided to head back.

'Come on, Alfie.' Despondently she retraced her steps as Alfie followed her with his tail down, and at last the lights of the house came into view.

As she stepped into the warmth of the kitchen her frozen cheeks immediately began to glow as she looked around. It was just as she had left it, and again she cursed softly. There was nothing for it but to phone the police now, so with shaking fingers she lifted the phone and dialled the number, then went to check on Jo who was thankfully fast asleep in bed.

'Now, Mrs Beddows, are you quite sure that there is nothing else you can tell us?' a policewoman asked almost an hour later. It was approaching midnight now and Jess was dropping with tiredness and despair.

'That's all I know,' Jess told her quietly. 'I've told you everything that Jo told me.'

'Perhaps it would help if we could speak to your daughter personally,' the young woman suggested.

Jess shook her head firmly. 'No, I promise you there's nothing more she could tell you and I really don't want her disturbed at this time of night. I checked on her when I came back in after going out to look for them and she was fast asleep.'

The WPC nodded in understanding. 'All right then. I'm going to get my colleague to radio for help now and they'll send some men out to have a scout around, although to be honest I doubt they'll be able to do much until it's light.'

Jess nodded dully, wondering what the hell had brought them all to this. Moving to this house was supposed to have been the making of the family, and yet it seemed to be the cause now of its falling apart. The worst thing about it was that she was powerless to change that now. It was too late to turn back the clock.

# Chapter Thirty-Eight

By seven o'clock the next morning the house was teeming with police officers. Jess had been up all night and her eyes felt gritty from lack of sleep. The young policewoman, who had introduced herself as Sam, had stayed with her throughout the long dark hours, but now she was due to go off-shift and had informed Jess that someone else would take her place as the police began their search.

'Try not to worry too much,' she said as she squeezed Jess's hand. 'I'm sure the men will find them both safe and sound.'

Jess wanted to believe her but somehow she couldn't. The terrible sense of foreboding had grown worse as the night progressed and now she was sick with fear.

Another young policewoman had entered the room now and Sam instantly introduced her. 'This is PC Moon, but I'm sure she wouldn't mind if you called her Donna.'

Jess nodded distractedly in the woman's direction before returning her gaze to the window. She could see the policemen fanning out across the lawn; it looked an eerie sight in the early-morning mist and she shivered. It had been a dreadful night, and if Mel and Simon had been out there she couldn't believe that they could have survived the freezing temperature.

'Jess, I was saying it might be helpful if we spoke to Josephine now before I go off-duty,' Sam said. 'She just might have remembered something that might help us with the search.'

'What? Oh er . . . yes, of course. It's time for Jo to get up now anyway.' Jess rose painfully from the chair where she had sat huddled all night and hobbled up the stairs.

'Jo, will you get up now, love?' she called as she tapped at her door before opening it. And then her mouth gaped open as she saw Jo's empty bed. It hit her like a ton of bricks: Jo had wanted to go with her to look for Mel and Simon the night before, but Jess had sent her to her room! Jo must have waited until she and Alfie had got back and checked on her, then slipped out to look for them herself. But where was she now? The stiffness suddenly vanished as Jess almost tumbled down the stairs in her haste before exploding into the kitchen.

'Oh my God, my dear God . . .' she babbled incoherently. 'She's not there! She must have gone out last night after I'd checked on her, to look for Simon and Mel.' Racing past the open-mouthed officers, she flung open the door to the utility room and her hand flew to her mouth. What she had suspected must be true; Jo's Wellington boots and her waterproof coat were gone. Jess thought of the fast-flowing swollen river. If Jo had ventured too close to that and slipped in . . . She let out a sob.

And then Sam's arm came around her shoulder and Jess allowed herself to be led back to the kitchen whilst Donna hastily put the kettle on. Meanwhile Sam was once again talking urgently into her radio as she informed the station of the latest developments. Jess rocked to and fro, her thin cardigan wrapped tightly about her, feeling guiltier by the minute. If she hadn't gone to Karen's, Simon and Mel wouldn't have rowed. And if only she had checked on Jo again when the police arrived, she would have realised that she was missing too.

'It's all *my* fault,' she wailed hysterically. 'I should never have gone out and left them.'

'Now you can just stop that nonsense this instant,' Sam told her firmly. 'You can't be with all of them twenty-four hours a day. Try and relax. I've sent for the doctor. He'll be able to give you something to calm you down.'

Donna was now informing the search-party that Jo was missing too as Jess slipped further and further into her worst nightmare. It had been bad enough losing her baby, but now it was beginning to look like she might lose the rest of her family as well.

More police cars were pulling into the courtyard, and two plain-clothes officers arrived and began to question Jess all over again.

'If you can think of anything – anything at all – no matter how trivial it might have seemed at the time, it might give us a lead as to why this has happened, Mrs Beddows,' the older of the officers said to her.

Jess had wracked her brains all through the night, but there was nothing more that she could tell them, other than what Jo had told *her* – and so now all she could do was wait. Police from Bedworth and Atherstone had now also joined in the search, and Jess watched fearfully through the window as they walked treacherously close to the edge of the swirling river looking for any signs of the three people who were missing.

A shout eventually went up outside, and Jess began to shake. And then an officer was racing back up the lawn and one of the senior officers stepped out into the courtyard for a hasty consultation with him, closing the door behind him. Jess strained her ears to try and hear what they were saying, but all she could hear was the faint mumble of voices.

Eventually, the officer came back into the room with the doctor who had just arrived.

'Mrs Beddows, I'm afraid I have some very bad news for you,' he told Jess grimly. 'One of our men has just seen the body of what appears to be a young girl in the river. They are trying to get it out now.'

'*No, no,* they must be wrong!' Jess whispered. It couldn't be true and yet deep down she knew that it was. But was it Mel or was it Jo they had found? Just the very thought of it being either of them was unbearable. She made to rise from her seat but Sam's restraining hand on her shoulder kept her firmly in place as the doctor approached her with a syringe in his hand. He was a short, unassuming-looking little man with balding, wispy grey hair and heavy glasses perched on the end of his nose.

'I'm going to give you a little sedative to calm you down,' he told her, and when she looked up into his eyes she saw that they were full of compassion.

'I don't *want* to calm down,' she said restlessly. 'I need to get down to the river. That might be one of my girls they've found.'

'Someone will come for us as soon as they've got them out,' he assured her, and then she felt the sharp prick of a needle and almost instantly began to feel as if she was floating.

All around were people talking in hushed voices, but Jess felt as if she was trapped in a world of her own; a world that was never going to be the same again.

It seemed an eternity before a solemn-faced policeman arrived and murmured something into the Chief Inspector's ear. The latter came and stood in front of her, saying quietly, 'They've managed to retrieve the body from the river now, Mrs Beddows.'

'I want to see it.' Determined not to be stopped this time, Jess rose from her seat unsteadily and made for the door as both of the young policewomen fell into step beside her. Sam, the kindly young woman who had sat with her all through the long night, had stayed on duty to offer support, and in that moment Jess was grateful of her company.

It was a dark drab day with scudding black clouds in the leaden sky as they walked across the muddy lawn towards a small white tent that had been erected on the edge of the river.

As Jess drew near, the officers silently parted to let her through and she swallowed deeply as she wiped her hands, which were sweating despite the bitterly cold day, down the legs of her jeans.

'Are you quite sure that you want to do this, Mrs Beddows?' one of the officers asked.

Jess nodded numbly as he drew aside the flap of the tent and waited for her to enter. There was something on the grass, covered with a damp white sheet, and as he lifted one corner of it, Jess gasped. It was Jo, still wearing her bright Wellington boots and her outdoor coat and looking for all the world as if she was fast asleep and might wake up at any moment.

'No . . . NO . . . NOOOOOO!!' The men bowed their heads as Jess screamed in anguish and dropped to her knees beside her daughter. She wiped the wet dripping hair from the girl's pale face and planted kisses on her cold cheeks, but there was no response. There would never be a response again.

Eventually, someone helped her to her feet and led her back towards the house. Jess went unresistingly, too deep in shock to do any other.

Pictures of Jo at different stages of her life were flashing before her eyes. The moment the midwife had placed her in her arms, seconds after her birth. She could still feel the maternal love that had flooded through her and the way Jo had stared up at her trustingly as if she somehow knew that this would be the start of a very special relationship. Jo taking her first robotic steps, her chubby hands held out in front of her. The day she had started school. The day she had managed to ride her first bicycle unaided and the look of triumph on her face. The day she had lost her first tooth. Jo making sandcastles on the beach. Jess was oblivious to everything else but there would be no more memories now. The very last one would be of Jo lying on the sodden ground staring sightlessly up at her, devoid of life, no more than an empty shell now.

They were halfway back to the house when another officer came haring towards them from the direction of Caldecote.

'Sir, we've found another body,' Jess heard him say to the Chief Inspector. She supposed she should ask whose it was, but she was too numb to care now. It was as if she had already accepted that all of her family were gone from her.

The two men continued to talk, their heads bent close together until Inspector Flynn turned and told Sam briskly, 'Take Mrs Beddows back to the house, would you, please?'

'Yes, sir.'

Back in the warmth of the kitchen, Donna quickly pushed another mug of tea into Jess's hand but she merely stared down into it, wishing she could drown in it there and then and go to be with Jo.

The Inspector eventually reappeared, looking harassed. 'Mrs Beddows, the body of a man has been retrieved from the river down by the stone bridge,' he informed her. 'We believe it to be that of your husband. He was found amongst the floating debris. It was that which had stopped his body being swept downstream.'

Jess stared up at him silently for a time before asking, 'And Mel?'

He shook his head, looking away from the pain reflected in her eyes.

'As yet there has been no sign of your daughter. My men are still searching now. Do you feel up to identifying him?'

He had expected tears and tantrums, but the pain Jess was feeling went beyond tears. Simon was gone from her too, and even though she had not seen the body, every instinct she had told her that it was his. She rose, and before she knew it she was walking across the lawn again in the direction of the stone bridge, flanked on either side by solemn-faced police officers.

In the distance yet another tent had been erected and Jess took a deep breath before entering. This time Inspector Flynn came in with her and it was he that drew the covering back from the man's face.

Jess stared down at him for a long time before whispering. 'That's him . . . That's my husband, Simon.'

The Inspector sighed. His heart was aching for the woman but he didn't know what to say to her. Words seemed so inadequate in these situations.

The rest of the day passed in a blur for Jess. She sat silently in the small lounge with Alfie's head in her lap, oblivious to all the hustle and bustle that was going on around her. The door seemed to be constantly opening and closing. Policemen bobbed in and out but it all went over her head as she waited for news of Mel. Mel was all she had left in the world now, and Jess knew that if anything had happened to her, she would have nothing left to live for.

It was tea-time when the door was suddenly slammed open yet again and a weary officer almost fell into the room.

'We've found the other girl, sir.'

Jess's eyes snapped towards him as she held her breath.

'Is she alive?' Inspector Flynn asked, and when the man nodded Jess felt tears of gratitude sting at the back of her eyes.

'Yes, but she's in a pretty bad way. She's been out in the cold all night and she seems to be in shock. She was lying in some bushes not far from the river and one of the dogs found her. They're putting her into the ambulance now and taking her to the George Eliot Hospital.'

The Inspector instantly turned to Jess to ask, 'Do you want to be there to meet her, Mrs Beddows?'

His words were unnecessary. Jess was already out of the chair. All the way to the hospital in the back of the police car she silently prayed as she had never prayed before. *Please, God, let her live. Please, please, please!*

They were just in time to see Mel's limp form being stretchered from the back of an ambulance, and Jess was out of the car and sprinting towards her before anyone could stop her.

'Mel!' She grasped the girl's hand, terrified at how icy cold it was. 'Can you hear me, sweetheart? It's Mum, I'm here and don't worry, you're going to be fine – you *have* to be.'

There was a nurse at either end of the stretcher and a doctor running along beside it, and it was all Jess could do to keep up with them. And then they were inside and before Jess knew it they had whipped Mel away through swinging double doors and all she could do was wait with a picture of the girl's terrifyingly pale face floating in front of her eyes. She had been ice-cold and shivering uncontrollably. What if she were to die too? It was just too frightening to contemplate.

She was led away to a small room where a nurse informed her that someone would be out to see her as soon as Mel had been examined by the doctors. Jess nodded numbly. There was nothing else she could do.

Inspector Flynn joined her after a while and stood with his hands folded behind his back staring from the window across the crowded car park as they waited for news. And then at last the door swung open again and a middle-aged doctor with thinning hair and a weary face came in.

'You'll be pleased to know that Melanie is going to be all right, Mrs Beddows,' he informed her. 'We're going to keep her in overnight for observation, but apart from a number of bruises and shock, she seems to be physically OK.' He didn't yet tell her that Mel hadn't spoken. It seemed more important right now to assure her that her daughter's physical condition was not life-threatening. From what he had heard, the woman had had a terrible time of it over the last twenty-four hours.

'C . . . can I see her?' Jess croaked with relief.

'I don't see why not, but I should warn you, she hasn't spoken yet. If you'd like to come with me I'll take you to her now.'

When Jess glanced towards Inspector Flynn as if for permission he nodded and she was surprised to see that there were tears in his eyes as he fell into step beside her.

And what he was thinking was, *Thank God for small mercies*.

At least this poor sod had *someone* to go on for now.

# Chapter Thirty-Nine

Jess approached Mel's bed with her heart in her mouth, wondering what she would see. The girl was lying quietly, and Jess was relieved to see that she had stopped shaking now, although her eyes were blank and lifeless.

She bent to kiss the girl's cheeks, careful to avoid the drip that was feeding into the back of her hand. 'What happened, sweetheart? Can you tell me?'

The doctor, who was standing at the other side of the bed, instantly stepped forward.

'I don't think she's up to being questioned yet,' he told Jess gently. 'We've just had to tell the police the same thing. But perhaps tomorrow when she's had a good rest? Melanie is deeply in shock, so I'm afraid I can only let you have a few moments with her for now. She needs to be kept warm and quiet.'

'Oh!' Jess choked as she looked back at Mel. The girl didn't even seem to realise that she was there. All the same Jess spent the next few minutes talking soothingly to her.

'Don't worry about anything,' she told her over and over again. 'We'll get through this together.'

Eventually, following a nod from the doctor, the Inspector took her arm. 'I think we ought to be going now so that Mel can rest, Mrs Beddows,' he told her. 'And don't worry. She'll be very well taken care of.'

Jess reluctantly stood up, and after giving Mel a final kiss she followed Inspector Flynn from the room. Her mind was in turmoil. How the hell could all of this have happened? She just couldn't think what could have brought them to this tragic situation.

Back at the house, she expected Jo to come running out to meet her with Alfie on her heels, but then it hit her like a slap in the face that this would never happen again now, and it was more than she could comprehend. She leaned heavily on the inspector's arm as he led her back into the house, and the first person she saw was Laura sitting there with tears streaming down her face, next to the doctor who had promised earlier on that he would call in again to see how she was.

'Oh, Jess.' Laura raced towards her with her arms outstretched. 'I'm so sorry, pet. I should have told you what was going on instead of avoiding you, and then all this might never have happened.'

Both Jess and Inspector Flynn were staring at her now and Laura flushed under their scrutiny.

'If you know anything at all that might throw some light on these events, I suggest you tell us immediately,' the inspector said, as Laura wrung her hands together nervously.

Her eyes tight on Jess's face, she falteringly began. 'Some time ago, Mel called in to see me one day on her way home from school and completely broke down. I cuddled her and asked her what was wrong, and she confided that . . .' Laura's eyes were as wide as saucers and for a moment Jess thought that she was going to clam up, but the woman visibly forced herself to go on. 'She confided that Simon had been sexually abusing her since shortly after you moved into the house. It normally happened on the nights when you went to see your friend Karen, and that's why they hadn't been getting on.'

Jess's lips trembled and she could barely speak. What Laura was saying was completely beyond belief. She had always known that Simon had a roving eye for the ladies, but the thought that he would use his own daughter in that way was unthinkable. She gripped the back of a chair for support.

'It can't be true!' she finally managed to gasp.

Laura wiped her eyes. 'I'm afraid it is. When I found out, my first instinct was to rush up here and tell you what was going on. But then, as Den pointed out, had I done that, it would have meant the break-up of your family, and you didn't deserve that on top of everything else that's happened lately. Neither did the girls. So that's when I started to keep away. We encouraged Mel to spend more time with us, as you've probably noticed. She needed support, and with all you've been through she felt she couldn't talk to you. Den got Simon alone and told him that he knew what was going on and warned him to stop. Between you and me, I think Den found it hard to keep his hands off him, Jess. We just wanted to protect the girl and we intended to wait until you were a little stronger and then we'd have told you what was going on, but as things have turned out, we never got the

306

chance.' She burst into torrents of weeping. 'If only I had, none of this might have happened!'

Even as Jess tried to deny it to herself, she felt as if the pieces of a jigsaw were finally fitting together. If what Laura was telling them was true, it explained a lot of things. The way Simon had always made Mel stay behind when she went to visit Karen. The state Mel would be in when she got home.

'I'm so sorry, Jess,' Laura sobbed as she saw her friend's despair. 'I'll never forgive myself for not telling you, but what would *you* have done in my situation?'

'Probably the same,' Jess admitted in a small voice, and then she too started to cry at last. Great gulping sobs that shook her whole body as the doctor hastily stepped forward again. There was another sharp needle prick and then thankfully she knew no more as a welcoming darkness closed around her, and she slept right through till the morning in the easy chair.

The police interviewed Mel early the next day before driving Jess to the hospital to see her, and the instant her mother stepped into the room Mel began to weep noisily.

'I'm so sorry, Mum,' she wailed as she held her arms out to her. 'I *wanted* to tell you, but I didn't think you'd believe me – and you were so sad already after losing the baby.'

'So what Laura said was true then?' Jess said dully as she cradled the girl's heaving body against her.

Mel nodded. 'On the night it happened you'd only been gone for a few minutes when Dad came to my room and I knew that he was going to hurt me again and I couldn't bear it. Somehow I managed to get past him and I just ran outside. I could hear him chasing after me, and before I knew it we were by the river at the stone bridge.' She trembled as her mind flashed back. 'He . . . he was shouting at me and threatening me and we started to fight. And then suddenly I heard a splash and when I looked around he was in the river. He was trying to swim but the current was too fast for him and I didn't stop in case he managed to get out and . . . and did *it* again, so I just ran and hid in some bushes. The next thing I knew was when the police dog found me and they brought me in here. The policeman told me that Dad is dead. I'm so sorry, Mum.'

'Don't be,' Jess soothed her as she hugged her. 'None of this is your fault. It's mine, if anybody's. I should have realised what was going

307

on right under my nose, but I never dreamed he would be capable of doing something like that. Especially to his own daughter.'

'That's not all,' Mel went on, and Jess shuddered. What else could there be?

'The . . . the drugs – you know, the ones that you found in my bag on holiday? It wasn't Emile who asked me to bring them back, it was Dad. He arranged for me to meet a man in the hotel foyer on the night before we flew home, and he gave them to me. I had to pay him with money Dad gave me before we left, and he said that if I didn't do as he said, he would plant some in my room for you to find so that you'd think I was using them.' Jess reeled with shock. It seemed that there was no end to the nightmare.

'So it wasn't Emile Lefavre,' she breathed as she recalled how awful she had been to him.

Mel shook her head, looking terribly fragile and ill. And was it any wonder, Jess thought.

'Had your dad ever asked you to do anything like this before?' she asked, and the answer when it came was what she had dreaded.

'Yes. Sometimes he made me drop packages off in the town after school. And sometimes I had to wag off school early to deliver them for him.'

*Oh Simon, how* could *you have been so wicked?* Jess's heart was screaming, but deep down she knew that he had not loved her for a long time – even before they had moved to Stonebridge House, if she was to be brutally honest with herself. It was she who had hoped that a new home would be a fresh start for them all instead of accepting that their marriage was beyond repair. And if only she had faced facts back then, she and the girls could have moved on, and none of this need have happened.

'The police lady told me that Jo is dead too,' Mel whispered brokenly.

'Yes, darling, I'm afraid she is. The police told me this morning that they thought her death was a tragic accident. I told her that she couldn't come with me when I went out to look for you, but she must have waited until I got back and checked on her, and then gone out to look for you and Dad herself. The police think she slipped on the mud and tumbled into the river and . . .' Her voice trailed away as pain enveloped her. *Beautiful, innocent Jo.* Her life was such a tragic waste. She'd had a whole bright future before her, and now all that was left of the family was Jess and Mel.

'We'll get through this somehow,' she murmured into Mel's hair, and then they clung together and sobbed as the policewoman standing discreetly in the corner bowed her head in the presence of so much grief.

Mel was discharged from the hospital two days later. Her bruises were healing but the mental scars would take much longer to mend, if ever. She had already seen a counsellor in the hospital, but that would only be the first of many sessions she would need to help her come to terms with what had happened.

Jess was delighted to have her home and fussed over her between endless interviews with the police. But at last the officers were satisfied and they left, leaving the house strangely quiet. Now Jess was faced with the unenviable task of arranging her husband's and her daughter's funeral, although neither of the bodies would be released for burial until after the inquest, which was set for the following week.

Jess didn't know how she was going to get through it and cried every time she thought of her darling girl lying somewhere on a cold mortuary slab. She tried hard not to even think of Simon, who had betrayed her shamelessly, and she knew that she could never forgive him for committing the ultimate sin in abusing his own daughter. She had forgiven him so much in the past, but this was beyond forgiveness.

She finally tucked Mel into bed and went downstairs to face her first night alone. Up until now the house had been swarming with police, and loneliness closed around her as she looked about the familiar room.

Jo should have been sitting at the table doing her homework or laughing at some programme on the television, but now she would never do either of those things again.

Jess made herself a drink but poured it away as she wandered around aimlessly, and when there was a tap on the door, she flew to open it, glad of some company, whoever it might be. It was too painful to be alone; it gave her too much time to think.

'Laura!' she exclaimed, almost hauling her into the room. 'Come in! I was just wondering what I was going to do with myself.'

'How are you?' Laura asked gravely.

'Oh, you know. Much as you'd expect. I still can't take it all in, to be honest.' Fetching a bottle of wine and two glasses, she now joined Laura at the table and Laura was shocked to see how ill Jess looked.

But then she supposed it was to be expected after the tragic events of the last few days.

'I er . . . I've brought something to show you,' she said, taking some sheets of paper from her bag. 'It's the research into the house I was telling you about, and I've discovered something quite amazing.'

'Really?'

'Yes. As you know, I've been researching into yours and Simon's family tree, and it seems that he was actually a descendant of the Fentons who lived here in Martha's time.'

Jess's eyes stretched wide with shock. 'Are you *quite* sure?' she gasped.

Laura nodded. 'Oh yes, I'm sure all right. I've traced right back to the child that Leonard and Melody adopted as their own after Grace died, and if you recall he was actually conceived when Jake Fenton raped Grace. The old man who died here before you bought the place was the last of the Fentons – or so I thought, apart from the distant American relatives who inherited the place.' She began to run her finger down a list of names as Jess looked on.

'There you are,' she said, stabbing a finger at Simon's name. 'There's no doubt about it. And I just wonder now if that's why Martha came back here – to try and warn you that Simon had bad blood in his veins?'

'I suppose it would explain things,' Jess said musingly. 'But how could she have known that a descendant of the Fentons would come back here one day?'

'Who is to say?' Laura shrugged. 'There's a lot more goes on between heaven and earth than we'll ever know.'

'Funnily enough, now that I come to think of it, I haven't heard her whispering since all this happened,' Jess said now.

'Perhaps she has no need to any more. If she was here to get her revenge on Simon, her job is done now, isn't it?' Laura pointed out. 'It's a terrible tragedy that Jo, too, became a casualty of that revenge.'

'You could be right,' Jess agreed, trying not to cry. Changing the subject she asked, in a shaky voice, 'How is Beth?'

Laura's face clouded. 'Not good, to be honest. I think the baby could come any time now.'

'It's all so sad, poor lamb,' Jess said dully.

'It's not something for you to worry about,' Laura assured her firmly. 'As far as Den and I are concerned, it's Beth's baby and we are responsible for it. He or she will be our grandchild. We'll have "father unknown" entered on the birth certificate and that will be an end to it.'

'But if there's anything I can do to help . . .'

'You just concentrate on getting through the next couple of weeks, eh?' Laura said kindly.

Jess nodded miserably as her eyes welled with tears again.

# Chapter Forty

It was now four weeks since Simon and Jo had died, and each day had been sheer torture for Jess to get through, full of pain and regrets. Karen had been a tower of strength, calling in daily, and Jess wondered how she would have coped without her.

Jo had been laid to rest in the small churchyard of St Theobald and St Chad's Church in Caldecote following the inquest, which had recorded a verdict of accidental death by drowning. Jess felt as if part of her had been buried with her. Sometimes the pain she felt was so harsh that she wished she had died too, but she knew that she had to be strong for Mel, and that was all that kept her going. That and the terrible guilt she felt because she hadn't realised that Mel was going through her own private hell. Now she had to somehow make it up to her.

Simon had been buried in an unmarked grave the day before Jo, but Jess had not been able to bring herself to attend the ceremony. Perhaps one day she would be able to think back to a time when she had loved him, but for now all she felt for him was hatred after what he had done to her daughters.

This morning was a particularly overcast day which matched her mood. She had got up early as usual after yet another restless night, and had then spent the next half an hour wandering from room to room. It was funny, but for the life of her she could no longer see what had ever attracted her to the house now. It was nothing more than a mausoleum, full of bad memories. But at least, she consoled herself, things couldn't get any worse. She was proved wrong, however, when Mel came down for breakfast with her eyes red-rimmed from weeping. But then that was nothing new. She had barely stopped crying since the day they had buried Jo.

'Toast, love? Or perhaps some cereal?' Jess asked, attempting to sound cheerful and failing dismally.

'No thanks, Mum. I'm not hungry.'

Jess sighed. Mel was scarcely eating enough to keep a bird alive but then neither was she; they had both lost their appetites.

312

'Mum . . .'

As Jess glanced across at her after fetching a jug of fresh orange juice from the fridge, she saw that Mel had something to say and so she sat down opposite to her and asked gently, 'What is it, love?'

'There's something else I've been meaning to tell you.'

'Then go on,' Jess encouraged although she was dreading what she might hear next.

'Well, the thing is – you know all those accidents that you had before Christmas? I don't think they *were* accidents. In fact, I *know* they weren't. The day you fell down the stairs and lost the baby, I saw Dad go up to the attic just before you did, and I think it was him that pushed you.'

'Oh, now come on, love. I know he was a swine but even *he* wouldn't be capable of that.' But even as she said it Jess's mind was working overtime as she thought of the enormous life-insurance policy he had taken out on her, and the way he had pressurised her to make a will.

'Yes, he would.' Mel looked back at her steadily. 'The day your brakes failed, I saw him tampering under the bonnet of your car just before you left. And what about the day you got the electric shock from the hairdryer? I saw him messing around with that too, and when I asked him what he was doing, he told me to mind my own business.'

'I think you're letting your imagination run away with you now, love,' Jess objected. 'Your dad couldn't have fiddled with it. He was on a stag do in London at the time.'

Mel shook her head. 'Oh no, he wasn't. He just wanted you to *think* he was away. He was actually staying with this woman who lives near the town centre. He's been seeing her for years. And what about how he rushed you into making a will? If anything had happened to you, he would have got everything – and he needed to because his business was in trouble. That's why he'd started dealing in drugs.'

As yet another piece of the jigsaw fell into place, Jess gasped with shock.

'Who was this woman your dad stayed with?' she asked, as she relived the day she had bumped into Abigail in the town. No wonder she had looked puzzled when Jess had mentioned the men in London.

'Her name is Wendy and Dad kept all his drugs hidden there,' Mel said wretchedly.

'Would you be prepared to tell the police all this?' Jess asked now, and Mel agreed. So all the time she had been battling like a fool to

313

keep their marriage going, Simon had actually wanted her dead. Shakily, she dialled Inspector Flynn's number.

The next day, following a police raid on the address Mel had given them, a number of people were arrested for drug-trafficking, including the woman with whom Simon had been having an affair.

Surprisingly, Mel seemed a little more like her old self after that and Jess hoped that now she had unburdened herself of all the terrible secrets she had been forced to keep, she might start to recover.

Mel even went back to school on a part-time basis the following week, and she seemed to be coping well with it, although the same could not be said for Jess as she rattled around the house all alone, counting the hours until her daughter would be home again.

'You should get yourself an interest outside of this place,' Karen and Laura urged her, but she was becoming reclusive as she tried to come to terms with all that had happened. The newspapers had been full of the story for the first two weeks following Simon and Jo's deaths, and it took Jess all her time to venture further than the end of the drive because she was convinced that everyone was talking about her.

It was one morning whilst Mel was at school that she took every single thing of Simon's that she could find, and dragged them out onto the field next to the copse, where she burned them to ashes on a giant bonfire. But Jo's room remained untouched. She had only ventured in there once to get the new jeans and the new top she had bought for her the week before she died. Jo had never got to wear them and Jess wanted her to be buried in them. And now the room remained shut up. It was just too painful to venture in there and see all the girl's treasures scattered about the place. She had, however, gone up into Martha's room in the attic, but the scent of roses was gone now, as were the whispers that had shortly before been her constant companion. Jess hoped that, if the girl had moved on, she was finally at peace.

And so one long day ran into another as Jess sank further and further into a depression. She was sitting in the chair one morning absently fondling Alfie's ears when she heard a car pull into the drive.

'I wonder who that can be?' she muttered as she hauled herself out of her seat and went to open the door. She wasn't expecting Karen until the next day. When she dragged it open she gasped with shock when she saw Emile Lefavre standing on the step.

'Now please do not shout at me,' he implored, holding his hands

314

out in front of him as if to ward off a blow. 'I do not know what I did to upset you so when we were in Paris, but I saw what had happened in the newspapers and felt that I should come and check that you and Mel are all right. I would not come straight away as I realised you had a lot to cope with, but if you are still angry with me I shall leave immediately.'

'Oh Emile, I'm so sorry for the awful things I said to you,' Jess told him. 'The thing is, I thought it was you that had . . .' She began to cry, and before she knew it, he was in the room holding her comfortingly.

'Now then, why don't you start at the beginning and tell me everything that has happened,' he prompted, and for the next hour that is exactly what Jess did. When she had finally sobbed out the whole sorry story, Emile whistled through his teeth.

'My God,' he exclaimed. 'You *have* been to hell and back.' He sensed that it was a relief for Jess to talk and so he was still there when Mel returned from school at lunch-time, with the rest of the day off.

'Emile!' she cried when she saw him, and Jess saw her smile – *really* smile – for the first time in a very long while. 'It's great to see you. Are you staying for dinner? *Can* he, Mum?'

Jess realised with a little jolt that she hadn't even thought of dinner. She had been too busy pouring her heart out to Emile.

'Of course he can,' she said uncertainly. 'But I've no idea what we're going to eat. Karen was going to do some more shopping for us tomorrow.'

'Then I shall cook if I am permitted,' he told her with a grin. 'I am known for being able to make a meal from nothing. Now, where is the fridge?'

In no time at all they were tucking into ham omelettes which Mel polished off with relish. Jess smiled. It was nice to see her looking happy again.

When they were done, Emile cleared away and told Jess, 'Now you make me a list of the things you need, and Mel and I shall go shopping for you, shan't we, *ma petite*? Just enough to tide you over until your friend comes tomorrow. I don't have to go back to school, and neither does Mel, so allow us to make ourselves useful, *n'est-ce pas*?'

Jess knew that she shouldn't really put the responsibility of shopping onto someone she barely knew, but anything was preferable to having to go out and face people and do it herself.

Emile and Mel were back within the hour loaded down with shopping bags after a quick trip to the local Asda.

'But there's far more here than I put on the list,' Jess objected as Emile began to efficiently unpack.

'You must eat and keep your strength up,' he scolded, and so she sat back and watched. It was nice to feel cared for again.

When he finally left, much later in the afternoon, Mel pleaded with him to come back soon. After glancing at Jess for her permission, which she gave with a slight nod of her head, he smiled.

'I shall be back on Sunday to cook you a good British roast dinner,' he told them, holding his hand up to stay Jess's objections. 'And do not worry. I shall bring all the ingredients with me.'

It was gone eight o'clock that evening when Jess realised with a little jolt that Laura hadn't called in. She had been so taken with Emile's visit that she hadn't given it a thought until now. She frowned. It wasn't like Laura not to call to see how they were, and she wondered if everything was all right with Beth. She was just contemplating whether or not she should walk down the lane to Blue Brick Cottage to find out, when Laura appeared, as if thoughts of her had conjured her out of thin air.

Jess saw at a glance that Laura had been crying but before she could ask her what was wrong, her friend burst out: 'I've just come back from the hospital. Beth has had a little boy.'

'Oh.' As she thought of the baby she had recently lost, a shudder ran up Jess's spine but now wasn't the time to think of herself and her feelings. 'Congratulations! Are they both all right?'

Laura nodded, looking frighteningly old and pale. 'Yes, they are now, but it was awful. Beth screamed the place down, poor love. She couldn't understand what was happening to her. Still, it's over now, and all being well they'll be home in a day or two. But how has your day been?' She felt uncomfortable saying too much about the baby under the circumstances, and was keen to change the subject.

Before Jess could answer, Mel began to tell her all about Emile's visit, and Laura smiled to see her looking more like her old self again. 'It sounds like you both enjoyed seeing him,' she said when Mel had finished.

'Let's just say he was a welcome distraction and we need all the distractions we can get right now,' Jess told her as she fetched a bottle of whisky from the drinks cabinet. Laura looked like she could do with a good stiff drink and Jess knew that, loving Beth as she did, the

316

birth must have been as traumatic for her as it had been for her daughter. It was never easy to see someone you loved in pain.

Laura gulped at the spirit gratefully, wincing as it burned its way down her throat.

'Cor, that was just what the doctor ordered,' she grinned when she had drained the glass. 'But I'd better be getting back now. Den is a positive nervous wreck. I only called in to check that you were both OK and to tell you about the new addition.'

It was as she neared the door that Jess caught her arm. 'Laura, are you quite sure that there's nothing I could do to help?'

'Ssh,' Laura said sternly. 'We've already had this conversation and I've told you, this is *our* baby now.' Impulsively, she leaned forward and pecked Jess's cheek. 'You just concentrate on you and Mel,' she urged kindly, and then she was gone.

Just as he had promised, Emile turned up on the following Sunday loaded down with yet more bags, which he promptly unpacked.

'Now you two shoo,' he told them, flapping his hands dramatically. 'You must not disturb a great chef at work. I shall call you when it is all ready to serve.'

The meal which followed three hours later was delicious, and Jess was thrilled to see that Mel ate every mouthful. Just as he had said, Emile was a surprisingly good cook. They dined on an enormous leg of pork covered in crunchy crackling, a selection of vegetables, and crispy roast potatoes all swimming in thick creamy gravy.

'Oh Lord, I won't be able to eat another thing for at least a month,' Jess groaned as she eventually staggered away from the table.

'Rubbish!' Emile exclaimed. 'You are far too thin. A woman should have curves.' Jess grinned. It was a very long time since there had been any light-hearted banter in this house.

In the afternoon, they watched the omnibus edition of *Eastenders* on the television, all curled up on the settee together, and then Mel went to her room to do her homework, leaving the adults to talk. It was then that Emile asked, 'Have you thought of moving from here, Jess?'

'Moving?' she asked blankly. 'But how could I? Mel has been through so much just lately. It would be unfair to expect her to move house on top of everything else.'

'But have you *asked* her how she would feel about it?' he pressed.

Jess had to admit that she hadn't.

317

'Then I should put the idea to her,' he said bluntly. 'It will be hard for both of you if you stay here. There are too many memories.'

Jess gave what he had said a lot of thought, and when he had gone and she and Mel were alone again, she put the idea to her over a light supper.

'Mel,' she began, struggling to find the right words, 'how would you feel about moving?'

'What? From here, you mean?' Mel's face lit up. 'I'd love it!' she said immediately. 'Even if you, me and Alfie just ended up in a little flat somewhere. I *hate* it here.'

'Right, in that case I shall get an estate agent around to value the place just as soon as possible,' Jess promised – and that is exactly what she did the very following day.

Beth came home from hospital four days after having the baby. Jess knew that she should go to see her but dreaded it. The pain she felt at losing her own baby was still raw and she couldn't imagine how she was going to react.

She was still struggling to come to terms with the fact that Simon had tried to kill her, and was missing Jo terribly, but she tried to remain positive for Mel, who still had very dark days when she did nothing but cry. The house also felt strangely empty without Martha's presence, and Jess kept expecting to hear the whispers start up again. Now she was looking forward to seeing the *For Sale* board go up and could hardly wait to be gone from there. It was no longer a home but just a place full of bad memories.

One morning, she waited until Mel had gone to school then set off to Blue Brick Cottage to visit Beth and the new addition to the family.

When she entered Laura's homely kitchen she found her sitting in a chair giving the baby a bottle whilst Beth sat at the window staring sightlessly out across the garden. Jess went over to the girl and planted a kiss on her head before approaching Laura, who smiled a greeting and said, 'I'll put the kettle on as soon as I've finished feeding his lordship here. Unless you want to finish him off, that is?'

Jess nodded mutely, her heart thumping as Laura rose and placed him in her arms. Jess's heart broke afresh as she stared down into his perfect little face. He was so like the baby she had lost that he almost took her breath away. The same blue eyes, the same shock of dark hair, but then Simon had always joked that all babies looked alike.

The baby snatched at the teat of the bottle greedily when she offered it to him and she cuddled him to her as her maternal instincts rose in her like a tidal wave.

'He's lovely, isn't he?' Laura whispered, feeling Jess's pain.

Jess gulped and nodded. 'Absolutely. Have you decided what to call him yet?'

'Den and I thought we might call him Lucas,' Laura replied. She could only begin to imagine how hard this must be for Jess, so soon after losing her own baby, and she felt for her. She had been through so much tragedy, it just didn't seem fair.

'And what does Beth think of the name?'

'Oh, to tell you the truth she doesn't even look at him,' Laura said as she glanced worriedly towards her daughter. 'It's as if now that she's given birth, it's over for her, but then we expected that. But that's enough about us. How are you and Mel doing now?'

'We're getting there. We just take one day at a time. To be honest, I can't wait to move away from here now.'

'I can understand that. And have you had any sign from Martha?'

'Nothing,' Jess told her as she dragged her eyes away from the baby. He had finished his milk now and she was patting his back as she winded him.

'I'm not surprised.' Laura frowned as she poured milk into two mugs. 'You've got to try and go on now for Mel's sake, and when you move you can make a brand new start.'

Jess nodded, but inside she was wondering how she would ever manage to move on. How did you forget a daughter and a husband who had suddenly vanished from her life in the blink of an eye?

'And how is that handsome Frenchman who's been visiting you?' Laura asked as she saw Jess becoming emotional.

'He's been a godsend,' Jess said fervently, then flushed as she saw Laura smile with amusement and rushed on, 'But there's nothing romantic going on, if that's what you were thinking.'

'I wasn't thinking anything,' Laura assured her. 'It's just nice to see someone being so kind to you and Mel. You need as many friends as you can get right now.'

'Sorry.' Jess looked suitably apologetic. 'I'm just a bit touchy at the moment.'

Laura lifted her grandson from Jess's lap. 'You'd be rather strange if you weren't,' she commented, and they then turned the talk to other things until it was time for Jess to go.

It was when she got to the door that Jess suddenly remembered one of the reasons she had come. 'I know we've passed on all the baby stuff we had, and you're very welcome to it, but I'd like you to accept this for him from me and Mel. You can either spend it on anything he needs, or put it into a bank account for him. Whatever you like.'

Laura gasped as she looked down at the cheque that Jess had pressed into her hand.

'B . . . but this is for five hundred pounds,' she gasped. 'I can't possibly take all this from you.'

'Yes, you can,' Jess smiled. 'I don't know what I would have done without you over the last few weeks. And it isn't for you anyway. It's for little Master Lucas there. He's just what we all needed. A brand new life after so much sadness.'

Laura's eyes welled with tears as she hugged Jess to her with her free arm.

'Thank you,' she whispered. 'I'm going to miss you so much.'

'I shall miss you too,' Jess said huskily. 'But just because I'm moving doesn't mean that we'll never get to see each other again. I shan't let you forget me that easily.'

She waved at Beth before slipping through the door, and as she closed it softly behind her, Laura gazed down at her little grandson, tears sliding silently down her cheeks. Life was strange, there was no doubt about it.

# Epilogue

'That's it then, missus. We're all loaded,' the portly driver informed her as he slammed the back doors of the large removal van. Taking his handkerchief from his pocket he mopped at his sweating brow as the hot July sunshine beamed down on them. At that moment, Mel bounced out of the kitchen door with Emile and Alfie close behind her, and Jess smiled at them.

'Right, you two, would you like to go on with the removal men and let them into the new house while I lock up?' she asked.

Emile nodded as Mel piled into his car. It was almost as if Mel couldn't get away from the place quickly enough, but then Jess supposed that this was understandable.

'Are you sure you wouldn't like us to wait for you?' Emile asked, glancing towards the house with a frown on his handsome face.

'No, honestly, I shall be fine,' Jess assured him. 'You two go on – I'll be with you in no time.'

Nodding, he slid into his car and she stood and watched as he pulled out of the courtyard with the removal van close on his tail. And then she stood listening to the birds for a while before going back into the house. It felt strangely empty although the majority of the furniture and all the carpets and curtains she had bought would be staying there. She had taken only the minimum of things, as most of them would be far too big for the tidy four-bedroom detached house she had bought for herself and Mel in nearby Hartshill. It was a lovely house although it was a complete contrast to Stonebridge House. It was very modern and airy, but both she and Mel had taken to it straight away. Now she wandered from room to room, running her hands along the polished mahogany furniture and staring from the windows. The new owners were a lovely couple in their mid-forties and they would be moving in the next day. They were intending to run a bed and breakfast business just as she herself had once intended to do, and she hoped that they would be happy there.

Alfie stayed close to her side as if he sensed that something was going on, and she bent to stroke him, whispering, 'It's all right, boy. You're coming too, don't worry, and we'll be right close to Hartshill Hayes so you'll be able to go for some lovely walks there.'

He wagged his tail as if he understood every word she said as she slowly climbed the stairs to pause in the doorway of Jo's old room. It still hurt her to go in there, but she somehow felt as if she should say a final goodbye. Not that she felt as if she was leaving Jo behind. She knew that the girl would live on in her heart wherever she lived.

It was as she was standing there that she heard footsteps on the stairs and the next minute Laura burst breathlessly into the room.

'Oh,' she gasped, as she leaned against the doorframe. 'I was worried that I'd missed you but then I saw that your car was still outside so I guessed I'd find you here.'

Seeing the tears in Jess's eyes she hugged her lovingly. 'Don't worry, pet,' she said gently. 'It will get easier.'

Too full to speak, Jess merely nodded, and then after looking around for a final time they walked downstairs together and once outside, Jess locked the door. Emile would drop the keys into the estate agent for her later that day.

'I suppose this is it then.' Jess looked at her friend. 'You take care of that lovely new grandson of yours and I shall be round to see you as soon as I've got straight in the new house.'

'You just make sure that you do.' Laura was sad to see Jess go, but she knew that she was doing the right thing. There was nothing here for her any more and it was time for her to move on. She smiled as she thought of Emile. He had been marvellous to Jess and Mel over the last months, and she had watched the closeness between them grow. Although Jess hadn't realised it as yet, he was obviously hopelessly in love with her, so who knew what the future might hold? Laura had a sneaky suspicion that Jess was beginning to return his feelings and hoped that when she finally felt ready to leave the past behind, the couple would find peace together.

Now she hugged her friend again and ushered her into the car. 'Go on then,' she ordered bossily. 'And you just be happy, do you hear me? That's an order.'

'I'll try,' Jess promised as Alfie jumped onto the back seat and she got behind the wheel. And then Laura stood and waved until she had disappeared off down the drive.

It was only then that she turned to look at the girl at her side, who was whispering in her ear.

Martha had appeared in Blue Brick Cottage the day that baby Lucas had come home from hospital, but then that was no surprise to Laura. She had been expecting her.

Her thoughts raced back to the evening she had gone to the youth club that Beth had attended to speak to the person in charge about the boy who might have had sex with her daughter, only to be told that Beth hadn't been there for months. From then on it had been easy to put two and two together. Beth had been with Simon, and when questioned, the girl had admitted that it was Simon's child that she was carrying. But how could she have told Jess that? It wasn't Jess's fault, after all, and Laura couldn't see the point in burdening her with any more worries. She had too many revelations to come to terms with as it was, without the added knowledge that her husband had fathered Beth's child. She could only pray that the boy hadn't inherited his father's badness, but only time would tell. And so the Fenton curse would live on, and from now on Martha would be her constant companion, just as she had been Jess's – unless she could find some way to break the curse and allow Martha to move on, that was . . .

Sighing, she glanced at Martha and side by side they set off towards Blue Brick Cottage.